Orcinus X

Orcinus X

Tyrus Wong

Published by Tyrus Wong

Designed by Vince Pannullo
Printed in the United States of America by RJ Communications.

Library of Congress Control Number = 2010936751
ISBN: 978-0-9829466-2-6

ACKNOWLEDGMENTS

FOREVER, I thank my parents, James Anthony Wong and Mary Louise Wong for their support and belief in me and in all that I've done. All of my stories are tributes to them because my heart, mind and hands had never known what to draw and write about without them. God Bless!

To my immediate and extended Wong family members, past and present. Many of you are named in this book because it was important to me to include you in some form and or fashion as a tribute to you all! God Bless!

To Captain Paul Watson and his Sea Shepard's; the inspiration for my like Sea Guardian crew, led by my closest friend and brother on the other side of the world, Mr. Darren Hall. I am the North American version of him and he is the Australian version of me. God Bless!

To my readers, thank you for selecting this book. God Bless!

I hope you enjoy it and I hope you'll take part in any of the on-going efforts that Captain Paul Watson and his Sea Shepard's support. Help to bring about the end to the Japanese "research" whaling activities in the Antarctic and Indian Oceans as well as to help abolish the abhorrent and ignorant culling practices in the Faroe Islands by the Faroese (approximately 200 miles north northwest of Great Britain); the traditional practice of the Grindadráp.

Initiated by people from one of my homelands as well; China. The killing of millions of sharks each year for their fins is a genuinely senseless waste and horrible behavior. I personally implore that the Chinese and other participating Asian peoples simply find a man-made substitute; something well within your power to do so, to replace this shameful waste of such amazing resources.

To me and to millions more, these practices are existing proof that some of mankind is ruining our world and shortening our time here.

To prospective traditional publishers and respective literary agents; I'm really trying here. With my father's tribute memoir, *My Father Died This Morning* completed in March

2011, I hope you'll consider this fantasy-fiction selection as further proof that I'm here, writing for the right reasons, sharing some engaging stories and making a true effort to become a successful mainstream author.

PROLOGUE

THE world has seen more than its fair share of super-predators but none compare to the time when *C. megalodon* ruled the earth. This ultimate shark was only rivaled, and only in the latter quarter of its long existence by one single co-super-predator; the progenitor of the Killer Whale called, *Livyatan melvillei.*

Much debate still remains today regarding *C. megalodon's* true origins. Some say *C. megalodon* is the ultimate earlier form of today's Great White shark (*Carcharodon carcharias*) while others believe *C. megalodon* was the last of its kind in the line of ancient sharks that began with *Otodus obliquus* approximately sixty million years ago (MYA) and that today's Great White shark is more closely related to an ancient line of Mako sharks, thus becoming the ultimate of that species.

One undeniable fact though; both *C. megalodon* and today's Great White sharks have serrated teeth while all species and sub-species of Mako sharks do not. We are clearly missing hundreds, if not thousands of pieces of evidence related to every species of shark in the oceans today but with the evidence we do have, these are the best conclusions we can reach. Variations in teeth for any animal take millions and millions of years to develop and evolve and the fact that *C. megalodon* reached its fantastic and terrifying size but died out directly due to its inability to adapt to colder waters tells many people one thing; the Great White shark is the ultimate form of all sharks past and present because they are the biggest predatory fish but not too big. They thrive today because of their ability to adapt and dominate in today's colder oceans.

Whales on the other hand came along quite a bit later on the evolutionary scale and as a result, they adapted to all water temperatures, thriving in the coldest regions as well as in the warmest. They also adapted a much more variable diet and this led to much faster brain growth, thus greater intelligence. Absolutely vicious in their earlier forms, all whales would have been considered *killer* whales, unlike today. The only advantage that *C. megalodon* had was her sheer size, simply dwarfing most "new" true killer whales but the early killer whale still had great-grandmother and great-grandfather looking out for them, in the form of *Livyatan melvillei.*

These two ultimate predators clashed many times. They learned from one another. They came from two of the longest lineages of animals to have ever lived and they lived and died together, always as combatants. For roughly three million years between approximately 13 MYA through 10 MYA, these two ultimate-predators traded devastating episodes of blatant and bloody attacks upon one another and upon anything else in their paths.

Fantastic predators were all over. So many sharks, impossible to count and the variety was unrivaled compared to anything that mankind has ever seen. The Great White was just making its way into the bloody theater; being so small in comparison to *C. megalodon* and with so many other giant creatures lurking about, all early Great Whites knew better than to challenge fishes easily three times plus their size. They kept to smaller and deeper areas of the ocean; preferring colder and darker waters where they were not challenged by the warmer water loving *C. megalodon* and her bigger rivals. The Great White simply adapted and chose colder waters and this is the primary reason why they exist to this day.

The ancient ancestor to the Killer whales also preferred warmer waters; drawing its tremendous energy from the richer oxygen content and more plentiful food supply at this time. Of course, any opportunity to dine on a *C. megalodon* was an extra-special event. *C. megalodon's* ancient ancestors of tens of millions of years previous to her had already engrained into the species, a set standard of behaviors and living. The chemistry of the world's oceans was becoming more oxygenated so predators were becoming more efficient, smarter, and in many cases, smaller.

Evolution is the ultimate engine that learns as it churns along. It improves upon its former designs but who's to say that any current form that we see today is in its best form. Has man evolved into its ultimate form or is there a better version of us just waiting around the corner a mere thousand or so years away? Time will tell. Many species were becoming more and more adaptable but some, like *C. megalodon*, were stuck in their old ways of seek-devour-reproduce-repeat. After millions of years, a new version based upon the former would appear and immediately take the throne as one of the supreme-predators for its time. See Appendix A at the end of this book for more details.

Whether you believe in God, Allah or any 'supreme being' or more so in Science and Darwin's theory of evolution, one fact is clear; there are rules to life. The very existence of so many varied forms of life simply means they all exist for a justified reason. This is the sole reason and perfect explanation for why mankind should stop being racist and prejudice against his own kind because if all the wonderful variations of mankind were incorrect, they wouldn't exist to begin with, right? Thanks to evolution, all animals, apparently except for human beings, live by their respective instinctive codes. Engrained in their DNA, they follow the exact same patterns, migratory paths, behaviors, and lives as their closest ancestors used to because these "Directions of Life" have been acquired and learned over tens of millions of years until they reached their refined versions in the animals we see today.

Who's to say if these rules have ever been broken? Animals may certainly have tried in the past but it's clear, due to their instincts for survival and their evolutionary paths that we can see and study for ourselves from their fossils, if and when they veered from their respective paths, they became extinct in pretty short order. They either lost the key elements to their continued survival or they simply weakened their kind and all died out. This is what extinction, without any human interference, means; the animal's inability to continue to adapt for whatever reason.

With improved exploration, human beings are constantly discovering new species of both plant and animal life. We have the intelligence and therefore the technology to expand our learning in so many different ways versus all other animals but the consequences of us playing God or trying to vastly accelerate the delicate balance that science and nature has taught us can and will have tremendous consequences. Even in our seemingly harmless hybrid plant life development, we are playing with fire. Again, there are rules. Ironically, we even named them the *Laws of Nature* but often, we don't follow or respect these laws ourselves.

Mankind has been on the top of the food chain for a paltry twelve thousand years at the absolute most. When we step down from our dominant position, which will happen in time, who or what will succeed us? Time will tell but certainly, when we experiment taking one creature with its own long-standing evolutionary path and try mixing it with another that came from its own unique evolutionary path, only one thing can happen— bloody regret!

CHAPTER ONE

JANUARY 9, 1985 – GUANGZHOU (FORMERLY CANTON), CHINA: JIMMIE HUANG'S HOME

ON this unusually warm morning, normal opportunity is in the air in recognition of the day's trade but there's something else in the air on this day.

Tai Huang awakens after a long night. He graduated the night before, six months ahead of schedule, with two degrees; a Master's in Science specializing in Marine Biology and a Master's in Chemistry, his childhood passion. At just twenty-five years old, he is on a path for success that few are able to handle. He drank heavily last night, like most others but he developed a secret cocktail that prevents all the ills of alcohol so he has no hangover. Built like his iconic martial-arts idol of the sixties and seventies, Tai is five-foot ten and one hundred and fifty pounds. He too is very muscular with a solid six-pack of abdominal muscles but Tai's love for his aunt's special deep-fried pastry treats will eventually take their toll on his mid-section. He grabs his face with both hands and rubs vigorously for a few seconds, slaps his checks, and is now ready to take on the day. His short jet-black hair is always sticking up strangely in the back but he doesn't care. It always takes his girlfriend or aunt to correct it or to at least remind him that he looks like a deranged peacock.

His best friend from childhood, Sik Yuen Zhang, also graduated early with honors, with the exception of the Master's in Chemistry. He too awakens clear-headed. They rise – surveying the floor of unconscious bodies and laugh, knowing they will all soon awaken sick to their stomachs accompanied by massive headaches and fits of violent projectile vomiting; the eventual accompaniment of having mixed beer, wine and other fermented spirits. A couple very attractive girls were given a shot glass full of Tai's secret hangover formula so they continue to rest comfortably but remain exhausted after several erotic episodes from the night before with Tai and Sik Yuen respectively.

Sik Yuen is twenty-seven, like his girlfriend Misa Tang. They grew up together and have always been a couple, since the age of fourteen. They share a love for all animals, especially sharks. Their respective degrees are in Marine Biology with emphasis on shark life, reproduction, and behavioral science. Misa has hair so black, it's blue. Sik Yuen is mesmerized by it and so is Tai but he'd never admit that to either of them. Misa is a classic Chinese girl of about five-foot four and all of a hundred pounds. Sik Yuen, whom everyone calls Yuen because "Sik" is his formal family name and is only used in more formal situations by his elders addressing him, is a well-proportioned but slightly stocky young man. He's five-foot ten, about one hundred and seventy pounds with short-cropped black hair and his forearms are tattooed up and down– compliments of his adopted uncle Jimmie Huang (Tai's father). Yuen is poised for a long and successful career at Tai's side because the two have been best friends since the age of five.

To some, Yuen looks like an infamous Chinese Triad gang leader with his deep stares but Tai knows the stares simply mean that Yuen is deep in thought and is likely about to offer something brilliant. They trust each other and they share the same goals and objectives in their lives; to vastly and quickly improve the lives of the local peoples that desperately rely on the health of the South China Sea and specifically, the Canton (Guangzhou) fishing ports. Fishing has been in both their families for over three hundred years. Consistently over time though, a terrible sickness develops out in Sea and overwhelms the Canton ports and many people have died as a result of an unexplained illness that grips the community. It has happened throughout their family's histories. In 1980, on Chinese New Year's day, Tai lost his mother (Mia) and youngest brother (Qin) to the mysterious illness and he vowed on that day to cure the illness that tore apart his family. It was this fierce determination that propelled him through college so quickly, taking on two extremely difficult subjects and mastering them in just four short years. He dedicated his graduation to his mother and brother and he remains vigilant as ever; striving to develop a cure that will once and for all, rid the Canton docks of this mysterious and deadly plague.

Tai and Yuen believe the deadly problems begin with the chemistry that exists in the South China Sea so they are preparing to travel once again down the coast to learn more about the fish life and geography of the area. Tai's father Jimmie has various favorite fishing holes located around and nearby various islands just south of the inlet that leads fishermen into the great port city of Canton (Guangzhou). Jimmie learned from his father decades ago about all the special fishing holes south of the Portuguese-owned city of Macau. Along that coastline, there are dozens of small islands, many submerged most of the year that Jimmie has visited over and over again. He always catches his fill of the standard resource; the beautiful array of Mandarin Fish (Chinese Perch) that inhabit the length of the coastline from Vietnam all the way up north to the Japanese Ryukyu Islands. Also present in these ancient waters of the South China Sea are many species of small sharks like the Pygmy shark, a wide variety of Dogfish Sharks, Lantern sharks and although rare for this far south, the occasional Cookie Cutter shark will make a brief and sometimes deadly appearance. In the deeper waters, an abundant variety of the more powerful and more feared sharks lie in wait; both species of Mako sharks (short-fin and long-fin), the wide variety of Hammerhead sharks including the Great Hammerhead.

The Great Hammerhead and all other larger sharks in the South China Sea continue to be harvested for their fins to accommodate primarily China's Shark-fin soup desires. This now shameful practice continues to go un-regulated and is reaching critical levels. One day soon, the world will suffer the dire consequences of these majestic and absolutely required predators being killed off from the world's oceans because they help to keep the delicate balance of the ocean's ecosystem in check. Without them, the ecosystem will eventually fall apart and we will all suffer those consequences in the form of new illnesses and new diseases for both mankind and for all marine life. The inevitable imbalances will have tremendous negative effects for all marine animals as over- population takes hold. Coupled with Japan's alleged annual 'research' on whales they conduct in the Antarctic and Indian Oceans, these disgraceful human behaviors will someday cause irreversible damage, if they haven't already. Thankfully with the fierce dedication from Australia's Sea Guardian's, hopefully their actions will one day bring an end to these shameful and disgusting practices; culling and the continued morbid practice of whaling.

The tectonic shelf around the coastline in this part of southern China extends out into the ocean for a few miles or so, generally, and not at tremendous depths. Then the shelf drops off sharply to depths that exceed fourteen thousand feet by the time you reach the middle of the South China Sea. These tremendous depths continue northward until you reach the southern tip of the island of Japan and they continue southward until you reach the Indian Ocean. The South China Sea is the second busiest waterway in the world and has been for thousands of years. Navigation in this part of the world is among one of the most challenging, right there with the likes of the Mediterranean. That also makes it one of the most mysterious bodies of water in the world because with that much regular traffic, no one has ever been able to study the ocean life as close as it should be studied. The awesome water depths in this part of the world are probably the only element saving hundreds of animal species from extinction by man.

Some strange occurrences have taken place for decades in this ancient Sea including various disappearances and some of the wildest looking fish ever seen. Mandarin fish, not to be confused with China's standard white fish resource, Mandarin Fish (Chinese Perch), are an amazingly colorful variety of highly sought-after small saltwater aquarium fish. They feature some of the most brilliant colorizations of any fish in the world. In Australia, they are referred to as LCD-fish, due to their wild and extremely bold colors and variations and they are among very few fish in the world that feature rich blue colorizations. Mandarin fish live close into shore so they are quite easy to see and observe in and around the shallow and brilliant coral reefs.

Fishermen down south, south of Macau, refer to certain areas of the South China Sea as "Dragon's Tears" due to a strange but wonderful scent that emanates from small areas just off shore. Amongst the many islands, it's hard to pin-point the exact source, especially given the fact that many of the small islands are submerged during various times throughout the year so you never really know from day-to-day or month-to-month what may grow and then quickly die off on these islands. In any case, it's a sweet smell mixed with a hint of ginger and it makes the fisherman hungry so most often when they detect this smell, they simply leave to get back to their respective villages for supper. The scent only resonates in the late afternoon to early evening hours and only on some days, not every day. Tai has heard these stories endlessly from his father Jimmie, who has travelled often down south in and around Macau and further south to catch bigger prey fish to feed his family. Jimmie has smelled this scent firsthand and has always warned Tai that just because something smells nice, doesn't mean that it is. Tai always smiles at his father's sayings and beliefs because of the obvious generational gap but Tai also knows his father is right. He will examine the area carefully and cautiously, just as he promised his mother and brother that he would. Tai is obsessed with finding an answer to the deadly virus plaguing the Canton docks and he will not leave the area or this work until he finds a solution.

When Tai turned sixteen, his father Jimmie shared a secret dirty joke with him that he always recalls and smiles at today. Jimmie told him, "Remember my story of Dragon's Tears Tai?"

Tai would nod and enthusiastically say, "Yes Poppy, why?"

Jimmie would grin and then say, "Well, the opposite is also true."

Tai's left eyebrow would extend up but before he could ask the obvious follow-up question, Jimmie would smirk and continue explaining, "Just because something smells bad, doesn't mean it is."

Tai knows there is a meaning to all this but he's not quite getting the intended joke. Again, before he could ask, Jimmie would burst out laughing and say, "Like your girl-friend's magic!"

Briefly embarrassed but then bursting out laughing together, Tai would run over to his father and they would happily embrace; laughing and confirming the fact together. They share an unbreakable and unrivaled bond as father and son and it would be moments like this between a man and his maturing son that would solidify their relationship for all-time.

Tai's twenty-five year old girlfriend Kim Tse awakens. She had been in Tai's bed the night before but for some reason she always gets up and finds another place to sleep. She doesn't mean to be so distant but she is. Maybe she sleep-walks and can't help it. Maybe she simply needs to get some sleep because Tai keeps her up all night; he has a voracious appetite for sex. Kim is stunning. With long black hair, she is five-foot six and built on a thin but muscular frame of about one hundred and ten pounds.

She's brilliant in her own right, earning a Master's degree in Chemistry, just like Tai and in some ways, smarter than him because she can understand even more possibilities of compounds than Tai can. They are a great fit for one another but due to their fierce dedication to their work, they are actually uninvolved most of the time.

By noon, everyone is up, slowly recovering from the party; the walking and dancing dead of the celebratory night before. Life now resumes and fellow graduates and friends begin to disperse back into their lives. Tai and Yuen make quick work saying their good-byes to many of their graduate friends and acquaintances so they can quickly re-focus on their pending South China Sea excursion.

Yuen calls out to Misa, "ehh Misa, you ready yet?"

She peeks upwards and across the room and nods, still too tired to actually respond. This makes Yuen smile devilishly.

Tai picks up on this and pats Yuen across the back and says, "See, for a change, you wore her out last night!"

Yuen grins wider and says, "You're right and I'm proud of it! What about you and Kim?"

"We destroyed each other and then, as usual, she left the bed." Tai's eyebrow rises up in continued wonderment and slight frustration.

"It's always been like this between you two?" Yuen asks.

"Always and she never explains it or even wants to talk about it so I stopped asking after last semester. She'd come into my room, we'd attack each other for an hour or so and then she'd leave."

Kim suddenly appears from the restroom at the end of the small village-style house and cheerfully says, "Ready! Let's go boys."

Tai and Yuen don't remember even mentioning the South China Sea trip to her but then Tai vaguely recalls mentioning it just before taking his secret shot drink and passing out the night before. Yuen confirms this and they both nod toward Kim in agreement. Misa then calls out, "You three go. I'm not ready." Kim immediately counters, "Oh come on Misa, and you've got to come with us. I want to learn more about your sharks and the guys won't tell me nothing but legends and other bullshit."

Tai and Yuen smile demonically and sass Kim back by mumbling under their breath, "Legends and bullshit. Legends, then bullshit. No sometimes bullshit first then legends. No just pure legendary bullshit!" The two laugh and slap high-fives then Yuen calls out to Misa and says, "Hey shark-girl, let's go. We'll tell Kim some new stories and maybe the future doctor will learn something too. It will be good to get the guy away from his beakers for a while." Tai looks over at Yuen and they trade a devious stare and then trade sarcastic smiles.

Tai quickly adds, "Hey, those beakers got me a full scholarship big guy and they also helped you graduate, right?"

Yuen quickly remembers all the help he got from Tai in Chemistry class in order to pass the course two years prior so he offers a quick "thumbs up". He readily acknowledges Tai's intelligence because he knows flat out, Tai is among the smartest people to ever graduate from the prestigious Beijing-based University. This foursome is the collective best and brightest the University has ever seen and the whole of China expects nothing but brilliance from this young and devoted team. Chinese government officials will keep tabs on the group because for one, they funded most of their studies; a normal practice for all high-performing students and athletes in China.

By 1:05 P.M., the two couples are ready for their trip. It's the first time venturing into the South China Sea for the entire group but like flipping on a light switch, once they leave the sneaky and challenging Canton inlet, everyone settles in for the long trip and begins preparing various instruments and experiments they have been developing days and a few weeks prior; water chemistry tests like various Ph. balance tests, other nutrient and foreign content experiments, fish scale sample tests (one of their favorites), blood tests on the variety of fish they will catch, other scale examination tests, fishing equipment tests to ensure testing consistencies and to track any anomalies that occur during the expedition, and most importantly to Tai, the chemical make-up and consistency of the water in various places along their route because he strongly believes that the big-picture issue could be related to the existing extreme pollution in the water.

Generally, disease and germs thrive in situations where they are left alone to multiply and adapt to their surroundings, just like anything else in nature but in this case, Tai believes the initial super-slime that builds up over time and creates the end-resulting deadly slime that people touch and unknowingly pass on to one another is what really needs to be addressed and resolved. On occasion, villagers ingest the virus from the market fish they consume and become deadly carriers of the virus like a short-term but deadly cold. The air-borne version that sometimes accompanies the virus is simply a double-deadly threat and Tai has no solution for that yet.

Fish that live in the area, like the Chinese Perch, feed and are immersed in that environment for years and when they are caught by local fisherman and brought to the docks for immediate sale, the resulting germs continue to build and strengthen into some kind of super-germ that becomes deadly to people. It may have a short life-span but being both air-borne as well as a contagious virus by that stage, it's nearly impossible for people to avoid catching and transmitting the virus to one another. It's like a perfect storm of chemicals coming together to consistently create this super-germ and because people have been fishing regularly in the area for centuries and bringing their respective catches to the Canton docks, it follows that the germ has the near perfect environment to consistently reform and attack unsuspecting residents.

The incubation period for the germ is very fast. So fast in fact, on some historical occasions, people have gotten sick and died in just hours. Tai remembers for his mother Mia and brother Qin, it took only a total of twenty hours for both to fall ill and die from kidney and heart failure. It sickens him each time he remembers back to that horrible day because what has always been a day of great celebration and joy is now and forever a day or great sorrow and pain for him and especially for his father Jimmie.

Jimmie and Tai share a very special tradition. Since the passing of his wife and youngest son, Jimmie has two authentic ancient Chinese coins featuring Chinese Emperor engraving's on them. They are easily worth over a thousand dollars each in today's collector market. He gives one to Tai and at the same time, they flip them into the air. They say a prayer and the coins fall to the floor in Jimmie's beautiful but simply adorned living room. Wherever the coins land, they remain until the following year.

It always amazes the two men how the coins somehow always find their way back close to each other after a year's time has passed. Jimmie believes the spirits of his beloved Mia and Qin remain connected and simply seek each other out in the form of these two coins. Having such a genuine scientist for an older son, Jimmie has never shared those conclusions with Tai.

The group takes various water samples and catch various small fish that properly represent the southern coastline. Kim and Misa take copious notes of each place, referencing their detailed maps and taking into account; direction, time and speed. Jimmie has taught Tai well over the years with regards to how far to go into the South China Sea, south of Macau and while not knowing for certain, Tai is usually able to stop within a mile or two every time where his father always tells him to stop for the bigger experiments and best testing environments. Right on cue, Tai again slows down the powerful but small research boat and drops anchor within a mere eighty yards from the spot he visited last season. They are very close to the continental shelf that features the last few hundred yards of sixty-odd foot deep water and then the drastic drop-off where in this area, the ocean floor is just a little over 14,000 feet below.

Completely unaware, at this same moment, the largest shark in the world is gliding by directly below them. The great female Whale Shark is on her way to the Indian Ocean about two hundred and fifty miles to the south and east of their relatively tiny research boat. She is newly pregnant and will give birth to four live pups that will each be about four feet long. No shark or any other predator, apex or not, dare bother her because with one quick movement of her gargantuan tail, she can shatter a shark's rib cage or concuss them so they drown with their eyes wide open. This majestic rich brown and white-spotted super-fish of over thirty-five feet in length is a true marvel to witness but being pregnant, she will not surface until she has travelled far enough to feel safe. The Indian

Ocean is her single focus so maybe the research team will get really lucky some other day and see her or one of her kind glide by in graceful rhythm.

After a few hours, the group has collected their samples and is wrapping up their experiments when suddenly Tai appears from the lower deck and demands to be taken to shore.

"Yuen, take us in!"

Startled, Yuen says, "Back to the docks? Yeah, I guess we're done for today huh?"

"No. Over to this shore! Come on man, can't you smell it?" Tai anxiously inquires.

Yuen and the girls take in a deep breath and in unison, they say, "Yes!"

Excited, Yuen floors the throttle propelling the boat towards the closest shore about a mile away. The mysterious and intoxicating scent follows.

During the hurried trip to shore, Tai shares his lower deck research findings and analysis of the water samples and fish dissections.

"Okay. Let me start by saying point-blank; I think we have a problem. I think we're about to see another virus strain on the docks and here's why."

Yuen and the girls move closer to Tai in growing anticipation and now in fear of the dreadful news. Tai has completed his analysis in record time and the threesome can't help but to be amazed and grateful for his amazing turnaround but at the same time, their guts tighten like vices because he has blatantly and honestly told them the news is not good. The group is used to such ultimate integrity from their former school days but Tai has always had the most forward and boldly honest approach with people, not wanting to waste even a moment of time with the standard pleasantries that usually precede difficult news.

Nervously, Misa demands, "What the hell did you find Tai?"

Like his presentations back in college, Tai calmly and professionally states, "The water samples came back with elevated levels of pollution, which I'm not really surprised at but the fish samples really tell the story. The cells in every fish we caught and that I dissected are damaged and in some samples, the cells are destroyed meaning that in a short time, if we hadn't caught these fish, they would begin decomposing from the inside out, basically liquefying. I'm not sure yet exactly how long it takes for the fish to begin liquefying because I'm also positive that just like other animals, some will suffer effects sooner than others and some will simply be carriers of the cell-destroying virus. Time will tell."

Yuen and Misa look over the fish samples. Kim returns from the lower deck with her microscope and looks over scale samples. Misa then realizes a terrible fact and exclaims, "We've got to try to catch a shark or something big like a shark to see if it has suffered or is suffering this same cellular damage as well because that's the major resource fisherman are bringing into the docks back home."

Yuen and Kim smile and Kim quickly says, "We're way ahead of you. We dropped some fishing lines as soon as Yuen dropped anchor to see if we could catch any larger fish and it's time to check those lines. Maybe we got lucky."

Yuen and Kim immediately begin reeling in their fishing lines and sure enough Kim has something on her line. It's a Chinese Snakehead; a nasty and voracious predatory fish. Jet- black with a thin white belly, this fish is a scavenger and survivor of the local South China Sea. At almost four feet long and weighing in at just over fifteen pounds, this fish is old and has lived in these waters for at least twenty-five years, possibly thirty.

On deck, Yuen and Tai marvel at the mutant-sized fish and Tai says, "This is what I'm talking about. Snakeheads aren't supposed to be this big. If this monster is in fact as old as I hope he is, no problem but I have a feeling he's not as old as he should be."

Yuen adds, "Yeah, and if he is relatively young, we're in deep shit, right?"

Kim quickly took a blood and scale sample from the Snakehead as Yuen extracted the hook from its mouth and she interjects, "I can already see issues in this fish's blood and his scales are slightly deformed as well. I think its cells are already in an advanced stage of decomposition but I'm not sure exactly how long this process takes either."

She glances over at Tai and grins. Tai returns the grin, walks behind Kim and quickly caresses her backside in acknowledgment and appreciation.

"Can you still smell it?" Tai asks of the group. "The Dragon's Tears?"

"Barely", Yuen quickly replies.

"It's fading. We've got to get ashore and see if we can find the source" Tai confidently says.

The foursome wraps up their deck work, secures their experiments and instruments and slips into the cool waters of the South China Sea. Armed with only fishing knives for protection, the dedicated team are all veterans of these waters but still quickly make their way to shore. They collect their breath and quickly survey the immediate area. Lush plant life is everywhere. Sixteen to twenty-foot high palm trees are scattered across the thin landscape. The tops of small bushes hidden amongst much larger bushes about thirty yards up shore are blossoming with small star-shaped blue flowers.

Pointing at Yuen and Misa and referring to an area about fifty yards down the shore-line from himself, Tai says, "You two check out that area and look for anything new we can use in our experiments and especially anything we can grind up and test in some Chem-experiments. Get our regular stuff too."

By regular stuff, Tai means, sea shells, coral (alive and dead), any dead insects, and any samples of fruits and vegetables and their respective leaves. Tai and Kim are experts at analyzing these items and creating new and regular compounds for a wide variety of medicines and topical aides for everyone back home. One in particular helps to heal scrapes, cuts and sores on people's feet as they walk up and down the Canton fish markets on the weekends. Tai's father Jimmie learned how to make the compound from his father and his father learned from his and so on going back to at least the early 1700's. This is one of Tai's favorite things to make for people, especially for the older women in the small village because they reward him with their deep-fried treats; donuts and other pastries.

Tai takes Kim by her left hand and leads her in the direction of the star-shaped blue flowers. They hug each other and kiss often before arriving at the small outcropping of colorful bushes. The smell is intoxicating and so is the moment. Tai knows he's just discovered the source of the Dragon's Tears scent. He lifts Kim up and through a small opening through the bushes and lays her down in the adjoining grassy field. She unbuttons her light green silk blouse and Tai attacks her strawberry-scented breasts and reaches his hands between her toned legs. She moans, smiles, and kisses him back as passionately as ever as he unbuttons her alabaster white shorts. She's already wet, something Tai loves about her because that simply means she's ready and really wants him inside her.

Tai slips her shorts off, holding her legs extended upwards and caresses the sides of her legs and hips. He presses his right hand palm into her slightly muscular lower abdomen and sweeps his thumb across the edge of her panties in several erotic passes. Then he takes a moment to simply look down at her, appreciating her slender and sweet-smelling body. Kim's silk green panties have a thin string that she quickly grasps and breaks away from her hips. She posts up onto her elbows and takes Tai's dark red University-branded cotton shorts down and he immediately complies by taking them off, grabbing and throwing them into the grass about ten feet away. He reaches down and grabs Kim's broken silk panties and tosses them over at his University shorts. She melts and aggressively wraps her legs around Tai's waist. She quickly flexes up towards him and sucks his tongue. Kim takes Tai's engorged member in her hands and caresses it methodically and repeatedly but after a moment he pulls back. He smiles and softly says, "Not yet; your turn first."

Kim's eyes roll back in her head in utter delight and appreciation as Tai caresses her legs open wide. He kisses and nibbles at her toned legs as she presses his face deep into her body. She sticks her fingers into his mouth and he sucks on her fingers briefly as she begins to climax for the first time. Then he starts to emphatically trace the Chinese numbers from one thru twenty inside of her. Once complete with those, he then begins tracing any other symbol he can think of as she caresses his short jet-black hair in increasing delight. She climaxes again as he finishes tracing the exhausting symbol for zero.

"Yes!" she exclaims over and over again, climaxing for a third and fourth time as Tai completes the Chinese numbers for a third time. She reaches down and caresses Tai's hair and then the sides of his face in exhaustive relief. She catches her breath and then motions him upward toward her mouth and she whispers, "Your turn My-Tai!" Tai smiles and settles in for what can only be described as the best oral pleasure he's ever experienced. Kim is as talented a chemist as she is a lover and she loves returning this erotic favor. Especially since Tai can climax and remain erect for sometimes, hours. She loves his smooth shaven body, just like he loves hers. It's cleaner and honestly more fun to pleasure each other without the bother of pulled or lose body hair. Tai has a very low tan line because he has always enjoyed laying out nearly naked in the sun on weekends back at college when he's waiting on experiment results to materialize or the like. He loves how the sun feels and the boost of vitamin D keeps his skin in great condition. Kim loves it because his tan line also accentuates his six-pack that she marvels and appreciates by caressing and kissing the muscular sections of Tai's abdomen.

In fact, in their freshman year, that's how Kim and Tai first met. Kim was told to visit Tai for some help she needed on a couple mathematics questions so she went up to his room. Tai's room featured a small patio leading outside; a much sought-after amenity by his fellow students. It was late September and still very warm outside. Tai was lying out in the sun with only a low-rise bikini on and applying Hawaiian blend sun-screen. The entry door was ajar so Kim just went inside. She looked around briefly and thinking that Tai was in the bathroom, she wandered into the small adjacent office room. The patio door was ajar and lying to the right side of the light-brown wooden deck was the nearly naked boy with the possible answers to her mathematics questions.

In that moment, the farthest thing from her mind was her math questions. She wanted to ask Tai if she could lick his abs and caress the gorgeous member that lay hidden horizontally underneath the remaining inch and a half of Lycra fabric. She stood there, frozen, staring at Tai's muscular bronze body. After another few moments of fantasizing, she snapped out of it long enough to clear her throat and knock on the patio door. Startled, Tai swiveled around on his butt to see who was behind him and when he faced the young girl, she was now boldly staring at him. He was about to be slightly offended and ask her what she wanted but in that same moment, he realized that his steadily hardening penis had peeked out past the side of his low-rise bikini and after another second, was now pointing right at her. She continued staring and cracked a wide smile as Tai repositioned himself and his member back into his bikini trunks. He grabbed his University-logoed beach towel, covered his torso and slipped on a tank-top. After another few uncomfortably quiet moments, they began talking about Kim's questions. When she left his room, she looked back at him and just said, "Very nice Mr. Tai!"

From the base of his neck to the tip of his pulsating member, she kisses and traces Chinese symbols across his smooth body, often finishing off the tour by sucking deeply on the top three inches or so of Tai's nearly eight-inch long penis. After fifteen minutes or so of erotica performed all over him and unable to hold off any longer, Tai ejaculates across a stretch of the long grass. Kim smiles and resumes her role as master massage therapist and erotic celebratory lover. This goes on for another ten minutes or so. Then Tai motions for Kim to lie back down underneath him. She complies and immediately her eyes roll back and she begins biting her bottom lip as Tai enters her body; still fully erect as if his release didn't even happen.

Rhythmically, they pulsate together for ten minutes in a classic coupling that they have always shared in these passionate moments and they both climax again together. Drenched in perspiration and surrounded by the intoxicating scent of the newly discovered Dragon's Tear bush, Tai and Kim wind down their union, temporarily drained of all energy but at the same time, they quickly become re-energized in a whole new way. They hold each other for a few moments and then trades smiles and quickly re-dress.

They shift gears and quickly refocus, taking samples of the Dragon's Tear bush; pulling various sized leaves from both types of bushes and a couple dozen or so star-shaped blue flowers.

It's been about an hour and a half since they landed on the shore and Tai figures Yuen and Misa have been experiencing the same thing and sure enough, a moment later, Yuen appears holding Misa's hand and leading her out of a grassy area behind a couple palm trees and bushes located in front of them. They re-collect their sample loot in their immediate area and the foursome makes their way back to the front of the shore where they had initiated from.

"Come across anything good?" Yuen asks Tai.

Laughing and smiling over at Kim, Tai sheepishly says, "At least three times."

Then he takes a deeper breath and states officially, "We found it! See these blue flowers? Allow me to speak for Kim (he nods over at her and she smiles back) as we introduce the two of you to Dragon's Tears!"

"Are you sure? I don't smell anything" Misa explains.

Kim smiles across at her guiltily and declares, "It's Dragon's Tears!"

Misa laughs, walks over to Kim and whispers, "You two were being nasty in those bushes weren't you?" The two girls hug and Kim confesses saying, "He was amazing! I came five times! And I think he ate my panties because I couldn't find them when we left!" Kim blushes and looks down, smiling.

"Five times and you're commando now too? … Fucking animals!"

The two girls giggle like thirteen year olds and stand ready to make the exciting swim back to the research boat. The group checks their loot one last time. Tai secures the Dragon's Tears items in a special Gortex covered cooler he bought during his freshman year at the Beijing University. He used it throughout school and never goes on any science excursion without it.

The two couples collectively take a deep breath and enters the South China Sea, heading back to their small research boat about fifty yards away. Swimming to shore was the easy part but swimming against the South China Sea currents to get back to your boat is a whole different story. The cool waters numb their arms after about five minutes and it takes on average about fifteen minutes to fight this fight. If the water and currents aren't enough, they still must remember, they're in the South China Sea; home of a great variety of predators including the Chinese Snakehead fish that will bite you if so inclined. Also, a wide variety of small reef sharks and there are also mid-sized to large Stingrays. Although timid creatures and generally wishing to avoid any contact with other animals, mankind included, if you are behind or beside one, they will flash their poisonous barbed tail at you. Electric eels are around occasionally and those are definitely best avoided under all circumstances because one shock from even a juvenile and you could be done. Of course, there are plenty of other threats lurking about but being only fifty yards off-shore in waters only thirty to sixty feet deep, chances are, the larger sharks are in deeper waters seeking larger and more abundant prey. Tai's father Jimmie has another favorite saying that goes, "As soon as you try to guess what a South China Sea creature will do, you have failed."

About sixty feet away from the boat, Misa believes she sees a fin. She calmly explains, "On our nine o'clock guys, I saw a fin."

Yuen stops dead in his tracks and nervously asks, "You think you saw a fin or you definitely saw a fin?"

Misa responds, "Why do you do that? Whether I think I saw it or definitely did, you still need to move your ass, right?"

Yuen begins digging through the cool water at twice the rate of speed and says something in older Mandarin Chinese, "Cu-cum-bak-kai-yigh", an ultimate-level cuss word; equivalent to someone having had sex with one's mother.

Misa laughs and strides towards the boat along with Tai and Kim, who are each now within a yard or so of the boat. They take turns quickly boarding the rear of the boat. Yuen is still about fifteen feet away when he feels something brush up against his right foot.

He freezes in place and then recovers enough to propel himself towards the rear of the boat. Almost leaping out of the water, he jumps aboard and shakes for a moment. Misa is ready with a towel and she wraps it across his broad tattooed shoulders. Yuen nods at her and Tai asks, "You alright buddy?"

Yuen doesn't want to respond but he knows the South China Sea can literally reach up from the depths and bite you in the ass, literally, at any given moment. He nods in agreement and heads down to the lower deck with Misa.

Tai and Kim ready the boat; quickly stowing their haul from shore in small compartments on deck and then pulling the anchor up. The team heads north, back to the busy and challenging inlet that leads them to their Canton fishing market docks. Navigating this water highway is especially difficult when you are anxious to share your catch with others or when you have just discovered something that you know everyone has been waiting to hear about for centuries.

On the docks, several people on the docks are beginning to cough and others are experiencing the cold sweats. An elderly couple who have been catching, preparing, and selling fish at the market for over sixty years, closes down their respective fish market tables and begins to head home. Ten yards away from their station, the seventy-seven year old gentleman collapses to the ground. His seventy-six year old wife immediately falls to his side and calls out to the rest of the market residents for help. Several people rush to the couple's aid. A middle-aged man picks the old man up in his arms and begins carrying the man over to his home, directly behind the closest end of the fish market. He can feel the elderly man's life slipping away and he begins to tear up. The elderly man's wife trails the twosome by several feet. In her heart she knows her beloved husband is gone. She pulls her short coat over her shoulders, just like her husband had always done for her when he thought she was cold or just in need of comforting.

The three reach the rescuer's home and he places the old man on a black futon-style bed. He braces the old man's head as he sets him deep into the middle of the thin white silk covered mattress. He then places a black and gold Phoenix-logoed silk pillow behind his head. The old man's wife collects her husband's hands and folds them solemnly across the man's thin-framed chest.

She kneels down beside him and softly says, "Thank you dear husband for a wonderful life. Xie-xie, Xie-xie. I will see you soon."

She bows three times and then steps away into an adjoining room where the middle-aged man has just finished placing a call to the local police station for an ambulance.

At the opposite end of the fish market, another one of the afflicted is fifty-one year old Jimmie Huang; Tai's father.

CHAPTER TWO

TAI and Kim trade smiles with each other like they both just got away with something they shouldn't have. With every glance, they can't help but to reminisce. Yuen and Misa are sneaking in a quick nap together in the lower decks and after Yuen's scare, Tai and Kim figure it's best to leave him alone and let Misa calm him down. That's exactly what she's doing. As Tai and Kim navigate the South China Sea getting the group back to the Canton docks, Misa is navigating Yuen's body with her unusually long tongue. She's like a female version of The Demon from the rock group KISS with that thing. There's nothing that Tai and Kim could have done but they still feel bad because maybe they didn't show enough concern in the moment. Tai figures if there was a real issue, Yuen would have said something and he also figures with Misa down there with him, he's probably not feeling too bad at all by now.

It's only another half hour until they reach the Canton docks. They can position their boat right alongside an entry point that is directly below where Tai's father Jimmie sets up his fish market tables. He always has three, never more and never any less and he always sells out everything on his table bringing in on average, about 1,200 Yuan; equivalent to about $320 US dollars at this time. Five miles out, Tai couldn't be happier. With his father's expert advice and constant support, he's found the source of the mysterious scent that local fishermen have wondered about for decades and he's excited to break down the plant to see what he and Kim can use it for, in support of helping everyone in the village. He's keeping his promise to his mother and younger brother by tenaciously seeking answers to the ancient and deadly village virus and that warms his heart as well. His passionate relationship with Kim continues and it feels like it has reached a new level. He thinks maybe it will finally translate into a more long-term relationship, especially since they will be spending so much time together developing new compounds and testing new exciting combinations of prospective medicines over the coming months.

Two miles out, Tai calls down to the lower decks, "Hey you two. We're almost in."

Yuen and Misa laugh together and Yuen quietly and sarcastically remarks, "I am!"

The couple finishes their quick union and begins to redress. Misa appears on deck first, her uniquely-colored hair clearly out of sorts in several places. Yuen accompanies her shortly after, securing his grey fish market T-shirt around his waist. Tai and Kim remain focused on the approaching docks.

Less than a mile out, the group's spirits collectively rise; glad to be returning home in general but especially with their haul of much needed known remedy ingredients as well as the new promising discoveries. Yuen and Misa can't wait to see what Tai and Kim comes up with because they know once they have that focus, they both have tunnel-vision when it comes to finding a great variety of new solutions very quickly. They usually begin their work with the known cure-alls and classic medicines they have been preparing now for almost a decade for their fellow villagers; since Tai was just twelve years old. Tai's excited because he knows a new batch of foot powders and creams will earn him at least a dozen fresh deep-fried Chinese donuts and other pastry treats. A couple hundred yards away from the docks, Misa notices that her favorite older couple's market tables and roof drop door is closed down. She had talked with them both just a few days earlier and they were both in high spirits so she's naturally concerned about them. Yuen notices this too and also becomes concerned. A few villagers see the approaching research boat and begin waving. The foursome is grateful because they can feel the appreciation being sent their way.

Curiously, Kim and Tai look at each other and Kim says, "A little frantic, right?"

Tai agrees and throws the throttle ahead another notch. Yuen says, "Hey brother, back down a little. You know how dangerous this inlet is."

"No, something's wrong. They aren't waving, greeting us back. I can see they are crying and waving us in!"

Yuen and Misa focus in on the old couple's table area and they can see now that Tai is right. Another small group of people continues to wave them in; they are crying. Another woman collapses to her knees.

Misa screams, "Oh God! Hurry Tai!"

Tai begins carefully but quickly positioning the boat to make port. He scans the market for his father Jimmie. As soon as he spots him, he watches his father collapse across his middle fish market table, sending it crashing to the ground and flipping over, on top of an unconscious Jimmie Huang.

Tai's eyes explode into tears. He screams out to the docks, "Poppy! I'm here now! Just hang on!"

The rest of the crew begins to cry and shake as well. In an amazing moment, the team completes all of their dock-side duties in a matter of seconds, usually taking several minutes; Tai cuts the motor and lassos the boat securing it to the docks in one motion; running off his own pure adrenaline. Yuen positions the boat and muscles it into its final resting position. The girls collect all of the group's discovered items and ready themselves for a long afternoon.

Jimmie Huang's body twitches in place as more small and mid-sized Chinese Perch fall across him and onto the ground. Jimmie's eyes are slowly closing.

Tai leaps onto the market deck and races over to his father, flipping the fish table up and away and off his father in an adrenaline-filled rage. The force knocks a small Chinese Perch out of Jimmie's mouth. Yuen joins Tai and the two young men carry Jimmie towards his home about forty yards behind the fish market area. The girls race ahead with all the supplies and open the door using Jimmie's not-so-secret hidden front door key; underneath his red dragon welcome mat that Tai got for him a couple years ago for his forty-ninth birthday.

Tai calms down, feeling the life force still present in his father and focuses the group. He announces, "Kim, prep the blue flowers and the leaves and break them down. Keep the leaves separate from the blue flowers until I get there. Yuen, get me a small bottle of Myst1 and some of that Compound-C from the kitchen. Dad always has some left over. Misa, can you get me a cold towel from the bathroom and some Aspirins?"

Everyone jumps to their orders. Like a seasoned surgeon and his triage team, they work most efficiently focusing on only what's needed and they come back together in a matter of moments.

Myst1 is a very special liquid potion Tai developed to help aid people who suffer from Diabetes Mellitus, like his father. The three-ounce dose bottles he developed have helped to save several villagers' lives in the past, including his father on two separate occasions. Compound-C is a powder Tai and Kim came up with back in school that serves as a super-boost anti-oxidant and mega-dose of vitamin C that compliments the Myst1 potion perfectly. The two elixirs generate an unmatched and unequalled boost of raw energy and positive chemical shock to a person's entire body, specifically, to their heart, lungs, and brain, protecting the unconscious or semi-conscious person from slipping into a diabetic coma or worse, suffering a heart attack and going into cardiac arrest. These two elixirs alone should warrant a Noble Peace Prize for Tai but as soon as Kim even mentions this real possibility, Tai always changes the subject.

Having propped him upright, Tai slowly and carefully works the elixirs into his father's mouth and down his throat. He can feel a strong pulse so he continues to feed his unconscious father the mixture. Kim is busy finishing grinding up the blue flowers and plant leaves, keeping them in separate grinding bowls. She has correctly mixed in another powder compound to each that is consistent with all of Tai's prepared medicines and treatments of this kind. Misa has filled a couple small containers of ice water and she brought the whole bottle of Aspirin as well as Jimmie's formal Diabetes medication bottle from his bedroom night-stand just in case.

As Misa passes by Tai, he reaches out and shakes and briefly holds her right hand. She squeezes back. Just then Yuen walks by swiftly, grabbing the bottle of Aspirin. He stops, backs up a step and opens the bottle. He dumps ten pills into his left palm and close-palms them down on the living room table next to Tai and his unconscious elder mentor. Yuen has six small bottles of Myst1 stuffed in his pockets and then he quickly makes his way back out to the fish market to aide a few more fallen villagers and their friends. This same event happened just five years earlier except a day later, the whole village and the Huang family was mourning the passing of Mia and young Qin Huang; Jimmie's beloved wife and youngest son.

Tai feels his father's pulse weaken slightly so he calls out to Kim, "Kim, take him. I need to work with the Dragon's Tears now!"

Kim and Tai trades places and Tai quickly scans the kitchen counter above his position, reviewing the prepared ingredients. From the scent alone, he figures Dragon's Tears can be some kind of a cure-all with positive properties so he grabs his smaller beaker set; there is always a couple sets around Jimmie's house because he marvels at what his son can do with chemicals and plus, he knows there is always a genuine need for Tai to be able to whip something up at a moment's notice in support of someone on the docks. Frantically now, Tai begins putting grounded compounds together. Kim watches this and grins slightly; delighted to watch Tai at his dedicated work but nervous too due to the growing desperate need. Tai drops in the last of the chemicals that will proof out whether or not his mixture is correct; trying to achieve a certain crystal blue color that is slighter cooler than room temperature.

Kim calls out, "We're losing him!"

The new elixir cannot be taken orally now because it would be too slow to help Jimmie so Tai prepares a Diabetic syringe retrieved from his father's smallest kitchen drawer. There is one left surrounded by a few dozen large grey blood test strips and a nasty looking needle poking element that Jimmie uses to prick his finger.

Tai draws the new elixir into the body of the syringe. He removes the thick rubber band from the daily newspaper lying on the floor next to living room table and wraps it around his father's right arm, high up above his bicep. The vein in Jimmie's bicep protrudes already but the vein opposite his respective elbow is hidden. After a moment, the vein appears and quickly but accurately, Tai injects his father with what he is already calling "Crystal Dragon's Tears", or "CDT" for short. In such an emergency, "CDT" is a lot better to reference when shouting out orders like Tai just did about a half an hour earlier when these proceedings began.

Critical moments pass and Jimmie remains unconscious. As a precaution, Kim is calling for an ambulance. The ambulance dispatcher responds back to her request saying, "Yes Miss. We are already on-site with a unit."

Kim asks, "What other unit? Here on these docks?"

"Yes Miss. They arrived on-site about fifty minutes ago."

"Are they still here?"

"Let me check for you. Just one moment."

After an uneasy couple of minutes, the dispatcher returns and says, "Yes Miss. They were just about to depart. I told one Tech to remain so he will find you shortly if you wait outside. My other technician will drive back to the station so we can secure the elder gentleman. I'm so sorry for your loss."

Kim bursts into tears and hangs up the phone. She makes her way back into the living room area where Misa and Tai are closely monitoring Jimmie Huang.

Misa quickly asks, "What? What's going on? Is it Yuen?"

Kim shakes her head from side to side, still crying and exclaims, "It's happening again Tai! Someone has already died. They wouldn't tell me who but there's an ambulance already here."

Misa runs to the doorway and screams, "Yuen!"

From the far end of the market, Yuen hears the call. Fearing the worst has happened; he gives the last bottle of Myst1 to a young boy, Jadei, who is assisting his fallen mother. Yuen heads back to Jimmie Huang's house. The boy of fourteen already knows what to do; how to prop his mother up in order to administer the elixir because he performed the same service for his aunt and oldest sister five years earlier.

Tai begins whispering to his father, "Come on Pop. I'm here for you. This will work or I'll join you right now, I swear!"

Tai's tears begin falling across Jimmie's face and down his neck.

"Kim, hand me some ice water and that cold compress."

Kim collects the items and passes them to a seated Tai, brushing through Tai's hair on her way. Just then, Yuen appears in the doorway. Misa immediately hugs his mid-section.

Jimmie's eyes open. He clears his throat and quietly inquires, "You guys back already?" He looks around, up and down, not realizing all that has happened to him and asks, "What? No fish?"

Everyone bursts out laughing. Their tears now are out of relief.

Jimmie squirms but Tai says, "Hang on Pop; Go slow. Do you remember anything?"

Jimmie says, "I remember watching you coming into shore and then I remember feeling like I had a fish in my mouth but I wasn't eating it. Does that make any sense to you?"

Tai smiles and says, "It makes perfect sense. Let's stay here on the floor for a bit longer and I'll take you outside later and show you why that makes sense."

The group takes a deep breath and Jimmie takes a deep breath too. After a few more moments, he drinks the rest of the ice water and stands up so he can sit back down more comfortably on his loveseat. Tai and Kim meet back in the kitchen area and begin mixing more CDT.

"Hurry up, right?" Tai says to Kim.

"I know." The couple starts to sweat.

The two are now able to focus on the fish market villagers who may still need help. A moment later, Jadei appears at the screen-door and screams, "Mr. Tai! My mom needs your help!"

Tai runs to the door and says, "Take me to your mom Jadei!" Tai calls back to his dad and asks, "Pop, you're good, right?" He looks over at him and Jimmie gives him a quick "thumbs up".

Kim sterilizes the lone syringe with a chemical that Tai and her developed; a time tested and proven sterilization liquid and quickly fills the syringe. She caps the top and hands it to Yuen who races out the door; the bottle of Aspirins jingle in his short's pocket.

Tai and Jadei reach Jadei's mother and Tai quickly props her up into his lap. He grasps her left bicep with his left hand and awaits Yuen. Yuen arrives and places the uncapped syringe into Tai's right hand. In the next fraction of a second, CDT is coursing through the women's veins. Yuen hands Jadei an Aspirin. The boy drops the Aspirin into the bottle of Myst1 that he left at his mother's side and shakes it vigorously. After a few moments, Tai reaches his right hand out again and Jadei places the bottle in his hand. Tai position's the women's head slightly up and back and slowly administers the semi-thick formula, allowing the women to swallow it slowly. She is awake but exhausted. After ten minutes, she's feeling better and bats her eyes at her son and at Tai to confirm this.

Misa has been in the area this whole time as well and has learned of the elderly couple. She rejoins Yuen and Tai and tells them the news. Yuen suggests they visit the elderly woman to offer their condolences and to see if she needs anything before the early evening hours set in. Tai shakes Yuen's hand and Yuen and Misa make their way to the elderly woman's small home; just yesterday, an elderly couple enjoying their long-time cottage and their twilight years but now a widow in a home she no longer recognizes.

Tai remains with Jadei and his mother on the ground at the fish market. A few moments later, Kim arrives with one of the small village-owned transport carts. During her rounds, she's already passed out a dozen more bottles of Aspirin-laced Myst1 and she found Jimmie's secret stash of extra new Diabetic syringes. Having prepared a clinical bottle to draw the new CDT elixir from, she also prepared like syringes for each person in need and by now, the timely and powerful new formula is well on its way to helping the afflicted survive this most recent scare.

Yuen and Misa arrive at the elderly woman's cottage home. It's been so long since they visited with her and her husband at length, they feel a little ashamed and embarrassed, especially given what has happened to her just about two hours or so ago.

They knock, too softly at first and then Yuen makes a final solid knock at the door. Being seventy-six, the young couple knows to allow a few moments for the woman to safely reach her front door. Those moments pass but then a few more minutes pass as the young couple quietly reflects on the day and watches the sunset sizzle into the South China Sea.

The Sun crashes into the horizon and shimmers in rich heavenly colors from high to low; red to dark orange and bright orange in the center to bright yellow and then finally dark yellow with the top colors quickly fading away as the sun sets. Now it is ready for the other side of the world to experience, marvel at and enjoy. It's been ten minutes now and the small lamp light on the front porch of the elderly couple's cottage home turns on. Yuen knocks firmly again and calls out, "Mrs. Kai? It's Sik Yuen and Misa Tang. Are you okay?"

Appropriately, Yuen uses his formal name. There's still no response so Misa goes around to the right side of the small cottage home to one of two small windows. She knocks appropriately so as not to startle Mrs. Kai. Misa walks over to the second small window and repeats her efforts. She waits for several minutes but still, no response.

Now Yuen is getting worried that maybe Mrs. Kai fell or something so he braces his right shoulder into the left corner of the front door and with one talented movement, he breaks the vertical door's threshold and the door swings open. Mrs. Kai is nowhere to be found, at least not in the immediate area. The young couple searches the other back rooms but nothing; no one. Actually, it doesn't look like she has even been home, at least not for a while. There is no green tea brewing, as is custom for the couple in the early evening hours and the top of her 15-inch CRT television set is cold. Yuen and Misa make the relatively short walk back towards Jimmie Huang's house but as they approach, they are greeted by Tai and Kim in the small market cart. The two are crying and this immediately makes Misa tear up. Yuen quickly asks, "What's going on? Mr. Huang?"

Kim looks down and cries harder. Tai tries to clear his eyes, blinded by his tears and says, "We took Jadei and his mom back home. She's better now. Mr. Kai was the one who died earlier today as we were heading into port with Dragon's Tears. Mrs. Kai waited with him in the ambulance just before they were about to leave so she could be with him for just a few more moments."

Misa frantically interjects, "Right, and then one of the technicians was going to stay behind and answer our call to help your dad and others in the market area, right? So what are you saying? Where is Mrs. Kai? Is your dad okay?"

Tai sullenly looks at Misa and continues, "I saw the Tech and waived him off because that's right when my dad came around. His partner called him back to the ambulance because he needed help."

Tai lowers his head and begins crying stronger and after a moment he says, "… Mrs. Kai had a heart attack sitting next to her husband. They weren't able to save her."

As the full evening settles in, the Canton docks have again suffered great losses. The village's grandparent figures have passed away; one from the still mysterious virus that continues to plague this small village and one from genuine heartbreak. A precious few were saved, thanks to a brilliant and surgically skilled team of four young adults who acted swiftly and effectively. Countless others were treated and saved with a powerful standard potion that most residents have come to rely on. Diabetes is a scourge upon mankind and it does not discriminate; rich or poor. It doesn't care where you live; whether it's in Denver, Colorado U.S.A. or Lisbon Portugal or in a small historic village just off the South China Sea near Canton China.

Exhausted mentally, physically and emotionally, the talented young foursome collapses asleep all over Jimmie's living room floor. Mr. Huang, fully energized and wide awake from his son's magical treatments, scoops up the local newspaper and heads to his back bedroom to read and rest. On his way past his son, crashed out and sleeping soundly, just like in his younger days when the two would return home after a long day of fishing, Jimmie kneels down and kisses Tai's right hand. He taps his son on the top of his head and then he proceeds to gently tap the heads of the rest of Tai's brilliant young team.

The spirits of the Kai's will forever remain in the small village. Now the elderly couple will look over the other residents with the hopes that the virus can be resolved. Mr. Huang still wonders deeply what happened to him earlier in the day but he's very content waiting until the following morning for those details. He takes a deep breath in appreciation of the moment; he whispers a short prayer in honor of the Kai's and then starts reading his newspaper.

CHAPTER THREE

JANUARY 10, 1985 – GUANGZHOU, CHINA JIMMIE HUANG'S HOME

THE sun begins to rise and like a built-in alarm, Tai awakens. Kim is nestled into Tai's chest and kisses his hand. Tai asks, "Was that you?"

She says, "Of course. I just did that."

"No. I mean last night. Did you kiss my hand last night?"

She rolls over, smiles and says, "That wasn't me My-Tai. That was your father."

She grins, tickles Tai's abs and goes back to sleep.

This is one of Tai's favorite times; getting up early in the morning and if his father is awake as well, which he usually is, they will fry some fish, prepare some white rice, boil some Bok Choy and snow peas and have breakfast together. Sure enough, Jimmie has quietly been preparing the vegetables in a white plastic bowl adorned with a blue dragon.

Tai gets up and approaches the kitchen. He quietly asks, "Pop. You look good. Feeling better?"

"Good son. Thank you. You're a great man. I raised a great man!"

The two gently bump fists and separate into their respective cooking duties.

Tai grabs some freshly filleted Chinese perch from the fridge and begins slicing it into smaller strips. He turns on the compact stove as his father prepares a special sauce that only he can complete, and always in record time. Some secrets remain undisclosed and Jimmie's sauce is one of them. Tai can smell the hint of ginger and standard soy sauce but there are a couple of other ingredients he's never been able to identify. Usually too hungry to care, like this morning, he again let's it slide and instead opts to indulge in the process of cooking. Still, the mystery drives him crazy, especially as an expert chemist. The two converge at the large Wok on top of the stove in the top left hand corner and Jimmie dumps the vegetables and sauce in. The mixture immediately crackles and flavored steam rises. It methodically crawls across the ceiling like a flavor-ghost, waking the rest of the living room floor up. Tai adds the white fish strips and now an even more heavenly scent begins to fill the kitchen and adjacent living room. Back in college, every student would sell everything they owned for food like this.

Normally to Yuen and Misa, a little shy of 6 A.M. means simply, 'cut that out and let us sleep' but not when Mr. Huang has prepared something for them because no one cooks like Mr. Huang.

Seeing the formerly unconscious awake, Tai proclaims, "Hey gang, breakfast is served!"

Tai and Jimmie prepare bowls for everyone and set them along the edge of the living room table. Father and son take up positions at the small marble-topped kitchen island. Small glasses filled with apple juice accompany each bowl. The living room threesome toasts and begins eating. The cooks toast as well and finish their bowls.

"This blue dragon bowl must be twenty years old Pop."

"It's twenty-five."

"You sound sure."

"I am. I bought it the day you were born and your mom bought our blue-dragon tea set right from the hospital's gift shop. They delivered it to us the next day. You had a sip of tea when you were one-day old; for good luck."

The rest of the group brings their bowls and glasses to the kitchen and begins rinsing everything out. Misa grabs Tai's and Jimmie's dishes and kicks them out of the kitchen area. She says, "You guys go check out the docks and Kim and I will clean everything up here, okay?"

The guys agree and step outside into the cool morning air. At fifty degrees, it's actually unusually warm for this early in the morning but after the previous day's horrible events, this warm morning feels great.

With Yuen trailing slightly, Tai and Jimmie walk over to Jimmie's market table area. All the fish have been cleaned up and two of the three tables are intact. The third table lies in ruins to the left side of the complete ones. Jimmie says, "So, you guys were headed into port and what, I passed out or something?"

"Exactly. We were only a few hundred yards away when we watched you crash dive across that table. It flipped over, pinning you underneath and it's likely a Perch ended up in your mouth, I'm not sure."

Tai continues, "All we know is that we set an all-time record getting in, tying everything down and rushing over to you. After that, everything is still a blur."

"You're telling me" Jimmie declares. "But there's something else you're not telling me."

Tai and Yuen look to either side of themselves and then Tai says, "Mr. Kai had been or got sick yesterday morning. They closed up and he collapsed and died just a little ways away from their tables. As paramedics were securing him in the ambulance, Mrs. Kai waited with him. She had a heart attack inside the ambulance and died alongside him."

Jimmie bows and says a quick prayer. His eyes tear up and he admits, "I do remember a commotion at the end of the market now. I had no idea that was the problem. That must have been when I was feeling dizzy so I sat down and continued scaling fish. My God, now I remember!"

Jimmie's eyes light up. Tai knows what that means. Tai immediately interjects, "Yes! Go on Pop. What else? What caused this? I know you know!"

Jimmie squints his eyes shut, digging deeper into his short-term memory banks. The haze from the day before is beginning to clear and finally he says, "Tai, you guys have some work to do!"

Tai again says, "What is it Pop? What's causing this?"

Jimmie settles his mind and then basically lays it all out for Tai and Yuen to hear;

"Okay. About a week ago, I brought in my catch; the normal variety, a few Snakeheads and a small stingray. The stingray was still alive so I was extra careful. I noticed its stinging tail was deformed and it had a greenish hue to it. I figured it was damaged from combat so I ignored it. But as I recall now, the Snakehead's mouth and teeth were also slightly green and its scales were slicker, slimier than normal, at least I remember thinking so at that time."

Jimmie begins to sway a little bit and Tai notices this so he grabs his father's right arm, braces his weight and guides him to a nearby bench. He figures Jimmie's energy will vary today, as expected, especially after yesterday's events combined with his father's ongoing struggle against Diabetes. Yuen races back to Jimmie's home to fetch another bottle of Myst1 and a few Aspirin, just in case.

Jimmie continues, "And the scales of most of my catch were the same; slimier, you know? I just figured it was from age and competition in our ancient seas. As you know, it's survival of the fittest out there for everything, every day."

Then Mr. Huang gets serious. He notices Yuen making his way back to them so he quickly states, "Son; whatever the hell this is, you fix it, hear me? This has got to stop and you and your friends are the only ones who can do it. You can make it right. Make it right son! For your mother and brother!"

Yuen approaches with the bottle of elixir and Tai and Jimmie adapt to the moment, carrying on a more standard and less serious conversation about the market and fishing in general.

Yuen picks up on the change of tone and the generalness. He's never asked what had been discussed because he understands and respects both Tai and his father too much to ask. It's none of his business, what is discussed between a father and son unless they want to offer.

Tai says, "Let's get you back home Pop. You should rest today before you think about heading back out to go fishing. Like you've always told me, the fish will be there waiting for you tomorrow and the next day and the day after that."

Tai motions to Yuen by waving his hand swiftly up and down, cutting the wind like a knife. Yuen knows what this means; ready the research boat.

The girls have cleaned up and have a nice aroma of incense burning throughout the house. Jimmie regains his strength enough to step into his home and immediately claim his favorite reclining chair. There are two but he prefers the one his wife used to sit in. As he would be out fishing, she slowly customized both arm rests with embroidered animals. Just before she died, she had been working on a blue dragon, Jimmie's favorite and all that remains to be completed are the mystical animal's back legs and claws. Jimmie has been trying to complete these areas himself but every time he begins, he's only able to work on them for a few moments before stopping and concentrating on something else. The back legs are completed with their intricate scale work but their five-digit claws are missing.

Tai quickly tells the girls that he and Yuen will make another trip out to get more Dragon's Tears plants and flowers and that they should remain in the village in case more people fall ill or need some other help today. The girls happily agree. In the meantime, Yuen has been preparing the research boat with supplies and two of Tai's chemistry beaker sets. He has also restocked Jimmie's Myst1 and left a new case of bottles in the small hallway in case the girls need to grab some for friends in the village.

The village consists of about thirty residents and has existed for over three hundred years; having been colonized by some of the resident's ancestors from the early seventeen hundreds. Traditions remain powerful and steeped, as with the rest of the whole of China; the great sleeping red dragon. But she is sleeping no more. Incredible building projects are taking place all over the country and plans are already coming together in Beijing to one day host the Olympic Games; maybe by the year 2004 or possibly 2008. Either way, there is much to be done because one thing is for sure, when China does host the Olympic Games, it will be unlike anything the world has ever seen or will ever see again.

Jimmie tells the girls, "It's great to have all of you here. I wish I could do more for you because I'm not used to being catered to."

The girls smile and then spunky Misa Tang says, "Well, you're very welcome Mr. Huang but that doesn't mean we won't kick your ass all day long playing Mah-Jongg!"

Kim Tse smiles brightly and settles in position at the living room table. She recognizes that look in Misa's eyes and that means only one thing; it's time to gamble!

Jimmie smiles from ear-to-ear and announces, "Oh, challenge accepted Miss Tang! Mix the tiles and put your money where your mouth is young lady!"

Knowing this would happen; Tai left the girls his milk jug-sized container of miscellaneous coins to gamble with because he knows this ritual all too well. A true standard all over the massive Asian population, Mah-Jongg is one of the oldest games in existence and is directly responsible for the creation of many other popular games around the world, including most famously, Poker using cards. Another classic Chinese game that may even be older than Mah-Jongg is called Pi-que; consisting of tiles featuring Chinese numbers and other symbols. It is possibly the pre-cursor to the larger and more complex game of Mah-Jongg. Both games are beloved by over three billion people.

Tai and Yuen wrap up their preparations in Jimmie's home and kiss their girls goodbye. Tai and Jimmie bump closed fists and the young men set off on their voyage once more. Jimmie's eyes tear up because he knows his son is going to do something special today; he's going to find the full cure to this deadly virus that continues to destroy lives in their small legendary village. He knows the next outbreak could be far worse and with less than thirty residents remaining, it really wouldn't take much of an outbreak to basically wipe out the whole village once and for all.

Jimmie yells out in Mandarin to the boys the equivalent of, "God's speed and good fortune!"

On their hour-long journey to the similar spot where they anchored off-shore the day before, Tai and Yuen talk about missing playing Mah-Jongg with Jimmie and the girls. Tai shares some of his favorite moments playing Mah-Jongg with his father with Yuen because Jimmie would always include such great stories of Chinese history ranging on everything from background on the various coins they were betting with to the great line of former Chinese Emperors. He would also sprinkle in even more personal accounts from when he and his young wife first met and Tai's early years in the village.

To this day, Tai keeps his beautifully embroidered red silk Happy Coat and black silk hat in safe storage. He plans on getting a garment frame for them one day so he can hang them on his wall in his own home back in Beijing. He hasn't told his father yet but he bought a home there about a month before he graduated and he plans on asking Kim to move in with him but with all that has happened since he got back to the village, he hasn't had time to share any of this news. Yuen knows but like a true friend respecting his friend's wishes, he's said nothing.

Jimmie wins the first match against the girls so Kim gets up to make another pot of naturally sweet Chinese white tea and to retrieve more of the groups favorite almond cookies. Jimmie is in gambling heaven as he rakes in his winnings; about sixty-nine cents.

Misa announces, "Double or nothing this round?" Jimmie and Kim quickly accept and the three combatants settle in for another match.

Like clock-work, Tai and Yuen arrive within fifty feet of their last anchored point, again about fifty yards off-shore directly across from the semi-hidden star-shaped blue flowered Dragon's Tears bushes.

To preserve the plant and nurture its continued growth, Tai has already calculated how much to take from it. He thinks about this during the swim to shore and Yuen is ready to do his part as well; pruning the plant from the backside as Tai has suggested back on the boat and during their swim. Tai brought along another compound that he and Kim developed that promotes fast growth in plants; the Huang's tomatoes, daikon (Chinese radish) and bok choy (Chinese celery) are legendary.

Tai wants to continue his experiments as before with this great resource but this time, he hopes to have more time to really come up with what he hopes will be a more in-depth and truly long-lasting solution. The few doses he and Kim put together before that helped Jimmie and the villagers was truly a 'heat-of-the-moment' thing that Tai wants to improve upon and document so larger batches can be developed.

Tai confides in Yuen and tells him about his father's fish from the day before. Yuen appreciates the follow-up. They both realize they are on the right path because they saw the destroyed and decaying cells for themselves yesterday on the boat. There is something going on in the water already and if they don't do something fast, another plague to the village is all but a guarantee; the only scary question is, when and if that next wave of the plague wipes out the entire village. It's horrible to think it but they are truly lucky that only one person died from the virus this time around. They feed off of the spirits of the Kai's in their research and Tai believes they are truly with him and Yuen as they do their work.

"The Kai's have to be the last Yuen."

"I know brother. I know."

Back in the village, Jimmie has won another match, this time raking in $1.38. The girls quickly respond with another challenge but first Jimmie offers a break so the trio can take a quick stroll around the market outside; a needed leg-stretch and the opportunity once again for Jimmie to pick Kim's mind about her feelings about Tai. Jimmie wants his son and Kim together but he knows relationships these days are more complicated, especially between two people like his son and this beautiful and bright girl. Still, he tries to sway things in that direction and all Kim can do is smile and blush.

Tai and Yuen are like robots when they reach the shore. They immediately walk up shore to the Dragon's Tears bushes and begin carefully pruning branches and taking samples of both leaves and blue flowers. Tai believes it's this combination along with a few other things back home that could be the correct mix for a new vaccine that could eradicate this plague once and for all. His eyes brighten up just thinking about the possibilities. Yuen is also energized because he knows his best friend is close to coming up with something. He's envious but proud at the same time. He wishes he'd paid better attention in Chemistry class because if he had, he'd be an even greater asset to Tai. Yuen's marine biology background and specialty with shark research hasn't really come in handy yet.

Tai senses this embarrassment and feelings of inferiority in Yuen. He pats Yuen firmly on his back and says, "Brother, what we do today, we do together; plain and simple. It will always be 'us', not 'me'!"

Yuen can't believe this statement. He gives Tai a big hug and then gets back to his duties. That statement means more to him than even Tai can know.

Tai continues, "As we work on this and other things together, for context and brevity, you'll hear me say, 'I' but know that I mean 'we' and I'll prove it by patenting our findings with everyone's names!"

Yuen nods in appreciation and then quickly assembles Tai's beaker sets and his small but very powerful microscope. He begins looking around the surrounding area for other standards that they typically collect on these trips. Tai begins grinding items up. He brought along a few small bottles of powder compounds as well to test and prove out or disprove his initial theories.

After twenty minutes, Tai seems cautiously optimistic. He calls out to Yuen, who is about a hundred yards away collecting shells on the shore. Yuen finds a dying Snakehead on-shore and drops it.

Tai sees this and quickly says, "No. bring it!"

Yuen retrieves the dying fish and quickens his pace back to Tai.

Kim blushes as Jimmie asks her if she plans on having children and if so, how many. Sensing the embarrassment, Misa quickly interrupts and offers, "Yuen and I will have two; a boy and a girl. Their names are Jiang, after my grandfather and Sadie. They will both be classic pianists and Mah-Jongg masters!"

Jimmie smiles and says, "Mah-Jongg masters huh? That sounds like another challenge."

Misa fires back with, "It is!"

The trio heads back to Mr. Huang's living room for their third Mah-Jongg match.

Back on the small island, Tai and Yuen are hard at work.

"I've mixed a new form of CDT and we can really use that Snakehead", Tai explains.

Yuen catches on very quickly. He asks, "Will you test CDT on the fish?"

Tai says, "Not yet. First I'll grind up some of its scales to see what's going on cell-wise and then I will inject it with a dose of CDT. We have to be careful though because too much will kill it and too little will tell us nothing or give us a false reading or false reaction."

"Good." Yuen says. "What else can I do?"

"See if you can catch another fish. It can't be sick like this one because maybe it's too late for this Snakehead. Our tests will work better on a fresher catch."

"Right. Okay. I'll be back."

Tai knows Yuen is an expert at catching fish where it seemingly looks like there are none to be caught. He'll catch something they can use so the promising experiments can continue.

Tai studies the Snakehead's scales. They are severely damaged but Tai notices something else, there is a strange heavy film he can see that surrounds the cells. Not just the usual slick that all fishes have; these scales are stained with dark green halos; exactly in-line with what his father had described.

Tai injects .65cc's of his newly formulated CDT into the Snakehead; just below its small pectoral fin. He sets the eight-inch long dying fish back into a rectangular-shaped plastic container filled with sea water. The fish bobs from end to end. It's showing very small signs of life left. Its pectorals are moving and its gills are moving but they are moving slower and slower with each passing moment.

Tai turns his attention to his other compounds and beakers, replicating his new CDT formula for another trial test on whatever Yuen catches.

Twenty yards down shore, Yuen calls out, "Fish on!"

Yuen reels it in. He brought his trusty rod and reel that breaks down into the size of a thermos. He holds up the ten-inch long Dog-shark for Tai to see. Tai waves and gives him a quick "thumbs up."

Back in Jimmie's living room, the group begins clearing the living room table of the Mah-Jongg tiles. Jimmie has raked in the winnings yet again. At game's end, his total take amounts to a little over five dollars. He smiles deviously and both Kim and Misa notice this. They move over to him and take turns giving him a quick peck on the cheek. Then Jimmie says, "You girls head into town and get us dinner, sound good?" He passes a fifty-Yuan note to Kim. The girls make their way out the door and Jimmie settles back into his favorite recliner, once again, attempting to finish the blue dragon's mighty claws.

Back on the small island, Tai takes the Dog-shark off the line and quickly scrapes its right side for slime. He places his findings in a prepared beaker. Then he scrapes the other side of the fish a little harder, peeling off some scales. Despite this small injury the fish is fine. He places it in another rectangular plastic container and sets it alongside the dying Snakehead's container. Tai prepares the small shark's scales just as he did with the Snakehead's before and studies them under his microscope.

Dark green halos again. Tai stands up and announces, "I think we have something here."

Yuen repositions so he can look at the cells under microscope too.

"So now what?" Yuen asks.

"I have an idea. We'll introduce some CDT to the slide and see what happens to the scale cells."

Tai does this and waits a few moments. He bends back down to the microscope situated on a fallen palm tree serving as a make-shift table and delights, "The halos are gone! They're gone!"

"What? Let me see."

A moment later, Tai looks at the slide again and he sees that the dark green halos are gone, dried up and the cell structures actually appear to be repairing themselves. He grabs another slide and tests it again. Same result. Then he tests another; and another. This goes on for another hour. He switches back and forth between fish samples and tests them over and over; same result. The green halos dry up each time. Then the two young men stretch and take a moment to enjoy their early success. Yuen sits back down. He can't stop smiling. His right index finger rests slightly into the rectangular-shaped container featuring the dying Snakehead.

A moment later, Yuen jumps up from his position, holding his right index finger in momentary pain and yells, "Hey! Fucker bit me!"

Tai jumps up and laughs.

"You're laughing? This damn fish bites me and you laugh?"

Tai responds, "Yeah, that DYING fish bit you so yeah, I think that's great!"

He continues, "That thing was almost completely dead when I took samples from it just over an hour or so ago. It was barely moving and should have died moments later but look at it now. It's lively and apparently, pissed!"

Yuen adds, "Yeah, and hungry too! Shit!"

The experiment has worked. Tai came up with a formula based on his original CDT. He was able to spend some decent time learning more about the Dragon's Tears plant and flowers. He adjusted and added some of his other powder compounds and now he has developed something that appears to have cleaned up the slime that builds up and that was slowly killing these fish. Tai figures that this slime must then transform into the virus that has been plaguing the village; something to do with either ingesting the fish or simply their topical slime that ends up on fishermen's hands that they must transmit to their eyes and mouth when they step through their duties on the dock.

All of this then gets shared at market as everyone buys from everyone else depending on what they want to eat over the course of the next few days. People are cordial; they kiss each other on the cheek and they shake hands all day long with one another. Like any cold virus, that's how it is spread in any community around the world.

Tai beams with pride. He announces to Yuen, "Damn, I think we did it! We really did it!"

Energized, Yuen says, "Yes! What now boss?"

"Let's wrap all this up and get back home. I've got to get with Kim and make a ton of this new formula because I think we can mass produce this and use it as some kind of fish cleanser before people take their food home with them or maybe even something we can ingest ourselves to prevent from getting sick in the first place that would last longer, or better yet, maybe even a vaccine."

Tai is so excited, he's about to hyperventilate.

The two high-five and wrap up operations. Tai injects the Dog-shark with .65cc's of the new CDT formula and he releases both test fish.

The fish scamper off parallel to each other at first and then dart off in different directions.

Tai nods and says, "Thanks guys! You just saved us!"

Yuen quickly adds, "Yeah, thanks, you bastard shark! Have a nice day!"

He gestures with his middle finger from his right hand and waves it in the air for a moment.

They make their way back to their small research boat and head back to the village; with phenomenally promising news.

CHAPTER FOUR

THE girls arrive back from the larger town markets and begin putting things away. Jimmie gave them a small list with the fifty-Yuan note and told Kim to just hand it to a certain clerk in the store that would know all about it. She did just that and now she has these funny looking orange labelled jars along with the rest of the food they selected.

Misa notes, "The guys aren't back yet? It's past four. I hope they hurry because the sea starts getting pretty rough soon, right Mr. Huang?"

"Exactly right Misa." Mr. Huang confirms.

Then he asks, "Another couple rounds of Mah-Jongg girls, until the boys get back?"

Misa immediately accepts but Kim explains, "Thanks but I think I'll take a shower and be ready for Tai when he gets back. I have a feeling we'll have a lot of work to do tonight and tomorrow."

Mr. Huang nods and says, "Very good Kim. Misa, the tiles, and break out the coin jug again because this time, I'm going to take it all!"

"Yeah, yeah, we'll see", Misa replies, smiling from ear to ear.

Jimmie gets up and turns his small black radio on. It's always on his favorite 50's and 60's classic American Oldies station; the only one. He genuinely loves the music but considering that the other stations are talk and older Chinese slow music stations, this is his favorite for those reasons as well.

The two focus on their pending tiles and strategies as Kim makes her way up to the upstairs bedroom and adjacent bathroom. Throughout, the floor is appointed with beautiful marble tiles and small area rugs. It's like a museum.

Kim begins to undress. First her pink and white flower-print half sleeve length shirt. She carefully repositions her favorite dolphin pendant necklace. Tai bought it for her about a month after they first met and she's never taken it off since. She shower's with it on and always has.

She unfastens her satin-lined black dress pants and they drop to the floor in a collapsed funnel, shimmering to the ground next to her flower-print shirt. She bends down and picks them up, tossing them across the left hand corner of the pearl-white covered futon bed. Her light pink bra and panties are silk and with the cool late afternoon air, her small crimson nipples quickly harden. She walks into the adjacent bathroom and shower room and pauses at the half length mirror.

The small single-sink counter comes up to about two inches below her naval so from there and upward, she can see her slightly muscular lower abdomen with nicely defined upper four-pack muscles; Tai's abs are very similar but on his frame, she admires them all the more. Ironically, this is exactly what Tai adores about Kim's figure. She reminds him of the amazing gymnasts he used to watch on television on weekends at home and back in college. Those young women were such gorgeous and crazy-talented athletes, he always hoped to meet and date one of them when they came of age but being such formally trained expert athletes, they were always under high supervision and never really accessible to meet.

Kim's sleek legs are perfectly in proportion to her arms and torso as well. She could have easily been an elite gymnast but she opted for science instead because she knew a career in science will always greatly outlive any career in competitive amateur or professional sports. Still, she is an athletic woman and solid athlete. She loves American soccer, volleyball, and she runs regularly when she's back home in Beijing, where her parents live. She has two younger sisters that also love to run with her but only if their studies are complete. As with almost all Asian families, a child's studies always come first.

As she pauses at the mirror, she can't help but to fantasize about Tai. She begins to masturbate. After a moment, she stops, remembering that she's in Mr. Huang's home and how inappropriate it makes her feel. She enters the shower unit. The flooring is standard but the walls are all a beautiful grey and pink marble, matching the main bathroom floor outside of the shower unit.

Comfortably warm water cascades down her lightly tanned and toned body, finding every mildly strawberry-scented crevice. She pours a small amount of her own special blend of strawberry body wash and blends it through her fine black hair. Then she sweeps it across her neck and breasts. Her rib cage and oblique's get attention and then her smooth shaven privates. She makes a couple quick passes across the top of her clitoris and then she sweeps by the sides of her small and firming outer labia. After a moment, she makes several passes with both hands across her backside and then she returns to her abs and rib cage. She makes one final pass inside herself. Now fully aroused she sits down and finishes herself off. She can't help it. A vibrant young woman; why not. It's her body and she's just as entitled to feel good and stimulate herself as anyone else in that private moment. She misses Tai performing these erotic tasks for her though.

The guys are just five miles out now as the Sun begins to set lower and lower in the increasingly colorful sky. Hawaii has nothing on Canton's setting sun and the marvelous sunsets that the village experiences each evening. Even in the winter months, the sunsets are simply magnificent.

Tai and Yuen have been relatively quiet the whole return trip; normally discussing other fishing trips, sports, or most often, the girls. It must be the anticipation that is keeping them tight-lipped. They're still saddened by the passing of the Kai's and Tai is determined more than ever to resolve this issue.

Finished showering, Kim redresses. Downstairs, she can hear the coin container empty onto the living room table some more; meaning someone is paying up again. Misa calls upstairs, "Kim?"

She answers back, "Yes!"

"Come on, we're holding the next match for you."

Jimmie is in the kitchen making his own version of deep-fried donuts for the group; small donut holes like in the United States but these have a decidedly different flavor. They taste like that special New Year's Day cake that everyone is accustomed to but they have a little punch of lemon-ginger to them.

"All right dear?" Jimmie asks Kim.

"Yes, thank you." Still a little embarrassed, she looks down.

Just then, Misa says, "My turn at the shower." She motions to Kim and continues,

"See if you can win some of Tai's money back from Mr. Huang because I still haven't won a match!" She smiles and heads upstairs.

The two new combatants grin at each other and begin selecting tiles.

Tai and Yuen approach the docks. Tai cuts the engine and shows Yuen how he maneuvered the boat into place so quickly yesterday because he still can't believe he did it. The trip was enjoyable and it's about to get really exciting again but this time, Kim and Tai will have some time, hopefully, to take their time and discuss what exactly the approach should be.

Tai needs Kim so she can flush out in her mind his ideas of either the topical "fish cleaner" solution that would be used every day in the market by everyone and a longer-term 'vaccine' that would be given to everyone in the village. Tai can't wait to reproduce the results he saw back on the beach for her because he knows she will really be excited and grateful. Plus, he can't wait to get her alone again so they can share some more erotic moments together.

Knowing Mr. Huang's passion for fishing, no trip into the South China Seas would be complete without some fresh catches. Before they set out for the shore to collect more Dragon's Tears samples, Yuen set out a couple multi-hooked and baited fishing lines. When they returned to the boat, the effort paid off with six skillet-sized Chinese Perch.

Tai and Yuen return to Jimmie's home and right as they enter, Kim exclaims, "Mah-Jongg!" and she holds up the coin container loot in triumph.

Yuen responds with, "Dinner!" and he holds up the fish loot in triumph.

Tai asks, "What? You actually beat him?"

Jimmie's head playfully drops and he admits, "Yes. She beat me!"

Tai asks, "How much did you take him for?"

She looks down at the pool of coins and quickly calculates and says, "Five-hundred and"

Before she can finish, Tai interrupts and says, "Five-hundred?" This makes Tai nervous because he knows his father has always had a gambling problem but he didn't figure he'd have a problem playing Mah-Jongg with the girls and with just a half-filled jug of coins.

Then Kim finishes her sentence and says, "Yes, five-hundred and twenty-four CENTS. We doubled the last game and I finally won one for the girls!"

As Misa descends the stairs she sees Kim's winnings.

"Yes!" She proclaims and sends a smirk over towards Mr. Huang.

He winks back and says, "So, after all that, we all broke even on the day. How did you guys do?"

Tai sits down. Yuen takes the fish into the kitchen and sets them in the sink. He runs water over them, filling the sink up half way. Yuen rejoins the group and sits next to Misa.

Kim senses big news from Tai as well so she sits down next to him and they all face Mr. Huang.

Tai explains, "Pop. We still have a lot of tests to do. And I'm still not sure about a few things; what might work best, doses and final mixtures, all that stuff. Still a lot of testing to do, you know?"

The rest of the group is on the edge of their seats, including Yuen, who already knows what's coming but he's still enjoying the moment. Tai is such an overly dramatic and great story teller, everyone is engaged.

Jimmie smiles and says, "And?"

Tai continues. Kim grabs his hand and squeezes. He squeezes back. Yuen and Misa trade the same gestures across the table from Tai and Kim. Jimmie moves up from his former reclined position.

"Yuen and I collected more samples and I mixed a new form of CDT. Yuen found a dying Snakehead stranded on the beach. Then he caught a Dog-shark. I ran tests on the scales of both fish and they both had dark green halos under magnification; the foundation of the virus in slime form. It must combine with something else once the fish come to market and with our handling of the fish and touching our eyes and mouths, I think that kicks off the sickness that people end up contracting."

"We shake hands with each other, kiss each other on the cheek, etc. and this spreads it just like any other contagious cold virus, right?"

Everyone nods.

"Plus, we ingest these fish and of course, that gives us an even larger dose of the virus that truly becomes viral in our bodies."

Everyone nods again.

"So, I placed a droplet of the new CDT formula I made on the test slides of each fish and the dark green halos slowly disappeared and seemed to even dry up and disappear."

The group starts getting restless so Tai continues, "But wait, this is the most exciting part! After a few moments as I looked at the Dog-shark's scales, the scales actually looked like they were repairing themselves!" Then I tested them again. First the Snakehead's scales from the dying Snakehead right? Same thing; its dark green halos cleared up. Then I injected the dying fish with .65cc's of the new CDT and placed it back in its container. It was still dying and should have died any moment after that."

Misa quickly inquires, "It should have died?"

Tai says, "Yes, it should have died. I returned to testing the Dog-shark and got the same good results so Yuen and I celebrated briefly. He sat down and had his right index finger in the dying Snakehead's container when…"

Yuen stands up and exclaims, "Yeah, when the little fucker bit me!"

Everyone bursts out laughing as Yuen sternly looks around and sits back down. He shows the bite to everyone. The fish's teeth broke the skin in two places and left indentations on another finger.

Jimmie peers over at Yuen's finger and smiles.

Yuen mumbles under his breath just barely out of range of everyone's hearing, "Great, I get bit and everyone laughs at me…"

He's kidding. It's his sarcastic way of being funny in the moment that he should actually voice louder, just in case he is misunderstood.

Tai continues, "Most importantly remember; the scale cells began repairing themselves. That was with just a droplet of the new CDT formula I made and used. Now imagine that on a larger scale."

Tai smiles and continues, "Imagine what that means if we can make enough formula to develop a new fish cleanser; a wash for everyone to use to combat the slime that almost all fishes have on them when they come into market."

Tai's voice begins to get louder. Everyone wrestles about again and Jimmie starts to tear up.

Tai notices this and says, "Wait dad. Plus I am thinking about a much more permanent solution, like a vaccine that we can give to everyone that could build up immunity against the slime that I think results in the virus that has been destroying lives in this village for as long as we can all remember!" Tai points to the ceiling in honor of his mother Mia and younger brother Qin and breaks down.

Now everyone breaks down crying out of sheer relief and joy. Jimmie gets up and walks over to his son. They embrace and Jimmie squeezes the back of Tai's neck and says proudly, "I think you did it! I'm so proud of all of you kids."

Tai immediately adds, "Yes, we did it because I couldn't have completed the tests without Yuen and he caught the samples right when I needed them. It all came together because we worked together!"

Yuen and Misa hug tighter and Yuen looks over at Tai and nods in solemn appreciation.

Totally overwhelmed and excited, Kim joins the father-son embrace and whispers into Tai's ear, "I love you!" Tai hugs his father once again and then picks Kim up and spins her around in the air. He brings her close into himself again and softly says, "We get this fixed and then you marry me?"

Jimmie over hears the proposal and reconfirms, "Wait, what was that son?"

Kim starts crying and immediately shouts out, "Yes! I'll marry you!"

Everyone starts crying again and the whole group comes together. They hold each other and simply celebrate the amazing break-through moments of the day. After a moment, Kim and Tai break away to kiss and dance together. Yuen and Misa do the same. Jimmie heads into the kitchen to retrieve another pastry. Tomorrow will be a busy day and for weeks to come but right now, everyone rejoices.

Forty-three miles up the coast from Macau, the test Snakehead swims along darting around like normal. His full energy restored, he is invigorated like never before. Ever the predator, he seeks out new prey. He spots a small school of fish and quickly heads towards them. The fish's natural instincts are in over-drive since it received a shot of something from that human back on the beach. It closes in on the school and prepares its classic attack from below, just like a Great White shark preys upon its prospective meal. A moment later, a six-foot long female short-fin Mako shark opens its jaws and swallows the snakehead fish whole. The powerful Mako's eyes don't even move as she peers around for more prey. She had sensed this snakehead from about two hundred and fifty yards away and simply honed in on it; of course being the fastest fish in the ocean didn't hurt her chances for catching this meal either.

South and west about a mile and a half away from this predation, the test Dog-shark swims along. It feeds on individuals from a small school of squid swimming by and then darts down into deeper waters. It follows its instinctive pattern of hugging the nearby coastline, just as the laws of nature and instinct have ordained for hundreds of millions of years for so many marine animals, including sharks. A rogue like most sharks except hammer heads in the open ocean, the solitary small Dog-shark enjoys the cooler depths.

Huge predators lurk below the small Dog-shark. It can sense some of them but being one of the smaller species of sharks and being just a juvenile of only eighteen months old, his senses are not nearly as keen and powerful as the rogue short-fin Mako sharks that are swimming below. The whole highway of predators and prey below perform their dance, just as they have done since the oceans became full of life. Moments later, the Dog-shark's movements become labored. It's struggling. There are no immediate threats around him. There are no predators plotting against him. It climbs from the deeps to get to the surface. When it reaches the surface, the fish is dead. It bobs along the surface like a small empty black thermos. Birds of prey approach it. They smell the new carcass and immediately fly away from it.

Just then back on shore, directly across from where the test Dog-shark had been wading in its plastic container, a four-foot long squid washes on-shore. It's dead. Its tentacles are tinged dark green as waves move the dead invertebrate back and forth across the rocky shoreline.

An hour passes and the female short-fin Mako that swallowed the test Snakehead has swum closer into shore. She swims closer to the sea floor. As she does, she startles a three-foot long stingray that jets it poisonous tail at her repeatedly. Too far away to do any harm, the female Mako ignores the effort. She quickly weaves in and out of an outcropping of sea weed and continues to glide along effortlessly. Fifty yards away from her, another larger male Mako picks up on struggling signals. It changes direction and heads towards the source.

As the larger male Mako zeroes in on the struggling source, his appetite grows. He extends his short but powerful jaws; they jet outward as he looks forward to his initial bite. There's no need. He backs off and in a flash he veers away and dives deep back into the abyss. After a few moments, the six-foot female Mako begins tipping to her left side. She struggles briefly to right herself but a few moments later; her once vibrant and powerful body floats to the surface like a six-foot long silver casket. Her once focused black eyes are tinged slightly green and her once ferocious jagged white teeth are also tinged and jet out from her once lethal jaws. Birds of prey from on-shore fly toward her and approach. They smell this newly dead fish and alertly fly away.

CHAPTER FIVE

June 6, 1985 – Yokohama, Japan 11 P.M.

IN a lavishly decorated room featuring two six-foot tall salt-water aquariums in half-moon shapes and sacred Samurai swords resting in the center of each wall in various patterns with the traditional empire of Japan red sun on each wall, Japanese Yakuza leaders receive word that the young Tai Huang and his friends have created a new multi-purpose elixir and they want it for their own docks and for possible "research" on whales in the Antarctic Circle.

Japan's on-going struggles versus Australia's *Sea Guardians* keeps them very busy and often, preoccupied. Their four-ship fleet, called the *Misha Katana* (#1 through #4), are led by Commander Eishi Torusan. The first ship is the factory ship that features a huge slipway for bringing harpooned grey, humpback, and sometimes even blue whales onboard. The other three ships all feature the latest in technology with regards to tracking and reporting their profits back to their port headquarters at Yokohama. It is rumored by both the Chinese and Australian governments that Eishi Torusan and his fleet are financed by the Japanese Yakuza but of course, there is no direct proof of this organized criminal relationship to date.

Australia leads all efforts to have these practices banned because Japan is ruining the ecological systems throughout the Antarctic and Indian Oceans and in every other area of the southern Pacific. Whaling has been formally outlawed in these areas but Japan claims they are conducting 'research' so that's how they are skirting the current international laws for the time being.

The dedicated efforts of Australia's *Sea Guardians* headed by Captain Darren Hall continue to derail Japan's hopes for harvesting their annual quotas. The *Sea Guardian's* fleet features four ships as well; a Command ship led by Captain Hall, a twenty-five year retired veteran of the Australian Royal Navy. The second and third ships both feature the most advanced GPS tracking and on-deck high-resolution video recording to capture these horrible whaling activities. The recorded events are then sent directly in real time to Australian government officials for their review in determining illegal activities being conducted by the Japanese *Misha Katana* fleet. The Sea Guardian's fourth ship is a very special speed boat outfitted with custom-made propeller failing devices the crew calls, 'prop-failers'. These devices consist of very heavy gauge ship's anchor-type rope with a variety of small metal objects hanging along the edges. The speed boat operator and his small crew of two or three launch this device whenever they close in on any one of the *Misha Katana* positions. They deploy these heavy gauge ropes by throwing them across the intended path of the Japanese whaling ships but they primarily target the factory ship.

Several times in recent seasons, the *Misha Katana1* or one of the other protective ships has literally run over the *Sea Guardian's* speed boat and this has caused great anxiety and anger amongst both fleets. Captain Hall has personally commissioned the building of new speed boats for the past decade in support of his fierce dedication to stopping these illegal whaling activities and in 2010, he actually paid for one of the speed boats out of his own savings; a little over $100,000 Pounds Sterling. He christened it the *Kill Switch*. Each season, the *Sea Guardian* crews love hearing him proclaim, "Throw the Kill Switch" whenever they close in on the Japanese whaling fleet.

All of the *Sea Guardian* ships feature a wide variety of other implements used to deter the Japanese whaling activities; on more of a mano-y-mano basis. These implements include custom cocktails that can be thrown at the illegal Japanese whaling vessels in an attempt to sicken the crew. The cocktails feature a variety of rotten ingredients that upon contact will certainly prevent that Japanese crew member from carrying out his or her regular duties. The Japanese crew responds by throwing an assortment of items including alkaline batteries and firing their water canon back at the *Sea Guardian's*. This behavior goes on for hours as long as the combatant ships are within range of each other.

One of Captain Hall's favorite devices this season is the new cocktail cannon he made. It fires the rotten cocktail bottles high into the air and over new netting that the Japanese have devised to combat this ongoing threat to their 'research' activities. At the conclusion of each season Japan sues the Australian Captain and his crew for damages but Captain Hall fires right back with documented whaling activities when Japan is able to land a few whales on their factory ship's slipway. Captain Hall is also very careful to document the Japanese factory ship's processing plant activities that are directly forward and to the right of the slipway; proof that these 'research' efforts are in fact simply food processing and packaging activities. Captain Hall even has proof from an insider who infiltrated the Japanese crew. She has physical and further video evidence showing the packaging tape and cans that are used to package a wide variety of whale products.

With his boom microphone and video cameras high up on several masts and his on-deck high resolution digital cameras, the *Sea Guardian's* document everything. Unfortunately this also includes the Japanese mercilessly shooting several great whales with their cannon-like harpoon. The devastating explosions rock the whole area as these deadly implements strike their targets. The whales scream out in horrific agony and their death throws can be heard for miles as they slowly die. Then they are systematically repositioned and loaded onto the *Misha Katana1's* slipway to be processed. To witness this horrible event take place even once is something no human being will ever forget but to the Japanese, it's simply *'research'*.

Back in the lavishly decorated room, a large man stands at the front of an onyx-clad Executive table. As he stands, the rest of the Japanese Yakuza leaders take a quiet deep breath in and briefly hold it. It's Boss Saitonaka and he's about to announce that his gang will oversee the "Tai-son" project. His grainy deep voice and ominous dark look rivals that of Hades himself.

Boss Saitonaka is a direct descendent of Japanese Samurai's that decimated parts of Northern China and Outer Mongolia in centuries past and he richly believes that this is how business should sometimes be conducted today; just cut off their heads and be done with it.

He is always seen carrying his trusty black and white snake-headed cane that is actually a sword. Custom built for him when he was only twelve by his father, Boss Ito, this sword's scabbard features intricately carved ivory and is topped off with a 24k gold trick locking clasp with his initials engraved into it. No other man's hands have ever touched this sword and no other man's hands ever will; unless they don't value their hands and their head.

Boss Saitonaka says, "Gentleman! What we embark on today will set a new course in history for the Empire of Japan." The room erupts with applause.

Boss Saitonaka's eyes squint and darken. "Tai-son Huang will give us his formula and then I'll feature his young head on the mantel behind you for everyone to give thanks."

A demonic laugh emanates from Boss Saitonaka as the rest of the Yakuza leaders glance over at a special display area against the far wall. It has a blue light that cascades down from the ceiling and a small shelf decorated with banzai trees at the moment. The other leaders all sense a chill in the air as they turn back around.

"I will lead this effort and each of you will show your respect by doing whatever I ask of you, whenever I ask, without question!" The room again erupts with applause.

"I make this point clear to you all right now; if I don't get this formula because of your group's interference, your heads and the heads of your families will adorn my new blue-lighted shelves before Tai-son's head does! My nephew Eishi Torusan anxiously awaits this new formula and I will not have my sister wait any longer for her son's return speaking of his successes in the Indian Ocean, is that also clear?"

Boss Saitonaka does not expect any responses and as usual, he does not get any; to do so would be an insult. What he has said and 'asked' is simply accepted and understood.

Boss Saitonaka sits down; carefully re-positioning his cane to the left side. The room applauds as six women appear from behind the adjacent wall. They are carrying platters featuring various kinds of sushi and two of the women are carrying small white futon-style cushions. They lay them across the floor and lie down on them. All of the women are naked. The rest of the Yakuza leaders push away from their positions at the formal onyx table and make their way to the cushions and intimate entertainment area. Boss Saitonaka remains in his seat at the table. The women undress the men and several engage in oral pleasures on them. The group then helps themselves to the variety of sushi and saké that is featured on small tables that more naked women have returned with from the back room kitchen. Light traditional Japanese music begins to play in the background as Boss Saitonaka looks over at the crowd and smirks. He claps his heavy hands together and the music stops. Everyone in their current positions of undress and activity stops.

Two more naked women appear from the back wall. They are armed with Japanese short swords that they hold in front of their shapely chests. Boss Saitonaka rises from his chair and the women rush to meet him. The women place the swords in each of Boss Saitonaka's hands and they begin undressing him. The trio makes their way over to a new red silk futon-style cushion that has been placed on the floor for Boss Saitonaka and they slowly lay him down on it.

As one of the women massages Boss Saitonaka's penis, he selfishly declares, "I am the top Yakuza Boss now and in perpetuity!"

The other men stare at him like deer caught in headlights and say nothing.

He continues, "I have always been smarter than each of you so it is truly my rightful place and privilege. I know some of you may very well plot against me so let me just say this, do whatever you're going to do, right fucking now or shut up because this is as weak as you'll ever see and catch me so you might as well make your move now while you have this opportunity!"

He squints his eyes for a moment and then throws one of the short swords into the void of the room. The sword sticks and rings out, having found it's intended target. Everyone in the room turns slightly and witnesses the sword sticking in the wall directly behind one of the now former banzai trees that had been resting on the top shelf under the blue light. One naked woman rushes over to retrieve the sword and as she does, Boss Saitonaka releases the second sword. Just as she arrives at the shelf unit, the sword whips by her right side at hip high; slicing her skin on its way. She doesn't wince or even acknowledge the wound. She retrieves both swords from the wall and makes her way back to Boss Saitonaka.

She bows and places the swords at his feet. Then she approaches him. He smiles and licks her wound. Other than their slight head turn to see the sword stuck in the wall, everyone in the room still has not moved from their earlier positions. As Boss Saitonaka savors the woman's blood, he climaxes. He sighs and then claps his hands. The room resumes as they were before. The orgy goes on for hours.

CHAPTER SIX

JULY 4, 1985 – GUANGZHOU, CHINA; JIMMIE HUANG'S HOME

AS the United States celebrates her Independence for the two hundredth and ninth time, Jimmie Huang wakes up early to begin celebrating his son's and future daughter-in-law's pending wedding engagement. Having accepted last night in front of him and Tai and Kim's best friends and co-scientists, Sik Yuen and Misa, the group is energized like never before. With the group's discovery of a new CDT-based elixir that has proven to repair a fish's scale integrity as well as helping to bring a dying fish back to life, the tight-knit group begins to plan their momentous day. Impromptu weddings are not common but since they want to share this with their families as soon as possible so they can get back to their dedicated work, Mr. Huang has arranged for a quick wedding ceremony with the local magistrate, a friend of his, for July 7; in just three days.

The next morning, Tai and Kim awake and playfully wrestle around for a few moments. They enter the shower room together and go through their favorite rituals. They kiss passionately under the warm water and caress each other's bodies, reaching into every visible and hidden place. Kim takes Tai's pulsating member in her hands and caresses it with increasing pressure until he nearly collapses in delight. Recovering quickly he throws Kim up around his waist. She reaches down and spreads herself for him. Then she rears back almost going unconscious as he enters her, moving her up and down on himself. After ten minutes of this fantastic water-torture, the two climax together. Kim carefully slips back down to the shower floor and makes one more pass under the now lukewarm water. As she exits, she splashes water back onto Tai, brushing across his member. Tai exits the shower and Kim greets him with a dry towel. He drops it to the floor and grabs the wet towel from around her waist. Still erect, Tai picks Kim up and lays her across the bed. She massages him and again he enters her, taking the time to caress her smoothly shaven lower abdomen along the way. After another ten minutes, Tai senses her impending scream. He places his pinky and middle fingers from his right hand in her mouth. Just as he does, she climaxes and bites down on his fingers. He extracts his fingers and his exhausted member and smiles deeply. Tai reaches down for the wet towel and brushes it across his body. He walks over to the clothes hamper and deposits it. On his way back, he hangs the dry towel back up and turns around. Kim greets him with her classic abs tickle and then she kisses his defined stomach muscles and runs her hands along the tops of his thighs. The couple dresses each other and kisses often. Kim leans over and offers a whisper into Tai's left ear, "My-Tai!"

"So, I'll head back to Beijing. I can't wait to tell my folks!" Kim exclaims.

Tai says, "Okay. That will be great. I'm happy for them too! I get to make an honest woman out of their stunning daughter!" Kim fires back a quick smile and a wink at Tai.

Tai continues, "I'll get to work with Yuen. We'll have everything ready for you when you return so you can help me with a vaccine, deal?"

"Check, mate!"

"Clever girl."

Kim heads downstairs and runs across Misa who is just finishing her breakfast of steamed Chinese Perch, rice, and vegetables, compliments of Mr. Huang.

"I'm heading to Beijing Misa. Come with?"

"I really would but I thought I could help Yuen with his experiment setups and then Mr. Huang gave me that look he has for a Mah-Jongg rematch so…"

"Gotcha. You guys have fun. I can't wait to see my mother's face!"

Tai heads downstairs and catches the end of that conversation. He brushes by Kim, tickling her back and shakes her left hand as he heads into the kitchen for a breakfast plate.

Misa asks, 'You'll eat first right?"

Kim says, "No thanks. I'm too tired."

Misa covers her mouth and laughs. Yuen also laughs.

She recovers and says, "I mean, thanks but I'm not hungry."

Yuen mumbles under his breath, "You were hungry earlier but Tai took care of that hunger!"

Kim waves goodbye to Mr. Huang and blows him a kiss. Jimmie Huang smiles and waves back. He says, "Take care sweetheart. We'll see you and your parents real soon?"

Kim smiles and says, "Very soon!"

Finishing up his breakfast, Tai joins Kim and the couple head to Tai's new silver coupe; Jimmie Huang had it delivered to his home in anticipation of his son's graduation and resulting visit. He tosses her the keys and says, "Drive careful. Treat YOUR car well."

Kim starts crying and says, "But your dad just gave you this car."

"Think of it as an early wedding gift from him and I'll work on your ring!"

Kim's speechless. She just cries and hugs him deeply and just stands there. Tai holds her hand and tickles the inside of her right hand palm. This signals her to just get in the car before they both explode into tears. Kim drives away and honks the horn as she turns the corner to head up to the main road.

Tai and Yuen quickly resume their work and Misa begins assembling the various beaker sets, canned powder compounds, and various other instruments that Tai and Kim will need when she returns. Tai quickly starts making new CDT base formula in preparation of the new revised CDT formula that he and Kim will need to test on more fish. This new formula will help to immediately combat the slime that is present on all fish caught and brought to market. As the fishermen handle the various fish, they can simply wash their hands and the fish with this formula and that will help to greatly reduce the transmission of any possible bacteria that could turn into an infection. Yuen reminds himself to remind all of the villagers to wash their hands thoroughly with the solution and to always properly cook all of their food, preferably well-done.

Jimmie motions over to Tai, signaling to him that he's going to go fishing for the afternoon. So proud of them all, he just looks back and says, "You fix things up here and I'll go and catch dinner."

Yuen and Misa give a 'thumbs up' and Tai says, "Right Pop. Hurry back so we can explain everything we've done in excruciating detail…" He smirks and winks.

Leaving, Jimmie Huang says, "Yeah, save that for everyone that can follow it!" He smirks and winks back at his son.

Armed with a new case of Myst1 and a big bottle of Aspirin, the team heads out to see all villagers to make sure they have their monthly supply of Diabetes-combating medicine. This gives Yuen the opportunity to give his cooking preparation speech that he's been practicing all morning. Misa can sense the mild stress he's suffering so she runs her hand underneath Yuen's shirt and gently scratches his back as they walk toward the first group of resident fishermen.

As soon as they get within ear shot, Yuen just blurts out, "You have to cook your food very well done!" The small group turns and smiles at the approaching threesome. One of the men asks, "What was that Yuen?"

Tai offers, "Morning everyone! We have more Myst1 for you all and some Aspirin to protect your hearts!" Yuen walks behind Tai and in appreciation, pats him on the back. Misa and Yuen then distribute the elixir and a handful of pills to each person. With some of the villager's homes nearby, Tai offers to take their supplies over there and the residents all nod in approval.

"We'll just leave them on your porch and you can bring them in later after your day of fishing and trading."

Exiting the inlet that leads in and out of the Canton docks, Jimmie Huang smiles and directs his boat through the crazy waterway; this port may be the second busiest port in the world but for Mr. Huang, it's simply business as usual. As usual, he's in a fishermen's heaven.

Tai hid another surprise for Kim in the passenger's seat of her car; a plane ticket and a parking pass. Instead of having to drive all the way up north to Beijing, now she can relax and fly back home to collect her things and her parents. She puts the plane ticket in her small handbag and then she looks at the parking pass. It's a three day pass for airport parking in the VIP section, as close as you can get to her Departures gate. On the reverse side of the parking pass, it says "Open the glove-box baby!" on a small sticky note.

She smiles as she reviews Tai's crazy near-illegible hand-writing and opens the glove-box. She sees a black leather box with a silver lace ribbon around it and a couple 14k gold dragon pendants attached to it. She's just approaching the turn-off to the airport so she shuts the glove box and completes her drive. Her heart begins to race; almost matching the car's engine.

Thirty minutes later, she arrives in the VIP parking lot of the Canton International Airport. The car is shut off but her heart continues to churn. She opens the glove-box again and grabs the black leather box. There's a small note on the outside of the box but when she sees the two 14k gold dragon pendants, she starts to cry. After a moment, she reads the note;

"My-Kim! The dragons are for your parents. Ready to open your box?

Love, Your-Tai!"

She kisses the dragons and puts them in her dark blue silk jacket pocket. She opens the box and immediately explodes into tears. There, staring back at her is a four-karat diamond engagement ring; like nothing she's ever seen in her life. It's simply the most stunning ring ever. The silver pillow that supports the ring is coming out of position so she moves to reposition it when it comes loose. As she pulls it away, she notices another small note folded underneath it.

She shakes in complete nervousness and delight as she tries her ring on for the first time. It's a perfect fit. After a few moments of being completely lost staring at her engagement ring, she wipes her joyful tears away and reads the second note;

"Your plane leaves in thirty minutes so move your sweet ass!"

She bursts out laughing.

After a moment, she collects her things and makes her way into the airport check-in and then on to the terminal. She's spent about two seconds looking at where she's actually walking and the rest of the time staring at her left hand ring finger.

In the early evening, Kim's plane arrives on time at Beijing International Airport and her parents, Bruce and LuAnn Tse are waiting with hugs. They have no idea she's engaged. As Kim approaches her mother, the two burst into tears. Bruce looks up into the air as if to say, "Oh boy, here we go."

The two women can't stop crying and hugging each other and after a while Bruce begins to get uncomfortable. He's just standing there as his wife and daughter carry on. After a few more moments, he's feeling left out because Kim hasn't even acknowledged his presence. Finally, the two women separate a little and Bruce says, "Anything left for me?"

Kim raises her left hand and Bruce starts crying. They embrace one another and continue laughing and crying together. A couple walking by sees the ring on Kim's finger and they start clapping. The proud parents and bride-to-be collect themselves and walk out to Bruce's car.

A few hours later, back at their family home, Kim has told her parents about almost everything except Tai's hidden gifts and how he must have planned all of this out way in advance. Her parents agree and Bruce offers, "That Tai. Clever young man!"

LuAnn adds, "So sweet and generous!" She starts crying again. Kim adds, "And sneaky, My-Tai! I had no idea he had a ring already made and fitted for me! He even threw me off by saying that he was going to work on it while I was gone!"

Kim looks up into the air and says playfully, "Oh, he's gonna get it when I get back!"

Bruce interrupts, "Easy girl!"

Blushing now, Kim says, "Dad! You know what I mean."

Blushing a little now too, Bruce says, "Yeah, I do know what you mean!"

After a moment, Kim adds, "And Mr. Huang. Amazing man! He gave me and Misa fifty yuan each to get groceries that only came up to twenty dollars or so and he makes his famous Chinese Perch, rice and vegetable breakfast for us all every morning!"

Bruce repositions in his seat and says, "Hmm… sounds good."

"It really is and he makes this special sauce that I can't even describe. You'd have to taste it to believe me."

LuAnn adds, "Jimmie has always been such a great man. I miss his wife and son so much; Mia and Qin."

She breaks down in grief and runs into the bathroom.

Bruce wipes tears away and says, "You know Kim. We used to live close to the Canton docks where Mr. Huang and Tai grew up but I moved us away from there about twenty years ago. You and Tai actually used to have play dates together until we moved when you were both five."

Kim starts crying and says, "I didn't know that."

She gets up from her chair next to her father and falls into his lap. He hugs and holds his daughter, never wanting to let go but then after twenty seconds or so he remembers, she's an engaged young lady now so he props her back up on her feet and says, "Ok. Tomorrow's a big day; a lot to do and very little time. Get some rest now sweetheart."

Kim leans back down and kisses her father on the cheek and says, "Night Dad."

Early the next morning, July 6, 1985, the Tse's are filled with electricity; their alertness and readiness for the day is in hyper-drive. Bruce stayed up all night making calls to family and friends and calling in some favors for his daughter's wedding and LuAnn has been nothing short of a woman possessed, arranging for her daughter's wedding dress, flowers, and the reception hall. In the eight hours overnight, everything is ready. It may have come together so quickly for a very small gathering and ceremony but this will be one of the more memorable weddings in recent Canton times; the Tse's and the Huang's will be one.

Kim's parents bring her up to speed on everything they've arranged and again, she's speechless.

Bruce and LuAnn take turns declaring, "Your cake is being made right now. Your dress and the cake will be shipped Next Day to Canton in the next few hours. Your flowers are ordered and will all be delivered the next day. The photographers are ready and will meet with Mr. Huang first thing tomorrow morning. We've called everyone so we'll have a second reception for you when you two get back from Hawaii."

Taking all that information in, Kim cries and then asks, "Hawaii?" Bruce and LuAnn smile and the threesome start to cry again. Bruce says, "Two weeks; Maui, then to the Big Island and both sides, Hilo and then Kona! Just like your mother and my honeymoon!"

Kim hugs her parents and then reaches into her travel bag. She pulls out the two 14k gold dragon pendants and says, "From Tai!" LuAnn covers her mouth and Bruce immediately just says, "Amazing young man!"

LuAnn collects herself long enough to give her daughter one more hug and kiss on her cheek and asks, "Do you want me to call Mr. Huang so he or Tai can pick you up at the Canton airport?"

Kim cries again and says, "I have a car at the airport parking lot. Tai gave me his new car that Mr. Huang just bought for him!"

LuAnn hugs her daughter again and runs back into the house. Overwhelmed but keeping it together a little better, Bruce hugs Kim and says, "Wow! Ok. Let's get you to the airport. Your mom will be fine here until we head out later today so let's go or we'll have to go through all of this again at the airport!"

Bruce and Kim make their way to the Beijing International Airport.

11 A.M. at the gate, Bruce hugs Kim and says, "Travel safe. We'll see you tomorrow afternoon sweetheart!" Then he whispers, "Congratulations baby!"

Kim hugs her father back and smiles. She waves back as she walks down the airport connection tunnel. Bruce starts crying as he walks away from her view; his little girl is going to be married tomorrow and that fact just hit him.

During her flight, Kim thinks of all the things she wants to do and get for everyone who put all this together. She starts sketching ideas for a custom-made silk suit for Mr. Huang that he can relax in during weekends and evenings and some brand new fishing gear; everything she's seen in his current arsenal plus about ten new things she knows he'll love, including a new set of scaling and cleaning knives.

For Yuen and Misa, she decides on a slick new kitchen appliance; a new stainless steel refrigerator will do the trick. For Tai, a custom-made 24k gold wedding band featuring three small diamonds signifying; her, him, and them. And of course, a new batch of strawberry-scented body wash for her, that's actually for Tai. She blushes in her window seat as the plane taxis to her arrival gate.

4:15 P.M. Kim makes her way to the parking lot and gets into her new silver coupe. She can't wait to get back to everyone and the seventh can't get here soon enough. She pulls out of her parking space and proceeds down the single lane exit. As she pulls out a black van with tinted windows pulls out from a space a few places behind her and another black van pulls out from a block ahead of her.

As the three cars approach the airport exit gates, the van in front of her stalls and stops; she waits, patiently at first but after a few minutes she honks her horn. Nothing happens. The van in front doesn't move. After another minute, she honks again. Getting really frustrated, she honks a third time but still nothing. Finally, she exits her car and approaches the van in front of her.

As she reaches the van's driver side door, the black van behind her hits her silver coupe. She jumps to the side and looks back in shock. There are no other cars coming or going in or out of the airport.

She walks back to look over the damage to her car and as she does, the driver side door to the van in front opens. Two men exit the van in back and begin apologizing but they are talking so fast, she can't make out what they're saying. One thing she knows for sure, they are not speaking Mandarin or Cantonese Chinese. As the two apologetic men continue rambling on, the man from the van in front is approaching her from behind. She senses this and just as she turns around, the man puts a damp cloth over her mouth. Five seconds later with very little struggle, she's unconscious.

JULY 7, 1985 8 A.M. – KIM AND TAI'S WEDDING DAY AT JIMMIE HUANG'S HOME

With the ceremony in just four hours, everything is set. The photographers arrived early at 6 A.M. and began setting up cameras in Jimmie Huang's home as well as outside for the new bride and groom's wedding pictures.

The flowers are already arriving as well and Jimmie is at the front door signing off on Kim's wedding dress and the wedding cake from very special delivery. Tai is on his way to the airport to pick up Kim's parent's Bruce and LuAnn. Yuen and Misa are handling the rest of the decorations in Jimmie's house and greeting various guests who are arriving. In all the commotion and fire-storm of activity, no one has asked about Kim this morning. They each figured the other had talked to her so no one has asked.

At the airport, Tai picks up Bruce and LuAnn. The older couple can't stop hugging the young man.

Bruce shakes his hand and says, "Tai. Thanks so much for everything son. Kim gave us the gold dragons. You didn't have to do that."

LuAnn moves in and practically picks Tai up in her short but powerful and adrenaline-filled arms. She starts crying and says, "The ring was so special; so amazing! I'm so happy for you two!"

Tai rights himself and smiles. Then he asks, "Did Kim take a later flight or is she staying with a girlfriend this morning because we haven't seen her yet."

Bruce immediately says, "No. She was on her scheduled flight yesterday. I took her and watched her leave. She should have touched down a little after four."

LuAnn adds, "And she told us what your dad and you gave her; too generous. I can't wait to see that car!"

Tai adds, "Did she call you this morning then because now I'm getting worried."

"I'm sure she's fine. You're right. She probably is staying with another girlfriend so she can relax before this afternoon." Bruce seems confident in what he says but underneath his breath, he's nervous too.

10 A.M. – just two hours to go. Tai is pacing the house and starting to get upset. His senses are in overdrive and not with the regular wedding jitters everyone knows and hears about. He feels something is genuinely wrong but he doesn't want to upset Kim's parents. Jimmie starts calling some of his friends at the airport; asking them if they saw Kim earlier this morning. It makes him feel bad to ask but maybe Kim got cold feet and took off on some other flight.

CHAPTER SEVEN

11 A.M. – Guangzhou, China; Jimmie Huang's home

JUST one hour to go. Now everyone is concerned. The remaining guests are arriving and are immediately learning that the beautiful bride is nowhere to be found. Even the ordained local magistrate is worried because he's known these two families all their lives and he knows Kim would not have second thoughts without at least telling her mother. Yuen and Misa start calling the airports again, both Canton and Beijing International.

Bruce and LuAnn are in shock. Jimmie Huang paces throughout his home trying to figure out what is going on and as he circles around his son, for the first time in a long time, he can't think of one single thing to say to help calm his son's mind and spirit. What was to be one of the village's highest moments ever has turned into an abyss of depression and doubt.

Around this same time – Somewhere in Japan

Kim starts to come around; slowly recovering from the effects of the chemicals that knocked her out a few hours earlier. She wakes up naked on the top of red silk covers in a small bedroom adorned with flowers on the two end tables next to the bed. There's a dark figure sitting in a lounge chair directly across from her smoking a cherry-scented cigar. She picks up on the scent first and immediately wraps herself up in the silk covers.

The figure speaks. "How do you know I didn't already have my way with you, several times?"

"Who the hell are you? Where am I you bastard?"

"You're safe, for now. Japan. How long that stays true is up to you Kim."

"Who are you? How do you know my name?"

Just then she starts feeling an awkward and terrible pain. She winces and reaches down to touch herself. When she brings her hand back up to her face, she nearly passes out. Her clitoris has been pierced and is still bleeding.

Frantic now, she starts crying. "What did you do to me you fucking bastard?"

"Bastard? Me? No. You're one of MY girls now and I'll give you the same choice I offer to all my girls."

"Fuck you! Let me out of here! I'm supposed to be getting married right now!"

"I know Kim."

"Fucker, stop calling my name!"

"Rude; such language from a sweet and tight young lady. My offer is simply this; I take you now and often and you marry me..."

Kim reaches over to the end table on her left side and grabs the vase of flowers. She throws it into the corner at the dark figure. The vase and flowers explode upon impact on the wall behind the dark figure.

"Let me finish. I take you now and you marry me soon enough or I don't take you and in return for my generosity, you never see your family or fiancée again. How's that?"

Kim reaches over and grabs the flowers on the right side end table. She throws them into the dark corner. As they near their target, Kim hears the distinct sound of a sword being drawn. In the next second, the vase and flowers are sent all over the room in a thunderous explosion.

"I see. You need some time to think it over. I understand. You have until Noon. The exact time you were supposed to be saying 'I do" to that little fucker Tai Huang!"

The dark figure exits the small room. Kim collapses to the floor, rolls up in a fetal ball and cries. Small shards from the vases start to cut her right shoulder, side, and leg. She passes out from the extreme stress, grief and pain.

NOON – GUANGZHOU, CHINA

Jimmie Huang's home is silent. Completely filled with over thirty guests and another eight people directly supporting elements of the wedding, people mill around like the walking dead; no one knows what to say or what to do.

LuAnn hasn't stopped crying for the past hour; her daughter is nowhere to be found on her wedding day. Misa is in shock and is crying now because she can't imagine any scenario where Kim would have changed her mind and would not have told someone by now. Misa, Yuen and Tai have called everyone they know in Beijing; former classmates, friends, and even the restaurant and bar owners where they used to hang out as students. Tai collapses into a chair in the living room where he was supposed to be standing and getting married to his girlfriend of the past five years. Instead, he's wondering where she is and if she's okay. Jimmie joins his son. Guests begin moving outside to give the Huang's and Tse's some space. Bruce Tse staggers for a moment and then clutches his chest. LuAnn immediately calls out for help and several friends and guests come to their aid; they help Bruce to the living room sofa and a lady brings him a glass of orange juice. Jimmie sees his magistrate friend and excuses himself.

Yuen has been very busy. He's been making calls from the Kai's home to various places in China, India, Australia, and Hong Kong. First he heard Kim was in Shanghai. Then ten minutes later, he got a tip that she was in Dubai. Finally, a senior member confirms that Kim is in Yokohama, Japan. She's alive, for now. Yuen reconfirms this information and demands to be kept informed at this number.

Noon – Yokohama, Japan

The door to the small bedroom swings open. The man who had been harassing Kim an hour and a half earlier enters the room and walks over to the bed; he's naked. Two women accompany him pushing an ornate cart. Another man enters behind the two women balancing a coffin propped up on a dolly. The two women help Kim back up on her feet and then they begin cleaning up the room. The man with the coffin places the ominous black box in the corner behind the door. He exits the bedroom.

The naked man sits down on one side of the bed and the women sit Kim down on the other side of the bed. One of them hands Kim a warm wet towel as the other washes her body down with another wet towel. They carefully but quickly remove the small shards of ceramic from Kim's right side and clean up the dried blood. One woman stands Kim up. She kneels down and begins washing off Kim's privates. Kim allows this because all she can think about is the black box sitting in the corner. As the woman continues to wash Kim, the naked man starts masturbating. Kim starts crying and says, "What is this? What the hell do you want from me?"

The naked man climaxes and one of the women rushes over to him and pats him down with a clean warm wet towel. Then, she begins giving him oral pleasure and he says, "See? These are my girls. Since you are now too, let's re-cap."

Kim can't stop crying and looking at the black box. A moment later, the box shifts and settles into a small rut in the floor. The sound jars Kim to her core. A small urine stream begins to run down her left leg.

"I gave you two options earlier; I take you now and we are married soon or I don't take you and you stay with me, never to see your family and fiancée again. Which is it Kim?"

Still on opposite sides of the bed, she spits over at him.

"Just for that, I'm adjusting my offer. Now, you either give yourself to me or you finish off what this bitch started…"

He starts to laugh. Kim notices a change in the pitch to his voice.

"I'd rather die than fuck you!"

"I thought about that as you slept earlier but I'd never take the head off of such a beautiful girl. I'd much rather get head from you but if you want to die, that can be arranged!"

He continues, "In fact, as I pierced your perfect clit, I thought about taking you over and over but I knew if I did that, you'd kill yourself so I didn't. You're welcome!"

The man's voice went from sounding much younger and cleaner to more raspy and deep. The change sends chills down Kim's naked body.

"Leave us." The naked man dismisses the two other women in the room. Kim stands at the foot of the bed and the man stands up, erect.

"Now, choose! Either lay down for me or finish this off!"

Kim's eyes explode with tears. She looks around the room but no matter where she looks, all she can really see is the coffin.

She wipes her eyes clear. She takes a deep breath and says, "Did you kill him? Tell me."

"Why should I tell you anything?"

"Tell me and I'll do this. I'll stay with you but I have to know if I have anything to live for."

The man turns toward the end of the bed. He contemplates and then after a few moments he says, "Tai is fine, sort of. Right about now, he's collapsed into a corner crying his little eyes out worried about you."

Kim makes her way over to the naked man. She kneels down and takes him in her hand. She looks up and says, "This is all I'll ever do with you or I'll kill myself and if you ever make me do anything else, I'll bite it off the first chance I get before you can kill me."

Actually pleased, the man says, "You'll stay and never try to escape?"

She starts and nods. His head falls back. She thinks about biting him but she knows she has something even more special to live for, growing inside of her, so she finishes him off quickly and walks into the small bathroom to throw up. When she enters the bathroom, there is a box waiting for her; her clothes have been washed and there is a black silk jacket with a small orange and white Koi logo on the chest.

She throws up again, rinses out her mouth and quickly dresses. As she re-enters the bedroom, the black box in the corner is gone. The man is dressed in a black suit coat and tie with dark grey pants. His black suit coat has the same orange and white Koi logo on the top front pocket.

Kim says, "What about my parents? Can I ever call or write them that I'm okay?"

"Bruce and LuAnn live. Tai lives. You contact any of them and they die before you die, deal?"

Destroyed, Kim nods in agreement. She's twenty-five and decides in this moment that with a long life ahead of her, maybe she'll get a chance to make things right some day and if not, she'll join her loved ones because she doesn't believe what this man is telling her anyway. Time will tell.

JULY 8, 1985 2 P.M. – GUANGZHOU, CHINA; JIMMIE HUANG'S HOME

Tai wakes up after one of the most miserable and exhausting days of his life. It's all a blur initially but unfortunately, it's starting to come back to him now; his fiancée has been missing for two days. All the wedding decorations have been removed. Bruce and LuAnn, crushed by their daughter's disappearance, have already flown home to Beijing. They hope to hear something from the local police offices in either Canton or Beijing because at 1 P.M. yesterday afternoon, Bruce officially declared his daughter missing and filed all the required reports to have police help find her.

The Canton fish market community is crushed as well. They have to get back to work preparing their catches and returning to the South China Sea to catch more fish to sell. Jimmie sees the initial activity and walks upstairs to talk to his son.

"Tai?"

"Yeah Pop?"

"I know this is all so terrible and I wish I had an answer or anything to offer to help but we just have to wait."

"I know Pop. I just can't understand this. If she wasn't ready, all she had to do was tell me. I just pray it's not something worse."

"The best thing now is to keep busy because if you constantly think about all this, you'll go crazy and that won't help her, you or anyone else, right?"

Wiping tears from his eyes, Tai nods and says, "I do have a vaccine I can test now so I'll look into that with Yuen and Misa and that will help them keep busy too."

"Good man. I'll keep making calls and let you know if I hear anything."

Just then, Yuen and Misa enter Jimmie's home. Yuen has been making more calls from the Kai's home.

"Where have you two been this morning?" Jimmie asks.

First he nods with respect and then Yuen says, "Outside helping set up tables for folks." Misa bows and excuses herself to the kitchen area.

"Tai ready?" Yuen asks.

"Give him a few more minutes," Jimmie says.

Jimmie continues, "Hey, you can help me gather some things for your vaccine tests, right?"

"Right."

Yuen and Jimmie start collecting a few things for the first vaccine trials. Misa joins them and helps locate a few more things. The threesome waits for Tai.

Upstairs, Tai can't stop crying. The last seventy-two hours have been exhausting and were supposed to culminate with a flight to Maui for his and Kim's honeymoon. Instead, he's hoping to learn that she's alive somewhere, anywhere.

JULY 29, 1985

Tai, Yuen and Misa continue their vaccine trials, doing anything to keep busy. They try to reminisce about earlier times but before they get too deep into those conversations, Misa explodes into tears and runs away. The vaccine tests are going very well and Tai believes it is ready for human testing. Yuen volunteers to be the first, along with Tai and Misa. If successful, Tai's father Jimmie will be the first Canton villager to receive the potentially life-saving new drug.

Tai focuses in on his work because while devastated by Kim's disappearance, he still has a promise to keep to his mother Mia and younger brother Qin. And to Kim because he knows she would want this work to continue because of all the people it will help.

Still, something is missing; a void that Tai can't quite put his finger on but he knows something's not right. He's comfortable with the first two test fish and thrilled about those results. He had a witness to corroborate the results; In fact, his witness got bit by a dying test subject. He would have loved to test more subjects but judging from the two successes and repeated microscope results, he can't help but to move forward with his current vaccine test plan. He figures another few days, and he'll be ready to test out the new vaccine on his father, himself, Yuen and Misa.

CHAPTER EIGHT

July 29, 1985 – Yokohama, Japan.

KIM is escorted to a room at the end of a long hallway; there are ceremonial masks and helmets adorning the walls. She recognizes them as being Japanese in origin; a samurai helmet with a small katana sword behind it, a ninja mask and silver throwing stars in a half moon shape around it, and another samurai mask but this one is ancient and is enclosed in a glass case hanging on the wall.

"Friends of yours?" she inquires.

The man walking behind her laughs and says, "Your suite, my dear. Anything you ever want or need, except to leave, just ask. I'll see you tonight for dinner and my pleasures."

Kim rolls her eyes and says, "Ok dear. Have a good day honey." Kim spits on the floor outside the door to her new apartment.

"Hey, just on the floor now. You're adjusting. Very good!" The man braces her back and pushes her forward into the extravagant room.

Emphatically Kim says, "Yeah, I've adjusted to the fact that I have to suck your little dick a couple times a day but for the three minutes or so that it takes, it's not so bad."

"Feisty! I love it! But careful girl, don't go losing your head, if you know what I mean."

Kim has grown accustomed to how far she can push him so she leaves her last comment stand. She enters the room and is stunned; the entryway features a giant plush black rug with a huge orange and white Koi airbrushed on it. There are small black marble tables aside each of the four doors; two bedrooms, a formal living room, and the bathroom.

As the man takes her on the tour of her new living quarters, she's well aware of the fact that he's trying to buy her love, thinking that one day she'll actually accept him as her mate. There are various paintings along the walls; koi of course. Framed in mother of pearl, they are amazing. The two bedrooms are the same with the exception that Kim's bedroom features an ornate dresser and elaborate mirror. On top of the dresser, there is a wooden jewelry box stocked with various bracelets, necklaces, rings, charms, and a ladies Presidential Rolex watch.

"Awesome. Now I can dress up my hands and wrists when I'm jerking you off. Which do you prefer, a ring on my right hand or a bracelet on my left wrist as I stroke you dear?"

The man just smiles as they continue the tour. The bathroom has a broken white marble pattern and as soon as Kim sees it, she breaks down crying; it reminds her of the last morning Tai and she spent together in Mr. Huang's home. The man wants her to notice the rest of the bathroom decorations including the shower and tub that features an orange and white koi on the wall and floor of the tub. It's clear that everything here is brand new. This whole place is brand new. Kim figures that this guy has to be Japanese Yakuza but she can't figure out why he would be after her.

The tour concludes with the formal living room. Off to the right, there is a seating area for six; midnight blue Birds of Paradise and white roses adorn the black glass table. The rug underneath is dark grey with the expected orange and white koi design in the center. The chairs are black with dark orange accents. To the left, a fully stocked bar with three high-rise bar stools. Kim can see every type of saké and imported wines from around the world and there are numerous decorative bottles with special liquors in them. There are two bottles of wine that have the orange and white koi logo on them.

During this whole tour, ten associates of the man have been re-securing each room and stand guard outside of each room as well as at the entrance. Kim has noticed this but has said nothing because she's already figured out that this guy is Yakuza so she knows that level of security comes with the territory.

Sick of the charade, Kim asks, "So what is all this really? You didn't kidnap me just so I could suck your dick, right?"

"Smart girl. No, actually, I brought you here with us for your mind." The man laughs deeply and then adds, "Ha! Imagine that! I do love you for your mind! Your other skills just happen to be an added bonus my dear."

Kim asks, "My other skills?"

The man laughs deeply and says, "Your hard body and your sweet little apple of an ass!"

Kim laughs back at him and says, "Ok, but just you remember, you're just three inches and one bite away from oblivion!"

"Hey! Relax!"

"You fucking relax! You took me away from everything and everyone I loved and all this shit is supposed to make me forget. Fuck you! Fuck your marble floors, fuck your flowers and fancy fucking rugs! And, fuck your orange and white Koi all over the fucking place, you fish-fucker!"

The man stands still, half in shock and half in delight over Kim's fiery demeanor.

"And what the hell is your name anyway?"

"That's not important right now dear."

Frustrated by his continuous games, Kim runs into her bedroom and slams the door.

Depressed and mentally exhausted, she collapses into her bed and after a few moments, she passes out from all the stress and anxiety.

The man excuses himself from the living room and starts walking all the way out of the apartment complex. His ten men walk ahead of him, escorting him to the front door.

JULY 31, 1985 – GUANGZHOU, CHINA; JIMMIE HUANG'S HOME

Tai was ready to move forward with the first vaccine tests but something has been delaying his efforts. The fact that it's been over three weeks since Kim disappeared hasn't helped his mindset either. He and his team have kept busy but naturally, nothing is the same. Jimmie has kept a cool head, fishing and supporting his fellow villagers at the fish market. His daily fishing trips have been a welcome break for the group.

Tai keeps busy with existing and new experiments and Yuen has been a big help in re-supplying the villager's with Myst1, aspirin, and supporting their fishing exploits as well. He even helped to fix the hull of one of the villager's boats that was damaged from a recent storm.

Tai has noticed Yuen's distance but he figures it's just how he is trying to cope with things so he hasn't asked about Yuen's frequent trips back and forth to the Kai's former home. Everyone deals with stress and anxiety differently.

Misa has been very busy, basically rearranging Jimmie's entire home for him. Jimmie knows this is what makes Misa happy during this stressful time and he actually likes having his home rearranged to give it a more modern layout and look. She's upstairs finishing up Jimmie's bedroom and careful not to make too many changes when she calls out to everyone downstairs, "Everyone, come here!"

Yuen is at the Kai's again. Tai and Jimmie head upstairs. Misa immediately says, "I found this under the bed. At first, I didn't want to open it but then I could see it was Kim's." Misa reveals the diary.

Tai reaches for it and reluctantly, Misa hands it over. Everyone wants to hold on to anything from Kim for as long as they can. The red cover has various small sketches across it. Tai turns to the last page. It reads, "Heading home to see my folks and then back to marry My-Tai!"

Tai explodes into tears and drops the diary. Misa quickly recovers it and reads the last page for herself. She joins Tai on the edge of the bed and the two grieve together. Jimmie pats his anguished son on his right shoulder a couple times and excuses himself. Just then Yuen enters the front door and sees Jimmie walking downstairs. Jimmie just nods upstairs so Yuen heads up. Misa greets him with a quiet "hi" and passes him Kim's dairy.

Respectfully but hurriedly, Yuen asks to speak with Tai alone. Misa obliges and heads downstairs. Yuen closes the bedroom door.

"I'm so sorry Tai."

"I know. We're all still so sad."

"No, I mean, I'm so sorry I couldn't tell you until I was sure."

"What? Sure of what?"

"Okay." Yuen pauses and takes a deep breath. "You have to promise not to tell anyone else or she could be killed."

"What? What the hell are you talking about? She could be killed... who's 'she'?"

"Kim!"

Tai stands up and says, "Jesus, you know where she is? Where is she?"

"I do but wait. I have to tell you how I know. And again, you can't tell anyone because if you do and they start making calls, it will get back to the wrong people and they will kill Kim!"

"Ok. Come on."

"I used to get into a lot of trouble when I was a teenager. You know this. But what you don't know is that, I stole some guy's car and got caught by him later that night. I was fifteen years old. He told me I was either stupid or lucky, and to choose. I told him I was lucky I wasn't stupid. He laughed and gave me an American $500 bill."

"He said, you put those skills to work for me and you'll see a lot more of those bills son. I told him my car stealing days were over so he asked me what else I could do. I knew he was Triad so I honestly told him that I could collect and his eyes widened. It was exactly what he was looking for at the time so he told me about a few collections that were needed and I did them. No big deal. I'm not proud of it but it was working out and I knew if I did this for a few years, I'd have the money I needed to go to school so like I said, I'm not proud of it but that's how I afforded my end of my school expenses. And it's the reason why we're friends today."

Tai is a little shocked that he truly never knew about any of this so he just sits and listens to Yuen.

"After our junior year, I got a call to visit Hong Kong over semester break, remember?"

"I remember that. You said you had to visit your parents because an uncle was sick and you came back three days later and didn't remember your uncle's visit but you showed off your sword tattoo to me and Kim. Ok, so that was all bullshit?"

"It was. I'm sorry but for a valid reason. I was being inducted as a full member. The tattoo was my initiation, well, that and drinking a shot of King Cobra's blood."

"Okay, so what's going on?"

"Okay, so being a member has a few advantages; contacts all over the world. Yes, being in a gang is the dumbest fucking thing I've ever done but what's done is done. I didn't have anyone in my life to talk to, to learn what all this life is really about and by the time that happened, when I met you, it was too late so here I am."

Tai stands up and gives Yuen a hug and says, "I'm sorry brother. I really didn't know."

"I know. It's my fault but today, it comes in handy because my point is, Kim is okay, as far as I can tell."

"Shit, what does that mean?" Tai sits back down, preparing for bad follow-up news.

"Kim was kidnapped when she returned from visiting her parents in Beijing; right in the fucking parking lot at Canton International Airport just as she was about to drive back to us."

"Fuckers! Who did it?" Tai demands.

"I'm not completely sure what gang but I know it was Yakuza. I'm just not sure what family and what Boss yet."

Pissed off and motivated like crazy Tai says, "Alright, I know you know a lot of people. All day, every day until we find her and get her back! Whatever it takes and whatever it costs! Just do it!"

"I hear you and we're working on it. We know she's in Yokohama but not the exact location. The problem with that location is that, that's where the top Boss, Saitonaka, lives. Talk about bad news. He wrote the book!"

Heartbroken, Tai asks, "Just tell me now; is this Saitonaka going to kill her? Am I ever going to see her again? Fuck, what the hell is this man?" Angry and exhausted, Tai breaks down again.

Yuen reaches down and grabs Tai's hand and says, "Trust me when I say; we will find her and get her back if it takes my last breath to do it! Kim's a sharp girl. She'll know who these people are and what buttons to push and what buttons not to push. They want her for a genuine reason. That's what I'm trying to figure out now because if that wasn't true, she'd already be dead."

"Fuck! This is my fault. This is all my fault!" Tai exclaims as he stands up covering his face.

"What do you mean?"

"Oh my God! A week before finals I got a call to meet someone around the corner at the bar. I didn't think anything of it because I was exhausted and trying to get ready for our chemistry final. I met with him a few hours later. This guy casually asked me about the Myst1 I had been making for my dad and the Canton community and how I had helped to enhance it. I told him that Kim and I had been experimenting with several different versions until she nailed the mixture we were looking for. He simply got up and left, before our drinks even arrived so I stayed and drank them both. Kim met me later and then you and Misa met us and we had a great night together."

"I think that's it! That's the reason why they kidnapped Kim. You two have been top-of-the-class in chemistry for years and the new formula you developed for Diabetes must have been the reason. The Japanese culture hasn't normally had this issue but with all the development since World War II, new generations, and wild technologies, the growth in the professional sector has grown out of control. So has their appetite for anything US-based, including fast-food."

Yuen continues, "Obesity is a bigger problem in the US but in Japan, they have been trying to do something sooner rather than later and with such a small country, they have been trying to develop something for over twenty years. Your formula gives them a long-standing cure for their people and instead of just developing it on their own, they kidnapped one of China's top students who'll make it for them for free, and of course, the Yakuza will profit big-time from it!"

Tai stands up in shock and says, "Jesus, if they know about our work now; CDT, the enhanced CDT we're using on fish… I'll never see Kim again!"

"Exactly so we've got to track her down and arrange to get her back before that happens! If she's under Boss Saitonaka's heavy thumb, it's going to be pretty tough because he doesn't give up on anything until you're dead."

"Ok. I won't tell anyone about the Triad. You work on getting her back for us and I'll take care of everything else because we still have to get this vaccine up and running for people."

"I keep getting updated information from my contacts so I'll let you know when I know but we have to make sure your dad, Misa, and everyone else doesn't find out what's going on. If Boss Saitonaka even gets a whiff of this, he'll start chopping heads off and I'm not kidding. It's what he does when he's stressed and wants a quick solution. People simply lose their heads around him!"

"Understood. I'm going to read through Kim's dairy and see if she mentioned anything that could help you locate her."

Confidently, Yuen says, "We'll get her back!"

Tai and Yuen shake hands and hug like brothers in arms. Tai is beyond relieved to learn that Kim is alive and in Japan. He's going crazy not being able to share this news with anyone because he knows how much it's tearing Kim's parent's apart as well as his father but in order to protect her, he has to do the right thing for her safety and for now, that means keeping his mouth shut. At least for now, he can concentrate on the tasks at hand. He has some peace of mind and hope. It fuels his determination and desire to complete his experiments. His mind goes into 'auto-pilot' mode where all he does all day long is think about Kim; his work simply gets done without question and without a second thought.

CHAPTER NINE

AUGUST 1, 1985 – YOKOHAMA, JAPAN

KIM wakes up and is startled. She winces and tries to focus her blood-shot eyes and realizes a dark figured man is sitting next to her. Trying to collect herself, she realizes her nightmare is a reality. She has been kidnapped, again and she is still far away from her family, friends, and fiancée.

She curls back up and closer to the top of the bed, away from the man.

Sternly and in a very sharp and serious voice, the man states, "I am 'Hey Sun'.

Kim nods.

The mysterious man continues, "I'll tell you why you're here but again, you tell no one what I tell you, ever." Kim nods again and is about to speak when the man looks at her with the tops of his eyes. She keeps quiet.

"I work for the Chinese Government; a special team that helped you to attend school and now it's time for your work to see the light of day. We had to take you from your family and friends but I promise, only for a little while. You are the true brains behind many compounds and experiments. Tai Huang was in your shadow and trying to patent several things without your knowledge."

Hey Sun passes a folder to Kim. She looks through it briefly but when she comes across the patent form for "Enhanced Myst1", she looks harder. The form only has Tai's name on it and it's stamped 'APPROVED' across the top in big block red letters with a respective patent number next to it. She's shocked.

The man continues, "See. You may also notice that he put in a request for something called 'CDT' and that form also has only his name on it. We assume you were the true head of this project as well. No more games and no more courtship Kim!"

Kim is about to interrupt and offer some input when she realizes there's something wrong with that last patent form; they just came up with CDT in the past few months.

There's no way the completed patent would already be granted. She sits quietly and lets Hey Sun continue.

"Now I know what you might be thinking; it takes longer to get a patent. Well, being in the Chinese Government has many advantages and one of them is when you want something like this done, it gets done!"

Kim looks down to the floor in disappointment; she was hoping to have tripped the man up on his story but his explanation makes sense. The she quickly reconciles the fact that if Hey Sun is Chinese Government, what the hell is she doing in Japan?

The man continues, "Now you might be wondering if I really work for the Chinese Government, why the hell are we in Japan?"

Kim's eyes wince. She thinks to herself, "What the hell is going on? Is this asshole reading my mind now too?"

He continues, "We have a few friends here in Japan that agreed to secure this location for you, for a price. The Chinese Triads were about to kidnap you as well and we prevented that from happening. China is a hell of a lot harder to find someone in than in Japan so that's why you're here."

Again, that makes sense and she can't help but to feel a little grateful. Hey Sun's story is checking out so she stands up and finally asks sarcastically, "So, are you here to help me get away or do I have to suck your dick now?"

Hey Sun grins and says, "I am rescuing you, sort of. Now, you answer to me, so yes, it is my dick now for you to suck!"

Hey Sun pulls the bedroom door open, exposing the hallway. Another man enters holding a black box. He places the box in front of Kim on the floor and exits.

Kim looks down and says, "For me?" Hey Sun says, "Not exactly but if you'd like to open it, go ahead."

Kim hesitates and Hey Sun says, "Allow me." He pulls the top off the black box and grabs Kim by the back of her neck and says, "This is the business we are all in, yourself included! Understood?"

The eyes of the decapitated head are looking up at Kim who quickly covers her mouth in horror.

Hey Sun quickly dismisses the severed head and continues, "Here's your deal; you'll work with Tai Huang but he won't know it's you he's talking to. We need the two of you to continue working together but apart, understand?"

"But..."

"I'm not finished. Listen. You will talk together working on several new projects but you can never tell him it's you. Your voice will be disguised on his line but if he ever asks, the line will hang up and if he does it again, we'll kill him. Trust me when I say, he will know these same rules very shortly."

"You two work well together and we don't want to lose that but he can never know it's you. As far as he knows, you've disappeared and that's it. People disappear all the time. Trust me when I say, he'll understand. People can continue to just disappear!"

"What I need to know from you right now is if you kept any kind of journal or diary where you shared any experiment thoughts, notes, ideas, new concepts, drawings, details, anything that has to do with Myst1 or CDT or anything else."

Kim does not hesitate. "No. I don't have any journals. There was never any time to write it all down."

A total lie that she sells beautifully with her eyes batting down in servitude and she believes, she has convinced Hey Sun.

"Good. So, I'll let you know when we're ready for your next steps. For now, just enjoy your suite and let me know if there is anything I can get for you until next we meet; next week."

Exhausted but amazingly relieved, she jumps back into her bed and covers herself up. She knows that Tai is alive, she's alive, and she's going to be able to talk with him soon. She can't wait to tell him so many things because she and Tai share something that absolutely no one else, not even Yuen and Misa, knows about. In their former Chemistry classes, they would be so busy; they derived basically, their own language using chemistry symbols, scientific names, phrases, etc. By simply calling out an element out of sequence that only they would know is out of sequence, they'd really be saying something else. This is how they communicated during the most difficult times in class to help each other out and to share intimate thoughts as well for when they got back together at the end of the day. To the layman, it was all scientific garbage between two aspiring young scientists.

She knows it will work against Hey Sun so she's happier than she's been since her kidnapping the day before her wedding. At this time, Hey Sun boards a private jet bound for Tokyo. He'll be there for one week getting some last minute details in order.

Just before his private jet takes off, Hey Sun waves down one of his men. The man runs back to the small staircase on the front left side of the plane.

"This little bitch is lying. She has journals. As soon as we get the formulas for Myst1 and this new CDT, I'll kill Tai myself and you can have your way with her but don't kill her until I get back. I want one last round with her before she's done! Got it?"

The man immediately nods and bows one time. He closes the small staircase back up and the plane begins to taxi to the runway. The tail of the aircraft sports an orange and white Koi fish with the red sun for the Empire of Japan in the background.

Tai reads through Kim's diary and finds a few things that catch his eye so he copies them down. Most importantly, he finds a few pages that she wrote immediately after the couple's erotic moments behind the Dragon's Tears outcropping. When they got back on the research boat, she described a couple more options and quantity changes for a possible enhanced CDT that Tai could test but they never got around to it once Tai had come back from Dragon's Tears Island with Yuen with his solution.

Tai sits on the edge of the upstairs bedroom and cries with joy. His gorgeous bride-to-be has done it again; she's added the 'spice' that she has always added helping to make something that he developed, better. Her suggestions and adjusted ingredients for the enhanced CDT are nothing short of brilliant and he knows immediately that for one, she's right, and two, that it will work. All this time, he's been waiting for some kind of sign or something. Thankfully Misa ran across Kim's diary just in time because now he believes the proposed vaccine will work even better than it did on the test fish.

Tai immediately calls for Misa and Yuen to help him set up new testing beakers and materials and for Yuen to get him a couple new test fish. Tai heads downstairs to retrieve his notes and samples of the current enhanced CDT. A few moments later, his dad walks in, having returned from his morning fishing trip just outside the Canton inlet. He's holding a variety of fish for sale at the market and some for dinner. Tai notices two smaller Chinese Perch and says, "I know those are for our dinner but I really need them." Jimmie immediately un-hooks them and hands them to his son. Jimmie senses his son's genuinely relieved state and after all that has happened he's glad to see him settle back into his work and routine.

Tai starts testing and immediately confirms the original issue; green halos around the fish's scales. The bacterium is present on test fish number one. Test fish number two is the same and actually worse; in an advanced stage. Yuen is out trying to catch a more lively fish and he's taken a test tray half full of sea water to preserve his catch for Tai. Yuen quickly hooks another foot-long snakehead; a perfect specimen and a fish that normally lives farther out in the South China Sea. That gives them a better estimate to predict the bacterium's range.

"Yuen. Misa. Look at this." Tai demands.

"The cells are repairing but now, with Kim's version of this formula, the areas around the cells are clearing up as well where with my version earlier, this wasn't happening." Tai takes a moment to reflect.

He sits down and says, "Jesus, that means it might have appeared to have worked but maybe it really didn't. Damn it! And I checked for false positives too. I wonder what happened to those first two test fish."

Yuen looks through the microscope and says, "Doesn't matter. This is better, just like Kim hoped. That's why she left you her notes and that's all that's important." Yuen and Misa walk over to Tai and the three trade hugs. Then Tai runs downstairs.

"Dad! Don't sell those fish and tell everyone at the fish market to wait on eating any fish tonight. By tomorrow, I'll have a real cure for everyone that will work because Kim blessed it herself!"

Jimmie nods and tours the market telling everyone the latest news. Yuen comes in with a fresh catch but the snakehead appears to be dying already; it's already turning on its side. Tai grabs it and takes a blood sample. He injects the fish's blood into another solution and waits.

After four minutes, Tai grins and says, "Perfect. This fish was going to die within the day. His blood cells show me that he has advanced bacterium issues. I'm going to keep with the .65cc's injection but using Kim's formula, watch what happens."

Tai injects the twelve-inch snakehead and places him into a half-filled custom aquarium that Jimmie had set out in the living room. Misa dumps the rest of the seawater into the tank.

The fish looks to be dying; it continues to turn to one side and its struggle to right itself is a weak attempt at best. Yuen and Misa begin to look disappointed but Tai appears confident. A few minutes pass and the test fish still leans to one side but his gills are still moving so that's a positive sign. Jimmie returns from his market rounds and pats Tai on his back on the way to the kitchen.

Jimmie announces, "Tonight, a special treat for you all. I'll prepare my special sauce over rice and vegetables. No fish but instead, steak I picked up from the town markets. I have just enough for a stir-fry!"

Everyone perks up and moves into the kitchen area. Most of the furniture has moved around from one side of the house to the other but not Mr. Huang's favorite chair with his former wife's embroidery; that remains as it was. Yuen and Misa glance over at the fish and see that it's not making any progress; still appearing like its dying. Tai remains confident and completely ignores the test fish. He attends his cooking duties with his father. After thirty minutes, everything is ready and the house smells amazing. Misa sets the table and Jimmie starts serving. Tai excuses himself and heads to the restroom. On his way, he diverts into the back bedroom where his father keeps his Diabetes supplies; he's looking for some injection needles he can use to deliver the new vaccine that hasn't fully proved out.

The four enjoy their dinner together. An hour passes and Tai has not once looked over at the aquarium. Yuen and Misa have several times and as far as they can tell, nothing has changed but they didn't want to bring this up during dinner. Yuen and Misa begin clearing the table and Jimmie settles into his favorite chair. He grabs the newspaper on the floor next to him and starts reading.

Tai says, "Ok. Let's have a look now."

Tai submerges his right hand at the back end of the aquarium and looks over at Yuen. He gives the water a little splash and in an instant, the snakehead swims over to the distraction. He pulls his hand out just as the twelve inch fish was going to bite him. Yuen and Misa are shocked. They smile and they have that classic look of wonderment on their faces. Jimmie smirks and returns to his paper.

"How? What did you do?" Yuen starts to ask. Misa jabs him in the rib playfully and Yuen stops talking.

"It was Kim! I read her diary and the changes she described. I made her changes and this truly works now. I can't honestly say what happened with our first two test subjects and I take blame for that but credit for this goes to Yuen for catching the test fish for me as quickly as he did, to you Misa for helping gather everything up to perform the tests, and to my dad for telling me how to find Dragon's Tears! I just put it all together."

"Oh sure, it doesn't bite you!" Yuen shakes his middle finger at the little snakehead. Everyone smiles.

Smiling, Yuen says, "So what's the plan now Boss?"

Tai states, "Ok. I've got to dissect the formulation and start over to prove this works and we need time to see how this little snakehead does, just to make sure before we start injecting people with this stuff. Plus, I thought the same dosage was sufficient but it's not. Kim pointed that out for me and I believe she's right. The amount to administer should vary just as people vary so I'll have to come up with a height, weight, and age scale for a safer vaccine."

Tai gets serious. Jimmie sits up in his chair and Yuen and Misa also take notice of his change in demeanor.

Tai sits down and says, "Right now, in front of you all, I say this."

Yuen's getting nervous. Tai stands up and paces around the living room table. Yuen's getting more nervous.

Finally Tai says, "The work we're doing and the work we will do together. No one can ever know about it. It's what Kim would want."

Yuen's guts settle back into his belly. Tai winks over at him.

Misa tears up and immediately offers, "Agreed; for Kim!"

Everyone else repeats, "For Kim!"

Misa says a quick prayer and grabs Yuen's hand.

Tai adds, "And if anyone ever asks about patents on our formulas or anything like that, just say you don't know. That's their trap because I'll tell you all right now, I have never even filed for a patent on anything we've ever done and that includes going back to the stuff Kim and I started back in school. I swear to you all this is true, in front of my father! You all know how I sign my name so if anyone ever shows you any patent papers, look for the karat above my alleged last name because I'll guarantee you, it won't be there!"

August 15

Tai has completed the complex vaccine matrix representing each person in the village. It has their height, weight, age and respective proper measured dose to be administered. He has tested everything thoroughly and he's confident this custom vaccine will completely prevent the bacterium from forming into the deadly virus that has been plaguing this village for centuries. Jimmie again volunteers to be the first to be injected. Yuen and Misa have been passing out invitations to everyone in the village earlier that morning and people are now starting to visit the Huang home for their vaccinations. The dosage also takes into account those individuals who have various known medical conditions like Diabetes or high or low blood pressures and before each person gets their shot, Tai's team reconfirms any other medications each person may be taking at this time and if those medications are short or long-term.

Tai and Jimmie get their shots together from Yuen and Misa and then Tai and Jimmie return the favor, administering Yuen and Misa's shots. The foursome toasts with shot-glasses full of plum wine and they hold each other's hands in a moment of silence for Mia, Qin, the Kai's, and for Kim. Tai squeezes his father's hand and Jimmie squeezes his son's hand back as their eyes begin to tear.

Misa walks between Tai and Yuen and gives Mr. Huang a big hug.

"Thank you dear." He says.

The girl's mesmerizing hair demands the guy's attention and when Yuen picks up on this, he pokes Tai in the ribs and then Tai pokes his father in the ribs. The men laugh together.

Tai reminds Yuen and Misa, "Everyone's 'blood-soup' is different so be sure to ask each person about their current meds and any recent conditions."

Yuen and Misa give a 'thumbs up' from their 'station' on the immediate left side of the living room and Tai and Jimmie are ready at their 'station' on the right side of the living room. As people enter Jimmie's house, they choose a line. Once they receive their shot, a shot-glass of plum wine is waiting for them if they wish and a new bottle of Myst1 with two baby Aspirins attached to it.

An elderly couple enters. They were close with the Kai's. They nod and bow toward Jimmie and the elderly man shakes Tai's hand. The elderly woman hands Jimmie a small basket. It's a pyramid-shape arrangement filled to the top with home-made pastries; Tai's mouth waters. He smiles, nods and bows back at the couple.

Jimmie sets the basket down and walks with the couple to their place in line. "I'm so sorry about the Kai's. I know the four of you were very close."

The elderly man says, "Your son and his friends are helping us all and we can't thank you all enough. I only wish Miss Kim was here today with us to celebrate this blessed success."

The three hug each other and Jimmie heads back to his 'station' near his favorite chair. He taps the embroidered arm rest.

By 6 P.M., everyone in the village has received their vaccinations. The group has reminded everyone to always wash and cook their fish and all food thoroughly because the vaccine is a preventative measure and a great one at that but it doesn't replace common sense; always prepare your food carefully and fully, period.

Tai motions to Yuen and the two walk outside. Tai says, "I'll tell you this now because as things heat up, you have to know what helps to make this work in case something happens to me or Kim. You have to become the chemist or all of our friends here will die."

Yuen nods.

Tai continues, "In Kim's notes, I learned something and it's key to the Enhanced-CDT. With the right set of compounds, it generates a very small amount of ascorbic acid, vitamin-C and this is critical for the vaccine to work correctly. That's also why the dosage must be staggered according to a person's size, weight, and age but also adjusted for their current meds and conditions. Too little and it will have no effect and they would still be susceptible to the bacteria and virus. Too much and it could cause an adverse reaction with their other symptoms and maybe even kill them."

Yuen listens intently. His heart begins to race as the importance of these instructions hit him like a ton of bricks.

"I've coded everything! Only Kim will know what this all means but now, you'll learn our coding so you can help in case something happens to me or Kim as we try getting her back. I know things can go bad quickly so I've already prepared my mind for that. It's Yakuza; I get that. I just hope your Triad contacts can find her before anything bad happens."

Tai and Yuen return to Jimmie's house where Jimmie is preparing his favorite dinner for everyone and Misa has already broken out the Mah-Jongg tiles and coin jug. It looks to be a long enjoyable evening for the group. The other village residents all rest comfortably enjoying their evening as well; eating dinner, sewing, playing Mah-Jongg, reading the daily newspaper, watching television, etc.

CHAPTER TEN

AUGUST 30, 1985

TAI decides to head back to Beijing to visit the Tse's. It's been almost two months since they've talked. Yuen and Misa accompany him. The three will visit the Forbidden City and the Great Wall as well as their former university.

Tai calls out to his father, who's occupied in his back bed room behind the kitchen area.

"Ok Pop. We're heading out. See you in about three weeks."

Jimmie responds, "Ok. See you later son! Take lots of pictures for me!"

As Yuen and Misa load Yuen's rental car, Jimmie and Tai quickly meet up in the living room. They bump fists and smile. Jimmie returns to the back bed room and Tai leaves his family home and enters the rear passenger seat of Yuen's car.

Kim has remained patient but she can tell that Hey Sun is growing more and more impatient with his business lately. She still hasn't been asked to perform any of her science tasks and it's been three weeks since her and Hey Sun last spoke of it. Just before dinner, Hey Sun calls for her to join him in his room. Knowing what this means, she dresses appropriately and readies herself for another 'quickie' session with her 'accepted' new captor.

"Not this time. I have news for you."

Kim stands back up from her kneeling position and sits on the edge of his bed.

"Your parents…"

Kim bursts into tears. "Wait. Let me finish. Your parents are fine but I have relocated them for the time being."

"Why?"

"Why? Because you're lying to me! You have chemistry notes, don't you? Tell me now or who knows what can happen in this big wide world to such a beloved couple."

"I swear I don't! I left all that behind in school because it was for experiments we did there that are over now. None of those notes would mean anything to you or anyone else. The school doesn't keep any of that but check for yourself if you want."

"We did! They have nothing. Ok, I just hope for your sake you're telling me the truth. Actually, I hope you're telling me the truth for your parent's sake!"

"Where are they?"

"No! This is how this is going to go! You create or develop something for me and I share details with you. We trade back and forth until I have what I want before you get what you want. Got it?"

Kim has no choice but to accept Hey Sun's terms.

So far, Hey Sun has kept his promise not to force Kim to have sex with him; just her usual duty. But he has added a little flair to things prior to his climax.

Hey Sun asks, "Are you ready for my appetizer?"

She nods.

This 'performance' doesn't bother her at all because for one, it helps her relieve her own internal stresses and two, it's amusing for her to see Hey Sun lower his guard and basically make a fool of himself during this time.

The forced couple leaves Hey Sun's room and heads down the hall to the formal living room. Hey Sun grabs his crotch in anticipation of the next hour or so.

The doors to the formal living room open and two of Hey Sun's men stand guard, eagerly awaiting this particular show themselves. Hey Sun only allows a select few of his men the privilege of watching the dinner performance and this will be these seven men's first time and something they'll never forget.

Naked women adorn a large rug placed in the middle of the floor away from the formal dining table. Traditional Japanese music plays in the background with the occasional strong drum beat coming at the end. A two-tiered low-profile black onyx table is moved into the center of the rug and small square black sushi dishes are placed around the lower tier. The upper tier of the table sits up about six inches above the lower tier. With the music already playing, Kim enters the room dancing in small circles, changing her direction every now and again. Hey Sun and his men immediately make their way to the large formal dining table located to the left of the two-tiered low-profile black onyx table. The guards stand their ground, on the inside of the entry doors, that are now closed. Soft blue light falls across the room in waves, like it's raining inside and the music almost matches the blue light's movement perfectly.

Kim continues to dance seductively in front of the small black onyx table as the men seated at the formal dinner table watch and occasionally take drinks from their logoed saké cups. Kim's head falls back; she's in her trance now – completely enveloped in the moment. This is what Hey Sun loves about her; the girl gets absolutely possessed in this state and she's shocking and wild to watch. She'll do things that even these men probably haven't ever seen before.

She begins to undress; first, her black and white silk robe comes shimmering down to the ground and covers the top right corner of the low-profile black onyx table. A naked attendant quickly removes it, repositions the sushi dish and returns to her position against the wall. There are three of these women who consistently serve this dining room for Hey Sun and Kim. Kim begins placing her hands and fingers intermittently inside her orange and white silk panties, seductively digging down in them like she's slowly firing an American Western revolver.

One of the men at the table nearly passes out. Just before he does, he ejaculates in his pants. Hey Sun's eyes brighten and he quickly refocuses them on his captive mistress. He smiles and pounds his saké cup down. An instant later, the cup is filled and a new bottle is placed for him on the table. Kim's panties are wet so she takes them off slowly. She twirls them on her right index finger and then places an end in her mouth and just stares and dances toward the formal dining table. One of the other men slips off his chair and falls to the ground. A naked woman from the wall runs over to him and helps him back up. As he retakes his chair, he yells out, "Banzai!" and then he repositions the front of his pants. Kim immediately grabs his saké cup and wraps her panties around it. He looks like he just won the country's biggest lottery. Stunned and dumbfounded, the rest of the men at the table glue their eyes on the man's saké cup; wishing it was theirs. Hey Sun laughs deeply and then motions with his right hand to Kim.

Kim returns to the front of the small low-profile onyx table and continues her seductive blue-light dance. All the men and women in the room are sweating because while Kim has given great performances in the past, this is by far, her best dance to date. She is truly possessed tonight.

"Set!" Hey Sun proclaims. Kim sits down in front of the onyx table and is still. The blue-light converts to a much brighter but soft white light that fills the room. The music stops. The men around the formal dining table take their seats and turn away from Kim. The naked women against the wall attend to Kim; giving her water, some ginseng, and they feed her sushi and rice. This goes on for ten minutes; it's intermission.

At this same time, the men are served a variety of the hottest sushi hors d'oeuvres anyone has ever tasted. The men were all already sweating from Kim's initial performance but these appetizers could make them pass out before she finishes her routine.

Exactly ten minutes after he said, 'Set!' Hey Sun announces in Japanese, "3-2-1!" The music starts up again. The lights dim and the mystical dancing blue lights begin again. The men turn their chairs around toward Kim. Kim's head sweeps back and forth. She begins crawling toward the center of the small onyx table and when she arrives, she spreads her legs open and lies on her back, sprawling across the entire table. The attentive naked women place sushi selections across her body including over her nipples and over her naval. There are short strips of flavored sea weed across Kim's ribcage and inner thighs and smaller pieces across her amazing abdominal six-pack muscles. She's also wearing a very low-rise sea weed wrap as a bikini bottom. The attendants used special sweet edible glue that will keep all the morsels in place throughout her performance, maybe. She looks so amazing; the women against the wall are getting aroused as well. The orgy will commence soon enough so they watch and wait.

Just then Kim begins to dance as if she were standing upright. Hey Sun's mouth opens. He can't believe how this girl is letting go with all this erotic action. Kim snaps her fingers and a moment later, a naked woman hands her a small pitcher. Kim is fingering herself and then she begins pouring the pitcher all over her amazing horizontal muscular body. The pitcher is full of a sweet and sour orange liquor.

One of the men at the formal dining table says something but even Hey Sun can't make it out. It included the words, 'Holy shit' but in Japanese and then something else. Hey Sun just laughs and motions over to the man who nods and smiles deviously back at him. Now, a variety of sushi including both yellow and blue-fin tuna, a variety of sea weed wraps and rice and other ginseng-topped sushi selections are being placed on the square dishes around the low-profile table. This is clearly now going to be referred to as Kim's table.

Kim begins spinning in the center of the table, sending small waves of the orange liquor across her body and onto the sushi dishes. Then she starts to spread her legs apart as she does this and one of the men at the table stands up and shouts, "Oh, yes girl!" Then, he collapses. The three main naked attendants rush over to him and take him back behind the split wall; to the hidden kitchen area. He's dead. Hey Sun's eyes widen again and he grabs the front of his pants and gropes himself repeatedly. He proclaims, "Go!"

Kim stops spinning and lies across the table resting on her right hip and facing the formal dining table. The rest of the men and Hey Sun adjourn from their positions and kneel at a position around Kim's table. The music changes to a slightly more up-beat pace and sound and the blue lights dance across the room a little faster.

Unexpectedly, Kim reaches down and grabs a piece of sushi off of Hey Sun's plate. She licks it, sweeps it across her left nipple, then down across and beyond her naval and then returns it to his plate. The other six remaining men watch in shock. Hey Sun looks on in overindulgence as well. He reaches down and picks up the seduced piece of sushi and devours it. He kisses his right index finger and offers it to Kim. She sucks on it for a few moments and then returns to her former position on her right hip.

The men begin eating from their sushi dishes around Kim's table and the attendants serve them saké as they desire. One man pours his dish into his saké cup so he can savor the eroticized orange liquor that Kim seductively served. He nearly passes out as he performs this maneuver. All the liquor is beginning to take its toll. One man stands up and starts dancing to the music. He points at the blue lights and waves towards Kim. Hey

Sun looks over at the man and smiles but after a few minutes of this behavior, he claps his hands together. The man promptly sits back down and quietly takes a drink of his saké.

Kim repositions herself and offers up her left side ribcage to one of the men. Shocked, he is frozen. He's not about to eat the flavored sea weed from off her gorgeous body. He wants to desperately but he knows if this is taken by Hey Sun as a form of disrespect, it'll easily and quickly cost him his head. He toasts her with his saké cup and waves her past toward the next man at the table. Slowly, she moves down the table and this time offers up the inside of her right thigh. She puts her fingers in her mouth and winces. The man wets his pants, falls backward and passes out.

Hey Sun crazily shouts out, "Go on Kim! Kill another one! Fuck!"

Kim moves to the other side of the table. The man there is sweating profusely. He can taste this girl, in fact, in a way, he has. He wants to partake in what he believes is a bona-fide offer to eat off of her but he's not sure. The liquor in him is sending mixed signals. If he's wrong, it could cost him his head. He knows this but the liquor and his identity are telling him not to care. Kim scoots over to him on her tiny apple of an ass and then she spreads her legs right in front of him and rests her right leg up on his same shoulder. He dives in.

The man begins kissing Kim's sweet and sour orange-stained tits. Then he slurps the sushi off from each of her erect nipples. Hey Sun does nothing. The man continues, bending Kim's body back as he scoops up several pieces of flavored sea weed from across her ribs and upper abs. He reaches for his saké cup from around her waist and takes a drink. He exclaims, "Banzai!" and returns to Kim's ribs.

A moment later, the doors to the formal living room open and the guards stand on the outside of them. The music hasn't stopped playing. The blue lights continue to dance across the entire room. The rest of the men kneeling at Kim's table remain still. The man in Kim's lap can't taste anything. He can't hear the music anymore and he can't see what's clearly in front of him anymore. Kim pushes the man off of her and immediately runs out of the room and down the hall to her bedroom. She runs right past her bed and into the shower.

With this performance officially ended, Hey Sun draws his cane sword back. He wipes off the blood from the top eight inches with his silk dinner napkin and as he does, the man's head finally falls to the floor with the rest of his shocked body.

In her shower, Kim washes off the evening's dinner selections. She's directly caused the death of one of her co-captors and she's caused the death of another through her seductive dancing and offerings. Tai would certainly be shocked by her behavior but he'd also be proud of how she is using these people against themselves as well; thinning the herd. She intensifies her movements inside herself as she imagines Tai's hands and throbbing member inside of her. She screams out, "Tai!"

Just then, Hey Sun enters her bedroom and hears her cry out. He walks to her bathroom door and says, "Kim? You're okay?"

She smiles, not embarrassed in the least and quickly offers, "Yes. That was just shocking is all."

Hey Sun nods to the closed door and says, "I'm sorry. People must learn that alcohol is no excuse for disrespectful behavior. He crossed a line that he'll never cross again."

"My fault?"

"No! Never think that! If a man can't handle his liquor while eating his dinner and watching a beautiful performance, that's his fault. The treats on you were for me and if he's too stupid to know this, he's better off dead! You just clean up and I'll see you in about two weeks."

"Can I ask who he was?"

"This one time. His name was… Saitonaka. A foolish man that no one will miss."

"Oh, okay. Goodnight then." She's relieved that he'll be gone for two weeks after all this.

Hey Sun shrugs with delight that Kim is being so orderly and now, so amazingly erotic around him. He thinks maybe this forced relationship has turned a positive corner.

CHAPTER ELEVEN

SEPTEMBER 12, 1985 – BEIJING, CHINA

HEY Sun arrives at Beijing International Airport. His men await him at Arrivals in his silver limousine.

Tai, Yuen and Misa have been having the greatest time. With the success of their Enhanced-CDT and with their fellow Canton villager's happy and healthy, they are spending some real time seeing the many ancient wonders of their homeland; The Forbidden City and the Great Wall of China. During their school days, there simply wasn't time to really visit these great places and soak up all the rich history.

After a long day of walking and incredible site seeing, Tai places a call to his father.

"Hey Pop!"

"Hey, world travelers!"

"Pop. We're still in China."

"Ha, that's right but how many people get to visit the Great Wall?"

"True. How are you?"

"Good. Very good in fact. Yesterday, I caught the largest Dragon Fish ever, right off the coast of Dragon's Tears Island."

"Great. And everyone else. How are they?"

"Very good. Busy catching and selling fish like usual."

"Good. So no issues with the vaccine or anything?"

"Not one!"

Tai breathes a huge sigh of relief.

"Okay! Hey, we're going to head over to our former school now and stay for maybe a few days and then we'll be heading back. Yuen says 'hi' and Misa says, 'get the tiles ready!'"

"Great! You all take care and I'll see you soon."

"Ok Pop. I'll bring you back to see Emperor Qin's mountain tomb; amazing!"

"Yes! Very good. Okay, bye my great son!"

"See ya Pop!"

SEPTEMBER 16, 1985 8 A.M.

Hey Sun locates the hotel where Tai and his team are staying. After a few moments preparing, he places a call to Tai's room.

"Hello? Can I speak with Mr. Tai Huang please?" Hey Sun settles back into his hotel room chair.

"Yes, speaking."

"Mr. Huang. My name is Hey Sun. I work for the Chinese Government as the new Director overseeing your former course work from Beijing University."

Excited, Tai perks up in his bed and says, "Yes Sir. How can I help you?"

"Well first, I'm afraid I have some bad news to share with you. Your father is Mr. Jimmie Huang, correct?"

Tai's heart begins to race. "Yes. What about my father?"

"He passed away last evening."

Tai starts shaking. He throws up. He explodes into tears and throws the phone across the room embedding the lower half of it into the wall.

Yuen hears the thunderous damage against his adjoining wall and opens the shared door. "Jesus! What was that? Tai, what's wrong?"

Tai can't even open his eyes to see where he's walking. He walks right into the bathroom door and falls backwards. He cuts his head on the corner of the small ottoman in the bedroom and just stays collapsed in agony.

Yuen calls over to Misa, "Misa! Quick!"

Misa runs into the room and sees her close friend Tai collapsed on the floor crying his eyes out and slamming his fists into the thin floor carpeting.

She starts crying and screams, "What happened? Tai, what's going on? Please, tell us!"

Tai can't speak yet. His heart weighs a thousand pounds and he's having genuine trouble breathing. Yuen quickly fills a glass of water from the adjacent bathroom. Misa goes over to Tai and falls to the ground with him.

"What is it Tai? What happened?"

Yuen begins shaking. He knows this could be news he would be terrified to hear as well. Again Misa tries to coerce any information from Tai.

Yuen sits Tai up and gives him a little but stern shake and says, "Tai, tell us!"

Tai finally opens his eyes. He barely makes out the glass of water Yuen is holding and takes it. He takes a drink and immediately chokes on the cold water. He waits a moment and takes another drink and catches his breath. Yuen and Misa give him some space. They sit back and then up on Tai's bed but Tai remains on the floor.

After a few moments, Tai says, "I just got a call. Someone named Hey Sun from the Chinese Government overseeing our school work. He told me my father passed away last night!"

Tai again collapses in grief; not believing what he just said. All Tai can think about is the fact that he just spoke with his father yesterday evening and his father said he felt very good and was in very high spirits.

Misa collapses in grief as well and Yuen is stunned. Something defiant in him stirs and he stands Misa up and walks her back into their room. He closes the door quietly and picks Tai up off the floor.

Tai hugs his friend and says, "We just talked! How can this be?"

"Tai! Please! Tell me what the man said again; every detail and even how he sounded."

Tai pulls away and stops to think. Then he says, "He introduced himself. He said he was with the Chinese Government looking over our former school work. Then he asked me to confirm who my father was and then he said he died!"

"Okay. Wait. How did he sound when he introduced himself?"

"What?"

"Did he sound pleasant or stressed out like he knew he had bad news for you?"

"Jesus! I don't know Yuen. The man just said my dad died!"

"Did he sound pleasant to start? It's important."

Tai takes a drink of water and sits up taller in his bed. "What are you saying now?"

"Okay. I'm saying if this guy sounded pleasant but then had such a terrible thing to tell you, he's a liar and what he said is probably bullshit too!"

Tai's eyes brighten up. His mind starts to calculate what Yuen is telling him; maybe his father isn't dead like he's hinting toward. He stands up and shakes his head.

Yuen walks over to him and Tai grabs him and says, "What kind of sick fucking game is this?"

"Yes! Exactly. A sick fucking Yakuza game brother! This is what they do!"

"Jesus! Are you telling me that there is a genuine chance that my dad isn't gone?"

"Yes! I'm saying that this sounds to me like this guy is using a classic scare tactic and what he's saying is bullshit! The trick now is to figure out why he's saying it."

"Fucking bastards!"

"Yes but trust me. These bastards are good at these games because it's all they really do. We have got to be really smart and I'm not talking about book-smart either. One mistake on our end and you're dad will be dead because they obviously know who he is and of course, they already have Kim."

Tai wipes his eyes clear and says, "What do we do?"

"Okay. This guy will obviously call back because you buried your phone in your wall. He knows you're freaked out so you have to play along with that and let him set the course for us to follow. That gives us time to see what's really going on, who all is involved, and where everyone is before he starts showing his cards."

"Showing his cards?"

"There's always a much bigger reason why these guys pull these stunts and it almost always centers on money. Right now, he's bluffing but before we call him on it, we've got to play his game and make him think we're playing it with a losing hand."

"Money always, but what else?"

"Revenge! Okay, so this guy will call back. Record him if you can or let me know so I can listen in on the call. Maybe I'll recognize his voice."

"Okay."

"He's got you in a tough spot so again, you've got to play to that; it'll suck having to act like your dad is dead but you've got to do it. I swear on my eyes he's okay. You've got to trust me. I'll call my Triad people right now and get him away from his home and sent away so he'll definitely be safe."

Tai grabs Yuen's hands and shakes them. Then he gives Yuen a big hug, lifting the larger man off the ground as his eyes tear up and he loses it again. Just then Misa knocks on the shared door.

Yuen quickly explains, "We've got to bring Misa into this now because we have no choice. And after this morning, she needs this!"

Tai nods and says, "You make your calls and I'll talk to her about everything we've talked about, right?"

"Everything. She'll be so glad to hear about Kim too!"

Yuen exits Tai's room, letting Misa in.

He turns and says, "Sit and talk. I'll be back." He closes the shared door behind him.

Misa is still crying but when she sees that Tai has recovered, she feels a little better but also uneasy.

Tai winks at her and says, "Shit. Where do I begin?" He smiles and this relieves all the tension in her shoulders, face, and stomach. The two hug each other and Tai gladly buries his face in Misa's so-black-it's-blue hair.

"Tai? What's going on?"

"I wish I had a drink to share with you because trust me, we both need one!"

"What? Come on. You're making me nervous again."

"Okay. Just flat out, my dad is fine and so is Kim."

Like a deer in headlights, that's too much for Misa to handle. She breaks down crying and Tai hugs her and says, "I'm serious. My dad is fine and Yuen and I know where Kim is."

She hugs him back and starts to wipe her eyes and cheeks. "I don't understand."

"Me either but Yuen told me and I trust him like you do." Tai stands up and prepares for this difficult speech.

"Okay. First, Kim was kidnapped. She's fine. She's in Japan. I can't tell you exactly where and before I tell you anything else, look at me. I have to be very clear with you. You can't tell anyone; not one word about her or my dad, got it? Or they will be dead and I'm serious about that; deadly serious!"

"What is this?"

"I'll get to that. Promise me. Promise Yuen. And promise for Kim and for my dad or you'll be helping to kill them."

"I promise! I promise!"

"Misa, I'm serious! No one can know until this whole damn thing is over because it's much bigger than anything we've ever seen or even knew about probably."

Misa breaks down and finally offers a solemn promise that Tai knows is real.

"Kim was kidnapped the day before our wedding and taken to Japan by the Japanese Yakuza. Yuen found this all out because he is Chinese Triad, how's that for starters?"

"What? Shit! I didn't know that!"

"He's kept that secret for a long time but in this case, I'm glad he called his contacts to help us or we'd never see Kim alive again because after they get what they want from her, they probably will kill her. That's why we've got to be so careful, smart, and lucky at the right time."

"And your dad?"

"Yeah, that almost killed me and I swear on my eyes, I'm going to get this guy back for that one!"

"Who?"

"I got a call earlier this morning. You might have noticed the phone stuck in my wall."

Misa looks over and smiles.

"This guy, Hey Sun told me he works for the Chinese Government and that he's overseeing our former school project work. He doesn't say what projects and then he simply tells me that my dad is dead."

Misa nods as Tai continues. "Yuen asked me a strange question but when I thought about it and when I think about it more now, it makes sense. That kind of news is always delivered with sorrow and empathy, not statements of fact and not led by a formal project introduction that obviously means nothing when you're about to tell someone one of their parent's has just died, right?"

"That's sick!"

"Exactly but you see the kind of person we're dealing with? Anyone willing to do that is willing to do a lot more to get what he wants so Yuen says we've got to play along until this sick fucking game is over."

"Fuckers!" Misa stands up and gives Tai a hug and then she steps away.

"I swear! I will do whatever I have to, to help get Kim and your dad back!"

The two walk over to the wall and excavate the room phone from the wall.

Yuen has been making several calls from his room.

"Yurii?"

"Hey, Yuen! So, what's going on?"

"Listen. I need something right now and I mean now."

"You got it. Who?"

"Not a hit. A safety, got it?"

"Safety. Got it. Who?"

"Mr. Huang; get him right fucking now! Take him somewhere safe and I'll call you later. No noise on this one because they're watching!"

"They're always watching."

"No; a new mark this time. Name's Hey Sun. Check him out and keep it quiet because this guy is running things for now."

"For now, got it. Later!"

"Thanks Yurii!"

Yuen re-enters Tai's room. Misa runs over to him and playfully grabs the front of Yuen's shorts.

"So my gangster lover, what now?"

Yuen stares over at Tai. "I guess you told her?"

Tai nods and finishes getting dressed. "Okay, listen guys. I'll play this up like Yuen says but Misa, you have to now too. Whenever this guy Hey Sun is around, I want you breaking down and running out of room all the time because if he thinks we know what he's up to, he'll make a call, you know?"

Misa agrees and then Yuen adds, "Update. Kim is fine. Mr. Huang is being picked up by new friends soon. But some bad news too."

"What?" Tai and Misa both ask at the same time.

"The Yakuza has the Tse's too; Bruce and LuAnn."

"Why?"

"The game; to get Kim to really do whatever they want, they have her parents to drive their point home and if she refuses, they'll suffer for it. We have to start thinking like them to get that one step ahead at the right time."

"Shit! This is going to get really complicated!"

"Oh, we're just getting started brother but remember, we'll have a few shots to take of our own. We just have to get a little lucky and have near perfect timing and we can put them in some serious spots."

"You enjoy this, don't you?"

"Not the kidnapping parts but the game, yeah, does it show?"

"Uh, yeah!"

"One more thing; they make big moves, really big moves so we've got to be prepared for that and I'm talking about big swings in momentum, or so they'll think. Either way, it has to be done their way for now."

"Hey, whatever it takes because this is all about getting Kim back and keeping my dad safe; whatever it fucking takes!"

NOON

By this time, the hotel has replaced the phone in Tai's room. Hey Sun calls Tai back.

"Tai Huang?"

"Yes?"

"This is Hey Sun Tai."

"Mr. Sun, yes?"

"I am so sorry young man. My sincere condolences."

"Thank you Mr. Sun. Can you tell me what happened?"

"Heart attack brought on by some kind of vaccination that Mr. Huang had received recently I'm afraid."

Tai breaks downs and says, "Jesus! No! That's my fault!"

"Your fault? How could that be your fault Tai?"

"Oh, that's a long story Mr. Sun. I wouldn't bother you with all those details. I'm sure you're very busy."

"No, please. I'm here to help."

"Okay. Maybe we can meet later tonight because my friends and I are making arrangements for my father."

"Oh, well that's why I was calling because I needed to inform you that due to some suspicious circumstances, the police were called and they have already taken your father's body into their care and custody for testing."

"Testing? What the fuck does that mean?"

"Now Tai, please. Calm down. Let me explain. It means there was evidence of possible foul-play so they are just following proper procedure in their investigation. This is normal and I have asked them to keep me informed as to the results and they agreed so I'm looking out for you son."

"But that's sick! There's no foul-play. That's bullshit!"

"Maybe but we have to let them perform their duties and then we'll know the whole story. Now, you did say it might be your fault. I need to know what that means."

"Mr. Sun, I appreciate your help but maybe I should talk to a lawyer first."

"Sure. That's always an option but let me say this. Can a lawyer prevent you from going to jail for the rest of your life? Especially if there is foul-play on your part."

"Jesus! What, are you a cop?"

"No. Just someone trying to look out for you. This is serious son and if we don't work together, I'm afraid you could be facing some real jail time. I should tell you there are more people involved as well."

"More people? Who?"

"Do you know an elderly couple that live close to your father named Tan and Wan Ching?"

"Yes, I do."

"Well, they passed away the same night as your father did and they are also under police care and custody."

"Oh God!" Tai pauses the phone and smirks over at Yuen and Misa who have been listening in this whole time. The three smile at each other. On the other line, Hey Sun's eyes darken with delight.

"Tai?"

"Yes. I'm here. It's just hard to hear all of this right now. With my father and now the Ching's. This is really awful Mr. Sun."

"Yes it is Tai so you need to talk to me before the police do so I can make arrangements to help you."

"Okay Mr. Sun. Let me get a few things settled here and I'll meet you tonight back at my father's home, okay?"

Immediately interjecting, Hey Sun declares, "No! You can't go to your father's home!"

"What? Why not?"

Realizing his over-reaction, Hey Sun settles down and says, "…uh, remember, it's part of the full investigation and if you're seen there, they'd likely arrest you on the spot for questioning."

"Oh, right. Okay. Thanks. Where then?"

"Beijing airport. My private jet is waiting for you."

"And my friends?"

"Yes, your friends too. You must all come and talk with me so we can work this out. Don't delay. Again son, I'm sorry about your father."

"Thank you Mr. Sun. I appreciate your help. I'll be sure to tell my friends about you and your offer to help us when they get back from lunch."

"Very good son. I'll see you soon."

"Okay."

Tai hangs up and looks over to Yuen.

Yuen narrows his eyes and says, "Perfect! Fucking perfect man! You sold it and this asshole bought it!"

Misa smiles, following everything as well.

"Again. I'm just telling you guys, this may take several years to flush out so just be ready and of course, in that time, we may never see Kim or your dad until all the cards are dealt and we force this asshole to show his losing hand."

Tai and Misa nod and then Tai smirks and asks, "I never knew you loved American poker so much."

Yuen smiles and says, "Sorry. That's how I learned about how these things work and the analogies have stuck."

"It's good. It suits you." Tai offers.

Yuen says, "Thanks. You've got another gift. You've got a touch for this already. I'm impressed."

"Hey man, I'm just pissed and motivated so I'll try anything and I know I have to be great at it, or else so, let's go!"

Hey Sun sits back in his room and laughs to himself. He mumbles, "Little fucker. I've got him and he doesn't even know it. And soon I'll be fucking his girlfriend while he sleeps in the room next to her!"

Tai's team exits their room and heads out to get lunch down the street. Three rooms down the hall, Hey Sun peers out into the hallway, pauses and then quietly exits his room and heads out the alley exit.

And so the game begins.

CHAPTER TWELVE

SEPTEMBER 16, 1985 4 P.M. – BEIJING INTERNATIONAL AIRPORT, CHINA

TAI'S team arrives at the airport and two men escort them through security and over to Hey Sun's private jet. It is the most stunning and amazing thing they've ever seen.

The pilot and the two security men are a little mysterious but other than that, the plane is spectacular; only two or three years old at the most, it's white with black stripes from tip to tail and for the tails' center section as well. Same design with the wings. Inside, the cabin seats six comfortably and there is a single bathroom in the rear of the plane. A small bar sits in the left center of the plane and it features a small table in front of it. All the seats are khaki-colored Italian leather with double-wide black stitching; very elegant. The two security men sit in the front seats. Tai and his team sit in the center-rear area of the private luxury jet. The trio can't help but to soak in every inch of the plane and commit it to memory. Tai decides to test the pilot.

"Mr. Sun joining us soon?"

The two security guards say nothing.

"Excuse me, sir? Are we waiting for Mr. Sun?"

A few moments pass. Finally, the pilot steps into the small hallway at the front and says, "No sir. Mr. Sun is already heading back to his offices. We'll join him there shortly. Please, be comfortable. Have a drink if you wish and we'll take off very soon."

"Okay. Thank you. Uh, our destination?"

The pilot returns to his cabin seat and closes the black cloth screen. The two security men directly in front of Tai turn their seats inward, effectively blocking anyone's attempts at walking forward to the pilot's cabin. A moment later, the private jet begins to taxi to its approved runway.

Misa overhears on the pilot's radio, "Yes sir, we're making our way to you now." Tai's team holds hands as their brains, hearts, and stomachs all move to the back of their bodies. The jet takes off, defying gravity yet again.

Hey Sun has been very busy; putting various documents together, making numerous calls, and packing three suit cases full of clothes, some convenience items, materials, and other supplies. He smirks as he steps through his tasks. He calls Kim from his new-fangled technology gadget called a cellular phone.

"Kim?"

"Hey Mr. Sun."

"Clever girl."

"Where are you now?"

"I'm meeting with a few people and then I'll be home to you."

"Meeting with who?"

"Just some people in my business. See you tonight and try not to kill anyone during dinner, huh?"

"I can't promise anything!"

Hey Sun's eyes widen and he chuckles to himself deviously and hangs up. Kim looks down at her stomach. She's worried. She can tell she's starting to show. Hey Sun can't know about this unless she does something quick to cover this issue. Pregnant with Tai's child from their time back on Dragon's Tears Island, she knows if Hey Sun sees this, he'll know it's not his and he'll assume correctly that it's Tai's. In the end, she'll simply receive a kick or punch in her stomach that will kill her baby. Kim starts sweating trying to think of a solution and after ten minutes of frantic behavior and ten million thoughts racing through her mind, she starts crying; she has a plan and she hates it. She hates herself for even thinking it but she knows it's the only thing she can do to save her and Tai's son or daughter.

6:30 P.M.

Tai's team touches down. A silver limousine awaits them on the tarmac. During their ride to meet Hey Sun, the driver tests them.

"You three from China?"

Tai perks up in his seat and leans forward. "Yes sir. Students last semester."

"You must all be the best because Mr. Sun doesn't waste his time with second best people."

"Oh, thank you. So where are we meeting Mr. Sun?"

"His offices downtown. We'll be there by 8 if the traffic isn't too bad."

"Sendai?" Misa queries.

Then Yuen asks, "Yokohama?"

The driver confirms, "Yes, Yokohama. Does that surprise you?"

Tai says, "No. It's just that we got all turned around and lost our sense of direction plus that plane was something else. I got horrible news from Mr. Sun that was probably very difficult for him to share."

"Oh?"

"Yes. My father passed away sir."

"I'm sorry."

"And some other friends of ours. On the same night."

"Family is such a blessing and friends are precious. I'm so sorry young man."

"Tai Huang. And these are my friends, Yuen and Misa. We all graduated as top scientist's very early last semester."

"Brilliant. I'm sure you can be of great aid to Mr. Sun and to yourselves. Listen to what he has to say to you."

"Yes sir. Thank you."

"Okay. Sit back and enjoy the ride. Have a drink from the blue bottle. It's a proprietary blend that Mr. Sun has had made special."

Misa and Tai look over to Yuen who is shaking his head from side to side slowly.

"Thanks, no. We don't really drink and I'm still really shaken up about my father and our friends back home."

"Understandable."

8:10 P.M.

Tai's team arrives at Hey Sun's downtown Yokohama offices. There is abundant activity outside but compared to regular business hours, the streets and building are quiet and dark.

Hey Sun's security men from the plane have travelled the same distance separately by motorcycle. They greet Tai's team at the front doors; ornate black onxy doors with light gold dragon's as handles.

Yuen comments, "Beautiful Chinese dragons."

One of the guards speaks this time. Smirking, he demands, "They are Japanese dragons!"

Yuen continues, "Chinese. See, they have five claws. If they were Japanese, they would only have three."

Misa smiles. Tai peers over at Yuen as if to say, "Relax."

Misa whispers to Yuen as they enter, "What if they had four claws?"

Yuen whispers back, "Everyone else; Korean, Thai, etc."

Misa smiles and squeezes Yuen's left hand.

The group of five enters the elevator. The other guard presses the 'P' button.

Tai asks, "Nice building. Is this an embassy building for China?"

The befuddled guard is about to speak again when his partner motions.

"Here. The Penthouse suite. You can meet with Mr. Sun now to answer your questions. Good night."

Tai's team exits the elevator and the door begin to close. As they do, the pissed off guard offers his middle finger between the doors as they close.

The front doors to Hey Sun's office are tinted glass. The reception desk and seating area is lighted with a small desk lamp.

Tai comments, "The guards just left us. How the hell are we supposed to open the doors?"

At the moment of his 'open the doors' comment, the doors open. The group enters and the doors quickly close behind them.

A voice comes over the small white embedded speakers in the ceiling, "Please veer to your left and find Suite A1. Thank you." The group complies.

Walking down the left side of the Suite, it's unremarkable and dark. Half way down, they see "A1" on a set of double doors. These doors also have the Chinese dragons on them. Yuen smiles. Misa smirks and pokes him in his ribs.

When the group enters, they see an executive desk in front of them, back a ways. It is surrounded by a six-foot high shelf full of books and various decorations including small lamps, vases, and several giant fish teeth located throughout the shelf in their own separate display cases. There appears to be no one in the suite.

"This is creepy." Misa says.

Yuen and Tai nod.

A moment later, soft white lights turn on and a man enters from the far right corner of the suite.

"Good evening! I'm so glad to meet you all!" The bald man prematurely extends his hand in a friendly and warm greeting about ten paces early.

"Mr. Sun?" Tai inquires.

"Yes. Of course. You are Tai Huang and this must be Yuen and Misa Zhang."

The threesome nods and Yuen and Misa both say, "We're not married."

Misa says, "Not yet", under her breath.

"Pardon my absence when you arrived. I've been busy getting things arranged for you."

Tai asks, "Arranged Mr. Sun? For what?"

"For your departures of course."

Disconcerted, Tai asks, "What departures?"

Tai continues, "Maybe now is a good time for you to tell us what's going on and why we're here because this has already been a really long day."

"I'm sorry. Of course. It's just that this will likely come as a shock to you all and I apologize for that but time is of the essence in your case."

"Our case?" Yuen questions.

"Yes. Please sit down and I'll explain myself better."

Tai's team sits down together on the burgundy leather sofa. Mr. Sun settles into his chair in front of them and to their right.

"Nice offices, huh? I just moved in here last week."

"Mr. Sun, please." Tai says.

"Of course. I'm Sorry. The police called me earlier this evening and said they have various accounts all confirming that you three personally administered a medical shot to everyone in your Canton village some time ago; maybe a month ago. Is this true?"

Misa demands, "Is this guy a cop or what?"

Tai immediately says, "He's trying to help us Misa so please, let's hear him out."

"Thank you Tai. Pardon me but as they test these folks and unfortunately, as they complete their autopsies of your father and the Ching's, I have a strong feeling they will then indict you three for manslaughter and maybe even third degree murder, depending on who gets the case. I'm working on finding that part out now."

Yuen and Misa look down to the ground and she starts crying. Tai tears up and says, "Please. Continue Mr. Sun."

"It is absolutely critical for you guys to tell me exactly what you did and how you made this medical compound. If I know before the police find out, I can do more to help you but if you wait, it makes my job much more difficult, understand?"

Tai offers, "I can write it all down for you but unless you are very well versed in chemistry, it won't mean much to you."

Amazed, Hey Sun asks, "Really? You can just do that off the top of your head?"

"Of course."

"Shit! Excuse me. I mean, yes, that would be great. Okay. Now for the serious talk. I know this is all going to hit you guys like a bullet-train but please, hear me out."

They nod. Yuen thinks to himself, "Here it comes…"

"I have worked very hard setting everything up. Believe me. It's time to act! Once those other results come back, the police will know and my help to you will become very limited. So, for the next two weeks, I have another place for you all to stay where you'll be safe. It's here in Yokohama but much safer than a downtown office building."

"Appreciated." Tai offers.

"After that two week period, we have to split you guys up. I'm sorry. You'll be in touch with each other so you can work together on your notes and such but I can't have you all together because that would just make it easier for the Chinese Government and police to round you all up."

"But wait, I thought you worked for the Chinese Government?" Yuen asks.

"I do and I can pull a few strings here and there when it comes to your work. Only, I have to be the first to know or it could be too late and my leadership would step in, see?"

"Ok." The group agrees.

"Plus, there is another bad factor to your work and the other formulas you guys have been working on."

"What's that?" Tai asks.

"The Chinese Triads are also trying to find you and if you don't know who they are, let me just say; they are on a completely different planet than you and I. I'm afraid of them as well! If they get involved, I won't be able to help you at all. They have their own rules for sorting things out and their answers start and end with various calibers of bullets and closer in, a blade!"

"We understand." Yuen confirms. Misa starts crying again.

"I know sweetheart. This is all probably very overwhelming for you all but just let me continue dear."

Hey Sun glances over at Misa; hungrily in Yuen's opinion. He sharpens his eyes towards his alleged protector.

Tai interrupts, "Sorry Mr. Sun. Go ahead."

"What we thought we'd do, and I have my leadership's approval for this, is to relocate each of you, just temporarily until the investigations die down and things get back to normal. We have arranged for very nice accommodations for each of you and again, you'll be in touch with each other so you won't be totally alone. In fact, we want you to be in regular contact with each other as you continue your work."

Tai inquires, "Our work Mr. Sun?"

Hey Sun counters with, "I assume you have various other experiments that you've been working on that you'd probably like to get back to?"

"Actually, no. We were on a break. That's why we were visiting the Forbidden City and The Great Wall when you contacted me. We were on vacation after the work we had just completed."

"Oh, okay. Very good. So you can write down that work for me. Did you happen to keep any journals or diaries, ever?"

"The University wouldn't appreciate it but we really didn't. There simply wasn't time and quite honestly, if I had, anyone could've just picked up on our work and said it was theirs."

"Never? Any of you?"

Collectively, "No sir."

Tai adds, "In fact we had another member of our team, Kim Tse. She would always tell us not to document our work for this very reason and in honor of her, we have continued that tradition."

"In honor of her?" Hey Sun asks.

Tai quickly adds, "Yes sir. She disappeared some time back and there's been no word of her since."

"Oh? I'm very sorry to hear that."

Yuen says, "Thank you sir. We were all very close."

Misa stands up and quickly walks out of the room and into the corner where Hey Sun initiated from.

Hey Sun calls out, "I'm sorry Misa. Not another word about your friend Kim. She must have been a special girl, like yourself."

Yuen says, "It's still very hard for us all to deal with that and losing Mr. Huang. Can you tell me and Tai what happened exactly?"

"Of course; we believe something in the compound that you gave people caused an adverse reaction causing them to become ill and in the case of your father and the Ching's, their passing. It was horrible. They had to have died in great agony."

10:00 P.M.

Hey Sun continues. "What I'm trying to do for you three is simply to save you from years of persecution and prosecution. I can keep this out of the press for a little while but again, we must split you up. In recognition of your sacrifices and current work, your University loans will be paid off so long as you all agree right now to work only for me."

Yuen immediately responds, "That works for me!"

Tai nods as well. Hey Sun excuses himself to go check on Misa.

As Hey Sun leaves the immediate area, Tai smiles and says, "Wow! No more loans!"

Yuen says, "Yeah but didn't I tell you there would be big moves?"

Tai says, "Yeah, but we'll be in touch with each other so that's cool."

"True but again, I'm just saying that nothing is as it seems, especially with these guys."

"The big thing for me is communication so we'd better have a backup plan."

"Good point. I expect these guys to change things up whenever we delay results on anything they want. What did you have in mind?"

"I can teach you how to make a radio transmitter." Tai quickly shares.

"That's perfect because I can guarantee you that all of our calls will be monitored and recorded. That's why Hey Sun wants us to talk to each other as much as we want initially. Once we start making the progress he needs, I'll bet our calling activities will become more controlled or canceled."

"Okay. So it sounds like we're going to have a couple weeks together before we are split up so we'll have to find some time to get that wrapped up. Whatever I show you, share it with Misa as soon as you can."

Hey Sun tracks down Misa in the backroom area of his main office.

"Dear, are you okay?"

"I'm fine. It's just hard to realize all the time that has past already. I don't think I'll ever see my girlfriend Kim again."

"You two were close?"

"Very. In fact, we were like sisters. We shared everything. We talked about everything."

She reflects for a moment and continues, "In fact, we used to sleep together and tickle each other until we passed out."

Hey Sun's eyes widen. This revelation makes him adjust his silk underwear as he and Misa continue to talk. Hey Sun puts his arm around Misa and pats her right shoulder. He rubs it gently at first and then applies deeper pressure as her stares down her shirt.

In a surprise move, Misa turns into Hey Sun and hugs his waist. Startled, he doesn't know what to do but he likes this behavior. Hey Sun looks off in the distance; putting thoughts together in his mind to scheme a new way to keep Misa with him as his second concubine lover. Then he figures, with Kim, the two of them would put on the ultimate of all erotic dinner performances.

Misa offers, "We appreciate what you're doing for us. We do. If you don't know already, Tai is brilliant and Yuen and I are together because we love each other."

Hey Sun pushes away from Misa and reconfirms, "That's right. You two are a couple. I'll keep you together in exile if you wish."

"Yes! Please! He's all I have and I promise, we'll work hard for you!"

"I've told the boys already. Your school debts are paid, compliments of the Chinese Government and my offices."

"That's so generous. How can we repay you?"

"Later. Let's get back to Tai and your Yuen. I've got a great place for you all to stay for the next two weeks until we can clear everything up that the Police are looking into. Then I'll get you three out of the country so you can work in peace."

Misa bows towards Hey Sun and the two walk back into the main office area where Tai and Yuen are concluding their radio transmitter lessons.

Energized, Hey Sun says, "Okay team! I just have your loan payoff documents I need you each to sign and we'll be done with that."

Hey Sun folds over the top ten pages of the large document he's holding. Tai notices the logo of their school appears on the first page he folded over and then Tai signs first, then Misa, and then Yuen. Just before Yuen signs, he notices the second page move up and it appears the edge of the title page says something like, "… patent." He signs and commits that page to his memory. At the back of the large document, Hey Sun has the three sign again.

"Okay. We're out of here! My limousine will take you three to your new luxury apartments so you can get settled in. It's been a really long day and I know you all must be very tired."

"Yes sir, we are." Tai confirms.

"I've got a few more things to wrap up here so let me just say goodnight and I'll talk to you all tomorrow afternoon." Hey Sun bows at the young group and excuses himself back into his office.

As the group settles into Hey Sun's limousine, Yuen belittles that same guard about the Chinese dragon door handles.

11:15 P.M.

Tai's team arrives at their safe-house location. The group is tired but they can't help but to remark on a few things they see.

"The masks and swords are unique. I think they're authentic." Tai remarks.

Misa says, "I love the marble flooring and the flowers outside of each of the rooms."

Yuen smells death. He's sick to his stomach and requests to get to his room ahead of Tai and Misa who are still gazing around at everything.

"What's in the room ahead of us?" Tai asks.

The guard says, "That's the formal dining room. It remains closed until the evening. Tomorrow evening, you will all be treated to a memorable dance before dinner, compliments of Mr. Sun and his favorite seductress."

"Oh, very nice. I can't wait." Tai enters his room and Misa enters the room across the hallway from Tai, where Yuen is heard throwing up in the bathroom.

"Goodnight Tai." Misa closes her door.

"Night Misa." Tai closes his door as the guards return to their positions at the front entrance of the suite.

In his upstairs suite, Hey Sun turns on several surveillance cameras. They don't feature sound, but they do feature high definition black and white imagery. There's one that covers the front entrance where the guards are located, two that shoot down each direction of the hallway, one for each of the bedrooms Tai and his team are in, two covering the formal dining room and a ninth that covers Kim Tse's bedroom.

Having cleaned up, Yuen attacks Misa. Hey Sun grins and looks on as the two make love. Hey Sun talks to himself under his breath as he grabs the front of his black and orange sleeping pants, "Get your last licks in you chubby bastard because soon enough, that beautiful bitch of yours will be mine!"

Hey Sun masturbates as he watches Misa ride Yuen, up and down in a slow rhythm. He looks over at Kim's monitor. She's fast asleep. He looks over at Tai's screen. Tai is also asleep. Hey Sun thinks to himself and then says, "Ah, now it's time to add a little guilty spice to the mix! Shake up these chinks a little bit!"

A half hour later, a knock comes to Tai's door. Groggy, he gets up and opens it. Standing in front of him, naked, is one of the dining room attendants. She smells of lilac and pushes past him. She walks over to the bed and sits down facing Tai who is closing his door.

Embarrassed, Tai immediately offers, "I can't."

In her sultry voice, she says, "It looks like you can!" admiring his growing erection.

She runs her hands underneath his thin grey silk boxers and caresses his inner thighs. He gasps for air as he watches this gorgeous woman work his legs, all the while staring deep into his weary eyes. On her way up and down his leg, her path is interrupted by Tai's engorged member. She repositions his underwear so his erection projects out of the center hole. She strokes him slowly at first and then quickens her pace before beginning to suck on it hard. Exhausted but thrilled in this moment, Tai ejaculates but remains erect. The naked attendant continues to attend to him. She reaches between her legs and massages her clitoris with deep circles and a slap every once in a while. She's so turned on by his continued hardness, she begins moaning and massaging him all over. He starts to moan now as well. When she starts to kiss deeply and lick his lowest set of abs, Tai climaxes again. She loves his completely hairless privates so much that she shoves her fingers inside herself and self-climaxes right after Tai does. Tai begins to fall back but catches himself as the woman continues to weaken his manhood. After a few more minutes of strong and gradual rhythm and pressure, Tai climaxes yet again and collapses onto his bed. He passes out a moment later. The naked woman smiles from ear to ear, stands up and kisses Tai on his cheek and then exits his room. She offers up a 'thumbs up' to the camera in the hallway and heads back to her formal dining room quarters.

CHAPTER THIRTEEN

SEPTEMBER 17, 1985 9:00 A.M.

TAI awakes, feeling appropriately guilty. He showers, dresses, and sits in the single chair in the corner of his bedroom. Yuen and Misa are in the shower together. They take turns washing each other off and getting each other off and washing each other again. As they dress, Yuen confirms with a series of little pinches that Misa understood his radio transmitter instructions. She confirms. She actually had to correct one part of Yuen's instructions so it was good that she whispered those corrections in his ear before they moved on.

At 9:30 A.M., a knock comes to Tai's and Yuen's doors. It is breakfast served on respective carts; a selection of fruit and juices. Scrambled eggs, a small bowl of white rice and a saké cup filled with sweet liquor. On Tai's cart, there is a small notebook with a little note attached to it that reads,

"Please complete your notes for me in this notebook and return it to one of my security men at the front door when you're finished. Xie-xie (Thank you)."

Yuen and Misa conclude their meals as Misa tells Yuen what Hey Sun had said to her last evening. Yuen glares and then tells Misa to wait for some other big move that Hey Sun is sure to make soon.

Several hours pass and finally at Noon, there are knocks at the teams' doors again. It is lunch served on respective carts again.

Tai sneaks his head out the doorway and says, "Excuse me but where is Mr. Sun?"

The security guard nearest to Tai says nothing.

The one across the hall says, "He's away right now on business but he said that he'll meet with you all for the performance dinner tonight."

The guard finishes his delivery and attends Yuen's door, closing and locking it for him.

"Performance?"

"Yes; something very special. If you need anything else in your room, please just call the front."

"Okay then. Xie-xie."

"Excuse me?"

"Oh, that means thank you."

"Of course. You're welcome."

Tai's eyes brighten and then he narrows them. He thinks to himself, "How could this security member working for Mr. Sun not understand what 'Xie-xie' means?" He'd like to share this new information with Yuen but it'll have to wait until this evening because Tai quickly takes note that the security guard locked his door from the outside.

As he eats his lunch, Tai continues to write in Hey Sun's notebook. The formulas he wants to share at this stage are complete; the ones for his Diabetes-friendly Myst1 and an adaptation of his original CDT, taking out all references of Dragon's Tears. Tai smiles to himself as he writes out the extremely long-winded account in chemical terms for two parts hydrogen and one part oxygen combined with the respective ingredients that make up basic aspirin.

He does offer an adjusted chemical formula for his blue elixir but only in its base sugar form. He draws up several small pictures to complete the performance and even signs the right corner of each page, as if to personally 'approve' them. The descriptions for Myst1 alone take up a total of six pages. He smirks to himself again and begins writing his adaptation of his original CDT that he figures will take up about nine pages. For the rest of the ninety-page notebook, he figures he'll fill it with a variety of other experiment notes that he can easily recall from his former school days; past class experiments that will surely keep Hey Sun and his people busy tracking down. They are legitimate notes to offer because they could come in handy for the smaller resources he's pointing out but mainly, they'll help Tai buy some more time for things to play out.

Yuen and Misa eat their lunch and Yuen drives home the importance of this whole matter to her. He also explains himself in better detail regarding his Triad past.

"I just can't believe how you were able to keep that a secret and from me too."

"I know. It's made me feel awful but it was better for you all not to know just in case something happened, you'd really be able to say that you didn't know what someone was talking about."

Disappointed he didn't confide in her earlier but playfully, Misa begrudgingly says, "I guess. Still it was sneaky Yuen."

"Just please, never say anything about it at all around this Hey Sun guy or that'll be the end of us for sure! He's already made one really big mistake telling us that Triads are out to get us. I can obviously tell you that's not true!"

"I'm going to start calling you Sneaky Yuen instead of Sik Yuen." Misa smirks and winks at Yuen.

Misa continues, "You're a dangerous guy to know."

Misa says as she grabs the front of Yuen's pants and starts rubbing him. The couple finishes their lunch of assorted sushi, white rice and a four-pack of Tsingtao beer. Tai received the same and he has finished it all.

At 4:30 P.M., the familiar knocks come to Tai's team doors.

A guard hands a gift garment box to Misa and says, "We'll see you two in one hour." He closes and locks their door behind him.

The other guard tells Tai the same thing and then he asks, "I was told you might have a notebook for me?"

"Yes but I'd like to hand it to Mr. Sun myself before dinner."

"As you wish Mr. Tai." The guard closes and locks Tai's door.

At 5 P.M., the doors are unlocked and Tai, Yuen and Misa step into the hallway.

The elder security guard says, "Please wait here for one moment."

Yuen immediately comments, "Was it really necessary to lock us in our rooms?"

The younger of the two guards again says nothing.

The elder one says, "Mr. Yuen, Mr. Sun is a very private man. He doesn't want anyone to have the wrong impression of him so he asks that you be patient as we get things arranged for you all. It's in everyone's best interest then that you are safe in your rooms."

As expected, Yuen dismisses the long-winded explanation. He nods towards the elder guard as a show of respect. Misa admires the changing of the flowers that the dining room women are tending to.

She says, "They are so beautiful! I love Iris and Bird of Paradise!"

Misa doesn't even take note that the women are naked but Tai and Yuen do. Misa looks down the hall as the women continue replacing flowers and then she playfully but sternly elbows Yuen in his ribs.

At 5:15 P.M., the doors to the formal dining room open and swing apart. The guards escort Tai and his team into the room. To their immediate left far against the wall, a full bar complimented with very high-end high-top bar stools. In front of the bar is an eight-place dining room table. Underneath the black onyx and tinted glass table, there is a giant plush rug featuring several orange and white koi swimming in various directions; it's stunning. On top of the dining room table, the centerpiece is a larger arrangement of purple Iris and purple Bird of Paradise flowers. There are empty saké cups above each place setting. The place settings consist of rectangular black silk placemats with red silk napkins and dark silverware; tungsten. To their immediate right against the far wall, a shelf unit with small banzai trees adorning the multi-level unit. In every other position on the shelf, there is a large fish tooth in a white keep-sake case. The shelf unit itself is antique cherry wood; likely from an ancient Chinese or Japanese time period.

Misa points toward the shelf unit and whispers to Yuen, "Amazing!" Tai and Yuen are speechless.

A moment later, soft orange and blue lights begin dancing across the room. As they near a wall, they bounce back and automatically dance across the other side of the room. The effect is mesmerizing Yuen who is now a little sick to his stomach. He excuses himself and requests to go back to his bedroom. The elder guard escorts him back.

Tai and Misa take a seat at the front-side of the formal dining table. Their saké cups are filled by a naked female attendant. Hey Sun enters, trailed by a naked woman who attends to his dress jacket. He dismisses her to the back wall where she waits.

Tai stands up and quickly hands Hey Sun his notebook and whispers, "Mr. Sun; my notes sir."

Hey Sun smiles wide and takes the notebook. Tai returns to his seat.

"This being your first night, we wanted to throw you a celebratory dinner. One you will never forget, I promise you this. This dinner performance is in honor of each of your achievements in school and it's a toast of things to come!"

Hey Sun claps his hands and a flurry of activity commences. A low-profile black onyx and tinted glass table is placed to the right of the entryway, directly across from the formal dining room table. Another ornate orange and white koi fish plush rug is positioned first and the low-profile table is then placed on top of it. Tai can't stop staring at the orange and blue accented naked bodies crossing in front of him and neither can Misa. The women are all their ages and are as equally stunning as Misa. Misa laughs to herself and nudges Tai.

She whispers, "That girl looks just like me but with shorter hair. Maybe I have a sister!"

Tai agrees and whispers back, "Your twin." Hey Sun takes note of this as well.

Yuen returns from the bathroom and says, "Who the hell are you?"

The other man in the room says nothing.

Agitated, Yuen approaches him and again asks, "Who the hell…"

Before he can complete his question, he's out cold. A second man standing in the corner behind Yuen places a napkin laced with chemicals over Yuen's mouth and nose, rendering Yuen unconscious in four seconds. The guards quickly collect Yuen's possessions, throwing everything quickly into his carry-on-sized luggage. They scan the room for any last details and then as two other men carry Yuen out, the guards close and lock the bedroom door. They quickly head down the hallway away from the formal dining room area.

In her room, after a long hot bath, Kim is brushing out her long black hair as she sits on the edge of her bed. She prepares for her night. She can't wait for what's to come. She plans her moves out in her head with each brush stroke. She's wearing her favorite custom formula of strawberry body scents. Even thinking about the night to come makes her a little nervous but genuinely excited. She takes another stiff drink from her shot-glass.

Brighter but still soft white lights come on above the dining table and the flurry of activity continues. As various naked women attend to the bar and dining table, Tai is taken away by one of them to an area behind the bar. A woman approaches Misa with a white box featuring a black silk bow wrapped around opposite ends. She nods in appreciation and opens it. As Misa unfurls the orange and white silk robe, Hey Sun's eyes grow big and so does the front of his pants, which he repositions and settles back down.

Hey Sun says, "Please. Change here Misa."

"Take my clothes off right here, in front of everyone?"

"If you wish or just put the robe on over your dress if you like."

Never one to back down from a challenge and with Tai out of the room, Misa undresses and quickly redresses wearing just the stunning and cool silk robe. She retakes her former position at the table. Behind the bar, two women slowly undress Tai. One of them takes his shirt and pants off. She kneels and kisses his abs down to his shaved lower abdomen. His heart races and pumps blood into his penis causing it to immediately extend out and away from his silk underwear. She takes him into her mouth and sucks hard. After a couple minutes, he can't hold it any longer; her technique beats him. These moments are destined for Tai's own journal that he has neglected for years, since he met Kim but deserve their place in the brief erotic histories he's had. Before, Kim occupied all of these episodes but these escapades are definitely worthy of note and Kim would understand they were simply turns of events out of his control, especially under these unusual but exciting circumstances. Either way, he'd be happy to accept a few slaps in his face for them. After another couple minutes, he climaxes again but the woman refuses to release him. After a third round, he finally softens. The women then wrap Tai in his robe and send him back out to the dining room area. Exhausted, he embarrassingly sits down next to Misa and admires her robe. The area is robust with activity; stunningly attractive and naked women scurrying around everywhere tending to the dinner guests. One excuses herself from the room and rapidly walks out.

Hey Sun then says, "Normally, our dinner production is a little longer but this evening I think we'll get right to things in honor of our esteemed guests." He claps.

The orange and blue dancing lights stop for a moment as a woman enters from behind the wall nearest the banzai tree shelf. She's wearing a see-through orange and white silk robe that breaks at the bottom every time she takes a seductive step. Through her Zorro-like thin black mask, she can see her two targets this evening; a young man and woman sitting at the formal dining table. She smiles and continues her seductive slow walk toward them. As she approaches the low-profile black onyx table, the lights resume. Women start serving an array of small entrées including Chinese Perch and blue-fin tuna with white rice. They refill everyone's saké cups and leave the bottle for their convenience.

As the masked woman begins her erotic performance, Hey Sun motions to Tai and Misa to join him at the low-profile black onyx table.

Yuen comes to. He's in the back seat of the same limousine that brought them all to the retreat. He's alone in the car.

He bangs on the front glass concealing the driver, "Hey! What the fuck is going on?"

The glass descends and the elder security guard says, "I'm very sorry Mr. Yuen. That was me. We had to leave quickly and there simply wasn't time to discuss it. Please pardon my disrespectful behavior."

"Where's Misa? Where's Tai? Are they in other cars?"

"Exactly right. You'll all be in touch again soon enough. Please, have a drink of water and sit back as we make our way to the airport."

"The airport?"

"Yes sir. Didn't Mr. Sun tell you?"

"No. I don't remember anything about the airport." Yuen shakes his head clear a second time.

"Yes sir. Mr. Sun is beginning the relocations and we simply had to get you out first due to the police investigation. They now know from other sources that you and Mr. Tai administered the injections that killed several people, including Tai's own father."

Yuen shakes his head again and reminds himself, 'this is the game' so he pauses and then emotionally exclaims, "Oh God! So it's true then; the regular Diabetes shot Tai and I gave people killed Mr. Huang and the elderly couple?"

"Yes. I'm very sorry but remember Mr. Sun is helping you out. He's the only friend you three have now. I'm taking you to a secure location and after a while, you'll be back in touch with Tai and Misa okay? Everything's going to work out so don't worry."

"But how?"

"It's all taken care of."

"I'm so grateful. We would have all gone to prison… for decades. How?"

"That's true so just work hard for Mr. Sun and it'll all work out in time."

Nervously, Yuen settles back because it's all he can really do. He's anxious to know where's he's going and he hopes Misa isn't freaking out too bad. He hopes Tai can keep a cool head as well and play this game because like he said, the big moves are coming fast and furious now. If Misa and Tai can roll with the punches, they'll survive this ordeal.

A moment later, the driver brings the conversation glass panel back up and stops the luxury car. A scantily-clad woman enters and the car takes off. Yuen sits up in his seat.

The woman offers the back of her hand; the top of which is filled with a tiny mountain of white powder. He declines so she promptly snorts the compound up. She licks her lips and moves into Yuen's lap. He braces her gorgeous small backside and immediately takes note that she's not wearing any underwear. All of a hundred pounds, she's a little younger than Yuen. She digs slowly into his pants and begins massaging his penis. They kiss and the girl sucks Yuen's tongue hard. He turns her around in his lap and faces her away from himself. He kisses her backside as he wrestles his pants all the way down.

As he enters her, she begins wailing away saying, "Yes, harder! Harder Sik Yuen! Yes!"

This goes on for ten minutes when finally, the forbidden couple explodes together.

They settle into separate seats and Yuen says, "I have a girlfriend but she won't do it that way with me. I feel great and terrible at the same time."

The woman says, "Name's Mika, and that's your girlfriend's fault because you were great!"

"Mr. Sun told you my full name?"

"He told me a few things, why?"

"Mika? Your name is Mika? My girlfriend's name is Misa."

"Ha, so close, but … oh so far!"

Mika massages Yuen's member again and after a few more moments, the new couple is going at it again. The driver's turns the hidden camera back on, now that the frivolous talk has ended.

The masked woman continues her dance and teases her guests with the occasional half wrap around her body with her see-through silk robe. Finally, she motions for Tai and Misa to join her on the table. She lets her robe fall to the ground revealing her gymnast-like slender physique, complete with slightly muscular abdominal muscles. Pretty drunk by now, Tai can't believe it. They both look back at Hey Sun. He smiles and motions his right hand forward for them to join the masked superstar erotic dancer.

She positions Tai and Misa apart with herself in the middle. She kneels down and begins running her hands up and down and inside of their closest legs. This goes on for several minutes. Both Misa and Tai are going crazy. Their robes drop and another naked woman clears the clothes from the top of the black onyx table. The masked woman stands up and takes a step back, giving Tai and Misa a few minutes to glance over at one another; they do. Tai smiles because he's always loved Misa but never thought he'd get to see her amazing body. She's a slightly shorter and slightly less muscular version of Kim but that so-black-its-blue hair of hers has always made him crazy and in the dancing orange and blue light, he can't even describe it now. As the light dances across her ribs and lower abdomen, he takes a deep breath, unfurrowing his six-pack abs. He is now fully erect and his nearly eight-inch long penis looks amazing to Misa as well as orange and blue lights dance across it. During this whole time, a woman has been tending to Hey Sun as well. As she gives him oral pleasure, he can't help but to squirm a little bit in his chair as he watches the couple on the table marvel at each other. They are facing him so he can see everything and amazingly, they remain in their displayed separate positions, anxiously awaiting the next command from the masked woman.

She's ready for her next move. She slowly begins pouring slightly thick red liquor across the top of Tai's shoulders. It begins running down his body in cool thin strips until it reaches the top of the table. Then she does the same to Misa. As she finishes pouring it across Misa's shoulders, she hands the pitcher off to someone behind her and she begins licking the red liquor off the back and sides of Misa's tiny and muscular frame. Misa begins to moan and almost loses her stance. With her eyes closed in ecstasy, she staggers back into place.

Hey Sun announces, "Careful. The table is very wet now."

Misa whispers, "So am I!"

Misa regains her stance again and allows the masked woman to continue. She lifts her arms up as the masker superstar licks the liquor away from her breasts and abs. Tai looks on; he's pulsating now.

The woman behind the masked woman hands the pitcher of red liquor to Tai and whispers, "You should do as you wish with her tonight. Indulge yourself and I'll be back to finish you off myself!"

Tai begins pouring some of the red liquor on Misa's body, replacing what the masked woman has licked off. He can't believe he's doing this but he continues. Misa can't believe it either as she looks Tai up and down. She wants to attack Tai like she can't believe but she remains in place. She watches some of the red liquor scroll down the front of her body and into the small patch of pubic hair she sports. She closes her eyes tighter and climaxes on the spot. Then she opens her eyes and looks at the sexy vertical pattern of red liquor that has scrawled its way down and across Tai's abdominal muscles. She knew he was clean shaven from chest to toe but had never seen it for herself. She closes her eyes, brushes some of the red liquor inside herself and climaxes again.

Finally, Yuen and Mika have arrived at the airport. Passionately, they kiss and Mika moans the whole time. Yuen massages her back and sides as she moans louder and caresses him. She offers Yuen a stiff drink and he takes it. The fast couple laughs as they search for his belt and her left dress shoe. She takes a quick snort from a tiny bottle she has in her purse and then proceeds to suck Yuen's tongue like a lollipop. When the elder driver opens the door, Yuen is ready for his relocation like nothing ever happened.

The driver hands him his boarding pass and motions him to go to his left toward the check-in counters. Mika remains with the elder driver. Yuen was half thinking she'd join him but she is clearly the 'property' of Mr. Sun. As Yuen walks away, he notices the elder man's arm around Mika, resting on her lower right hip.

Yuen turns away and mumbles to himself, "It is what it is!"

He glances down at his boarding pass, searching for his seat location and more importantly, his destination.

Hey Sun can't believe how these two are carrying on but he loves it and of course, he knows his color video recording of the whole performance will likely make him millions over the coming years; that's what the orange and blue lights actually are. Beautiful and seductive lights that queue an overhead color video camera located on the light modules themselves. They also control other video cameras that turn on from hidden locations around the bar, mounted in the front of various liquor bottles. This way, several angles and various zoom effects are captured for every event. Also hidden and focused in on the small black onyx table from their positions, are several other video cameras located in the ceramic planters of various banzai trees on the far shelf. The eyes of the koi fish featured on the planters are the video camera lenses.

Just as Tai looks like he's about to make a move over to Misa, Hey Sun claps his hands. The diabolically sexy masked woman retreats to the wall behind the banzai tree shelf and the other naked women line up against the back of the wall next to the bar. Soft white lights now fall in the room as an engorged Tai and completely aroused Misa stand on the low-profile black onyx table naked and dripping in sweet red liquor.

Hey Sun simply excuses himself and the doors to the formal dining room close. As they do, the blue dancing lights return. Just as Tai begins to look over to Misa, she's on him. Tai throws his head back and almost falls as Misa tends to his red liquor-stained member. She makes quick work of him and then she lies down on the table. Tai kneels down and kisses Misa's breasts. The two are so hungry for each other they can't stand it any longer. Tai enters Misa and she slides off the table and onto the floor. The couple is together for almost ten minutes when Misa opens her eyes and says, "We have to tell Yuen. I have to tell him about this."

Tai says, "I know. I'll tell him too and if we ever see Kim again, I have to tell her."

"I know." Misa starts crying as she climaxes for the third time.

"She'll understand because she loves you. She'll know what this all was when we tell her about all of this someday. I just hope she can forgive me because you are fucking amazing!"

Misa winces in utter delight. She bites her bottom lip and moans louder. With every thrust Tai gives her, her inside muscle control grasps Tai's manhood, driving him insane.

Someone could ask him what his last name was and he'd have no clue. Misa climaxes for the fourth time.

"If I wasn't with Kim and you weren't with Yuen, I'd be with you Misa! I love you like a true friend and girlfriend tonight but never again, right?"

"Yes! I know! I love you too Tai! Never again but tonight, please, just stay inside me until we both can't move!"

The couple climaxes together again and continues on for another ten minutes.

Hey Sun enters Kim's room. He announces, "That was such an unbelievable performance!"

"You liked it?" She asks.

"My God. I loved it! I was going crazy just watching the whole thing."

In a strange romantic move toward Hey Sun, Kim moves over to him and grabs his right hand.

She pulls him over to her bed and says, "I've been thinking. You haven't hit me or made me do anything I didn't want to do and I want to show you that I'm grateful."

Hey Sun can't believe this change of attitude and he's not about to lose this chance. He sits down in the middle of Kim's bed and waits.

Kim continues saying, "So, I thought tonight, you can have me because I don't want you to ever hit me and because honestly, I'm lonely. I want to be touched in that special way but it's just sex, okay?"

Hey Sun smiles widely and says, "Not just sex. Sex with you Kim will be fantastic but I understand what you mean so just tonight, okay. Honestly, I'd never hit you but you have seen what some people do that makes me go crazy and I'm not going to promise you that I wouldn't react the same way."

Kim immediately says, "I know. If they don't do things to make you that mad, you don't have to react that way, right?"

"Smart girl! You lead. I want you to do what you want so there's no pressure at all."

Kim smiles and starts to dance for Hey Sun in front of the bed. She plays with her silk kimono; cascading it up and down her body. Her strawberry body scent is making Hey Sun hard. She lays him back on the bed and sheds her kimono. She laughs, flexing her abdominal muscles at him, making him fully erect. She begins tracing the exterior line of her pink and white silk panties; then the inside of them. Hey Sun begins to masturbate. She looks at Hey Sun and smiles. She reaches her arms up and back, floating her hands through her slightly wet black hair.

Completely entranced by her, Hey Sun claims, "Oh my God girl!"

She walks over and sits next to him. She grabs his free left hand and positions it over her right breast. He softly massages her breast and ribcage. Kim thinks to herself, "He's no Tai that's for sure but it'll do."

She crawls across the top of Hey Sun and positions herself on him. After two minutes, he's done. She couldn't be happier because that's all she needed and wanted from him. She smiles back at him and excuses herself to the bathroom. She turns on the shower and begins crying.

She holds her hands together and says a prayer, "Tai. I'm sorry but that was the only way to save your child. I pray for the day when I can apologize to you in person! Please forgive me!"

Hey Sun is completely spent and still lying naked across the middle of the bed.

Kim returns to the room after her shower and says, "And I wanted to thank you for allowing me to skip tonight's dinner performance. I needed the rest tonight."

Groggy, Hey Sun says, "You're welcome but I must tell you that young Camilla put on quite the show for our guests. She was wonderful and our guests really got into it!"

"Guests?"

"Yes. I told you... I had a couple of potential investors visit so I thought we'd show them a special time and Camilla really out did herself."

Kim smiles, winks and says, "I'll have to ask her for details."

Hey Sun smiles back, shakes his right index finger at Kim and says, "Now, you said yourself, these erotic dances are best kept to oneself. Your dances belong to you so Camilla's dances should belong to her, right?"

"Right you are." Kim wonders what special things Camilla did during her dance and for whom but since it was her idea to keep these dances a secret when she started dancing for Hey Sun and his guests, she'll abide by her 'show but don't tell' rule.

CHAPTER FOURTEEN

SEPTEMBER 18, 1985 9:00 A.M. – YOKOHAMA, JAPAN

TAI and Misa awake in their separate rooms. Tai is really feeling guilty now. He showers and just can't believe he let things get that out of hand last night. His head is pounding with an unimaginable headache. He stands under the shower head and just lets the water beat down on him; wishing Kim was there with him so he could really come clean with her. He so desperately wants to tell her everything that's happened so he can clear his conscience but that confession is simply not available. He reminds himself of what Yuen told him; that he must be more patient than he's ever been because this 'game' could last years. He can't wait to talk to Yuen about last night because he must know that he and Misa had sex at dinner last night. Even hoping to get that off his chest makes him feel better so he takes a deep breath, finishes his shower and gets dressed.

Misa rolls across her lonely bed. She sneaks a few peeks at the morning and then quickly closes her eyes again. She figures Yuen in already in the shower so she goes back to sleep. Eight minutes later, she wakes up again, expecting to hear the shower or Yuen wrestling in the bathroom like he normally does; his morning rituals are noisy to say the least. After a few more moments of nothing, the silence is deafening so she gets up and walks to the bathroom door.

"Sneaky Yuen?"

She knocks on the door. "Morning! Hey, please, don't use all the hot water."

She sits back on the edge of the bed. Five minutes later, she's starting to get frustrated.

"We need to talk so please finish up okay?"

She squirms around on the edge of the bed for another five minutes.

Finally, she walks over to the bathroom door and tries the knob. When the door opens, she looks down at the ground at first and then all around the bathroom. She's expecting to see some of Yuen's clothes, a wet towel, his small bathroom bag or something but the floor is perfectly clear of clothes and there are no traces of Yuen on the counter top or anywhere. She steps out quickly and looks around the rest of their bedroom; it's like he was never there.

Her mind races; does he already know about her and Tai's dinner escapade from last night? Maybe he felt better, came back to the dining room and saw the two of them going at it like a couple of wild animals. She covers her mouth with both hands and starts crying. She can only imagine how pissed off he must be and of course, he wouldn't say anything except to leave in humiliation and anger.

Rationalizing, she thinks to herself and screams, "Fuck! What's he going to say? Eh, excuse me Tai, could you stop fucking my girlfriend for a minute so I can tell you that I'm feeling much better so I'll step in now. Go jerk it off by yourself in the corner!"

She continues to rant to herself saying, "Shit! We were so stupid!"

She starts shaking and continues crying alone.

At 9:30 A.M., the two guards open Tai and Misa's bedroom doors and wait in the hallway with their respective breakfast carts. Misa opens her door and asks the younger guard, "Where's Yuen? Is he in another room?" The younger guard says nothing.

A moment later, Tai opens his door. He sees Misa and looks toward the ground. He squeaks out a quiet and formal sounding, "Morning."

Misa walks across the hallway and says, "Yuen's gone! He must have come back to the dining room and saw us all over each other and left!"

"You know this already?"

"Everything he brought with him is gone! He took everything and left! He must have seen us together last night!"

Tai asks the elder guard, "Where's Yuen? Is he in another room?"

The elder guard says, "Mr. Sun will be here shortly to speak with you both. Please, enjoy your breakfast. You can eat together if you wish."

Misa immediately says, "No!"

Tai looks over at the elder guard and says, "Thank you. We're fine until then."

He closes his door with Misa inside with him. The guards walk away with big smiles on their faces.

"Misa. Like Yuen told us; remember the game. Something's going on. I don't think Yuen's here and I don't think he knows about us."

"You don't? Why?"

"I don't really trust any of these guys but I think that elder guard is telling the truth when he talks to me about things. If Yuen was here, I think he would have said so."

"If he knows, I can imagine he's so pissed at us!" Misa explains.

She shakes her head and walks over to the edge of Tai's bed and sits down.

"Let's just wait to talk to Mr. Sun. I'll ask point-blank and hopefully he'll just tell us what's going on with Yuen. Okay?"

"Okay."

At 10:00 A.M., Hey Sun knocks at Tai's door. Misa runs over and opens it.

"Good morning you two; quite a performance last night I must say."

Misa narrows her eyes at Hey Sun and demands, "Where's Yuen? Where is he? Tell me!"

"Misa. Please. We all need to talk because I do have great news for you both. I need to go to my offices downtown. Please join me."

Reluctantly and already exhausted this morning, Tai and Misa agree.

Growing guilt prevents them from talking to each other at all so during the twenty-minute drive, they say nothing to each other. Hey Sun sits opposite of them in the company limousine. He can feel the new and growing tension between them.

The three arrive at Hey Sun's office and Hey Sun offers Tai and Misa some tea. They decline. Hey Sun plays his next card.

"So, let me ask you this; where do you think Yuen is?"

Immediately offended, Tai says, "What is that supposed to mean Mr. Sun?"

"No. No. I just mean the way you two were carrying on last night, do you think Yuen came back and saw you two?"

Misa's head drops down and she starts crying. Tai drops his guard and head in shame.

"I see. Well, I am sorry to tell you this but, that is what happened. Yuen came to me after seeing the two of you go at it last night and he asked to leave immediately so I simply accommodated his request and sent him back to Beijing like he asked."

"Beijing? I thought we were all going to new locations to avoid prosecution from the police investigations"

"True but with Beijing being so massive with population, I figured that was a decent relocation for Yuen, especially under the circumstances. He was quite upset. We fixed up the room and cleaned things up before Misa returned because I didn't want her slipping and falling on all the shattered glass and ceramic slivers on the floor."

"Oh God!" Misa says. She buries her face in her lap and cries harder.

Humiliated, Tai asks, "Will Yuen be back in touch with us for our experiments?"

"That's really up to him. He certainly has the means to do so but I can't speak to his will or interest in contacting you. I guess time will tell."

Further humiliated, Tai looks down to the floor again.

"Look. You two just try to settle down and I'll make sure the rest of your relocation details are taken care of. You will be quite comfortable I assure you and you can then get past all this and concentrate on your work, together if you wish."

Misa immediately says, "No! I have to be alone so send me to some other place."

If Tai couldn't feel any worse, he does now. He has betrayed his best friend's trust and he has dishonored his best friend's long-time girlfriend for one night of lust and weakness.

Misa requests to leave immediately so Hey Sun calls for his driver to take her back to her apartment suite. Hey Sun requests that Tai remain with him in the offices so they can talk about Tai's notes.

After an extremely uncomfortable few minutes waiting for the younger guard to come and pick up Misa, Hey Sun and Tai settle back into Hey Sun's office. Tai briefly admires the various books and then he notices the various large shark teeth encased in special glass display cases on the shelf.

Tai offers, "Yuen and Misa are something of shark experts you know."

"Really. I didn't know that. And yourself?"

"Novice but very interested. We all took the advanced chemistry courses but Yuen and Misa specialized in marine biology with emphasis on shark life while Kim and I focused more on chemistry."

"Good to know. Maybe we can work on a few new experiments I had in mind for you."

"Sure, just let me know."

"I must say Tai that your attitude has been quite pleasant throughout this whole matter. I want you to know that I appreciate that."

"I appreciate all your help too. Can you tell me now what happened with my father?"

"Yes; of course. I'm glad you asked because with Misa away, I feel we can get through this difficult time together and just know, I'm sorry in advance for what I'm about to share with you."

"He's at peace now but I still need to know what happened for my own peace of mind."

"Of course. As I said before, apparently something in the compound you gave him and the Ching's mixed poorly and caused them to react a few days after you left for your Beijing trip. The Ching's both died just hours apart of heart and kidney failure and your father. Your father, suffered a great deal for many days before finally succumbing to heart failure himself."

Tai breaks down, nearly falling out of his chair. Hey Sun gets up from behind his desk and walks over to console Tai.

After a few moments, Tai says, "I talked to him on what must have been his last day and he sounded just fine."

Hey Sun pauses because that is not the information he had received from one of his cohorts that reported back to him.

"Well, you see. The disease affects everyone differently. I think your father braved through how he really felt until it was simply too much for him. I'm so sorry."

"Can I visit so I can pay my respects at his gravesite?"

"Again, I'm very sorry. In order to put everything together the way it needed to be, both your father and the Ching's were cremated. It was the only way to keep that evidence away from the police."

Acting devastated, Tai kneels to pray and says, "Oh God, forgive me!"

Hey Sun pats his shoulder and grips the back of his neck.

After a few moments in grief, Hey Sun offers, "Son, what you can do now for your father is to help me. Help me understand more of what you wrote in this notebook."

Hey Sun walks back behind his desk and moves the notebook toward Tai.

"Of course. Anything! I owe him and the Ching's that and I owe you my life because we'd all certainly be in jail right now."

"Most likely, yes. So, help me by teaching me about your experiments and compounds so we can work to prevent this from ever happening again and maybe we can work on other projects together that will really help to make a positive change."

Tai points out the complex symbols and respective formulas that make up the generally simple end results. He expounds on his over-writing like it's all so crucial when what he really did was write and re-write the same thing multiple times, in various formats and layouts. Hey Sun is impressed how Tai can barely even glance at his own notes as he re-explains everything to its finest detail, adding additional comments here and there.

Hey Sun then moves over to the left corner of his office book shelf and takes one of the large encased shark teeth off the shelf. He hands it to Tai and says, "Now here's something to talk about Tai."

Tai stares at the awesome fossil and asks, "What is this from?"

"An ancient shark called Megalodon. That's just one of its 270-odd teeth!"

The tooth is amazing; over five and three quarter inches tall, measured from right (leading) edge to tip. The root of the tooth is pristine and the serrations along the edges of the tooth are immaculate. It's blue-grey in color and the burlette (area just above the length of the root) is perfectly intact and un-cracked. The tooth weighs a little over a pound. Tai's impressed because he knows full well what this tooth is worth and the fact that this tooth came from a fish the size of a double-decker bus.

The two marvel at the tooth but especially Hey Sun who is always in awe of his own collection of Megalodon shark teeth. His fascination with these ancient sharks began when he was just a little boy. His father used to tell him stories of the greatest fish to have ever lived in the ancient oceans over twenty-five million years ago.

"So, what's this tooth worth anyway?" Tai casually asks.

Proudly and immediately, Hey Sun claims, "I paid sixteen thousand Yen for it just a year ago and I'm told it's easily worth over twenty thousand now."

"Wow, that much? And you have what, another six teeth on your shelf. That's over a hundred and twenty thousand Yen worth of shark teeth on your shelf."

"Exactly!" Hey Sun smiles and places his prized possession back on the shelf. He grabs one of the smaller four-inch long teeth he has on the shelf and hands it to Tai.

"Here, you take this with you. This will give us something else enjoyable to talk about as we work together."

Tai nods and accepts the amazing ancient orange-tinted gift.

"That one is from Chile. That's why it has that amazing color to it because when it fossilized, the sediment around that part of the world had more iron oxide content in the water, causing the tooth to take on that orange pigment."

"You know a lot about these teeth Mr. Sun."

"Yes! Thank you! I have done my fair share of reading. I'm a huge fan! Just imagine if they lived today but it's actually a good thing they don't. There would be nothing left in the ocean for us to catch and eat!"

Tai just places the ancient tooth aside and thanks Hey Sun again with another nod.

"Wow, I get all wound up talking about sharks! So, let's head back to your suite so we can make your final arrangements for relocation and then you can settle in and we can get to work."

"Very good. Thank you again Mr. Sun." Tai gets up and starts walking toward the exit door.

"Don't forget your tooth Tai."

On the drive back, Tai asks, "May I ask where I'll be?"

"Of course. Ryukyu Islands. The main island of Amami Oshima. Very nice place and plenty of space for you to do whatever you need."

"Ryukyu Islands? Just south of Japan, right?"

"Exactly. You know your geography Tai."

"Yes sir. Growing up in Canton, you get to know your neighbors fairly well."

"Of course. Did you or your father ever fish the islands south of here? Around Macau?"

"No sir. My father's favorite place was always just inside and just inside the inlet to the Canton waterway. He always said fishing south and messing with the mighty South China Sea was too dangerous for him. He lost a lot of friends over the years to the Sea. When I was younger, I actually lost my mother and younger brother in an accident so we never returned for that reason."

"Oh, I'm very sorry to hear that; so much heart-ache in your young family."

"Yes sir."

The driver interrupts and says, "We're approaching Mr. Sun."

"Thank you driver. Tai, you go ahead back to your room. Be sure to check in on Misa. I hope she's better now. I'll see you later tonight for dinner."

Tai exits the limousine and turns back and says, "Mr. Sun? Thank you again."

"Of course son. See you later." Hey Sun pushes the button that sends his tinted window back up.

The limousine pulls away as another guard escorts Tai to his bedroom suite.

Hey Sun demands, "Check into his story about his mother and brother and get back with me before the night ends!"

The driver responds, "Yes sir!"

"Drive to Osaku Park and back. That'll take twenty minutes or so."

"Very good Sir. And thanks for letting us watch the show the other night Mr. Sun."

Hey Sun laughs deeply and says, "Horny little devils weren't they?"

"Definitely Sir! Misa is an amazing girl. I have a whole new appreciation for our red liquor brand now sir!"

"Yes! Don't tell the other driver but I'll send you the tape of Mika and Yuen from last evening as well! Mika loves it from behind, as you know!"

Hey Sun settles back into his seat and readjusts the front of his pants.

"Yes! Thank you sir."

CHAPTER FIFTEEN

SEPTEMBER 18, 1985 – YOKOHAMA, JAPAN

TAI gets back to his bedroom suite. He showers and redresses quickly so he can try to talk to Misa alone for a little while about the current state of things and to make sure she's still on-track regarding this whole 'game' of Mr. Sun's.

Tai calls to the front to request the security guard open his door so he can talk to Misa.

The guard responds, "Yes Mr. Tai. Would you mind waiting for Mr. Sun to return?"

Puzzled, Tai says, "I guess so, but why?"

"Thank you Mr. Tai. Mr. Sun will be back shortly to speak with you."

Twenty minutes pass. Tai begins feeling a little anxious.

In Hey Sun's private bedroom suite, Misa waits impatiently. She's been there ever since she returned from the meeting at Hey Sun's downtown offices. Finally Hey Sun enters the room.

"Misa dear. Are you feeling better? I know the whole Yuen situation is very troubling but being history, it cannot be changed."

Misa begins crying and says, "That's what Yuen would've said!"

"He must really hate me and Tai now and I can't say as I'd blame him."

Hey Sun appropriately pauses a few moments and then says, "He was not happy when he stormed out of your room that's for sure. That's why we cleaned it all up before you returned because it was too dangerous to walk back into."

Misa shakes her head, ashamed and hangs her head down.

"Okay dear. I hate to rush you but my offer still stands. Would you like to join Tai in his relocation site or would you prefer your own site? I'm happy to tell you where you'll go if that helps."

Misa shrugs her shoulders and says, "It really doesn't matter anymore now. I've lost my soul-mate! I don't want to be alone on some strange island either so I guess I'll join Tai wherever he's going." She breaks down again.

"Very good dear. I think that would be best as well and of course, I'll visit you both from time to time to see how things are coming along."

"Mr. Sun?"

"Yes?"

"I appreciate everything really but I'd really prefer not attending dinner tonight if you don't mind."

"Of course. I understand. I'll have a cart prepared and sent to you."

Hey Sun escorts Misa out of his private quarters and downstairs, back to her bedroom suite. Tai hears the door close and opens his door.

Hey Sun spins around in the hallway and says, "Tai. Please. May we speak?"

"Of course Mr. Sun."

"I just spoke with Misa and she's pretty messed up over the whole Yuen situation. As you can imagine."

Tai nods.

"I have yet to hear anything from him myself and it's nearing the time that we need to relocate you both. I talked it over with Misa just a while ago and she is devastated but she'd still like to accompany you to the Ryukyu Islands."

"Oh. I don't know if that's such a good idea Mr. Sun. After last night, living together would be very difficult, don't you think?"

"I agree but she said that Yuen is likely extremely upset with you both and she didn't want to be left all alone. We actually had to do quite a bit of cleaning to fix her room back up after Yuen practically destroyed it."

"Really?"

"Yes. All the broken glass and furniture would have been very upsetting for her to have seen. Not to mention the scribbles in blood on the wall..."

Tai hangs his head. "Blood scribbles? What have I done? Damn it! I should have controlled myself! This is all my fault! I wanted her but I should've stopped before things got out of hand."

"Probably, but of course these things happen. I have to say honestly, you were both magnificent. You were just caught up in the moment. No one could blame you."

"Yuen was my best friend and I betrayed him. I betrayed the love of my life Kim as well and I betrayed my friendship with Misa! I deserve to be hanged!"

"This is a very difficult time for you all. Maybe it is best that you two be apart for a while. Of course, at any time if you change your mind just let me know. I'll try to visit with each of you once a month or so to see how things are coming along and of course, you'll be documenting your various projects and progress for me, right?"

"Absolutely. Thank you again Mr. Sun. You've been a great new friend to us all. These new developments are very stressing. I know for myself, I'd rather not be around Misa because I'd simply be too ashamed to even talk to her. I just hope Yuen will contact me soon so I can tell him what happened and how things got the way they did."

"As you wish. If it helps, I'd be happy to accept blame because it was after all, my dinner invite but honestly, I had no idea that you two would..."

"Yeah, yeah, I know. Thanks but this is my failure; no one else's."

"I understand. I'll make the final arrangements and we'll get you two moved as soon as possible."

"Where will Misa be sent?"

"Honestly, it's probably better that you not know for now because of the on-going police investigations."

Completely distraught and distracted, Tai says, "Right. You're right Mr. Sun. Thank you again. This is all very embarrassing. My father would be ashamed of me and that's just killing me right now. Please excuse me."

"Yes Tai. Just take it easy and this will all get easier with time. Try to eat something and rest."

Hey Sun closes Tai's door and smiles deviously to himself. He's truly broken these young people and he's got them wrapped around his finger now. He knocks lightly on Misa's door.

"Yes?"

"Yes dear, it's Mr. Sun."

Misa opens the door and Hey Sun walks in looking solemn. At the same time, the elder security guard collects Tai and tells him they are ready to go now in order to make a special flight that Mr. Sun has arranged. Tai doesn't hesitate and the two leave. Tai heads to the Ryukyu Islands. No longer feigning it, mentally and physically exhausted and spiritually broken, he needs help boarding the plane.

The elder guard assists him on-board and says, "Mr. Tai, it has been a pleasure, really. Take care of yourself young sir." Tai nods and struggles to get to his seat.

"What's wrong Mr. Sun?"

"Well dear. This is awkward for me. I spoke with Tai."

"Yes."

"It seems he doesn't want you to accompany him." Hey Sun grimaces.

"What?" Misa exclaims in anger.

"Yes. He said that he knows he's to blame in part for you and he being together last evening but that it was really you who initiated the event."

"That fucker! That was his cock in my mouth but it was also his fingers inside me! If he wanted me to stop, all he had to do was stop what he was doing and step back. I would have taken the hint God damn it!"

"Now dear please. Calm down. I'm sorry for all this. I setup the dinner but of course, I had no idea you two would…"

"Stop! Stop! I know. We're both terrible but for Tai to say that this was my fault is total bullshit! I can't wait to tell Yuen what happened now!"

Hey Sun recalculates in his mind and says, "Maybe it's not such a good idea for you to be alone but I can tell you don't want to be with Tai, right?"

"Hell no! I'd scratch his fucking eyes out as soon as I saw him! Then he wouldn't be able to help you with shit!"

"I see. Let me make other arrangements for you then and we'll get you taken care of very soon so you can put all this behind you, okay?"

"Thank you Mr. Sun. I really can't thank you enough."

"You're welcome dear. Just relax and I'll be back soon to get you on your way. Sit tight."

Hey Sun slowly closes Misa's door as she heads into the bathroom to shower.

Hey Sun runs down the hall and up to his private room so he can watch Misa on his video screen. Sure enough she is in the bathroom undressing. Her shirt is already off. She drops her skirt and stands in front of the counter mirror. She starts crying and kneels down for a few moments. Then, she bounds back up, wipes away her tears and turns on the shower. She takes off her black silk panties and enters the shower stall. She briskly washes her hair with the shampoo she stocked before and then she detaches the shower head and starts moving it around her body. She bends over and power washes her hair again and then slaps her hair back to the back of the shower wall.

SEPTEMBER 19, 1985 9 A.M.

Hey Sun knocks on Misa's door, ready to take her to the airport. She's been ready since 6 A.M. Stressed and struggling with everything that has happened, she says nothing as the two walk down the hallway and out to the limousine. She doesn't even ask about Tai and his whereabouts.

"This is it dear; for a little while anyway. You just get settled in. My staff there will help you get adjusted. Just start on a few small projects when you're ready, okay?"

Misa nods and gives Mr. Sun a hug. "I'm sorry for all this Mr. Sun. You must be pretty disappointed in us."

"Not at all dear; things will come around. Relationships all take time and for some wounds to heal it may take more time but 'time does heal all wounds.'"

Misa is speechless. She just hugs Mr. Sun again and boards the charter jet. She doesn't know where she's going and she doesn't care. She's mentally spent and emotionally destroyed. She's menaced and haunted by what Yuen must be thinking right now. She wonders if the Triads have a punishment for member's girlfriends who cheat on them. Her mind is racing and this thought genuinely begins to scare her. She grabs a 750ml bottle of Jack Daniels from the small bar across from her seat and downs it all in a matters of moments.

CHAPTER SIXTEEN

September 19, 1985 – Ryukyu Island, Japan

HOURS earlier Tai's charter jet lands at Ryukyu Airport. He's drunk, having finished off the bottle of Jack Daniels near his seat as well. A couple of Hey Sun's men help him out of the plane and into a rental car. Tai passes out. They start the hour and a half long drive to Tai's new laboratory on the southeast corner of the main island.

Misa's plane lands at 10:15A.M. local time. She's on a remote island in Micronesia and she could care less. She struggles to de-board the plane and right herself. Her so-black-its-blue hair is all kinked and messed up and her shirt is crinkled across her left side where she passed out in her seat. A man walks past her on the tarmac loading up baggage for a different charter jet when she suddenly awakens and declares, "Hey, fuck biology and have a drink with me and Mr. my Sun you! Not in my ass though! Not in the fucking ass!" The man backs away and quickly walks around her.

Yuen has been flown around various places catching connecting flights for the past eighteen hours. First he was sent all the way to Dubai, then to Cairo. An hour later he caught a flight to Ankara and then on to Kuala Lumpur. He's been frustrated but he also knows this is all part of the game Hey Sun is playing now. He just hopes Tai and Misa are keeping their cool and wits about them because this is going to be a long ordeal. He can't wait to hear back from his Triad contacts how Mr. Huang and Kim are doing because it's been quite a while since he's been able to get any update. As he waits for instructions in the Kuala Lumpur airport he occupies himself with thoughts of how to build a radio transmitter so he can be back in touch with Tai and Misa as soon as possible.

Hey Sun gets word back from his pilot that Misa is extremely inebriated and prime for her next step in his master scheme. He tells the pilot to get Misa to the Kuala Lumpur airport so she can talk with Yuen to set up the next phase.

"Yes Sir?"

"Get that beautiful bitch back on the plane and make sure she has a new bottle of Jack for her flight. Call me with all the details and drama after you bring her back. That should wrap things up for those two for some time!"

Hey Sun laughs and pushes the 'end call' button on his huge modular cell phone.

Tai comes to just as his driver is approaching his new shore-front home; a straightforward one-level home with a fully stocked basement for Tai's experiments. There's a deep cove in front of his new property that he can stare down at and admire from his elevated back porch area. The cove is calm and reminds him of the southern-most section of his Canton fishing docks but this cove is quite a bit deeper; much deeper in fact. Inside, there are simple furnishings but they are nice; a black loveseat and sofa that folds out into a sleeper unit, a six-foot tower bookshelf in the far corner, and down the centrally placed main hall, the master bedroom and a spacious bath and shower room. The home features basic-level but nice hardwood flooring and there are several plants located in each major room and open kitchen area. In the open kitchen area that overlooks the outside cove, the refrigerator is fully stocked with several selections of fish and vegetables. There are basic pots and pans for cooking and even a wok sitting on the kitchen counter. In a small hallway pantry area, there are several large bags of white rice ready for cooking. Of course with the deep cove right in front of him, Tai will be able to fish every day and it also serves as the perfect resource for him to conduct further Enhanced-CDT experiments on the fish he catches. Scattered around the front and back of the property are tall thin palm trees and to the right of the cove, there's a perfect area to build up an observation deck so Tai can fish out into the deeper waters of the cove if he wants.

With all the anxiety and guilt he feels over his tryst with Misa, at this point Tai is just praying that Yuen will contact him soon so he can try to explain how everything got so out of hand. He still feels that the circumstances will help to exonerate him but he also knows he's earned a good ninety-percent plus power punch to his face or stomach from Yuen when and if they finally see each other again. Tai's also immediately aware of the fact that Misa is upset with him and that will likely result in one of her classic kicks to the groin that no one to date recovers from in less than a day. Tai experienced one of those classic kicks back in their school days when over-stressed and trying to make a strict project deadline, he rudely and very mistakenly called Misa a 'crazy bitch' – big mistake. Tai's left testicle paid that tab and it aches today if Tai concentrates on that painful memory for too long.

Tai looks around his new living space. He's excited but still exhausted. He notices the fold-out sofa and pulls it up and out so he can sleep off all the stress and refined spirits. The driver leaves him a modular cell phone and a small phone book and excuses himself. Over the next few hours, Tai wakes up every now and again, compliments of the distilled whisky running through him. Then his mind settles and focuses in on the real possibility that his father may be dead and this makes him break out in a cold sweat. All this time he's only been able to take Yuen's word for it that his father is actually alive but the possibility that he could have died, especially due to the Enhanced-CDT vaccine that Tai gave him is really starting to frighten him. In his drunken state, borderline delirious, he starts talking out loud in his new living room.

"I'm so sorry Pop. I can't make it right now. I've messed up so many things, I don't know where to start telling you about it all. I failed my friends. I failed Kim. I failed myself and I killed you!"

Tai blindly reaches out into the empty air and falls out of the sleeper bed. He hits his head hard on the hardwood floor and knocks himself out. Tai sighs as blood begins to trickle down from just above his right temple.

Misa's plane lands at the Kuala Lumpur airport. The pilot escorts her inside to the restrooms near the arrival gate. On the way, she spots Yuen. She bursts into tears and starts running down the corridor. She runs right into some woman's stacked baggage and crashes to the ground. The pilot helps her up and like nothing; she continues her race into Yuen's waiting arms. He can't believe it's her either. Plastered, Misa is crying harder and she's more and more out-of-control as she gets closer. She wants to jump into Yuen's arms but she's too drunk to send the appropriate signals to her legs; instead, she jumps too early. Yuen notices this so he closes the gap so she doesn't face-plant herself on the ground. The two cry together and embrace. Like confession, Misa just jumps right into the conversation that she thinks needs to take place.

"Yuen! I'm so sorry baby! I didn't want to hurt you!" She starts kissing him all over his face.

"I know you're really mad at us but just let me explain! The lights and the naked women served us. The red liquor all over and in me. She licked me over and over and then Sun clapped."

Yuen holds her and starts laughing because her story is as crazy as anything he's ever heard from her, especially when she's drunk.

"Then the lights stopped and the Sun clapped his hands again! God damn it, it was good! He poured the red over me and I came because I wanted you but you left and then you came back and saw me sucking his cock! Then Tai said it was okay and after all that saké and the naked dancing, the lights fucked me up. I was so drunk then he put his fingers inside of me and I thought about you. He fucked me right off the table! I didn't know where you were and then you saw us. Oh God, I'm so sorry baby! Please forgive me. I didn't want to!"

Yuen pushes back and tries to sift through everything Misa just said.

"What? What did Tai do to you? He fucked you? Tai fucked you?"

Yuen tries to gain Misa's attention but now she's crying even harder and she's completely unintelligible. Misa falls to her knees and covers her face.

"You two danced naked together and then Tai said it was okay to put his fingers inside of you? What the fuck is that supposed to mean? That happened? I'll fucking kill him!"

Yuen stands around in shock for a few minutes. Misa tries to stand back up but Yuen pushes her back down. She falls back and lies across the floor crying her eyes out.

Finally, Yuen stares down at Misa and says, "Bitch! Get back on your fucking plane and get the hell out of here, now!"

He spits on the ground in front of her and walks over to the other end of the departure gates.

The pilot pauses for a few moments and then finally helps Misa to her feet and she collapses into his arms. He picks her up, cradling her and walks back out to his plane with her. After securing her into a seat, the pilot taxis the plane and takes off; heading back to her new Micronesian island location. Even unconscious, Misa is destroyed.

As they travel, the pilot calls Hey Sun. "Sir."

"Yes. How did it go?"

"Miserably! Really awful sir. Miss Misa jumped into his arms and starting telling him what he saw. He never got a word in until he heard her broken descriptions of sex with Mr. Tai and then he got really pissed. He threw her back on the ground, spit on her sir, and walked away!"

"Brilliant! He really spit on her?"

"Yes sir, right on her. She lost it and I actually had to carry her on-board."

"Shit! This is easier than I thought! I've got them all now and I'm in no rush for them to get started on their work so we'll leave them be for now and just let all this simmer and stew in their little minds. No more contact unless you hear different from me. No trips and no requests, got it?"

"Yes. Of course sir."

"Come back home and take the rest of the fucking week off! Fuck Mika, she's all horny now!" Hey Sun laughs demonically and hangs up his phone.

Having thought about it for a long time, Kim fears that the very short encounter that she and Hey Sun had may not have been enough to convince him that she's pregnant so she decides to seduce him one more time to make sure she can protect her pending child. Once she really starts showing, he'll likely leave her alone and nurture her because all the while, he'll think it's his child so he won't want to upset her in any way.

September 19, 1985 6 P.M. – Yokohama, Japan

Kim calls to the front and requests to see Hey Sun. Hey Sun calls her back from his room phone.

"Kim? You're okay?"

"Fine. I thought I'd skip dinner tonight."

"Oh."

"Actually, I thought we'd skip dinner together... in your room."

"Really?"

"Yes."

"I'll send for you now." Hey Sun hangs up before Kim can.

He's been drinking his favorite saké but he's not drunk. Kim has been drinking from her new custom designed saké cup as well all afternoon. She is a little impaired. A security guard escorts her to Hey Sun's upstairs suite and he returns to his downstairs front entrance post. Kim knocks lightly at first and then, wanting to get this over with, she knocks firmly. Her eyes start to tear up.

Hey Sun opens the door and says, "Dear? Why do you cry? To see me?"

She shakes her head and says, "No. It's just that …"

He walks with her over to his small office area and sits her down.

"It's what?"

She starts crying more and shakes her head. Hey Sun gets her a glass of ice water and sets the glass next to her.

After a few moments, she takes a drink and continues saying, "It's Tai. How could he betray us? How could he betray me like that?"

Hey Sun consoles her with a small box of tissues.

"I mean, how could he sign those patent papers with only his name? He always told us this was our thing, our work, our discovery. That was all bullshit!"

Hey Sun's eyes grow taller. He likes where this one-sided conversation is going. He doesn't interrupt Kim. He just retrieves her some more ice for her glass.

"I was so foolish! You know I used to tell him his work deserved to be recognized officially. He always immediately refused and he never wanted to even discuss it. I wouldn't be surprised to learn that he had submitted some of our work for awards and just never planned on telling me."

"I'm sorry Kim. Relationships are tough things to balance when you're in school. There are so many distractions."

"What do you mean?"

"I really shouldn't get in the middle of things between you two, between all of you really."

"What the hell does that mean?"

"Okay. Maybe tonight is not a good night for this."

"No. I want to know now. What's going on?"

"It's awful. Are you sure you want to hear about all this now?"

Kim sits up straight in her office seat and just stares at Hey Sun. He can feel her anxiety and anger beginning to boil.

After a few moments, he says, "You know, maybe it's best if I just show you something. Now first let me say, I record my dinner sessions because most often, my meetings there produce real results in the business I conduct so it makes sense to tape the sessions."

Kim nods in agreement.

He presses the play button on his small remote unit and the recording begins to play. Kim's eyes are glued to the screen.

She sees Misa and Tai enter the room and her heart skips a beat. She smiles and starts crying.

"Where's Yuen?"

Hey Sun quickly says, "He got a little sick during lunch earlier and excused himself from dinner so Tai escorted Misa."

A little surprised, Kim says, "Oh." She re-focuses on the screen. She watches Camilla enter the room and admires her skills.

"You were right. Camilla is nice."

Hey Sun smiles and quietly laughs to himself as he anticipates what's next.

Misa starts undressing and Kim starts to blush a little. The girl is gorgeous and Kim has seen Misa naked before but not quite like this. Then the recording jumps to another camera. It re-focuses and zooms in on the area she knows as the wall behind the bar.

She smiles at first as she sees Tai but then as the naked women begin undressing him, her smile disappears. She watches one of the women, Mika, take Tai in her mouth and proceed to make him almost collapse to the floor in ecstasy. Kim sits back in her seat and glares her eyes at the screen; over and over, and over again.

Again, the video jumps back to the main dining room. As Kim sees Misa and Tai standing naked together on her low profile black onyx table, she starts sweating out of anxiety. She watches nervously as Camilla slowly pours the red liquor that Kim knows intimately all over Tai and Misa's shoulders. At first, she's thinks to herself, "nothing really awful has happened yet, except for Mika giving Tai world-wind blow-jobs so…"

She's still thrilled to see them both but as the recording progresses now, her stomach starts to churn with anger and bile. As soon as she sees Misa start sucking Tai's dick and then lays down for him, her blood begins to boil. When Tai literally pushes her clear off the table as he thrusts into Misa, she stands up and throws her water and ice glass at the screen.

She screams at the screen, "Bastard! He's fucking her now?" They come here so we can meet back up and the first chance they get, they fuck each other senseless?"

Hey Sun stops the recording and sits down in his office chair. He's struggling trying to contain his joy.

After a moment, Hey Sun says, "I'm sorry Kim."

Then he pushes the fast-forward on the recording to a preset marker and presses the play button again. Kim focuses and recognizes Yuen sitting in a limousine. There's a girl performing oral sex on him; her head appearing and then quickly disappearing out of frame over and over and faster and faster. She finishes and turns around in frame. Kim just passes it off because it's just Misa but after another second, she says, "Misa?"

Hey Sun stops the recording as the girl's face enters the full center screen.

"That's not Misa! What the fuck is he doing with her?"

Hey Sun says, "You see Kim. I brought them all here to reconnect with you and at first, they were happy but then they started drinking and carrying on about wanting to do new things and meet new people. That's Mika there with Yuen. I suppose she does look a little like Misa. Yuen wanted to take a drive during dinner so I sent him alone but he insisted my driver find someone to join him. Mika said she'd go so he could talk to her about sharks or something. Does Yuen know a lot about sharks?"

"Fucking dog! Fucking rat!" Kim yells at the screen.

She rests back in her seat and starts crying harder.

Kim starts rambling off stressful thoughts, "And we were going to get married and everything was going to be so great and now, everyone's turned into fucking bastards and whores!"

Hey Sun is about to switch to another scene involving Tai but he relents. He shuts the recorder off and hands Kim a box of tissues.

Hey Sun confesses, "Look. I felt bad when you told me that I took you away from everyone you loved and to make it worse, the day before your wedding so like I said, I brought your closest friends here to reconnect and my sincere apologies were going to include a gift from me by helping you and Tai get married."

Kim's head drops into her lap and she starts shaking.

Hey Sun continues, "But the first night, everyone had their own plans and they were coming and going at will so what was I supposed to do? I kept them away from you until it looked like they would settle down so I could get things prepared but by then it was way out of control, especially once Misa and Tai carried on during that first night at dinner."

Kim reaches across to Hey Sun's desk and grabs a large marker. She hurls it across the room. The tip explodes against the wall and marks the wall like a child's doodle.

Hey Sun confesses, "I really hate to make things any worse but you wanted to know and I want to be totally up front and honest with you because I still feel really bad about taking you away."

Kim clears the thick tears away from her eyes and says, "Let me have it."

"Okay but this is really difficult; maybe too much for you right now."

Exhausted, Kim drops the rest of her guard and says, "Just go ahead."

"I've learned that some kind of Diabetes shot that Tai and Yuen gave to folks back in their home village has actually hurt various people and some people have actually died."

Kim's heart almost stops. "Who? Who died? Tell me!"

"There was no easy way for me to tell you this either; Mr. Huang, Tai's father died and a couple named the Ching's also passed away as a result of bad reactions to the shot."

Kim falls out of her seat and starts crying uncontrollably. She pounds her right fist against the floor and just starts screaming, "No! No! No!"

Hey Sun goes to his small kitchen area and gets Kim another cup of ice water; not a glass this time.

Hey Sun rests the cup on the corner of his desk and offers to pick Kim up so she can sit back down. She braces against him and takes her seat. She taps his hand in appreciation.

He continues, "Okay. So awful I know but I'm trying to help them out now. It's time you knew who the hell I am and what the hell I really do."

Kim perks up a little bit in her seat because she's never expected to get this information from Hey Sun, especially after he flat out told her she'd never know and if she ever really pushed him for it, he might kill her. Hey Sun walks around his desk to his executive leather chair and sits down.

He sighs and says, "I work for the Chinese Government overseeing yours and Tai's former school work. Again, please let me apologize because your work has been nothing short of brilliant from day one. My people got a tip that the Chinese Triads might be after you and Tai in order to get your work so I had to step in as soon as I could and that day just happened to be July fifth. I'm so sorry but that was simply out of my control."

Kim takes a drink of iced water and sits up attentively in her seat. Hey Sun continues.

"A few days later I got a call from my leadership; a friend connected to the Chinese State police, and he told me about three homicides at the Canton docks, including Tai's father Mr. Jimmie Huang. I told him to alert me as to their progress and to help me find Tai and his friends so I could help them. It turns out they were on vacation spending tons of money in Beijing. In fact, Tai bought a house and paid off more than half of it in cash."

Kim's eyes widen and the anger and bile in her stomach increases. She covers her mouth and tries to swallow some air to prevent throwing up all over.

"So, we picked them up and after some careful maneuvering, I arranged to bring them here because the police investigations came back confirming through eye-witness accounts and from autopsy results on Mr. Huang and the Ching's that various substances directly contributed to their deaths. My police insider friend told me that Tai and Yuen were now officially under arrest and being sought by local Canton police."

"After all that has happened, I was able to settle everyone down long enough to tell them about the police investigations and the fact that they were now all wanted by the local police for, at the very least, third-degree murder or voluntary manslaughter. At a minimum, they each face thirty years and Tai and Yuen would likely spend the rest of their natural lives in prison."

Kim's getting sicker to her stomach by the minute but she can't leave because she wants to know about all of this right now. She nods for Hey Sun to continue or conclude his devastating story. She can't take much more.

"I'm also a lawyer and I arranged to pull quite a few strings as far as quick new passports. I'm fortunate to have many friends who were willing to help and since I stepped in at the right time to help, Tai offered to pay me from his father's estate. Let's just say it helped out a great deal to make the rest of the relocation arrangements for everyone."

"Relocation?"

"Yes. I've helped to relocate Tai, Yuen and Misa to places of their choosing. They all wanted to be alone and after all that's happened between them, I have to agree it's probably best; at least for the short-term. They can each come and go as they please and they each have a cell phone like mine to call me or you anytime, for anything."

"I told them it's best to stay quiet and not make any noise for at least a full year, maybe even two, until the local and State Police investigations slow down and eventually end. The mid-nineteen eighties here in Japan are crazy but not nearly as crazy as in China. You probably know that yourself."

"I asked Tai what he'd like to do in the mean-time and he offered to work on his experiments and formulas that I guess the two of you had started. Something called "mist" and a Diabetes shot. I think he's obsessed with figuring out what went wrong with the version that he used that killed his father. I couldn't get any notes from him on it or anything so maybe he'll figure it out over time."

Kim narrows her eyes. She wants to spit on the floor but she's not going to do that in Hey Sun's private suite.

Hey Sun continues, "As for Yuen and Misa, they want to keep busy as well but they didn't want to be together, which honestly surprised me but it was their choice. After what happened between Tai and Misa, I don't blame Yuen for being so upset."

Hey Sun takes six pictures out of an envelope and passes them over to Kim. Shocked, she glares at them, amazed at the destruction; all the broken glass and furniture and the bloody writing across the walls.

"I arranged for their relocations as well as I said and they agreed to work on several of the same experiments that Tai's working on but they insisted that their voices be disguised so he would not know it was them as they worked on things together."

Looking slightly ashamed, Hey Sun looks to the ground and says, "This is why I told you that same thing our first night because I was just trying to protect you from all that was going on between the three of them."

Kim stands up and drops the empty cup on the floor. She crawls across Hey Sun's desk and kisses him passionately and appreciatively.

Hey Sun wants to continue talking but Kim grabs the front of his pants and says, "I want you now! Take me the way you want me! The way you've always wanted me!"

Hey Sun can't get his pants off fast enough. He picks Kim up and wraps her slender toned legs around his waist. They kiss deeply as Kim rips the side of her skirt off. Hey Sun holds her up and walks with her to the side wall of his office. He braces her against the wall as he takes her pink and black silk shirt off. She reaches down and grabs Hey Sun's erection and rubs it across her privates. She's wet and Hey Sun almost loses control.

She pinches the top inch of his penis and yells, "No way! Don't you dare!"

She smiles while she sucks on his tongue. Hey Sun reaches down and moves her wet panties to one side and thrusts inside of her. She knocks her head against the wall and this just excites the energized couple even more.

After a while, Hey Sun moves her to his desk. He withdraws slowly from her and she climaxes. He sits her on the corner of the desk as he clears away larger harmful items from their path. She smiles in appreciation and repositions herself across the width of the desk; the perfect height for him. Instead, he kneels down and places her ankles on his shoulders. Kim screams like she's never screamed before. In complete ecstasy, she climaxes again and grabs Hey Sun's hair. She encourages his every movement.

He stands back up and kisses deeply into her slightly muscular upper and middle abs. Her body is unlike anything Hey Sun has ever experienced and he's not about to neglect a single inch. He massages her perfect small breasts and then motions for her to move off the desk. She moves down the desk toward him and he turns her around. They twist around like pretzels to suck each other's tongues. They experiment with various positions. She bites down on her left hand fingers as papers and folders start flying on the floor in pile after pile. Hey Sun braces wider against Kim and the desk. She starts wincing in erotic delight and every time they hit each other, Hey Sun gets closer. After a few more moments, he releases and falls back several feet; his right leg is cramping up. Kim is exhausted as well; she could easily just sleep on the desk but she finally moves, sweeping her hair away and wiping the sweat away from her face.

She stares at Hey Sun for a moment and then seductively sits in her former chair, legs apart.

She says, "Done?"

Hey Sun can't believe this girl. What an appetite. He slowly walks over to her and runs his right hand through her sweaty black hair. She grimaces in delightful momentary pain and turns him slightly. She starts massaging his exhausted penis. After a couple dedicated minutes, he's erect again. She takes him in her mouth and engulfs him. Hey Sun has had more than his fair share of women but no one like this by far. He starts to fantasize what Kim and Misa would be like together with him and he explodes. It's after 11:30 P.M. by now and the couple settles in together in Hey Sun's back bedroom. Kim turns into Hey Sun and crosses her left inner thigh across the top of Hey Sun's knees. The new couple will sleep until late-morning now.

CHAPTER SEVENTEEN

September 20, 1985 – Uruma, Okinawa

YUEN finally arrives at the Okinawan city of Uruma. Okinawa is an island situated about two thousand miles east and slightly north of Taiwan, about four thousand miles south and west of Tokyo and about twenty-five hundred miles west and slightly south of Shanghai, China. Uruma lies on the east side of the tiny island of Okinawa.

The driver unloads the car and Yuen begins checking out his new place. It's similar in layout and design to Tai's place on Amami Oshima Island, Japan but without the deep cove in the front. Yuen just looks forward to some alone time and here, isolated from pretty much everything and everyone, he's got it.

Time can be a hindrance or a true resource, depending on how one chooses to spend it. Like currency, time has intrinsic value but only if it's invested wisely. Yuen decides early on to spend his time growing his anger over what Misa described to him. He can't help but to visualize Tai with Misa together. His anger and anxieties grow and build quickly during his first few days in exile. He tries to distract himself by fishing but so far even that's not helping. He starts a regimen of exercise and this starts to help so at least for a while, he can begin to relax in his new surroundings.

September 30, 1985

Yuen's fitness program has peaked. He feels better physically but emotionally, he's still broken and disturbed. Not being able to communicate with Tai about what happened with Misa is gnawing at his heart and soul. Unable to take the stress any longer, he places a call to Hey Sun.

"Mr. Sun?"

"Yuen. Yes sir. How are you settling in? It's been what, almost two weeks now, right?"

"Yes sir. I'd like to get in touch with Tai. We have some things to talk over before I can begin working on any projects with him."

"Absolutely. Let me call him to see what he's up to and I'll get back with you if that's alright."

"That's fine. Thank you."

"Okay. I'll call you back shortly."

Three days go by as Hey Sun attends meeting after meeting involving the Canton fish market investigations into the Ching's deaths. Hey Sun grows more and more frustrated because Jimmie Huang is nowhere to be found and hasn't been seen since he told Tai that he killed his father. After a while, he begins figuring that maybe the man went out fishing and fell overboard or something so, issue resolved in his mind, and one less loose end to wrap up later. Hey Sun talks with everyone else at the fish market but no one knows anything or at least they won't say anything if they do.

Finally on October 4, Hey Sun calls Yuen back.

"Yuen."

"Yes Mr. Sun?"

"Well, I spoke with Tai and we went back and forth for the past week. He said he really prefers not hearing from you until he feels he really needs your help with something so I'm sorry son but I don't know what else to tell you."

"Shit! What's he so sore about? If I had slept with Kim, he'd swim here to kick me in my teeth and I'd deserve it!"

"Tai is a very unique young man, like yourself but he's really into his experiments and he said he really prefers working on them alone until he gets stuck."

"Fuck it! If that's what he wants, he can stick it! I've got plenty of other things I can work on finally so that works for me. It'll actually be nice to step out on my own and do some things I've always wanted to do."

"Oh, like what?"

"I don't know if you knew this about Misa and me but we are very knowledgeable about just about every type of shark, past and present! I love them and it's time for me to get back into my research and experiments with them. I was right in the middle of my research on Great White migratory patterns across the globe when I started helping Tai and Kim with their damn chemistry experiments."

"Sharks? That's terrific! I have a real passion for sharks as well."

"That's right. I do remember seeing several large Megalodon teeth in your office before we left Yokohama."

"You do know your shark's young man. Excellent!"

"The greatest and largest predatory fish to have ever lived; I absolutely love Megalodon Mr. Sun!"

"I'll tell you what. Maybe we can begin working on some shark research projects together because as you know, the area of the South China Sea and Indian Ocean that you're around features some of the greatest migratory patterns of all of the greatest predators in the world."

Yuen enthusiastically and immediately confirms, "Huge rogue Great Whites, the amazing schools of Great Hammerheads, majestic Whale sharks and just about every specie of whale; even Orcinus Orca visits this region from time to time."

"Impressive Mr. Yuen. You just named them off like nothing but Orcinus Orca? What's that?"

"Killer whales sir."

"Oh, of course. Very good. See, you're teaching me things already. I'm going to send you something Yuen. Call it a gift and a pact between us as friends."

"You don't have to do that Mr. Sun. You've done more than enough for all of us. I sincerely appreciate everything, especially now."

"It's my pleasure. I'll send it right away."

"There is something else Mr. Sun."

"Yes?"

"Honestly, Misa and I worked very well together in the past. I'm still really upset over that whole issue but I would like to be in touch with her soon so we could work on things together. She is every bit as talented as I feel I am and she's even more knowledgeable about feeding and breeding."

"Certainly. I'll call on her and see how's she's feeling about things. Is that okay?"

"I appreciate that."

"Very good. So, just relax and think about our sharks and I'll be back in touch very soon."

"Thanks again Mr. Sun."

OCTOBER 4, 1985 – LAOAG CITY, PHILIPPINES

Misa takes the last drink available from the last whisky bottle in her new place in Laoag City. Laoag City is directly north of the Philippine capitol of Manila. She has not adjusted well at all to anything since Yuen spat at her and left her on the floor of the Kuala Lumpur airport. She places a call to Hey Sun.

"Misah Sun!"

"Misa?"

"Misah Sun sir! I need more drink and more whisky too!"

"Misa. You don't sound well."

"I sound like I sound. So fucking what! More drink!"

Her cell phone falls to the floor and Misa passes out.

Hey Sun thinks quickly. He calls one of his contacts located near where Misa is living and has him rush over to look after her. The man goes by the name of "Saka"; short for his full last name of Yamishinosaka. He has a younger step brother who works as a research vessel captain by the name of Eishi. Eishi works on several projects for his uncle Hey Sun as well during various times throughout the fishing season so the two of them are only in touch with one another during those limited times; being early October, this is not the time.

Saka arrives at Misa's small custom home. It's different from Yuen and Tai's in that it is a tall two-story building like a mini-castle. Being circular in design has its advantages and disadvantages. On one hand, you can't fit most standard furniture in the home but that opens up very cool opportunities for uniquely shaped items to be featured in the home; like her half-moon shaped futon bed and half-moon shaped dresser.

There is no front entrance so Saka goes to the back patio door and knocks. After a minute with no answer, Saka knocks harder; still no response. He walks over to the single window and peers through the small gap between the curtains. He can see about twelve inches worth of a set of legs lying on the floor but that's it. He goes back to the patio door and breaks the small top window glass so he can unlatch the door. Saka walks up the small flight of three entryway steps and sees Misa lying on the floor semi-conscious and naked. He picks her up and sets her in the middle of her bed that she has moved out of her bedroom. She makes little moans as Saka moves her so he knows she's okay, just very drunk and tired.

Saka goes back to where she lied on the floor and retrieves the empty whisky bottle. He places it on the kitchen counter and looks in the fridge for a drink for himself. He finds a beer and pops the cap. A picture frame lies broken on the living room floor but there's no other damage he can see. He cleans that up and walks back over to the futon and stares down at Misa.

The girl is physically as stunning as ever with her soft white skin, small breasts, and small diamond-shaped patch of silky soft black pubic hair. For Saka, she's irresistible, as for any straight man. Her so-black-its-blue hair is mesmerizing as it falls across the white sheets of the futon bed. Finally, Saka can't stand it. He takes his pants and shorts down and lies on top of Misa. His mid-sized weight of one hundred and eighty pounds wakes her up enough to make her say, "Drink with me and I'll fuck your brains out Yuen!"

As far as she's concerned, Saka is Yuen. She grabs his erection and starts massaging it. She moves up on the futon bed and continues stroking Saka. He starts kissing her neck and then her nipples. She starts to moan louder and looks up at Saka.

"You're supposed to be Yuen but you aren't."

"Name is Saka."

She looks at Saka and continues stroking him. She looks down at his body and says, "You look like Yuen and you feel like him too. Can you fuck me better than him?"

Stunned, Saka says, "Really?"

Misa smiles and says, "Yuen doesn't want me anymore!"

She starts crying a little and continues, "Fucker spit on me and now I want you so let's go!"

As Saka takes her, Misa wraps her legs around him and says, "You are better than Yuen!"

Of course, with this new escapade being recorded, thanks to Hey Sun's technical associates who setup the new home, Hey Sun looks forward to reviewing this tape to see Misa's condition and behaviors for himself.

Saka and Misa finish their union and Saka helps Misa to her shower where she promptly throws up.

"I'm sorry. That's not you. That's too much Jack Daniels!"

Saka washes off the bottom of the shower door.

"Again?"

Misa nods and says, "I feel a lot better now."

The couple spends the next thirty minutes trading sensual favors in the shower. Saka can't stop smiling. Later, Misa helps Saka re-dress and Saka gets back into his car and leaves. He places his call to Hey Sun to report her status.

"Mr. Sun?"

"Saka. How is Misa?"

"Good sir. She's resting now; too much to drink earlier."

"Did you take pictures?"

"Yes sir. Her bedroom and her living room where she moved her futon bed to sir."

"Very good. Not too much damage?"

"A little sir; to the kitchen walls and the picture frame in the living is broken. I cleaned things up."

"Good job Saka. Anything else?"

"She did request more whisky sir."

"That can wait. Okay, head back Saka. I'll call on you later."

Hey Sun decides to wait a few more days before he calls Yuen back with a status on Misa.

OCTOBER 7, 1985

Yuen has kept busy writing down ideas for new experiments for his shark research. He's reinvigorated and looking forward to hearing back from Hey Sun about Misa. Finally he gets a call from Hey Sun.

"Mr. Yuen, how are you today?"

"Very good Mr. Sun. How are you?"

"Fine. Thank you. How is your shark work coming along?"

"Great sir! I've been working on re-writing my notes about Great White migration patterns so getting back into the whole swing of things has been really great!"

"Excellent! I look forward to reading what you've got, when you're ready to share it."

"Of course. And Misa, how is she getting along?"

"Not so well I'm afraid."

"Oh. What's going on?"

"I'm afraid she's drinking a lot and not eating. I may have to bring her back to Yokohama for a hospital stay before it gets any worse."

Yuen's heart falls into his stomach.

Desperately he says, "Please, do everything you can for her! She's a great girl! She doesn't deserve to feel so bad but she does and that's my fault!"

"Now you listen to me Yuen. This is not your fault young man. Things happened and people made a choice, that's all. I'm a little older than you guys and I can tell you from experience, time heals all wounds. The choices we make when we're younger always come back to haunt us when we get older no matter what. I say, enjoy yourself when you're young and when it comes to relations, younger people just need to relax and have fun. As soon as they feel committed, that's the trap because of course you want to be with someone you love but at your ages, that's a hell of a commitment and it almost never works out because there's so much you haven't done yet."

Yuen wipes tears and his depression off his face and says, "Mr. Sun?"

"Yes?"

"That's honestly the best explanation I've ever heard and that includes these types of speeches from my parents and other family! Thank you for that!"

"You're welcome Yuen. You're very welcome son!"

"You know what?"

"What's that?"

"I feel great! I'm going to grab a tall glass of ice, pour some whisky and go fishing the rest of the day!"

"That's sounds like a great plan Yuen. You do that and I'll call you later with an update on Misa and hopefully by then, you'll have caught your dinner three times over."

"Yes sir!"

Hey Sun hangs up. Yuen fills a decanter with ice and Jack Daniels and heads for his favorite new fishing spot in front of his new small custom home.

"Saka?"

"Yes Mr. Sun?"

"Go and get Misa right now and bring her to me! There's a plane ticket waiting for you."

"Yes sir!"

"Good man!"

Hey Sun sits back in his office chair and proudly laughs to himself. He plots how best to deal with bringing Misa to Yokohama with Kim and immediately, the possibilities are giving him a hard-on. He believes he'll use the classic little sister-big sister ploy and see if that works out like Misa described to him before when the two of them used to sleep and tickle each other. Three minutes later, he quickly cleans up his excitement from off his desk.

October 12, 1985 – Yokohama, Japan

Hey Sun has Misa with him now and the two have been getting acquainted over the past few days. Misa has shared more stories with Hey Sun about her school days with Tai, Kim and Yuen and she's shared a few more intimate stories about her and Kim, including the time when they showered together after a campus mud party.

Hey Sun has sent Kim to Tokyo for a couple of days to shop for new clothes, lingerie and to try to find some new colored lights for her dinner performances; of course with an escort but Kim doesn't mind. She's used to that by now.

At their own private dinner in the formal dinner room, Hey Sun presses Misa for more details about her now infamous mud party.

"So how did the mud party come about?"

Misa laughs as she recalls, "That was a great night! Some girls from the business school got the idea to hold their class outside. Since there were only six of them, their instructor agreed and looked forward to it himself because it was really nice outside. So, they setup their desks and chairs and were working. From our chemistry lab, Kim and I saw them. We completed our work together and asked if we could hang outside with the other girls and our instructor approved. We had a couple boys help move a couple desks outside for us and we sat in the sun with the other girls. Kim and I kept quiet so the class could go on and after about an hour some clouds moved in. Their instructor asked if they wanted to get back inside but the class said no. After another half hour, it started to rain lightly. Again the instructor asked about leaving but the rain was warm and felt great so we all chose to stay while the instructor went back inside." She smiles and deviously glares over at Hey Sun.

Hey Sun anxiously moves about in his seat. Misa starts to blush a little and says, "Then it happened. It started pouring! The rain was so warm, it was great! After a while some of the business class girls starting taking their light sweaters off so we did too. In America, they call this a wet T-shirt contest and this one was as good as any of theirs! Maybe none of us had the big chests of the American girls but just imagine eight young college girls running around and chasing each other, half naked and soaked. Then some of us started slipping in all of the mud and there you have it; the infamous mud party!"

Fully erect, Hey Sun says, "Tell it again?" Misa smiles and says, "There is more Mr. Sun."

"Oh please!"

"After about ten minutes chasing each other around the desks and wrestling with each other in the mud, Kim and I went back into our building and cleaned up in our rooms. The boys hadn't returned from their classes yet so we stepped into the shower together because we were cold too and didn't want the other to have to wait for the shower. At first, we just held each other with our muddy clothes still on but that felt strange so we took off our clothes. It was awkward at first but once we just started looking at each other for a minute under the warm water, we both liked what we saw. As the water washed away the grass and mud, we noticed small scrapes and cuts on each other's bodies so we started washing each other with soap to clean the wounds." Just then, Hey Sun ejaculates in his shorts.

"Like a curious younger sister, Kim started touching my breasts. I didn't have any cuts on me there but I guess she was interested so she started circling my nipples with her fingers. It felt great so I closed my eyes and let her continue. With my eyes closed, she gave me a kiss and I have to be honest by saying it was the best kiss I've ever gotten from anyone so I kept my eyes closed and kissed her back. Soft kisses at first and then I thought I'd test our collective interests so I started to suck on her tongue. She moaned so I kept doing it." Hey Sun's eyes are practically falling out of their sockets right now.

"We both started washing each other with soap, even though we were both already clean. I ran my right hand across Kim's upper and lower stomach muscles as she ran her right hand up and down mine. Then we switched and she started running both her hands up and down the front of my body as I hugged her briefly and ran my hands down the front and sides of her body. It was really amazing. When she reached my lower abs, she reached down and brushed across my clitoris and I came. After that, we just melted into each other. She put her fingers inside of me so I did the same. I knew Kim was smooth shaven but I'd never felt her all soaped up, wet, and coming. She was wonderful how she kept kissing me and moving her fingers slowly inside of me. Even Yuen hadn't done this for me yet and I remember thinking to myself that he would not be able to top what Kim was doing to me unless he had fingers of fucking magic or something! We were both having so much fun coming, we had to sit down in the tub and then I remembered that I had my purple dildo in my dresser drawer so I got out real quick to get it."

"Oh my God Misa! Stop! You're going to kill me before I eat my last meal!"

Misa blushes but she continues because the story brings back such a great and erotic memory for her and she needs this.

"As soon as I showed Kim my dildo, she put it inside of her half way and motioned for me to join her so I hugged her and sat down. Sitting forward with her legs bent, I bent my legs up and past hers and she inserted the remaining half of my purple pleasure inside me. We held each other and just moved back and forth for at least twenty minutes or so. I know I came three more times. As we laughed and kissed while we dressed each other, Kim said it was five more times for her. We winked at each other just as the boys entered the room and called out for us. They had no idea and as far as I know, Kim has never told Tai because I have never told Yuen about that night with Kim."

Hey Sun closes his eyes hard and yells out, "White flag! White flag! I can't take it anymore! I'm going to explode over here Misa!"

"Really?"

"Are you kidding me?"

"No. Come here and prove it!"

The two start kissing and Hey Sun picks Misa up and takes her over to the plush orange and white koi floor rug. The rug that Kim's low-profile black onyx dinner table sits on. Misa grabs Hey Sun's erection thru his pants opening and starts sucking it. Hey Sun rolls over on his back and Misa starts taking his clothes off. She pulls his black belt off with her teeth as he kicks his shoes off. She lifts up his dress shirt and starts kissing deep into his chest and lower torso. Hey Sun reaches up under Misa's thin flower-print shirt and massages her perfectly shaped small breasts; they are just like Kim's but Misa's nipples are a little bigger. She pulls away her black skirt and starts rubbing herself hard across Hey Sun's erection. He pulls himself out and away from his boxer shorts and rubs himself into Misa. She reaches down and puts him inside her, moving her black lace panties to one side; just like how Kim did before. Hey Sun is amazed that these two gorgeous girls have the same incredible erotic habits and he couldn't be happier.

They are together for twenty minutes before they both give up; completely out of energy and impulses to move anymore. Having forgotten to eat their dinner, they return to the dinner table naked and finish off their steamed fish, rice and vegetables. They cap the night off with a bottle of warm saké and a few seductive dessert treats that Hey Sun always has prepared for him; sweet decadent specialties made by his naked attendants.

CHAPTER EIGHTEEN

October 22, 1985

AFTER two weeks, Hey Sun finally calls Yuen back.

"Yuen."

"Mr. Sun. How are you?"

"Okay."

"Just okay? I've got some news. I've completed my Great White shark migration notes. I think you'll find them very interesting and I have to thank you for the tooth you sent me. It sits in the kitchen window so it's the only thing I can see when I look back to the house when I'm fishing. Who knows, maybe I'll catch the last Megalodon!"

"Ha. Not likely since they died out at least one and a half million years ago, right?"

"Yes sir. You know your sharks too! So how is everyone else; Tai and Misa?"

"I've been talking with Tai about his ongoing Diabetes experiments. He's still trying to figure out what went wrong with it. His 'mist' thing…"

"M-y-s-t-1 sir."

"Oh, okay, his Myst1 formula. He sent me some notes but I can't figure them out to save my life. They may as well be written in ancient Greek."

"I can help you with that Mr. Sun."

"That would be very helpful because I do need to re-compile that data so I can use it to get your on-going police investigations permanently stalled or called off."

"That's great. Just send it to me and I'll help decipher it for you."

"Good man Yuen. Now… uh, sit down son."

"What?"

"Sit down and promise me you'll just hear me out."

Cautiously Yuen sits down on his living room sofa and says, "Okay, what?"

"We lost Misa last night."

Yuen's eyes almost fall out of their sockets as tears begin pooling on the floor below him.

Hey Sun just continues, "As you know she had been drinking but I had no idea how much. Her home only had the same number of whisky bottles as yours and Tai's did, four and I actually took one of them with me when I dropped her off because of how drunk she was during her maiden flight and after she met up with you. The pilot called me, concerned, and told me what happened between you two."

Yuen throws up.

"So there's no way she drank herself to death. She hadn't been eating either and that's what I think contributed to her death; basically she starved herself to death."

Devastated, Yuen screams out, "Oh my God! Misa!" and falls to his knees.

"I know son. This is especially hard because I know how you really felt about her but like I told you before, this was not your fault. She was a grown woman and she made this choice herself."

Sobbing, Yuen offers, "But I spit on her Mr. Sun! I spit on her! She was already destroyed when I pushed away from her and called her a bitch but then I spit on her! Fuck!"

"You spit on her? I'm sorry I didn't know." Hey Sun pauses for a minute and then continues, "But still, you couldn't control what she'd do or how she'd act even after you did that to her."

Yuen wails in grief and just keeps saying, "It's my fault! It's my fault she's gone!"

Hey Sun waits another few minutes and then says, "I'm so sorry Yuen. If there's anything I can do, please let me know."

"I have to see her Mr. Sun. I have to beg for her forgiveness at her body. When can I see her?"

"Well, with the police still investigating you and Tai and Misa, I had no choice son."

"No choice for what?"

"She was just cremated about an hour ago."

Yuen throws his cell phone right through his back patio window. It explodes on the railing outside just as the rest of the shattered patio glass crashes to the floor inside. He collapses to the floor and passes out from the extreme stress and overwhelming grief.

In his office, Hey Sun sits back and takes a long drag from his illegally imported Cuban cigar; he just started a new box that contains thirty of them. A knock comes to his door and he says, "Come on." The elder security guard hands Hey Sun an off-white envelope and exits the private room. Hey Sun moves up in his chair, grabs his smaller scale katana sword letter opener and slices the short edge off the envelope. He unfolds the letter size document and sees the check at the bottom half. The check is from his underground video distributor and partner, Muta Osaka. Hey Sun laughs and starts choking a little when he reads the amount to himself; "One million five hundred thousand Yen."

In the letter portion of the document, it reads;

Mr. Hey Sun:

This check is for the Misa/Tai, Mika/Yuen, Mika/Tai, and for all of Miss Kim's dinner dance sales. It is net, minus the 250,000 Yen you approved that was sent to Boss Saitonaka's widow.

I expect another million Yen to come in by year's end. Great show Sir!

Banzai!

Respectfully,
Muta-san

October 31, 1985

Back in Hey Sun's office, he's deep in thought; how best to re-introduce Misa to Kim and how to end up with both of them as his dedicated concubines. He racks his brains trying to figure out how to manipulate the two young women. He smokes several of his favorite Cuban cigars and finishes off a half bottle of saké trying to come up with something that will work. Finally, he arranges for a special dinner but he asks that Kim join him at his table by his side rather than giving the lead performance herself. That's fine by her because she's not been feeling her full self as of late, especially mornings.

Misa has taken over Tai's former room and so far Hey Sun has managed to keep her completely unaware of Kim's presence. She has kept Hey Sun busy by sharing her insights with him regarding the fascinating work she used to conduct on sharks. Being the senior researcher on all former school projects regarding shark breeding, she has told endless stories to Hey Sun involving their breeding habits and this almost always results in the pair 'breeding' as well. Misa deeply misses Yuen and Tai as well but she's settled into her role and new life with Hey Sun now. He spoils her with anything she desires and once a month or so, he sends her to Tokyo to unwind, shop, and tour the vibrant and expanding city.

It's naturally not the life or lifestyle she thought she'd pursue but right now, it fits. She always thought it would be her and Yuen growing old together but after what happened between them, that vision died when Yuen's spite and spittle landed on the floor next to her back in the Kuala Lumpur airport.

"Ready dear?"

"Yes Mr. Sun."

Hey Sun smiles because when Kim refers to him as "mister" that usually means he's about to get lucky after dinner.

The couple walks downstairs, out of Hey Sun's private living quarters, where Kim now lives full time. They hold hands as they walk inside. Kim claps her hands and deeper orange and blue lights begin dancing across the room.

"Nice!"

"I thought you might like them. I found darker orange and blue lights in Tokyo a while back. Remember when you sent me there? It was great, thank you again!"

Kim kisses Hey Sun on the cheek. Against the back wall near the bar, Mika and the other two naked women attendants eagerly await the evening's festivities.

"By the way, the cameras? Sneaky touch."

Slightly embarrassed, Hey Sun just nods.

The naked attendants begin by serving the couple warm saké and small plates of seasoned shitake mushrooms. A course of oysters follows and the couple makes quick work of the aphrodisiacs. Kim asks for a small glass of club soda to help settle her grumbling stomach. After a while, she excuses herself to one of the bathrooms down the hall.

As soon as she exits the room, Hey Sun has Misa enter the room.

"This is nice. I like the darker lights."

"Misa dear. Please have a seat next to me."

"Actually, I thought I'd do something special for you tonight."

"Oh?"

Misa sees the place setting already present next to Hey Sun and wonders whom it's for but she's more focused on her surprise gift for him.

"Sit back and just watch."

Misa walks over to the back wall near the bar and disappears behind it. Just as she turns the corner, Kim walks back in and says, "Better."

Hey Sun asks, "Okay now?"

She repeats, "Yes. Much better. I just had a touch of indigestion I guess."

"I think your stomach is upset because your mind can't handle not giving us a performance."

"That too." Kim smiles and settles into her elaborately designed high-back dinner table chair.

A few moments later, subtle music begins to play and her darker orange and blue lights begin scrolling across the entire room. The effect of the darker lights is stunning. As they bounce across the floor and walls, they hit one of the lenses hidden in one of the banzai trees on the opposite end of the room and both Kim and Hey Sun just happen to be looking right at it when this happens. She slaps Hey Sun's right thigh and smiles.

Hey Sun tries to explain, "But now we can watch your performances and marvel at your gorgeous moves whenever we want and you can review your dances and make tantalizing changes if you wish."

"Yeah, you just taped me so you could jerk off!" Kim moves her right hand across the front zipper of Hey Sun's pants and squeezes him.

Cocky and without guilt, Hey Sun immediately retorts, "And you are perfectly welcome to jerk off to yourself as well!"

Clever and quick, Kim fires back, "It may come to that tonight!"

Hey Sun smiles and laughs vigorously.

Kim claps her hands and shouts, "Mika! Go!"

A second later, a masked Mika and one of the naked attendants appear from the far wall nearest the banzai trees. They walk hand-in-hand and kiss occasionally as they make their way toward the now famous plush orange and white koi rug. Another couple of naked attendants follow them carrying Kim's low-profile black onyx table. They set it on top of the plush rug and return to the back wall near the bar.

"Maybe it's time to retire your black onyx table Kim."

"Maybe." Kim grins and then says, "But not until I've killed another one of your business associate's on it watching me come, huh?"

Hey Sun's erection begins to grow. He dabs the sweat off his forehead.

"Easy young lady! The night's early!"

He smiles as Kim seductively glares her eyes at him.

Mika is wearing a see-through white lace top buttoned only at the highest button and white lace panties that feature an embroidered orange koi covering her privates. The other naked attendant is just as stunning as Mika but a little shorter. She's wearing a see-through orange lace top also buttoned at the highest button and orange lace panties that feature an embroidered white koi covering her privates. Hey Sun adjusts his crotch as he anxiously awaits their next move.

The two women continue kissing and caressing each other. They take turns running their hands all over each other and occasionally, they run their fingers through each other's long black hair. This excites Kim so she undoes Hey Sun's pants and starts masturbating him; slowly at first and then she pinches the top of his penis and says, "Oh, no you don't! You don't get off that easy tonight!"

Hey Sun was just about to release when the pinch did what it was intended to do. He motions up in his seat and starts over.

Mika has become a very talented young mistress and it's obvious she has been teaching the other girl a trick or two. They move together as one; it's stunning and mystical to witness. The two attendants against the wall quickly visit the black onyx table and supply two black pillows. They place them on each end of the table and return to their post. As Hey Sun and Kim look on, she feeds him mushrooms and the last few oysters. He takes the food in and kisses her fingers. Then Kim forces her right hand index finger in his mouth and he sucks on it before releasing it back to her.

"You are in rare form tonight my dear."

"This is nothing!"

On cue, one of the attendants comes out from behind the bar wall with a pitcher.

Hey Sun immediately says, "I can only hope to know what this is."

"Patience Mr. Sun."

Mika picks up the pitcher and is about to start pouring it across the other naked girl's back when a voice rings out; "Wait!"

This genuinely startles Hey Sun and Kim because they are the only two voices that ever need to be heard in this room. They both furrow their eyebrows and Hey Sun's anger begins to build. His security guards inside the dining room at the entrance even look over to discover the source of this completely unheard of outburst. Clearly the person responsible has no earthly idea what they are doing.

Hey Sun stands up and takes his red silk napkin in his hand. He's just about to throw it on the table when the voice calls out, "Sit down!"

Completely shocked, Hey Sun doesn't know what to do so he looks over at his elder guard and waves his fist.

The elder guard quickly walks over to the corner of the bar and approaches the source of these outbursts. Very dark in that corner of the room, Hey Sun and Kim can't quite make out what's going on. A few moments later, the elder guard appears with a highly decorative katana sword strategically forced and positioned in his mouth. The guard's teeth very carefully cradle the expertly forged razor-sharp blade.

The masked individual standing behind him says, "If this fucker even blinks in a way that displeases me, I cut and you'll have the top of his fucking skull for a very graphic dinner soup bowl!"

Outraged, Hey Sun demands, "What is this? An outrage! I'll have your head for my dinner soup bowl tonight as I feast on your fucking brains!"

A stand-off; for several minutes, no one moves a muscle, especially the elder guard, whose corners of his mouth now shows the signs of even just the slightest movements against the perfect blade. Time stands still for a moment as the foursome stares each other down.

Finally, the masked individual laughs and says, "Ha, you'll have my head?"

Hey Sun immediately confirms, "God Damn it! Yes, I'll have your head tonight! I swear it!"

The individual unfastens her black silk skirt, revealing a stunning body. Her small pubic hair patch glistens in the dark orange and blue dancing lights.

She poses for a moment and then says, "Wouldn't you rather I give you head tonight?"

The music tempo picks up and the lights dance across the floor in a wild and exotic pattern.

Hey Sun and Kim are completely speechless. Hey Sun sits down and decides to just observe this mysterious goddess of the night because he's never seen or heard anything like her. Kim squirms a little in her seat because this woman just made her a little moist. The masked woman kicks off her three-inch high stilettos as the elder guard laughs and retakes his place back at the entrance.

The masked superstar dances over to the masked Mika and the other naked woman and the three dance in a seductive circle; this is unprecedented and Hey Sun can't believe what he's seeing. Neither can Kim. She's still stunned at the superstar's blatant boldness with Hey Sun.

The masked superstar continues taking off her clothes; her short-cropped denim jacket, revealing a black lace teddy undershirt. Her slightly tanned and muscular stomach and oblique's are equaled only by Kim's slightly more muscular abs and oblique's.

Seeing her body, Kim is getting more and more turned on and Hey Sun is pinching the tip of his penis so he doesn't arrive too soon. The whole room is mesmerized as the three women continue their performance.

The dancing lights adjust and they now feature a soft white spotlight beam that pauses every now and again as the dark orange and blue lights continue their travels. Kim takes a stiff drink of warm saké straight from the bottle and starts nibbling on her left hand fingers. Hey Sun notices her enthusiasm and motions for her to join the dancers on her black onyx table.

Hey Sun thinks to himself, "Maybe this is the final performance Kim wanted?"

He smiles deviously and readjusts the front of his pants.

As Kim approaches, the non-masked naked woman bows and excuses herself. She returns to the wall nearest the bar and pats herself down. The three women stop to look at each other. Kim stands in the middle of her table and pans to her right. She looks Mika up and down and smiles. Mika smiles back. Then Kim stares down at the table and slowly looks up and down at the masked superstar. Their eyes lock and just as Kim is about to smile and look away, the soft white beam strikes the top of the masked superstar's head. Kim sees her stunning so-black-its-blue hair. Her eyes begin to tear. The masked superstar is already crying because the other side of the soft white beam is highlighting Kim's beautiful face. They don't know what to do – do they show Hey Sun they know each other or do they play it off and just continue their erotic dance?

They honestly don't know what to do and are frozen in place just staring at each other. An instant later, Mika runs her hands up and underneath Misa's black lace teddy. She gently lifts her seductive undershirt over her head and tosses it to the ground. As Misa's so-black-its-blue hair cascades back down and across her shoulders, Kim moves into her and kiss her deeply. They start sucking each other's tongues and hugging each other. Mika steps back and gives the two girls some space. Hey Sun's dream is coming true. No longer able to hold himself off, his eyes wince as he gives up his fight.

A few moments later, he claps for another bottle of saké and turns his dining room chair fully facing Kim and Misa's table; he'll definitely have to retire that table after tonight.

Mika takes off her white lace top and begins pinching her nipples. Kim takes off her pink silk dress shirt and unbuttons her black dress skirt. She stands in front of Misa and Mika wearing only her favorite pink silk panties. Mika stands in front of Kim and Misa wearing only her white lace panties and Misa stands there in front of Kim and Mika wearing only her black silk panties. Hey Sun looks on but all his exhausted eyes can focus on are the privates hiding behind the black, white and pink panties dancing slowly in front of him.

Mika grabs the pitcher and slowly starts pouring it over Kim and Misa; across their shoulders and breasts and down their torsos past their privates. The substance is a lime green and to Hey Sun's surprise, the liquor glows in the dark orange and blue light. What an amazing effect.

For a few minutes, the three naked women dance together as they take turns bracing one another so each of them can remove her panties. Stained in the lime green elixir, they toss them toward Hey Sun's position. Overly excited and sweating profusely, the elder security guard picks them up and hands them to Hey Sun. As he starts making his way back to his entrance post, he suddenly clutches his chest and dies where he falls.

Hey Sun stands up abruptly, laughs and says, "God damn it girls! You've fucking killed him! Fucking fantastic!"

Hey Sun shakes his fist over at the dead man and yells, "Banzai! Banzai! Banzai!" and falls back down in his dining room chair laughing.

The girls continue. Mika now stands between Kim and Misa; wanting to experience them both for herself. She kneels and starts licking the lime green elixir off Misa's inner thigh.

Then she switches and does the same to Kim. Mika slowly rises until both Kim's and Misa's navels are at around the same height for her. She licks the area of each girl as she caresses the other with a free hand. A moment later, Kim and Misa stand wider as Mika takes turns diving into them with her strangely long tongue.

To some, this is over-the-top nasty but to Hey Sun, it's business as usual and it's amazing to see these young women let go and enjoy each other, especially since no one is getting hurt and they obviously like and trust each other.

He thinks to himself, "Is this forbidden pornographic sex or just erotic fantasy pleasures by consenting adults?"

He shakes his head, laughs and declares out loud "It's fucking hot and it's going to make me a fucking fortune, that's what it is! Banzai girls!"

Mika, Kim and Misa continue kissing but harder now. Kim starts licking Misa's neck so Misa does the same to her.

Hey Sun whispers to himself, "My God! It's just like Misa said! I'm going to get my own private mud shower party… that fucking glows in the dark!"

He yells, "Banzai!" at the girls and tries to masturbate again.

With the top of the table very slick, the girls lie down and form a circle. Like a forbidden sex pretzel, the women begin kissing, caressing, and putting their fingers inside each other. Mika is inside Kim, who is inside Misa, who is inside Mika. The girls kiss their partner's everywhere they can reach and all three women have climaxed twice already. They are each equally insatiable. Hey Sun is about to lose his mind watching this historic sensual event. He just prays the recording is still running because they've been at this for over an hour and a half.

Three minutes later, the women simply stop. They trade kisses and Mika returns to her dressing room quarters behind the bar area. Kim and Misa bow towards Hey Sun and exit the dining room. They enter the first bedroom down the hallway. They start crying together and kiss each other out of sheer joy of seeing each other in normal light.

They should be completely exhausted but they are invigorated by each other's presence. Sticky and sweating, they carefully enter the shower together. Finally, Misa removes her mask and Kim explodes into tears of joy. A second later, so does Misa.

The two shake at seeing each other again. The pulsating hot water settles them down and they just stand in the middle of the shower stall and hug each other. They both let out big sighs of relief and Misa says, "I love that it's you!"

Kim says, "I love that it's you! You're supposed to be dead!"

"Dead?"

Kim wipes her face and steps back a piece.

"Hey Sun told me that you died from refusing to eat anything. He said all you could do was drink whisky on the island he sent you to."

"I was dead-drunk a lot of the time but I ate plenty. Then Hey Sun sent for me and I've actually been here for quite a while now. Hell, I fucked Hey Sun's brains out in his office a couple weeks ago!"

The girls laugh and kiss each other again.

Kim thinks and says, "He must have had a good reason to lie to me and now I'm really interested to know what the hell that reason could have been."

Then Kim smirks and confirms, "Yeah, he's proud of the middle of his desk isn't he?"

The girls poke at each other's middle abs and laugh hysterically.

Kim continues saying, "He can't do it like Tai could but it's pretty good."

Misa steps away from the water and starts genuinely crying.

Ashamed, she stares at the shower drain and then offers, "Me and Tai."

"What?"

"Oh God!" Misa turns the water off and says, "Please, we really need to sit down and talk. I have so much to tell you Kim."

The two girls put on their robes and sit on the edge of Misa's bed.

"I think back on it now and it's my fault Kim. Hey Sun brought the three of us here because the Beijing Police are investigating us all for manslaughter."

"Manslaughter? What? Who died?"

"Tai made a new vaccine shot that works. At least we thought it did. Tai and his father volunteered to take it first and then Yuen and me. We ended up giving the shot to everyone in the village and it was working fine. Tai found your notes and completed the new vaccine, calling it 'Enhanced-CDT'. A few weeks later, we were in Beijing taking a little vacation when Hey Sun tracked us down and brought us here. Hey Sun said that the vaccine ended up killing the Ching's and Mr. Huang."

"Oh God! No!"

Kim starts thinking how Tai must feel and she starts shaking.

Misa continues; "Hey Sun said the police conducted autopsies and can prove that we administered the shots so that's where the charges of manslaughter come from. Eye witness accounts back it up as well so the charges would stick. Hey Sun got us out of there and brought us to Yokohama to avoid prosecution and pressure from the Chinese Triads who were also trying to track us down."

"The Triads? For what?"

"So they could get their hands on some of your inventions like Myst1, the original CDT, the CDT fish wash, and the crown-jewel, your new Enhanced-CDT."

"But if it kills people…"

"Exactly, that's why the Triads want it; to eliminate their enemies. They could care less if it works or cures anything. Hey Sun said if it appears to help people and is backed up by you and Tai's experience and reputations, it will sell for big money. The fact that's its deadly is just a benefit to them."

"So Hey Sun really saved you guys?"

"Absolutely! We would have gone to jail for at least twenty years a piece and Tai would have gotten a life sentence for at least thirty years because he mixed and created the vaccine."

"But wait, I tested that formula myself when I was with my parents and it worked perfectly fine. In fact, I gave my parents the shot after I injected myself and look at me."

"Your parents; Kim, I don't know where they are."

"They're alive?"

"I don't know. Hey Sun has said nothing about them to me. What about you?"

Kim starts crying and feels ashamed that she hasn't once asked about them since arriving at Hey Sun's hideout. She lies back on the bed and just shakes with fear and guilt. As she falls back, her robe spreads apart, revealing her naked left side from her foot all the way up to her left shoulder. As she goes to cover herself back up, Misa caresses her naval and lower abs and says, "I thought I noticed that at dinner."

"Noticed what?"

"Come on Kim, you're showing."

Kim's guilty tears change to joyful tears and Misa starts crying too.

"Hey Sun's?"

"Probably."

"What do you mean, probably?"

"The night before we were supposed to be married, me and Tai."

Calculating, Misa says, "And that was July 5th so how many months are you along now?"

"Almost four months now. I was scared and I thought I was pregnant by Tai when I got here a few weeks later. The only way I could protect our baby was to quickly sleep with Hey Sun so he'd think it was his."

"So it could be Tai's?"

"It has to be but the one thing that scares me is, shouldn't I be showing a lot more than I am for four months?"

Misa calmly says, "Not necessarily. Every woman is different."

The two women smile and Kim sits up and hugs Misa.

"Oh God! Please don't tell…"

Before Kim can finish her sentence, Misa kisses her on the cheek and says, "Never sister!"

Kim wipes her tears away and sarcastically asks, "So, how did you end up fucking Tai anyway?"

The two girls laugh out loud and then Misa says, "It was at dinner our first night. Yuen got sick from lunch and excused himself. The lights, the music, Mika; then Hey Sun challenged me and Tai to dance naked on the table. Before we knew it, Mika was pouring that sweet liquor all over us and we just lost it. Hey Sun left and Tai and me were just standing there alone and dripping in red liquor. I have to admit, he looked amazing and he was rock hard so I knelt down and we got into it. It was pure lust and that's all!"

"Jesus! That had to be the night I really slept with Hey Sun." Kim explains.

"When you really slept with him?"

"Yeah, the night before, I danced for him in my room and I got him off quickly. I started thinking that might not be good enough so I thought I'd offer one more time because I'd been having morning sickness and I figured he'd notice that pretty soon."

"He's been good but nothing like Tai."

Misa starts to say, "Tell me about it…" when Kim says, "Shut up girl!"

The two smile and hug each other, making peace.

"It was the time, place, circumstances and that damn saké. It's my fault."

"It's no one's fault."

Kim pauses and lowers her head. She peers back up at Misa and says, "When I tell you this, you're going to be mad at Hey Sun but you can't say anything and you can't act like you know."

"What?"

"Promise me?"

"I promise, what?"

"Misa, I'm serious."

"Okay, I promise."

"Hey Sun tapes everything, especially the dinner dances."

Misa's blood pressure sky-rockets and she shouts, "Fucker!"

"I know but remember, you promised."

"Shit! Does he tape in other places too? The fucking toilet?"

"Not the toilet, I don't think but our former rooms, the limos, and I'm sure his bedroom upstairs."

"God damn it! I enjoyed his penny-perversions but I didn't know he was taping me, us! How did you find out?"

"He showed me the tapes of Tai and Mika behind the bar wall just before you two… and the two of them in his room, and the tape of you and Tai."

"Kim… I'm sorry."

"Don't be. We've all made some mistakes but like you said, it was the circumstances put in place that forced decisions and we just acted on them. Do I wish I could take them back? Absolutely, but I just think to myself; I'm supposed to be married and enjoying my time with you and Yuen and enjoying my life with my husband Tai and our child but that's not happening so I'm making the best out of a bad situation by protecting my life and my child's life. I hope to God I can make it right because we've already lost so much."

Misa nods.

"And Hey Sun has been nothing but kind, loving, and supportive." Kim perks up, laughs and says, "Did I tell you I killed a couple of his guys with one of my dances?"

Misa perks up and smiles.

"Yeah, my first dance, I used the mandarin orange liquor and went wild with it. One guy had a heart-attack and died on the spot and then as the men took their places around the black onyx table, one of them starting kissing and licking me. He found out moments later that Hey Sun didn't approve of his behavior."

"Who was he?"

"No one we knew. A 'Mr. Saitonaka' Hey Sun said."

Misa adds, "And then we both killed the elder guard earlier tonight!"

"Oh God, that's right! See? The circumstances."

"So, what are you going to do with Hey Sun now?"

"I'll show him and tell him so hopefully he'll be thrilled to think it's his and leave me alone. Like I said, I only slept with him to cover for Tai's baby. What about you?"

"Well, I have my own news to share with him."

Misa undoes her robe and caresses her own lower stomach. Bragging, she says, "Well… I've been a little sick mornings myself."

"Yuen's?"

"God, I hope so but I don't know. I'm not showing much either and if it is his, I would be about four months along now too."

Misa continues, "I didn't tell you what happened between us."

Misa explains the details to Kim and she interrupts with, "He spit on you?"

"At me, yes. It was terrible I know but I'm starting to wonder more about what Hey Sun might have told him versus what he had told me because some things aren't adding up when I think back about them. I don't know Kim. Like I said, a lot of shit has happened and I think we've all made mistakes."

"That's true. I hate all of this too but we have to protect our babies now. Hey Sun still helped us all through a lot so he deserves our respect and gratitude for that, but that's it."

Misa nods.

Then Kim laughs and says, "I'll get him off because that only takes a dance and about ten seconds!"

Misa smiles and says, "True! And he's going to freak out when he finds out I'm pregnant too; wow, big day for him thinking he's going to be a father two times over. I just pray this is Yuen's."

"Me too!" Kim says.

"Tell him together or separately?" Misa asks.

"Together; if we overwhelm him, he'll treat us the same. Ha! He'll probably send us to Tokyo to shop for baby clothes all the time!"

The two young women settle down in bed and hold each other; so happy to be pregnant together, they can't wait for this next chapter in their lives.

Over the course of the next five months, Hey Sun slowly withdrawals from contact and simply allows Tai and Yuen to self-destruct, if they so choose. He's gotten everything from them he wanted and more. After Yuen struggled for months trying to decipher Tai's chemistry experiment notes, Hey Sun just discarded them as being worthless and no longer worth pursuing. He's effectively and efficiently dismantled their relationships and he's destroyed their confidence, desire and will to really produce anything of value. Hey Sun now has both girls firmly under his control and wanton desires. The two of them and Mika have done things that Hey Sun only dared dream about.

March 12, 1986 – Yokohama, Japan

Hey Sun has been on cloud-nine; with the birth of his two children, as far as he knows, he and Kim settled on the name of 'J.T.' for their son who was born on March 10, 1986. According to her doctor, J.T. is one month premature but Kim asks her not to tell Hey Sun this fact. Misa gives birth to a baby girl on the same day, about an hour after Kim, and asks her doctor not to advise Hey Sun of her one month premature birth as well. As far as the hospital knows, Hey Sun's younger security guard is the father of Misa's baby girl, 'Julie'.

Time passes, as time does. In one final power move, Hey Sun has his favorite guards sneak onto Tai's and Yuen's properties in the early morning hours on January 9, 1989 and all but burn them to the ground in what will be officially determined as an 'accident' and an 'act of God.' The guards carefully plan their arson attacks. They plant various implements that are assured to be deemed the root causes for each 'horrible and tragic accident.'

Tai's 'accidental fire' is easy to arrange because with all of his chemicals around, he has already provided the root cause for investigators to discover after the fact. All of his project notes, most of his equipment, his modular cell phone, and his most recent secret work on Enhanced-CDT is all destroyed. Awakened just in the nick of time, he runs out of the house and down to the inlet cove. He watches his house burn and immediately realizes that the only picture of Kim that he had was on his end table in the bedroom and now it's gone. Tai is devastated and broken. He makes a simple request of the investigators to be given a small hand radio and various fishing magazines so he can just sit around on his beach and fish in the cove the rest of his life like his dad would have liked.

Setting up Yuen is much more difficult because all Yuen has done to date is gone fishing. There are no chemicals laying around so they bring some items that would be consistent with an 'act of God' having caused the blaze and to drive home their point, a metal rod is planted and camouflaged on the back corner of Yuen's home, Sure enough, investigators determine it was the source of his tragic fire; lightening had struck the rod and that caused the slow forming fire that eventually engulfed over eighty percent of Yuen's home. He was lucky to escape with his life but everything inside, including his modular cell phone and all of his shark migration and breeding research notes were destroyed. The lead fire investigator gives Yuen a small transistor radio for local weather and news updates. Yuen thinks for a moment that he recognizes one of the investigators but having just barely escaped this incident with his life, he refocuses on rebuilding his home and just settling in because he knows full well that since he's not heard from Hey Sun for months, this place, this 'temporary' relocation site is now his permanent home and he also recognizes one other point;

"Fucking check mate!" he says over and over to himself.

Hey Sun has delivered the killer blow he was afraid of and now there's nothing he can do about it to make things right. Yuen's estranged from his closest friend Tai. He's still very sore at Tai for his intimate encounter with Misa but he can't be angry at her because the beautiful girl is gone and he'll blame himself for her death for the rest of his life. The two men go into a hibernation state of mind and withdrawal from everything. Their wills and hearts are broken.

Possibly even crueler, time has a way of passing without one noticing. It's relentless because time never discriminates. Time doesn't care who you are, what your problems or challenges are and time doesn't stand still, contrary to popular belief. Time rolls on as it has done since those first Big Bang moments launched it and Space into existence. Mankind is fortunate to be able to contemplate and study time because to date, we still remain the only 'intelligent' life in the universe. The truth or lies; a game or reality, it's all a blur to Tai and Yuen now.

Mesmerized and burned out, Tai reflects back on something his father Jimmie told him, "Sometimes in life, time isn't your friend until enough of it has passed."

With that running through his mind as he surveys all of the damage to his home, Tai's content with time passing because for the first time in his life, he really can't think of anything else to do or pursue.

If it's true that, 'All's fair in love and war' then Hey Sun must love war. He is Sun Tsu to Tai and his group's utterly vanquished.

CHAPTER NINETEEN

BITTERNESS has consumed the two young men for over a decade but finally and ironically at nearly the same time, they each realize their anger was much more about their own self-doubt and genuine guilt. It is simply time to grow older and make an attempt to reach one another.

After almost fifteen years in exile, Dr. Tai finally completes his custom cell phone using parts from his former transistor radio. He has also passed his time rebuilding and steadily making improvements to his exile home and property. The cove that fronts the back of his home now features a long fishing deck with two ports built in for boats to dock. There is also a small, one-person observation deck where Tai likes to fish from and dive off from. He's kept in very good shape over the years and still boasts his thirty-two inch waist that he had fifteen years ago. He has re-wrote all of his chemistry and experiment notes and improved upon almost everything, save for being able to actually conduct some experiments on people; like with his Enhanced-CDT vaccine. Daily, he reminisces about his time with Kim, Misa and Yuen. He hopes they are all well and he hopes Yuen has forgiven him. He's made his peace with just about everything except for the very real likelihood that his father did pass away from the original Enhanced-CDT vaccine he gave him. He can't reconcile this in his mind until he returns to his former home to see and hear it for himself. If it's true, he may very well die the next day from heartbreak and he's fine with that.

Yuen has been piecing together a radio transmitter over the years, using the notes that Misa prepared for him. He holds her instructions like a 24k gold Buddha statue and never wants to let them go as he works. But every time he gets started, his grief over her death and anger at Tai overcomes him so he stops. He's destroyed several key elements for the signal so he's been slowly fashioning replacement parts out of things he finds around the house and that wash ashore on his small beach; bottle caps, other small pieces of metal, and even pieces from a long-discarded computer. Today, several fishing lines, hooks and lures washed up that will help him complete the critical parts and metal pieces he's needed and waited on for over a year.

JANUARY 9, 2001 AT 9 A.M. – AMAMI OSHIMA ISLAND, JAPAN AND URUMA, OKINAWA, JAPAN

It's Tai's forty-first birthday; Yuen finally completes his cell phone. It transmits in a special frequency and Tai reads the signal on his custom cell phone. He leaps across his patio deck to answer it before the signal stops.

Desperately and nervously, Tai says, "Hello? Hello? Please! Hello?"

Smiling easily at first, Yuen says, "Hey old man!"

Yuen's eyes begin to tear.

"Hey back! Long time Sik Yuen!"

"Fifteen years man… happy birthday!"

"Wait, old man? You're two years older than me!"

The two men continue to smile and cry on each end of the call.

Then Tai says, "I don't know where to start apologizing to you man. Hey Sun helped us big time but then, everything turned to shit. I'm still reeling a little bit."

"He may have helped us to start but you know, I haven't heard from him forever and I've been spending a lot of time thinking about things. If he ever wanted to keep in touch, we're each just a quick flight away from him in Yokohama, right?"

"Right. I thought a lot about things too but I can't deny the mistakes I've made. I just hope Misa and Kim are okay, wherever they are."

"Misa died Tai."

"What?"

Tai stands straight up but he can't remember his brain sending any signal to his legs.

"Oh God! No! When?"

"Hey Sun told me that shortly after he sent us away, she refused to eat after meeting up with me for the last time and after another week or so, she slipped away."

"You saw her back then?"

"Yeah. It was awful man. I spit at her."

"What? Why?"

"Hey Sun told me about the two of you. She was drunk, spread all out on the floor of the airport where I was waiting for my flight to get here and she told me about you two. I was so pissed; I called her a bitch and spat at her as she lay crying on the floor. Fuck! As soon as I got on the plane, I thought about what she said and it didn't make sense."

"Why? What did she say?"

"She said that I must have seen you two and that's why I left, because I was so pissed but that's just it. I didn't see the two of you. I never did… I was sick after lunch that day and went back to my room."

"Right. I remember that."

"So, after a while, guards came in my room and some asshole came up behind me and knocked me out with some vapor-laced rag over my mouth. When I came to, the elder security guard was sitting in the limo and telling me that he had to get me out of there without explanation. I went from airport to airport waiting for a final flight when I finally ran into Misa. I didn't even think about what she said. I just reacted. Then a few weeks later, Hey Sun called me back and told me she died from starvation. I lost it and buried the big cellular phone he gave me into my living room wall!"

Casually, Yuen adds, "After that, I was done. To make matters worse, lightning struck a grounding rebar at the back of my house and burned it down. I was lucky to get out alive."

"Shit! My house burned down too!"

"Really?"

"Wait, when did your house catch fire, do you remember?"

"Oh, it was back in early 1989, January, I know that."

"Like January 9, 1989?"

"Yeah, that's about right."

"Fucking bastard! He set us up Yuen!"

"How do you know?"

"I remember my house fire because it woke me up on my birthday! How could both of our new custom exile homes go up in flames on the exact same day and time?"

"The fucking game Tai, the fucking game! This has all been the game! Fuck! Now I remember! Remember when we were talking in Hey Sun's office and I told you to beware of this game he might play?"

"I remember that. But after everything that's happened, with me and Misa, that wasn't part of the game, right?"

"I'm not so sure now. You and Misa, me and Mika…"

"Wait, what? You and Mika? How do you know Mika?"

"We fucked each other's brains out the night I left for the airport, that's how I know her! I thought she was going to join me here but as soon as we got to the airport, she stuck by the side of that fucking guard like crazy glue."

"Jesus! The first night we were in Yokohama, she blew me just moments before my dinner dance with Misa and she said she'd come back later that night to finish me off, but she never did because Misa and I stayed in the dining room all night."

Tai continues, "So wait, you're telling me that even after all that, leading up to me and Misa, that was all a part of this sick fucking game?"

Embarrassed, Yuen says, "That's what I'm telling you. In fact, I'll bet you when I finally get back in touch with my Triad contacts, they'll have some interesting things to share."

"Okay, so wait. Are you also saying that Misa may not be dead?"

"Exactly; at least I pray that's true and like I told you back then, I didn't think your dad had died and I hope and pray he's been alive all this time too!"

"Oh God! I hope so but it has been fifteen years. Let's see, he's sixty-seven now and the men in our family don't tend to live too much longer than that! I'm grateful to Hey Sun for sending us away and keeping me out of jail all this time but then I think maybe prison would have been better. I don't know. It's all been messing with my mind."

"I know brother, I know. Look; it's been a long time and I'm just glad to hear your voice again. Let me try to reach my Triad contacts and I'll get back with you. At least with our own phones now, no one knows we're in touch with each other and we have to keep it that way!"

"Yes! I'm so sorry for all this. Talk again soon? Go catch a Great White and let me know what's going on when you hear."

"Thanks man! Will do! And don't be sorry. This was none of our fault and I promise you this, I'll find out whose fault it is! You go and mix up some new formulas for us to work on together!"

"I will. I have and I've also built a couple other cell phones so if we can track Kim, Misa or my dad down, I've got one for them. I just hope they're safe."

"I hear you. I just hope Misa is alive and has forgiven me because I should have listened to her. Things would have worked out so much better because then she would have come with me and been with me this whole time."

Tai consoles his long-time friend saying, "I know man. We've got some serious questions to answer. I'm looking forward to hearing anything your Triad contacts have to say! It's time we get back into Hey Sun's game and show him how we can play!"

"Right on brother! Sit tight and we'll talk soon. Happy birthday again brother! Keep it on this frequency!"

"Thanks, old man!"

The next morning, Yuen tries placing a call to his former Triad contacts. Yuen hasn't been in touch with his Triad contacts for such a long time, their leadership has changed; they figured he died some time ago. He tries a few old numbers he vaguely remembers and finally, someone picks up on the other end. His transmission is actually picked up on a shared line by two separate people; his long-time Triad associate Toma and Tai.

Yuen finds out where Mr. Huang has been this whole time but that transmission breaks up too bad for Tai to overhear it clearly. All he gets out of it is his father's name being mentioned. Yuen and Toma continue talking but Tai's line cuts out after another couple moments. Tai immediately starts trying to fix his reception issue as Yuen continues his call.

"Yuen! Toma here!"

"Toma! Good to hear you!"

"You too! It's been too damn long Sik Yuen."

"Yes! Too long and a lot of shit has hit us all. Let me tell you."

Yuen details all the past events and Toma brings Yuen up-to-date on a few things.

Toma immediately denounces some of what Yuen is saying and Yuen couldn't be happier to learn that both Misa and Kim are alive and well and both mothers now to boot.

Yuen calls Tai back and brings him up-to-date.

"Are you sitting down?" Yuen asks Tai.

"Oh, here we go. Alright I'm ready, I think."

"Right off the bat, going back to Hey Sun's downtown office. Remember what we signed?"

"Yeah, the loan papers absolving us of our school debts, right?"

"Wrong! That was all just a mock-up and the last page was actually a release of all current and future patents of Myst1, CDT wash, or anything else you might have developed during our school time. Hey Sun also made sure that basically includes everything you ever work on will have some link back to that time. Bottom-line is that he owns it all now and has since that fateful day in 1985."

"I don't care about any of that stuff."

"Got a drink?"

"What? Of course not."

"Well, you'll need one after I tell you this."

"Shit. What?"

"Remember your dinner with Misa?"

"What about it?"

"Let's just say you are now a home video porn superstar because Hey Sun recorded the two of you and sold copies of it all over the black market in Indonesia, Malaysia, southeast Asia and Japan. On VHS. You remember those?"

"Yeah, yeah, sick bastard!"

"Wait, it gets worse."

"Come on man!"

"You remember your times with Mika? Ditto and featured on the same VHS tapes that sold. Wait, there's more. My time with Mika in the limo, twice, is on what they now call video compact discs and I just found out another release has set an all-time record; it's of Kim, Misa and Mika!"

"Damn! Mika gets around!"

"Yeah, the girl fucked us all, literally!"

"No. Hey Sun fucked us all, she just benefitted from it! I remember Mika looked a lot like Misa back then."

"Good point. That's what my friend Toma told me. He saw them in Tokyo a while back and said they look like twins!"

"So she's alive! Thank God!"

"Yes! Alive and well and very tired."

"Tired? Why?"

"All that moving around; picking up stuff everywhere, cleaning up, it's exhausting brother!"

"What are you talking about?"

"Hey, cleaning up after my daughter Julie all these years has been quite a chore!"

"Your daughter?"

Tai stands up and wants to run. He wants to jump! He wants to yell! He doesn't know what he wants to do but he can't stand or sit still.

"Yep. I'm a poppy Tai. I'm a Poppy! She's stunning, just like her mother; they have the same so-black-its-blue hair too! Of course, you can't point that out or you'll embarrass her, her mom says! Teenagers!"

"How old is she?"

"Fourteen. She'll be fifteen on March 10. They were going to send me pictures but I told my contact to tell them not to."

"Don't send pictures? Why not? It's your daughter!"

"And if Hey Sun or one of his people find out, what do you think he'd do?"

Exasperated, Tai sighs, "Fuck! The game! I'm going to end this I swear! I'm going to punch a hole in Hey Sun's chest for this!"

"We'll get him together but there's more."

"So, the fires we had, that was Hey Sun's doing. The whole setup; I found out that Misa was on her own exile island of Laoag City north of Manila but Hey Sun sent for her soon after to take advantage of her drinking. That would be around the time that he had her meet up with me because he knew she'd spill her guts about anything that happened between you and her and that's exactly what she did. He's had her with him ever since. Julie may actually be his but she could be mine as well."

"She's yours brother! Either way, she's yours!"

"Thanks! So, the Chinese Government basically helped Hey Sun put this together as far as we can tell right now; how else could he have gotten all this past the police, end the investigations, have all three exile homes built, file and complete all the patent forms and changes, have Kim and her parents kidnapped and tucked away safe and manage to keep all of this so quiet all this time?"

"Okay but this has got to have cost millions, right?"

"A drop in the bucket to these guys, especially when you've got a Government body footing some of the bill and the rest financed with underground sales of various sex tapes. Then, it's actually pretty easy. I'm told a little over ten million in adjusted Yen on the videos and disc sales alone!"

"We'll get them back, all of them! Fuckers! Shit! Is there more or can I breathe now?"

"There is a little more. Are you sitting down?"

"Should I?"

"I would."

Nervously, Tai sits down.

After a few moments, Yuen finally breaks the tension and says, "Relax, dad!"

Tai smiles and then says, "Wait, what the hell was that?"

Yuen explains, "I found out where Kim is. She's with Misa and she's doing very well but she has been extremely busy too … managing your son J.T.'s amazing school career!"

Tai explodes into tears. Sitting on his back patio, he falls back in overwhelming joy.

Yuen continues relentlessly, "He's fourteen like my Julie and if and when we ever see them, if you wish Julie a happy birthday on March 10, make sure you look at your son and tell him the same thing!"

"Both born on March 10?" Tai reconfirms.

"Yes! Isn't that great?"

"So wait, if they were both born March 10, 1986, they would have to be ours because; do the math! March tenth minus nine months or so means they were each conceived back when the four of us were definitely together and there was no bastard Hey Sun in our lives! It would be late May through maybe early July at the latest, if Julie and J.T. were say a month premature. Maybe I'm reaching a little bit there but it's possible, right?"

"Right! I'll try to find out more; based on what my people overhear or can find out."

"Oh man! We both have a new lease on life! I'm a Poppy too! I can't believe it and I know, no pictures. Just knowing after all this time, makes my life almost complete brother!"

"I know. Congratulations Tai!"

"Congratulations to you too! My God, we're fathers! I love it! Thank your contact for me, please."

"I will. I'm going to hang up now so you can take another call. Take care man and congratulations again! Trust me; you want to take this call."

With no other fanfare, Yuen hangs up on Tai.

A moment later Tai's custom cell phone rings for the second time.

CHAPTER TWENTY

"SON?"

Tai is frozen in place and speechless. His hands start shaking. He has a million things to say to his father but he can't catch his breath and he can't form any words. Jimmie can hear and feel his son's anxiety and grief over the phone and starts crying. After several minutes of relative silence and listening to each other cry over the phone, Jimmie finally says, "How are you my son?"

Tai takes as deep a breath as he can and says, "I'm fine Pop."

Tai looks up to the majestic sky above him and says a prayer.

He continues, "I don't know what to say to you and I don't want to ever stop talking to you."

"I know son. I'm so proud of you!"

Tai breaks down again and says, "I love you Pop but I don't think you'd be so proud of me over some of the things I've done." Tai starts to recount some things.

"For one, I thought I killed you with the vaccine. It killed the Ching's?"

Jimmie immediately says, "Son, the Ching's died of old age, that's it. Yuen's friends came and got me just as I was planning their funerals. They told me I had to leave everything behind and to not even talk about you because if I did, you might be killed. I said a prayer to your mother and younger brother and promised to keep you as safe as I could so I kept quiet and prayed you'd survive and you have!"

"You've been okay with them then?"

"Except for getting my ass kicked almost every night at Mah-Jongg, I've been fine. I make breakfast for everyone most mornings and in the evenings I read the paper and think about you and your friends. I know Kim and Misa are alive and doing just fine but I'm not told where they are and before you say anything, I don't want to know either; one less person who knows, the better."

Tai tries to compose himself as his sixty-seven year old father continues.

"I'm just so sorry that this all happened right before you and Kim were to be married. What a different world it would have been for all of you."

Jimmie gets serious and says, "Tai. More than ever before in your life, be careful! Don't worry about me. We can talk all the time now and we will but you and Yuen have to make this right son. It's a mess, I know but you can do it. This 'Hey Sun' is not who he appears to be and I fear even worse things are still to come."

"I will Pop. I promise!"

"As for the past; that's life son. Don't deny it and don't regret it, that's all I can say. You didn't put those events into motion so I don't blame you for anything you might have done. Everyone makes mistakes but some mistakes are unforgiveable. What Hey Sun has done and said to you all, what's he's taken from us all and what he still may say and do is unforgiveable! And, he has my grandson so as soon as you can, fuck him up for me!"

Tai bursts out laughing. His father almost never cusses, especially in English. To drive home his frustrated point, Tai overhears his father repeat his classic Cantonese expletive phrase, "Ku-Kum-Ba-Kai-Yigh!

"You must now be more patient than you ever thought you could be! Proof of Hey Sun's game is that he's content making wastes of your lives. Don't waste them. Be strong, think strong. Act strong! Things have a way of balancing themselves out, no matter what and sometimes, this takes a lot of time."

"Thanks Pop!"

"Look at me and fishing. I think of it this way; time is not your friend until enough of it has passed."

Tai stares up to the sky. After a moment, he closes his eyes and tears pour down his face in complete gratefulness and relief.

"God! I remember you telling me that before and I've remembered it ever since. I can't tell you how great it is to hear you say that to me again! That is so amazing Pop! Where did you come up with that?"

"Your grandfather used to say the same thing to me."

"Oh yeah, there is one other thing."

"What's that son?"

"Your grandson is brilliant! Like grandfather, like father and like son!"

As his tears fall off his face, they soak his daily newspaper. After a couple minutes, Jimmie finally says, "What does he like to do?"

Tai's eyes water up and he smiles with tremendous pride and says, "J.T. will be a lawyer. Chemistry and marine biology are just hobbies!"

"Hobbies?"

"Yeah, he's so sharp and well-adjusted, it's scary. I still don't know what his name stands for yet but I hope to soon."

"Doesn't matter. He's yours and Kim's son and my grandson! That's all that matters!"

"And I don't know if you knew this but Yuen and Misa have a daughter; Julie."

"That's wonderful! Tell Yuen congratulations for me and a happy birthday to little Julie!"

"That'll be easy because J.T. and Julie share the same birthday; just an hour apart on March 10, 1986!"

"Hey! March 10! That was my younger brother's birthday; your uncle Robert!"

"Yes! They are in great birthday company!"

"Hey! Speaking of birthdays, happy birthday, my son!"

Father and son continue talking but most of what Tai hears just goes in one ear and out the other; he's just overwhelmingly grateful to be speaking with his father after all this time. Much of Tai's heart is mended and his spirit is lifted for the first time in over fifteen years; he's a father himself, his friends are all alive and doing well, and he's speaking with his father who he thought he'd killed almost fifteen years earlier.

May 4, 2001 – Away on 'official' business in Beijing, Hey Sun instructs his now seasoned head security guard (the former younger of the two) to have Kim retire to her former room downstairs. He also instructs Misa to stay in the room across the hall from Kim and to keep their respective doors open.

"Ladies, please. After dinner, please retire to your respective former rooms in the main entrance hall."

Puzzled, Kim questions the request. "The main hall? We haven't stayed down there for some time. What's the point? All of our clothes are in Mr. Sun's room upstairs."

"Mr. Sun requested."

Misa asks, "Okay but which room are we to take?"

"I'm told it doesn't matter. Thank you Miss Kim… Miss Misa. Goodnight."

Kim says, "Go on ahead Misa. I have my call in five minutes."

Misa says, "Okay. Tell him, all my love."

Kim is distracted by her regular call with her son J.T., who is now fifteen years old and excelling at everything he does. He's already attending the same prestigious Beijing University that his father, mother, aunt Misa, and uncle Yuen graduated from fifteen years earlier.

"Morning son."

"Morning mom. How are you and aunt Misa?"

"We're good. Tell Jules to call her mom after class tonight, okay."

"Okay. I will. She's just finishing up a couple experiments in the lab. I can run and get her."

Kim starts crying and says, "No. That's okay. Let her finish."

"What's wrong mom?"

"You and Julie remind me of your father and me when we were in school together. Working on experiments together, always staying and working late."

Sarcastically J.T. says, "Yeah, and then jumping each other's bones!"

"J.T.!"

"What? We're hot for each other mom."

Kim calls her son's bluff and asks, "Really?"

Caught, J.T. says, "Mom!"

Mother and son wrap up their regular call with their favorite prayer in the hopes of seeing Tai someday soon. Kim has reminded J.T. to never speak of his father around anyone except Julie, who has the same rules regarding her father as well. The two kids share very special bonds of family and friendship that are enduring.

Misa enters one of the rooms in the main hallway and is shocked. She starts crying and can hardly catch her breath. She immediately walks back out into the hallway and screams for Kim.

From her position upstairs in their regular room, Kim is startled by Misa's screaming. As she runs downstairs and down the hallway toward Misa, she sees Misa standing outside her door, crying.

"Misa! What's wrong?"

"Look in your room. On the bed."

Kim turns around and stares inside, bracing herself for anything. The room is a little too dark to make anything out. If there's anything or anyone sitting on the bed, the black silk sheets covering the bed make it impossible to see. Kim goes inside and searches for the light on the corner wall. There's a strange smell that un-nerves Kim a little bit so she begins backing out of the room when Misa runs up behind her and screams, "Gotcha!"

"Shit! What are you doing?"

"Scare ya?"

"Yes damn it! And what's that smell anyway?"

"What? You don't like that filthy smell?"

"See. You can smell it too, right?"

"Oh, I smell it. It's filthy!"

Confused and still a little nervous Kim says, "Filthy, yeah. I guess it is a filthy smell."

Then Misa finds the light, flicks it on and says, "Yeah, filthy fucking rich!"

Sitting on Kim's and Misa's beds are clumpy shapes of American currency about four feet tall. There is $250,000 for each of them. Misa's eyes are practically bugging out of her head. Kim isn't so impressed because she immediately knows where all of this money came from.

"Misa."

Completely distracted and over-stimulated, Misa doesn't respond.

"Misa!"

"What?"

"It's from our dinner sex show."

"So what; it was amazing and we earned it, right?"

"No. It was private and something between us to share but thanks to Hey Sun and his people, now half of fucking Asia owns it!"

"You're right but we should do something with this money, right?"

"I'm going to send it away for J.T. and when he's eighteen, I'll tell him about it and he can then do what he wants with it."

"Where will you send it so Hey Sun doesn't find out and take it back?"

"I talked to some people from Perth Australia when I was in Tokyo last time. They'll help me and they'll keep it quiet too."

"Can you set up an account for Julie too?"

"Done. Just make sure Julie doesn't know either until we tell them together. At least then, this money will pay off their loans and get them started on a clean slate."

"Thanks. Can I ask who your friend in Perth is?"

"A conservationist ship captain and expert marine biologist. His name is Captain Darren Hall. His Sea Guardian fleet of ships helps to patrol and protect the Indian and Antarctic Oceans from Japan's bullshit 'research' fleet."

"Jesus! Are they still doing that?"

"You've heard of them?"

"Of course! Their murderous Misha Katana fleet captures and kills hundreds of pilot, minke, finback and right whales every season! The scourge of Japan remains her illegal whaling and culling activities and the scourge of China is her illegal shark finning and sea turtle slaughters! It makes me sick! Selfish, stupid, and completely irresponsible! With every campaign, we all lose face."

Kim adds, "Yeah, remember when honor meant something? Now, it's all about money. I'd love to burn the money Hey Sun left us but that would be irresponsible. When we tell J.T. and Julie about it, I'll bet they will come up with something truly resourceful and important to use it for."

In complete agreement Misa says, "They will!"

On September 12, 2001 at 8:46 A.M. EDT, the world remains in shock exactly twenty-four hours after the first hijacked terrorist plane struck the World Trade Center towers in New York City, New York U.S.A. Trained terrorists from Al Qaida commissioned by Osama bin Laden and financed by Iraq's President Saddam Hussein viciously and foolishly attacked the people of the United States of America on September 11,

2001. They chose to send their message of terror to the rest of the world when individuals commandeered several American-owned airplanes and crashed them into both World Trade Center towers in New York City. A third was crashed into the Pentagon in Washington D.C. and a fourth was intended for an additional strike somewhere in either New York City or Washington D.C. but it was diverted by the brave passengers from many nations and cities from around the world. This plane crashed into a field in the Borough of Shanksville, Pennsylvania. *God Bless the positive people in the world today and forever God damn the negative people!*

SEPTEMBER 16, 2001 – YOKOHAMA, JAPAN

From his part-time contacts on each island, Hey Sun receives word that Dr. Tai and Sik Yuen have been in contact with each other in secret so he orders his men to Amami Oshima Island, Japan to kill Tai and to Okinawa to kill Yuen.

Kim overhears the demand and pleads with Hey Sun not to follow through. He agrees but under one condition; that she remain with him forever.

"Why should I retract my command? I don't know what they've talked about and for how long. Who knows what they're up to?"

Kim counters with, "Why do you care? After all this time, they are broken men and simply want to be in touch with each other because it's all they have now."

"If I show mercy, it makes me appear weak. If I show pity, it sends the wrong message as well."

"Being merciless will have far greater consequences and I'll do everything in my power to leave you, I promise you that!"

"Even if that remark costs you your son?"

"You'd kill your own son, over me?" Kim poses the right ethical question to Hey Sun.

"Okay. I'll leave them alone but in consideration for my possibly foolish generosity, you agree willingly to remain with me forever."

"That's fine. My life is here with you and has been for some time anyway so that's fine with me. Shake on it?"

"Clever and sassy as ever; you'll dance for me again tonight?"

"Nope; it's Misa's turn."

SEPTEMBER 21, 2001 – AMAMI OSHIMA ISLAND, JAPAN

Tai and Yuen have been discussing a wide variety of plans for revenge against Hey Sun and the Chinese Government but they lack the true resources or a strong enough platform to launch their plans. They need a spark that can turn into its own powerful plan for revenge and it would have to be something that Hey Sun would immediately be intrigued by, but what?

Tai contacts his father at their usual time.

"Hey Pop!"

"Son!"

"How was fishing today?"

"Very good but I've noticed that slime build-up again. Where I am and no, I can't tell you because it's best you don't honestly know, the slime is as it was back home; thick and killing off several fish quickly after they're caught."

"Sorry. I have no way of producing more CDT where I am and getting it over to the docks back home."

"Many people will die again son if something isn't done soon."

"I know Pop but what can I do?"

"I hate to suggest it but maybe it's time to reach out to Hey Sun. He could arrange for supplies to be delivered to you so you could produce enough CDT wash that could then be delivered to our friends in Canton."

"Sure, if you trust that's what he would do with it. What prevents him from keeping it and selling it on the black market?"

"Nothing. But what if you convinced him to send it to Canton on the promise that you'd make him more that he could sell for himself?"

"There you go Pop; always a step ahead!"

"Hey, I may be getting old son but I've always had a clever and sometimes devious mind. I just chose to use that energy to catch fish!"

"Good thing for the rest of us!"

"You got that right!"

Tai smiles just as Jimmie smiles on the other line. Father and son absolutely cherish these conversations but it's Jimmie that cherishes them the most. At sixty-eight, he knows his best years are behind him now.

Seriously, Jimmie adds, "And remember; there are some things you can say to Mr. Sun now and some things that must wait."

Tai appreciates his father's advice, as always and then he adds, "And happy birthday Pop! I didn't forget. It's just with this phone of mine, sometimes the signal doesn't come in or I have to mix a new charging solution for the battery I devised."

"Thanks son! Thanks for another great day!"

Tai contacts Hey Sun and the two come to an agreement to have supplies sent to Tai so he can make huge batches of everything his father's home village needs.

Relentlessly, time passes by once again, as it has for eons.

CHAPTER TWENTY-ONE

February 7, 2008 – Year of the Rat on Amami Oshima Island, Japan

TAI places a call to Hey Sun using his 'unauthorized' custom cell phone.

"Mr. Sun?"

"Tai Huang. It's been a long time Tai."

"It's Doctor now."

"What do you want?"

"We've got a lot to talk about Mr. Sun."

"Talk? No! You and Yuen abandoned our deal so as far as I'm concerned, we've been done talking for a long time. I still regret helping you make all that CDT wash, aspirin and your Myst1 back in 2001! I made a little money but not as much as you promised I'd make."

"I can't help it if you don't know your markets, right?"

"Like I said, we're done!"

"Shit. That's too bad. You would have loved these shark experiments I've been conducting; some big money probably."

"Bullshit!"

"No bullshit! I've been in touch with Yuen and he's been teaching me all about shark migration patterns and breeding. Hell with not much else to do, I've gotten pretty good at this."

"With no texts and no note paper?"

"Don't need it with Yuen; he's an encyclopedia and as sharp as ever. Between the two of us, I'd say we easily have the knowledge to fill twenty volumes or so and my memory is just as good as it was when I was twenty-five!"

Hey Sun grimaces and then says, "Go on."

"Here's the deal; you deliver to both of us, the supplies we need and we'll continue to produce our CDT fish market wash for you to sell on the black market for whatever you can get but only as long as you supply my hometown Canton docks with their own full supply first, just like you did back in late September of 2001."

"I'm listening."

"Plus, we'll both write complete volumes of our shark research for you that you will own and can patent, just like how you fucked us over on my Myst1 and CDT formulas, right?"

"Right! Smart man. You accept defeat like it's natural for you."

"Fuck you, Mr. Sun!"

"I'll let that one go since you called me mister, but don't push it!"

"Whatever! So, do we have a deal?"

"Deal! But this time I want real fucking results or I'll cut your heads off and serve them to people you used to love!"

"What is that supposed to mean?"

"You don't want to find out now, do you?"

"We'll have your results Mr. Sun but after that, all I want is five minutes alone with you!"

Hey Sun laughs but deep down, he can feel Tai's hatred for him through the phone.

He says, "All in good time. We'll dance someday before we both get too old."

"Good! So, we agree we hate each other but we'll work together so you can profit?"

"Exactly right! So I will profit on my formulas because let's be honest, they are mine!"

Tai casually counters with, "For now, Mr. Sun; for now. One more request Mr. Sun."

"Are you serious? I should just send my men for your head now and be done with you!"

"As you wish, if they don't mind my field of acid bombs that will melt them down to shit in a matter of seconds!"

Hey Sun doesn't know if this threat is real or not but considering Tai and Yuen are brilliant and have had more than ample time to concoct such weapons, he has no choice but to take Dr. Tai seriously.

"Okay then. You're proving to be a slightly better opponent now than when you were just a cocky smart-ass kid. This intrigues me. What do you want?"

"I want Yuen here with me on Amami so we can work together and quite frankly, because I don't trust you and what you might try to do against him after we deliver our work to you."

"Absurd! You can have no such thing!"

"Our research notes alone will make you tens of millions. You don't have anything that can make you that kind of money and you know it!"

Hey Sun smirks to himself and laughs. "Maybe, but I can always use more!"

Hey Sun has plans to take over several other businesses and he knows this money would buy him the CEO's and primary stakeholders he needs to take over their operations. All he can see now are dollar signs.

After thinking about the bigger picture, Hey Sun says, "In honor of the New Year, I'll make this deal with you but just remember, don't fuck with me on this work or I promise you will live, briefly, to regret it, doctor!"

"Deal! Make it happen so we can get started."

"I'll have Yuen to you by week's end. But I have a condition of my own doctor; you can never leave Amami Island!"

Tai thinks hard and then says, "Accepted, with one exception?"

"Shit! What is it now?"

"To visit my father's home in Canton to pay my respects and to personally deliver CDT wash to everyone in my village; this would be the only trip annually Yuen and I would request."

Hey Sun thinks hard and then distastefully says, "Agreed but not right now. I'll get Yuen to you straight away so you can start your work. After you've shown me some real results and progress, then you can visit. After all, what's the rush?"

Tai stares out his kitchen window and prays for something epic to come along so he can make Hey Sun pay for all his treachery. The contempt in Tai's eyes for Hey Sun could burn a hole through lead right now.

After a moment he says, "Agreed, but now I want ten minutes alone with you Mr. Sun!"

Hey Sun rears back in his office chair, draws on his Cuban cigar and confidently says, "Accepted doctor! And after I'm done with you, if Yuen would like some time, just let me know! I wouldn't want my sword to get too lonely or cold!"

"Oh yes sir! I can promise you Yuen will accept! In fact, we'll probably have to fight to see which one of us gets to dance with you first!"

"Good show doctor. Maybe now you can be a worthy adversary!"

Hey Sun can't wait to tell Dr. Tai about his relationships with both Kim and Misa but the timing isn't quite right yet. He's actually become more patient over time himself.

February 14, 2008 – Amami Oshima Island, Japan

After twenty-three years apart, the two friends finally come back together. They've talked through everything countless times and laugh about it all now; having mended all of their differences and forgiven each other for their past indiscretions. As father's now and almost twice their age when they were together last, they have one single objective; to find their soul-mates and live the rest of their lives with their families. J.T. and Julie are now twenty-one and they'll be twenty-two on March 10 of this year.

Yuen brings Tai in to share his calls with his Triad contacts directly. Toma confirms the patent scams and offers to work to get them reversed over time. Toma also shares details that the Japanese Yakuza have been accepting and depositing huge sums as of late into new off-shore Japanese bank accounts. A copied deposit slip bears the signature of a certain "Mr. Hey Sun". Yuen asks Toma to work on settling this score first. Toma immediately agrees, knowing that by doing so, he and many of his other Triad brothers may be killed in the process but it's what they do.

"Toma!"

"Yuen! Good to hear from you!"

"I have a great friend, my brother, Dr. Tai Huang here with me now. He knows about this so it's okay."

"Yes! Dr. Tai. Hello!"

"Toma. Thank you for all your help!"

"Of course; hey, your father is quite a character!"

"He is!"

"And just so you know, he owes me about 4,200 from Mah-Jongg."

"Dollars?"

"Pennies!"

"Of course!"

"Okay, what do you need Yuen?"

"Hey Sun?"

"Still checking but things aren't checking out so sit tight on this one."

"Okay. Our original patents and anything new we develop?"

"That's a tough one because Hey Sun has the patent office in his pocket so that'll take time but once we get something going, I'll let you know."

"Good. Now what about Hey Sun's off-shore funds?"

"That's big-time! Over six million yen to date! Hey Sun and the Yakuza; something's not right there and absolutely no one here with me knows anything approved between them, know what I mean?"

"So, what's next?"

"We're asking around and if I have to, I'll check with a former friend and see if he might shed some light for us."

"A former friend?"

"Back in U.S. school, we knew each other and hung out until his uncle told my father that his nephew could never be friends with a Chinese rat!"

"Asshole!"

"Tell me about it! One of the top two Yakuza Bosses; Saitonaka, I think."

"Good. Keep me informed on this "Saitonaka." Let me know how he knows Hey Sun because these two characters working together is not good for anyone; Triads or Yakuza!"

"Exactly! Anything else?"

"Not right now. We've got to conserve our resources."

"Solved! I just sent you brand new cell phones; untraceable so keep an eye out in your cove. They'll be thrown off my speed boat at night in the next few days, three at the most. Sorry about the last ones. I didn't think a shark would eat them."

"You wrapped them in sea-weed and dock string."

"Hey, I said I had a great idea. I didn't say it was brilliant!"

"Thanks Toma!"

"Always my friend!"

"And thanks for all the updates on Misa and Kim. We'll get word to them soon but like you said, someone's always watching so we'll have to wait. Just remember, worst case, get Julie and J.T. away safe and then just let the fucking bullets fly if you have to! Don't hold back and make sure Hey Sun gets a couple between the eyes!"

"My pleasure!"

Tai quickly adds and asks, "Thanks Toma! And my father?"

"Simple; he's king here! I wish I had a father like yours!"

August 8 - 24, 2008: China hosts the Games of the XXIX Olympiad. Tai and his father celebrate it together over the phone.

"Almost ready?"

"Oh yeah! This is going to be very special son! I never thought in my lifetime, I'd see China host the Olympics. The new Beijing National Stadium (the Bird's Nest) and the Beijing National Aquatics Center (the Water Cube) facilities are absolutely amazing!"

"I heard how difficult it was to get all those beams bent and put into place for the National Stadium; incredible!"

The opening ceremonies bring tears to Jimmie's eyes. Never before and never again will an Olympic Games feature such an awe-inspiring greeting to the people of the world. With over half the world's population either watching or directly hearing about the Games, this event sends chills down everyone's spine. For the next two weeks, father and son hold extra calls between them so they can review and discuss their favorite moments from the past day's events. They are up at all hours during the day and night.

The events are spectacular and there are several surprises in many events including the Men's 400 meter free-style swimming relay where the Americans captured the gold medal by the smallest margin over the Germans. As excited as they are to talk to each other, Jimmie has been struggling recently with his Diabetes and finally, it has taken its toll on his kidneys. Tai can hear it in his voice; his weakened state and fatigue.

Knowing there is nothing he can physically do to help his father, Tai is heart-broken but he also knows that he can be there mentally, emotionally and spiritually for his father because that means the world to Jimmie, and to Tai too. Their connection as father and son will live beyond their bonds on earth because they've dedicated their lives to one another. They'll reconnect as they pass from this life and into the next because it's the only thing they want; to be reunited with each other and with Mia and Qin, for all-time.

As their phone call visits gets shorter and shorter due to Jimmie's increasingly fragile nature, Tai knows he's going to lose his father soon but he can't help to feel so grateful to God and to his father for His mercies and for his father's tremendous will to live as long as he has.

Controversy exists in Women's Gymnastics as the Chinese team is under investigation by the OCC (Olympic Competition Committee) for having under-aged athletes compete in these Games. The closing ceremonies are impressive as well as the Olympic Torch is passed on to London for the 2012 Games.

September 6, 2008 - Jimmie requests that the Triads take him back to his Canton home so he can be surrounded by his life-long friends and to see his beloved fishing docks one last time. Yuen tells Toma to get word to Kim so she can demand to see him since Tai and Yuen can't get there.

Kim happens to be in Tokyo. Toma travels there and creates a series of distractions in the streets, backing up traffic for miles. As Kim and her bodyguard sit and wait in their limousine, one of Toma's men grabs her from the car and runs down the crowded street with her before her bodyguard can catch up with them. Her bodyguard recognizes Toma's man as they leave so he immediately places a call to Hey Sun.

"Hey Sun sir!"

"Yes?"

"Miss Kim and I are still in Tokyo but some people just took her out of the limo and ran away with her!"

"God Damn! Who was it?"

"I'm not sure but I thought I recognized one of Toma's men sir."

Exhausted by his stupidity, Hey Sun says, "Fuckhead! Why are you still talking to me? Get her back, now!"

"Yes sir!"

"Wait. Are you sure it was one of Toma's men?"

"Pretty sure Mr. Sun."

Hey Sun thinks to himself, "Shit! I was right. The Triads are after her! Okay. I'll make some calls and see if I can find out what's going on. Keep this quiet for now and just try to get her back!"

"Yes sir."

With Kim secured in a building a few blocks away, Toma talks with her for the first time.

"Miss Kim. I am a friend of Sik Yuen Zhang. We have been in touch for a while. He is with Dr. Tai Huang on Amami Oshima Island, Japan."

Kim starts crying and holds her hands together in prayer.

She asks, "My Tai! And Yuen! How are they… Amami Oshima Island, Japan, where is that?"

"Miss Kim. I know you have questions and I have answers but right now isn't the time. You have to get back to Hey Sun's limo but before you do, you have to know something."

Kim wipes her anxiety and tears away and takes a deep breath. "Okay, what's going on?"

"Yuen and Tai have been away for a long time. They know the truth about many things now that you don't know but I'll tell you this; Tai's father, Jimmie Huang has been alive this whole time but now, he is dying. We arranged his capture and he's been living with us this whole time. Now, he's back in his home village of Canton and could die any day now. You need to request to see him so he can meet his grandson J.T. and so we can try to arrange for your safe capture away from Hey Sun. He's not who he says he is Miss Kim! You and J.T. and Misa and Julie are in great danger! I'm sure you've seen those signs and signals over the years but now it's time to set some things straight."

"So who are you really?"

"My name is Toma and you need to tell Hey Sun that, if he doesn't already know from your driver. More important, this game of Hey Sun's is about to get very serious and very dangerous. You need to play along if you and J.T. and Misa and Julie are to survive. Say what we tell you to say and be ready to move when we say it's time to move or this won't work, got it?"

"This is really it? We can all finally be back together?"

"We're trying Miss Kim. This is no simple task. By no means. I've got connections inside that Hey Sun doesn't know about but if we make any mistakes, he will know and trust me when I say, he'll spare no expense to find you all, kill you, and in a way that will be most entertaining for him and I know you know what that means; during a dinner dance perhaps…"

Horrified, Kim covers her mouth and cries. She knows exactly what could happen if she or Misa make a mistake or if Toma and his men make any mistakes. The very detailed thought makes her throw up. Kim is dizzy by all this detail but she knows in her heart, Toma is telling her the truth. It pisses her off to learn that Hey Sun lied about Mr. Huang all this time and has forced him and Tai to be apart for so long. She's honored to know where Mr. Huang is and to be able to introduce J.T. to his beloved and gracious grandfather.

Toma escorts Kim out of the Triad-secured building and gets her back on the path to her limousine. She confirms her true understanding and goes right into her performance piece of Toma's elaborate plan.

Running down the middle of the street between all the motionless cars, Kim calls out to her driver, "Help!"

"Miss Kim! Are you okay? What happened?"

Kim starts crying and blurts out, "It was terrible! The man who took me forced me into an alley and then another man joined him! I hate to think what they wanted to do to me! Then they started to argue over who was first and I broke away. See? They tore my dress and shirt trying to grab at me but I got away!"

"Thank God you're okay Miss Kim! Let's get out of here and get back to Yokohama. I'm going to call Hey Sun right now and tell him you're okay."

"Okay. Thank you!"

Kim settles back into her back seat and calms herself down from her performance. She immediately starts to plan out her conversation with Hey Sun about Mr. Huang and the fact that he's been alive this whole time.

At 6 P.M. Kim arrives back at Hey Sun's compound. She immediately heads for his upstairs bedroom suite and slams the door behind her. Hey Sun is in his office on the phone trying to get details on her location.

"Lying bastard!"

"Kim dear. You're back. Are you okay?"

"Okay, I'll say it again; you lying bastard!"

"What are you talking about?"

"Mr. Huang! Jimmie Huang, Tai's father, remember him?"

Before Hey Sun can speak, Kim continues, "He's alive and has been all this time! You told Tai he died and that the Diabetes shot that Tai gave him, killed his father! How could you be so God damn heartless?"

"Now wait, there are things you don't know. Tai made many promises when he was in school. Didn't he tell you? He promised to deliver his formulas over to the school so they could patent them and use the money to fund the school but after he graduated, Tai changed his mind and decided he wanted all the research and work for himself. I showed you the patent forms that he filed showing only his name, remember?"

"Go on." Kim demands.

"When he changed his mind, that's when I got involved and together with the Chinese Government, we worked very hard to isolate and prevent Tai and his friend Yuen from getting control of the school's patents and money. I was a little late because he's got money spread all over the place, see?" Hey Sun shows Kim his computer screen with a laundry list of off-shore accounts collectively holding over two million Yuan.

Kim reviews the screen for herself and asks, "Why aren't the accounts in his name?"

Hey Sun scrolls to the bottom of the page and shows one account in Tai's name that holds a little over 100,000 Yuan. Kim sees this and hates to believe it but its right there in front of her. Then she looks closer at the fine print that Hey Sun can't see for himself. It's a subscript note that reads, "From video and still-picture proceeds; master backup at \\saitonaka001server01\roomvideos."

Acting embarrassed, she says, "I'm sorry but then why would you tell Tai his father was dead and that he caused it if Tai was the one manipulating that whole thing?"

"Simple. To put stress and pressure on him so he'll make some kind of mistake. That's how all crooks eventually get caught; they slip up and leave some sort of evidence trail we can pick up on or they simply can't keep covering up their trail of lies."

She thinks carefully to herself, "Why would Hey Sun's computer backups be called 'Saitonaka' if he's dead? Did he take his accounts over or what?"

Her eyes widen as she thinks to herself, "Is Hey Sun this Saitonaka?"

At the very least, that server address is very suspect.

She refocuses and says, "Fine but the fact remains that Mr. Huang is about to pass away. I want to visit him to pay my respects because he was so generous and thoughtful to me growing up. I wish I could tell him his son is fine; is he?"

"As far as I know, Tai and Yuen are fine. In fact, they are working together on several things for me and I'm working hard to get all the patent work straightened out for the school. They created a real document mess so I'll be travelling a lot back and forth to Beijing to clear it up. You can go to visit with Mr. Huang but I want you back in two days."

"I want to take J.T. as well."

"Out of the question!"

"Why should it matter as the man lies on his deathbed? Are you incapable of showing mercy to the man you kept away from his son for so long? And what lesson is this to teach your son?"

"Okay but that's it! You have worn out your welcome here with me and quite frankly, I'm having more fun with Misa now anyway!"

"Go to hell!"

"Fine Miss Kim. You go and see Mr. Huang, the crinkled old man and take J.T. with you to see this stranger that is so fucking important to you but know this; when you return, it will NOT be to my home but to a new exile location and J.T. is to be sent to another. That's the deal. Take it or leave it!"

Crying and infuriated, Kim storms out of Hey Sun's room and partially covers her mouth as she says, "Fuck you, Saitona…!"

Hey Sun summons Kim's bodyguard to quickly move Kim out and to get her on her way to Canton to visit with Mr. Huang. At the same time, he instructs Saka to collect J.T. from his school location in Beijing.

"Pack this Chinese bitch up and take her to the airport! I'm done with her! She's visiting Mr. Huang in Canton and then take her to our place in Uruma, where she can rot! I have Misa and Julie now! And if the boat you take to Uruma port were to suddenly and tragically tip over, I understand Miss Kim is not the best swimmer among us…"

"Yes sir. I understand."

"And then bring my son J.T. back here to stay with me. If she asks during the flight or short boat ride where J.T. will be, go ahead and tell her he's staying with friends of mine in Pyongyang; that'll get that little heart of hers pounding a little faster before she drowns!"

"Yes sir."

"Ah, a tragic end to Tai's little Kim. Then I can share the intimate details her and I shared over all these years with him before he and I dance! That should just about do it for our doctor friend!"

On September 7, 2008, Kim and J.T. arrive at Jimmie Huang's Canton home. Toma and his Triad brothers have situated Jimmie's home to make it as comfortable and convenient for him as it can be; placing his upstairs bed downstairs in front of his window so he can watch over his beloved fish market each day. He has a variety of drinks well within his reach and three times a day, villager's stop by to check in with him for anything else he may need.

Jimmie genuinely appreciates their support and attention. He's grateful to them and for having been able to spend so much time on the phone with his son over the years. He's ready for the next process.

Kim walks in first and sees Mr. Huang sitting in his favorite chair. She immediately starts crying and says, "I see you finished the embroidery. It's so beautiful!"

"Yes. Finally; it was time. I had to have something to show Mia or she'll be upset with me!"

Jimmie laughs but then he starts to cough.

With the tears in her eyes now falling off her beautiful face, she takes a step back and says, "Poppy, please meet your grandson, J.T."

The look in Jimmie's eyes as he starts crying is priceless to Kim because she knows what this means to him. She bends over and kisses Jimmie on his cheek and whispers to him, "James-Tai!" then she excuses herself so J.T. and his grandfather can get acquainted.

Jimmie looks up with the greatest solemn pride and honor at his grandson and says,

"James-Tai! Such a great young man you are and a lawyer I hear. Be a great man because you want to be … and learn Mah-Jongg!"

J.T. explodes into tears. He bends down and hugs his grandfather for the first and last time.

"I love you Grandpa!"

Jimmie raises his grandson's head up and looks deep into his eyes.

"I wish you a great and long life! Find your father and tell him I had a wonderful life."

Jimmie smiles like only he can (his eyes smile) and this image burns into J.T.'s memory. He's only just met his grandfather but already, he feels he's known him for a century; such a classic and genuine man.

Jimmie gleams with great pride up at J.T. and then slips back into semi-consciousness.

In the meantime, Kim has made her way to the upstairs bedroom. She enters the shower room; it looks just like it did back in the spring of 1985. She notices a loose marble tile in the top left hand corner and extracts it from the wall where she hides a note.

Kim tells Tai everything in her note; it's coded so only Tai can read it.

My-Tai, my love!

I was pregnant one month with your son J.T. (James-Tai) when I was kidnapped at the airport by the Japanese Yakuza the evening before our wedding.

Your son J.T. is an international ecology lawyer now. He studied and just graduated from our former Beijing University.

The Chinese Government official calling himself 'Hey Sun' is really the top Yakuza boss named, Boss Saitonaka! His headquarters is in Yokohama, where you, Yuen and Misa all visited. His downtown offices are real and so is the hideout apartment suite that you know.

This Boss Saitonaka killed the other top Yakuza boss, Boss Shigemura, so he could run everything and as far as I can tell, he does. I stole the recording of him killing Boss Shigemura because it happened during a dinner dance performance that I gave that night. It is here for you or for someone you can trust to take and share!

Misa has a daughter she believes is Yuen's and her name is Julie. She also just graduated from Beijing University with J.T. They make quite the team and couple, just like us, my love!

I've done things that bring great shame to me and for them, I ask for your understanding

> and forgiveness. If we ever see each other again, I'll know when I look into your eyes if you can forgive me but just know that I only loved you and I've missed you terribly.
>
> I know about you and Misa and Mika and let me just say, that was a long time ago and under terrible circumstances. I don't care about any of it!
>
> Your father knows these truths because I told him! He loves you so much and has missed you terribly. I'm so glad you two have had the chance to talk to each other over these many years. It has done his heart so good to hear your voice!
>
> If we can be together again, we will do what your Poppy says to do, "Fuck this Hey Sun/ Saitonaka up!" For all he's taken away from us all! I swear it with my last breath as I know you have done as well! I love you My-Tai! I hope to see you soon or beyond and forever!

The next evening on September 8, 2008 at 9:35 P.M., Jimmie Huang dies but not from any ill-effects from the vaccine he received years before but from complications from his on-going Diabetes Mellitus; a heart-attack brought on by both liver and kidney failure. Having had a long life that culminated with being able to see his favorite girl and seeing her get older in Kim and having the solemn honor of hugging and speaking with his grandson, who's named after him and his son, Mr. Huang dies peacefully with a smile in his eyes.

Surrounded by all his friends on the Canton docks, everyone honors Jimmie Huang – bowing three times before him and placing various gifts in his casket. There are stunning condolence flower arrangements and elaborate and ornate plants everywhere. Even distant relatives from the United States have travelled to pay their respects to this classic and genuine family man. He'll be buried in the city-managed cemetery on the top of the hill, overlooking the entire Canton docks and the glorious sunsets that Jimmie Huang admired throughout his life.

Kim taught J.T. everything about his father growing up, including how to sign his father's name. J.T. signs his grandfather's Visitation booklet with his name and he sketches his father's name using Tai's favored Old English writing style that he liked using back in school. Kim notices Toma has signed the book. She signs the last page in the booklet and adds one word, "Xie-xie (pronounced *Shay-shay*)."

Kim and J.T. stay another day and share stories with the villagers. The locals all marvel at J.T. because he looks, sounds and acts just like his father Tai. They have missed him terribly over the years too and hope one day to see him again. As they prepare for their return trip, Kim notices the recording she hid in the shower wall is gone but her letter to Tai is still there.

The next morning on September 9, 2008 at exactly 6:50 A.M., Tai wakes up in a cold sweat. He knows why and bursts into tears. He knows his father has passed away. He sits in the shimmery early light of dawn shaking and crying uncontrollably. Yuen sits with him and the two men grieve together as they honor their iconic father and beloved father-figure.

Later that morning, Tai places a call to Hey Sun.

"I'd like to pay my respects to my father now! It's been so long since he passed away, I owe him a visit so I can ask for his forgiveness."

Hey Sun got word the other evening that Mr. Huang has actually passed away so now, he's open to the visit.

"I understand. You've waited long enough. I'll arrange it but it will take a few days. You can wait?"

"I can wait but I can't wait for some things Mr. Sun."

"Yes! I know. Okay. Let me make a few calls and get you setup for a flight out on the twelfth, how's that?"

Tai hangs up his fancy new (untraceable) cell phone, compliments of Toma. Yuen has one and two other cell phones that he hopes to get to Misa and Kim someday soon.

At this same time, a small charter jet awaits J.T. According to their deal, the pilot is taking him back to Yokohama but he'll tell Kim that he'll be staying with friends of Mr. Sun's in Pyongyang North Korea; a highly dangerous and military-controlled fortress city that does not welcome visitors under any circumstances; especially Chinese. Ironic and foolish since Mongols are the progenitors of all Asian people.

"I'm here for J.T. Miss Kim."

"Please! Don't take my son away. Can't you help us? You don't trust Hey Sun either, I know this from all the time we've spent together over these years. You hate the man as much as I do. Please!"

"We've talked Miss Kim but I value my head too. J.T. will be safe, I promise you that."

"Where are you told to take him because I know its bullshit before you even say it. Where?"

"Pyongyang."

Kim starts crying and almost collapses on the floor. J.T. pushes past the bodyguard/pilot and helps his mother to stand. He says, "I'll be okay mom. I have something for Mr. Sun myself."

"No!" Kim exclaims. "Promise me you won't do anything! Promise me!"

At first, reluctantly, J.T. finally says, "I promise mom… I love you!"

J.T. walks to the awaiting car and gets in. As he enters the car, Kim's former bodyguard winks at her and enters his driver's seat. A moment later, they drive away and Kim collapses to the floor again in grief. She knows she might have made a horrible mistake by accidentally calling out most of Hey Sun's real name right in front of him. She knows this could mean she'll never see her son again. In Hey Sun's control and with his powerful Yakuza connections, he was able to manipulate and cost Tai and Kim and Yuen and Misa over half their lives. At forty-eight, Kim and Tai can ill afford to wait on their son's return after another twenty-five odd years.

Another one of Hey Sun's men, Izu, anxiously awaits outside of Jimmie Huang's home. He's travelling with Kim and making sure she gets to her new exile location, far away from everyone she loves. Kim can barely breathe as she makes her way into the car for her trip. She knows things are very different now because her former bodyguard has already left with her son J.T. when he would normally always escort her everywhere she went. With that sense of genuine fear and despair in the air, she collapses across her seat and cries the whole way to the airport. When they land in Okinawa, Izu arranges for a small boat to transport Kim half way around the island to her final location of Uruma on the other side of the island; in the same area that Yuen stayed at before, but rebuilt now. Izu has orders and fully intends to abide by them.

Instead of making the much shorter drive to the city, Kim asks why they will travel by boat.

"Wouldn't the drive be safer and a lot faster?"

"I have my orders Miss Kim. This northern route around the top of the island and back down to the city will be more scenic anyway. This way, you'll get to see this whole half of the island from the boat."

Nervously, Kim looks around and then sits down in the rear seat of the custom speed boat. She's never liked boats but her passion for marine biology and research has always had her around them. Izu just stares blankly ahead as he steers away from the beginning port and heads out into the expansive East China Sea. With the exception of the various small islands; Amami Oshima Island, Japan to the north and slightly east and Laoag City to the far south and slightly west, there's absolutely nothing but crystal blue shimmering water and every possible predator lurking just a few feet below the surface in every possible direction. Speeding across the surface about a mile off-shore, Izu maneuvers the speed boat through the choppy waters. Kim has already thrown up twice and can't wait to make port at Uruma.

As they reach the northeastern tip of Okinawa, Izu sees two other small speed boats in the distance, about a mile away. He feels the back of his tucked shirt and confirms the presence of his 9mm hand gun. As the other two boats close in on their position, Izu recognizes the shape of their Uzi sub-machine guns. White with fear, Kim stares across the water at the approaching threat and then she looks to Izu for any kind of response but he's silent and has his eyes fixated on the approaching boats. Less than a quarter mile away, the two men on each of the approaching boats ready themselves. One man commands and positions his boat as it cuts through the waves and the other stands ready with his Uzi ready to spray the deadly projectiles in every direction. Kim is dizzy with fear and in a flash, it all goes down; a fire-fight in the open East China Sea!

The lead boat races across Izu's path and fires, forcing him to steer hard right.

Izu yells at Kim, "Get down!"

Not able to reach for his hand gun yet, Izu tries to maintain control of his small vessel. These aren't the waters to fall overboard into. As he barely maintains control, Izu spots the other speed boat approaching fast from behind his position. Their bullets riddle the right edge of the boat closest to Izu and continue on cutting through the choppy water. Izu waits and then abruptly turns left to avoid the impact. Kim slides on the floor of the boat on her back from one side to the other. Frothy sea water now fills the bottom two inches of the boat so she moves to stand up.

Izu yells at her again, "Stay down! Fuck!... here they come again!"

The two boats create wild waves and deep ruts around Izu; keeping him off balance and unable to reach for his weapon. They fire but with all the choppy water and three boats in such close proximity, bullets dart all around each boat. One of the men throws a small object encased in hard plastic at Izu. He ducks and the black-encased object falls into the corner of the boat. Frantically, as he wipes the stinging saltwater away from his face, Izu sees an opportunity to break away so he makes several strategic cuts with the boat left and then sharply right and then he throws the throttle full and guns his boat hard left, heading back to where he began. One of the other boats immediately follows and continues firing at Izu.

Izu looks back and laughs saying, "Fuck you! You missed!"

He finally reaches his weapon and fires backward at the oncoming boat. Then he smiles and looks down at Kim's position but she's not there. The water in the bottom of Izu's boat is stained pink.

Izu makes it back to port and immediately calls Hey Sun.

"Mr. Sun?"

"Izu! Yes?"

"There was a problem in Uruma sir."

"Oh?"

In his office, Hey Sun stands up. A moment later Misa enters and he motions to her to have a seat.

"Two other boats approached us and I defended our position. I made it clear of them but Miss Kim was shot and fell overboard... she's gone Mr. Sun."

Hey Sun smiles and thinks to himself, "Exactly as I had instructed."

Then he says, "What a shame; a tragic accident. You can come back home now Izu-san… good work."

Hey Sun sits down and cracks a wry smile. Then he breaks the news to Misa. She throws her drink across the room. It shatters into a thousand pieces on the opposite wall as she runs downstairs and into her former room.

With her clothes on, Misa steps into her shower and turns the water on full blast. She starts crying but as the water mixes with her tears, she's not grieving. Soon her tears turn into bouts of blatant laughing and giggling. She looks up to the ceiling and says a prayer and then continues laugh-crying out of joy.

As a boat nears the Uruma port; wrapped up in a thick dark blue blanket, Kim pokes her face out. Looking like a Jedi-Knight preparing for an altercation, she smiles and narrows her eyes as she looks over at Toma and her other rescue boat savior.

"Great job Miss Kim! When did you learn how to swim so well?"

"I've been taking lessons for years and today, they finally fucking paid off!"

She drops her blanket and gives Toma a big hug and kiss. Then she repeats the same for his friend.

The trailing boat catches up and ties down at port first. They help Miss Kim depart her boat and she gives them both a big hug and kiss on their cheeks as well. One of the men hands her a Band-Aid for her bleeding lip and her back is a little sore from crashing against the bottom and sides of Izu's boat but all-in-all, she's perfectly fine and can't stop smiling.

Toma says, "That really couldn't have gone any better!"

He congratulates his men and says, "Great job guys! Nice gun work too; to just riddle the top right edge of the boat passing along Izu's boat and then the whole ménage battle in the middle, that's was really beautiful! Really well done!"

"So how long before we can go?" Kim asks.

"This was a big move Miss Kim so I think we'd better wait and just let things settle down. I'll get you over to Amami Oshima Island in a few days, maybe a week at the most, how's that?"

Beaming with joy, Kim just smiles back at Toma. Toma nods and the group walks up the deck and into a small establishment to rest and to have an early dinner. Toma raises his right hand up and waves to the place's owner, Sing.

A moment later, six pitchers of Buddha brand beer are brought to their two tables and Kim toasts the men by saying, "Xie-xie and God Bless you!"

Toma and the men bow toward her and one of them says, "Now, we'll drink you under the table!"

Kim immediately responds, "Not tonight! I can out-drink anyone!"

Finishing her first serving to prove it, she slams her beer mug on the table and fills it right back up. She takes a deep breath and thinks about J.T.

J.T. wrestles about in his seat. The small charter plane is about three hundred miles north and east of the Island of Taiwan, headed back to Yokohama, Japan. A few moments later, the pilot, another one of Kim's former close bodyguard's suddenly experiences an alert in the cockpit; several red lights flash on and off signaling a failure somewhere in the electrical system so he quickly diverts the plane and heads for Okinawa to make an emergency landing. The pilot makes a call to Hey Sun, who is still basking in his office.

"Mr. Sun?"

"Sika! Come on!"

"I've got some warnings in the plane so J.T. and I will land in Uruma to have the plane checked out."

Hey Sun laughs to himself and says, "Be sure to feed the young man and tell him to buy some flowers for his mother but don't tell him she's lost at sea."

Sika says, "What? What happened to Miss Kim?"

"She's gone Sika. As I had predicted, remember?"

"God damn it! Is that why you had me take J.T. and Izu take Miss Kim?"

"I had to Sika. I wasn't totally sure you'd pull it off so yes, I sent Izu."

"She was a great woman Mr. Sun. She didn't deserve that end!"

"True but she knew who I was and I couldn't take the chance she'd tell others so now, she's not a problem anymore. Bring me my son and I promise I'll make things right with you. You can have Misa, hell, maybe even Julie too; she's ripe now."

Sika sighs deeply and wipes tears away and says, "We'll be in repairs for a while Mr. Sun so we'll take off again in the morning."

Oblivious to his anguish, Hey Sun says, "Very good. See you tomorrow afternoon then."

Frustrated and anguished, Sika simply says, "Yes sir."

Sika taxis to the small gate at the Okinawan airport and wakes up J.T. They make their way into a small restaurant and Sika orders a pitcher of his favorite Kirin beer. He fills a glass half way and slides it over to J.T.

"I've known your mother for a long time young man and I've cared for her like a sister so this is not easy for me to say to you. I also know how you must feel about Mr. Sun, me and this whole arrangement."

J.T. accepts the drink but then immediately pours it out on the outside patio floor. In the corner of the bar, a man places a call from the side wall phone.

"Toma?"

"Afa!"

"Hey we're over at Jos' Grille. Come on over and drink with us! Hey Sun's man Sika is here with a young man. My friends are working on his plane so I can stall him but you should get here now!"

Toma thinks quickly and says, "Stall them! We're on our way!"

Toma motions to two of his men and they immediately get up and head to a waiting car.

Kim asks, "And where are you sneaking off to?"

"Miss Kim, wait here. We'll be back soon."

Kim pours another drink from the pitcher and quickly finishes it off. She smiles thinly and says a prayer quietly into the early evening air. During this time, Izu has viewed the video disc that Toma threw into his boat.

Uruma is only thirty-odd minutes away from the Okinawa airport. Toma shakes his fist and punches the steering wheel as they make their way to the other side of the island. Toma steers the car much like he commanded his speed boat earlier in the day.

Thirty-one minutes later, food arrives for Sika and J.T. and even though he's disgusted by Sika's presence, he is hungry so he picks up his chop sticks and captures a few pieces of steamed fish and vegetables from the family-sized serving plate. Sika finishes off his fourth beer and requests another pitcher. Then he starts mumbling, "I loved your mother son!"

"What? What about my mother?"

Sika wails back in his chair and continues, "She was a great lady and so damn smart. You take after her, don't you?"

"Stop it! Stop talking to me about my mother or I swear!"

Just as Sika is about to tell J.T. about the accident earlier in the day, he excuses himself to the restroom.

Toma motions to his men and they make their way cautiously through the restaurant and over to J.T. who has his head down staring at the outside patio floor. They grab him by his arms and at first he clinches his fists but then he looks over at Toma, who is giving him an 'okay' sign. Toma stands outside of the restroom door. A moment later, Sika comes out. Toma grabs a concealed 9mm and strategically places his double-sided switch blade in the place of Sika's now former weapon. The two walk slowly back to Sika's table.

J.T. asks, "Who are you?"

"Friends. Let's wait here in the car for a little bit and then we'll be on our way?"

"On our way where?"

"To meet up with other friends."

Anxiously, J.T. sits back in the rear seat and peers out, into the dark patio corner where he was sitting.

"I'll say this once Sika and only once."

"The boy is coming with me."

Sika nods.

"You know what Saitonaka is about and you know what's he's done, right?"

Sika nods.

"Now, do yourself a favor and talk to Izu before you two return to Yokohama. I gave Izu something earlier today that others need to see as well before you decide what's best for either of you and trust me, Izu understands."

Sika nods.

"I have a strange feeling your plane is ready so leave and talk with Izu."

Sika nods and then quickly asks, "But where is Izu now?"

"Turn around."

Izu is standing next to Toma's car outside. Izu is furious; he looks like he could body-slam a four hundred pound sumo wrestler in one easy move.

Toma removes his knife away from Sika's rib cage and hands it and his 9mm back to Sika.

Then Toma says, "Do what you have to Sika and tell Izu thanks. His account in Perth is flush."

Toma gets in the car and he and his men drive away with J.T., heading back to Sing's restaurant.

Toma asks J.T., "Okay?"

"Yes sir. Thank you! Where are we going now?"

"We're going to Uruma to have a drink."

J.T.'s eyes water and he says, "The pilot?"

"He's fine. He's thinking things over."

"No. I mean I think he was about to tell me something horrible about my mother."

"Oh, like what?"

"I think he was going to tell me she died."

"Oh, she's dead alright… dead drunk by now and waiting for you so she can smother you with kisses!"

J.T.'s heart jumps but when he recalls, 'dead drunk', in Toma's description, he smiles and laughs.

"Oh and just so you know ahead of time, we're definitely going to record the two of you… so your FATHER can enjoy the spectacle later this week when he sees you both!"

J.T. explodes into tears and says, "My father!"

"Yes! Dr. Tai is waiting for you both just about five hundred miles away on Amami Oshima Island!"

J.T. is speechless. He can't believe after all this time; he's finally going to get to meet his father.

J.T. and Toma's other men high-five each other. Then J.T. rolls down his window and yells into the night, "Yeah! We're coming home Pop! We're coming home!"

Sika and Izu sit back down in the bar. Izu's eyes are red with rage.

"You knew about this and didn't tell me? I should kill you now!"

"I know Izu. I know. But you have to understand something; living around Boss Saitonaka is very different than being away and running errands for him."

"You should have told me! Eishi's a close friend and when he finds out, he's going to call for war, you know that!"

"And he should! Saitonaka has acted out like this for years."

"Yes, but killing another Boss, and the elder Boss at that, he'll pay for this with everyone's blood and heads that follow him if we don't do something!"

Sika thinks for a moment and then sits up tall in his chair. "I know what I have to do. I'll take care of my end. You just make sure Eishi sees that video disc so he knows what really happened and can then prepare whatever he needs to do."

Izu stands and bows at Sika. Sika bows back and shakes Izu's hand, holding it a fraction longer than normal.

Izu excuses himself from their table but Sika remains and places a call to Boss Saitonaka (Hey Sun). Saitonaka is trying to console Misa behind her bedroom door when another guard tells him that he has a call waiting for him in his upstairs office suite.

"Sika?"

"Yes Mr. Sun."

"No need for that shit anymore, how's J.T.? Are you two making your way here?"

"No sir. There was a problem."

"A problem? What problem?"

"… he's gone sir."

"Gone? What do you mean gone?"

"We were waiting for the plane when he broke away from me and started running down the dock towards some boats. He wouldn't stop sir."

"And…"

"And I had no choice sir. I shot him and he fell across one of the boats and into the water. We've searched for him for the past hour but we can't find him sir."

"Imbecile Fuck! Search again and then if you can't find him, search again! And then search some more! Search until your fucking eyes fall out of your fucking head!"

Sika can hear various items from Boss Saitonaka's office crash against several walls as he continues to scream expletives at his veteran security guard. Sika doesn't hang up the phone on Boss Saitonaka. He just lets him carry on until the line either cuts off or until Boss Saitonaka hangs it up. After a few minutes, Sika hears the phone whiz in the air and then go dead.

After a few moments, Sika gets up and heads for the small parking lot. He gets into the car to go back to the airport. Izu returns from the restroom and notices Sika isn't at their table so he heads to the parking lot as well.

Izu feels a little guilty that he hasn't told Sika that he too has helped Toma's efforts. He figures, it will give them both something to reconcile on their way back to Yokohama.

As Izu approaches the passenger's door, he sees that the inside of the window now features a fair sized circular-shaped crimson stain. Blood steadily streams down the shattered window glass from numerous points inside the shape as it slowly deforms. Izu walks back around and enters the driver's side. He closes Sika's eyes and whispers, "Banzai" to him as the last remnants of life leave Sika's body.

Izu drives the short distance to the air-field where Sika's plane is ready for takeoff. Izu carefully extracts Sika from the car and carries him into the plane. He sits him down in the closest front seat and fastens his seat-belt. Izu stares at the plane's carpeting for a moment and sighs. He retrieves a small blanket from the cupboard and wraps it around Sika's fatal head wound. Then he enters the small cockpit and taxis the small charter jet down the runway. He takes off, bound for Yokohama.

Afa has called the owner of Sing's and told him to get some club soda into Miss Kim so she'll be a little more alert for her guest when he arrives. Intrigued, she sips a little more beer and then starts drinking her club soda.

"That's it Miss Kim. Just drink the club soda now okay?"

"Yes sir, mister sir, thank you Sing!"

She laughs and rights herself in her chair. Sing's bar manager places a plate of steaming hot fish and white rice in front of her.

She celebrates it by pointing at it and then at him and says, "Bak-fan! Bak-fan!"

As Toma's car approaches Sing's restaurant, J.T. can hardly stay in his seat. Before he's even finished parking, J.T. jumps out of the car and runs up the small flight of stairs into the restaurant. He looks around with huge bright eyes and the second he sees his mother, she sees him. Kim falls to the floor crying. J.T. runs to his mother and tries to pick her up. Kim grabs her son and wraps her arms around him. She buries her face in his chest. Mother and son cry together sitting on the floor and after a few minutes, J.T. raises his mother up and gives her a kiss on her cheek.

Kim stares into her son's tear-filled eyes and whispers, "It's going to be okay now! We're safe, finally, we're safe!"

Toma didn't have a chance to tell Kim that they are actually leaving in the morning to be reunited with Dr. Tai. Remembering he had to leave without telling her, he patiently waits for her and her son to separate from their reunion embrace.

"Coffee here please."

Toma requests a couple coffees for Kim and J.T. Then he prepares to explain the day's events and next steps.

"Okay; stay with me here."

Kim and J.T. grab their coffee mugs and nod at Toma. Kim's still crying but it's with a smile on her face that she hasn't had for a long time. She drank heavily at Sing's earlier so she couldn't think too much about possibly having given her son a death sentence by inappropriately using Hey Sun's real name. Now, she's full of joy and smiles because her son is sipping coffee sitting next to her as she holds his hand in hers.

"My friend Yuen contacted me so I went to work. I called our other Triad brothers and tracked you two down."

Shocked, J.T. whispers to his mother, "Uncle Yuen is Triad?"

She nods, understanding this fact only now herself.

"You know Hey Sun is Boss Saitonaka now; he runs his Yakuza family out of his Yokohama business offices and palatial apartment complex."

J.T. can't believe what he's hearing. It's like the crime-dramas he used to watch in school but this is real and happening all around him. He can't wait for Toma's next sentence.

"Boss Saitonaka consolidated some things, mainly Yakuza leadership by killing a rival Boss and thanks to Miss Kim, I was able to retrieve the recording she hid and got it to one of Saitonaka's men who doesn't really see eye-to-eye with his infamous Boss."

"Damn mom! You're a fucking badass!"

Kim slaps her son's right shoulder for cursing and then smiles and says, "Yeah, I guess I am a fucking badass!"

"The video was crucial because I know Izu and I knew your former bodyguard Sika, Miss Kim."

Kim looks confused by Toma's description of 'knew', past tense. She may still be drunk but she caught that reference immediately.

Before she can ask, Toma confirms, "If I'm right and things are going like Izu told me, Izu is travelling back to Yokohama to meet up with Saitonaka directly at the airport so he can present him with Sika's body."

Kim starts crying.

Toma continues, “I’m sorry Kim but it’s what Sika wanted. Izu didn’t kill him. It’s just the game we play and when someone has played their final card and the winnings aren’t for them, they make their final play. I don’t really know what Sika would have done; if he would have delivered J.T. back to Yokohama or not but he made his choice and thankfully for us, it plays into our next move.”

Kim interrupts and says, “But Hey Sun, I mean, Saitonaka told me he was sending J.T. to Pyongyang.”

“An easy and convenient lie; Saitonaka doesn’t know anyone in North Korea and besides, their President would never allow Japanese Yakuza to setup shop in Pyongyang or anywhere else close. Their continued focus unfortunately seems to always be harassing and threatening Seoul South Korea. It’s been that way for decades.”

Kim remembers, “Sika did wink at me when he took J.T. but he still seemed distant. I made the mistake when I last left Hey Sun of calling him by his real name. Then, I noticed it by accident on his computer when he showed me various bank accounts – I saw the directory path and server name; it said ‘Saitonaka’. It’s a bad habit of mine but he showed me his computer screen to prove to me that embezzled accounts belonged to Tai. I memorized the account numbers because it’s a weird trick I learned back in school in order to remember a long or complex formula."

Toma stands up and confirms, “Shit! You memorized all the account numbers?”

“Sure. Why?”

“We can really hurt Saitonaka if you can write all those numbers down for me. In order to make the moves he did, he needs a lot of money for payoffs but without it; he’s a dead man! You know he stole all your patents for your former school work and set them up as his own for all current and future work, right?”

“No. He showed me that Tai re-assigned all of the patents to himself. I saw the forms myself.”

“Were they signed and dated?”

“I don’t remember but I saw them myself Toma.”

“Forgeries, I promise you Kim!”

“Let me ask you this; was there a medallion stamp on the first page? Do you remember seeing a large ‘International Patent’ stamp?”

Kim thinks and recalls that there was no stamp that sticks out in her mind.

“No but I remember Hey Sun said that the forms he had were preliminary forms for pre-approval.”

“Good! Wrong! There is no pre-form that people fill out. You’re either filing for a patent or you aren’t and any approved patent form will have that stamp on it along with a patent number! You didn’t see any numbers did you?”

"No and I'd remember seeing any numbers because I would have looked at them once and memorized them forever because I can't help it."

"There you go! Now, I gave that video disc to Izu and he watched it. The man Saitonaka killed on the recording was the elder top Yakuza boss, Boss Ito Shigemura. He has a son named Eishi that leads a seasonal 'research' fleet in the Indian and Antarctic Oceans. When Izu tells his friend and mentor Eishi what happened to his father Ito, the shit's really going to hit the fan in the Yakuza! All-out war for what Saitonaka has done!"

Kim sits up tall in her seat and confirms, "Yes! Misa told me about Eishi and his 'research' fleet. They illegally hunt whales, right?"

"Exactly! We have friends in Perth Australia that help to fight against Eishi's fleet. They're called…

Before Toma can name them, Kim says, "The Sea Guardians!"

"Right Kim!"

"Captain Darren Hall, right?"

"Right on mate! Misa told you a lot. So the whole fire-fight in the boats earlier today was staged and went off perfectly. I reached out and talked with Izu beforehand. I told him about the video disc I had and he said if what I was telling him was on the disc was true, he'd do whatever it took to help us out. Honestly, I wasn't sure he'd go through with it until he refused to fire at us as we approached because if he had wanted to, he could have put bullets between all of our eyes without missing a beat."

One of Toma's men reaches out to shake Kim's hand and she meets him in the middle of the table.

He says, "Nice work Miss Kim! You really held your own out there!"

J.T. pushes at his mom's shoulder and mumbles, "Badass!"

Kim nudges her son back and smiles.

Then Kim confesses, "When Toma grabbed me in the streets of Tokyo, he told me a few things that I could use to test Hey Sun out with and the first thing I did when Sika and I returned to Yokohama was to ask Hey Sun what his name meant. He stumbled and quickly changed the subject. All names translate into something, either a description or a place; for example J.T., your father's name 'Tai' roughly translates to mean 'king' and your last name, 'Huang' means 'yellow'".

J.T. quickly follows up with, "So, what does 'Hey Sun' mean or what is it?"

Kim's eyes tear up and she starts crying hard. J.T. hugs his mother and again asks, "What? What is it mom?"

Everyone in the room bows and J.T. can hear Toma recite a short prayer. He and his men wipe their eyes and start taking long drinks from their Tsingtao beer bottles. The room is so silent, it's eerie.

After another few moments, Kim lifts her head as tears stream down her face and she says, "Sweetheart, Hey Sun is the village where your grandfather grew up and it's where your grandparents, Jimmie and Mia Huang raised your father and his younger brother, your uncle Qin."

Toma and his men toast Mr. Huang and quickly order a new round of drinks.

Then Toma waves over at Sing, the restaurant and bar owner and says, "And bring that special shot-glass for young J.T.! Tonight, you join the legends young man!"

Kim stands up and steps back a few paces. She's seen this ritual before when Tai went through this in front of her with his father doing the honors.

Sing places a crimson filled shot-glass in front of J.T., bows, and leaves.

Toma walks over to J.T. and stands directly behind him. He braces J.T.'s shoulders and says, "Tonight, we honor a great man in Mr. Jimmie Huang. We celebrate with this young man's mother, Miss Kim and we look forward to finally meeting Mr. Huang's son, Dr. Tai very soon!"

Kim bursts into tears because she had no idea that was coming up next. She kneels down to the ground as Toma continues the rite.

"This young man earned our trust and support for all-time and we hope the day never comes when he needs to call on us but if and when he does, we'll be there because he is blood now."

Toma and his men bow toward J.T. and Toma motions to J.T. to take the drink. J.T. can feel this moment and what it really means; he's not joining the Triads but he is availing himself of their support, advice, and assistance if needed because they are offering it to him freely; this bond and secret circle of trust. J.T. picks up the shot-glass full of snake's blood and drinks it. The snake's former salty life-force streams down his throat and in that moment, Toma approaches J.T. and shakes his hands and then raises them up.

Kim is still recovering from hearing the news; she'll finally be reunited with her soul-mate Tai Huang and her life-long friend Sik Yuen Zhang. The three haven't seen each other for over twenty-five years.

Toma says, "Oh, one more thing Miss Kim."

Kim is in a daze and exhausted after the day's events.

Toma slaps down five-thousand Yuan (renminbi) and calls out to the bar owner, "Sing, another couple rounds and we need two more full dinner plates. The rest is a tip, compliments of the Tse's!"

Kim can't believe what she just heard. She staggers and J.T. has to catch her before she falls out of her seat. A moment later, Kim's parents Bruce and LuAnn walk in. Like the school girl of her younger days, the forty-eight year old Kim springs up from her chair and runs over to her elderly parents. The Tse's share an embrace denied them for over twenty-three years.

After several minutes, Kim guides her parents over to the group's tables and with renewed energy; full of respect and pride, she excitedly says, "J.T., says hello to your grandparents, my parents!"

The Tse's hug again and LuAnn just stares at her grandson and cries her eyes out with joy. Bruce reaches to shake J.T.'s hand but before he can, J.T. hugs his grandfather and grabs his grandmother so the three can share a group hug. Kim holds her son's face and all four hug each other.

By now, everyone in Sing's restaurant and bar is crying their eyes out, including the owner Sing.

One of Toma's men wipes his face clear and says to Toma, "We did good boss?"

Toma hugs him and says, "Yeah! We did great!"

Toma and the rest of his men step outside to smoke a cigarette but mainly to get out of the emotionally-charged room because they don't want everyone else to see them crying their eyes out too.

After ten minutes, Toma comes back inside, sits down and addresses Kim.

"If you can handle it, I'd love to tell you how we found and brought your parents here Kim."

With tears streaming down her face again, Kim grabs a beer, toasts the air toward Toma's team and says, "We're okay, finally we're okay so yes, I want to hear it! We need to." Then she quickly adds, "You know, you're going to have to repeat all of this for My-Tai tomorrow, you realize this?"

"Gladly!" Toma toasts the room and says, "First, I want to say how sorry we all are for everything that's happened to you. We're dealing with some of the most dangerous and unpredictable people there are so we have to continue to be careful, with eyes wide open."

Kim and her parents toast Toma and then they turn around in their chairs and toast Toma's men. Kim quickly stands up and hands Toma the list of off-shore bank account numbers as she shakes his hand.

Calmly but most appreciatively, Toma continues, "Okay. This was pretty straight forward. We got word that Yuen was on his way to Yokohama and that raised the only red flag we needed to put eyes on your parents Miss Kim. I had some friends of mine out of Shanghai monitor your folks in Beijing. My instincts proved out almost perfectly. We figured Saitonaka's men might try to take you while you were in Beijing with your folks or once you got back to Canton. When they made their move against you at the Canton airport, I made a call and had my friends collect your parents because we knew they were the next target. After a while, we decided to move them to Hong Kong. Between those two cities, we knew it would be impossible for Yakuza to track them down and we were right. I'll let Mr. Tse tell you where they stayed while they were in Hong Kong on and off over the years."

Bruce smiles and says, "Toma arranged it for us to stay in the former neighborhood where Bruce Lee grew up and we were able to visit his gravesite on several occasions. It was very special; especially for me because I'm the same age as Mr. Lee would be today. God Bless the man, his father and his teacher for bringing their art to the world!"

Kim asks, "You made a call after they kidnapped me in the Canton airport parking lot?"

"Yes. I was there Miss Kim. I had to let things play out because we didn't know why they wanted you but we knew it had something to do with your former school work, and Tai's too. You two were the very top two students the University had ever seen."

LuAnn inquires, "Were?"

Toma nods over at him and says, "Yes. Both of Dr. Tai's top scores were improved upon and your top marks Miss Kim were also improved upon recently."

Kim smirks a little and asks, "By whom?"

"By a certain Mr. James-Tai Huang and by a certain Miss Julie Zhang."

The room erupts in celebration and applause for J.T. and the Tse's. Bruce walks over and gives his grandson a big hug and Kim grabs her son's face and gives him a kiss on both cheeks.

Then Kim pauses and asks, "So what about Misa and Julie now? Can you arrange for them to get away from Saitonaka too?"

Toma looks down at the floor and says, "That's going to be difficult Miss Kim, for several reasons."

Kim listens patiently but her stomach begins to become unsettled.

"We're hearing that Miss Misa doesn't want to leave. She didn't want to risk it at the time when we approached her in Tokyo. Remember when the two of you were in the light shop?"

Kim immediately says, 'Yes."

"The two men standing across from you and Misa were with me. You had stepped away to find some other kind of colored light when we talked with Misa and offered to take her with us before you came back. That way, you could have honestly told Saitonaka that you didn't know what happened to Misa and he would have believed you. We had to be especially cautious and very quick in Tokyo because we might have some friends looking out for us there but naturally, Saitonaka has more."

Bruce comments out of amazement, "This is so intricate; the world you live in and live with Mr. Toma. When I was growing up, you simply learned how to fight to protect yourself but as you grew older, you moved on from these things."

Toma nods and says, "Yes sir but some of us couldn't make that critical adjustment for one reason or another. I told Dr. Tai that I wished I had a father like his to guide me and share his thoughts and advice with me as I grew up because I might have been destined for better things but as I learned from Mr. Huang, 'it is what it is' and I honestly have no regrets. I remember my past and I've learned from my former mistakes but life moves forward so, so have I."

"Good man Toma. Don't have any regrets and move forward because we only get this journey in life once."

Toma nods towards Mr. Tse.

Kim nudges her son and whispers, "You beat your dad's scores?"

J.T. smiles and whispers back, "By two points."

Kim hugs her son and then asks, "What about Julie, how many points did she beat me by?"

"Oh, she destroyed your scores mom! By three points!"

Kim smiles, kisses her son on the cheek and says, "That just means she's three times smarter than you guys because I beat your father's score by a single point."

Toma quickly adds, "So we missed our opportunity with Misa once and then I got word that she wanted to stay with him so we had to leave it at that until I get another chance to talk with her. Maybe with a little more time, things may change with her because I'm sure there is a lot she still doesn't know; like the fact that Izu reported back to Boss Saitonaka that Kim was lost and likely drowned in our speed boat fire-fight earlier today. Once she thinks that Kim is dead, maybe she'll think differently. It depends too on whatever Sika told his Boss about J.T. He indicated to me that he might fall in-line with us and our plans but I'm not sure, especially since the man is gone now. I have a feeling he did the right thing by us but I'll check this out later to make sure."

Then Toma adds, "Hey everyone; it's been a very long day for all of us. I'm sure you're ready to rest so why don't we pick up on our conversations again tomorrow morning."

J.T. leans over and whispers something into his mother's ear. She looks at him with surprise and great solemn pride.

She whispers back to him, 'You tell Toma."

"Mr. Toma?"

"J.T. Yes?"

"I would like to do something for you and your men but I want it understood, like my oath earlier tonight."

"Of course J.T. What is it?"

"I can't speak for Julie but there's now over 250,000 Yen in an account in my name in Perth that I'd like to give to you and anyone you deem who needs it to say thank you for looking out for my mother and grandparents all this time. I'm so grateful to you for protecting them for me before I was even born. And for helping me to finally meet my father so we can all be together."

Toma and his men face young J.T. and bow. Everyone raises their glasses and toast each other and the day's events one more time. Then everyone helps rearrange Sing's tables and chairs for him. J.T. makes his rounds around the floor shaking everyone's hands and stops to assist his grandparents make their way out to several cars waiting for them in the parking lot. In the corner of the bar, Toma is already back to work making several calls to arrange security for the pending logistics and flight to Amami Oshima Island, Japan.

Izu has made it back to Yokohama but before visiting with Saitonaka, he stops by the Yokohama docks and talks to his childhood friend and mentor, Eishi Shigemura on his main 'research' ship, the Misha Katana1.

"Izu my friend! How have you been? I hope my uncle hasn't been too difficult."

Izu bows in front of his elder friend and mentor. "Eishi. Good to see you again my friend."

"You look upset Izu. Please, sit and talk with me."

"I have upsetting news."

"Is it my uncle? Is he okay?"

"There is big trouble with Boss Saitonaka; it's very bad."

"Nothing my father can't fix, right?"

Izu looks down at the ship's deck completely ashamed. He knows his news will hit his friend like a bullet-train and he hates to have to tell him but he's the only one that could possibly deliver this kind of news.

"Not anymore Eishi."

"What do you mean?"

"Your uncle, Boss Saitonaka kidnapped Dr. Tai Huang and his bride to be back in the mid-eighties, right?"

"Right. I knew that but they're all okay right?"

"Yes, but only thanks to their own survival instincts and recently, thanks to the Triads help. Dr. Tai or one of his friends has very powerful friends. They rescued Miss Kim and her son J.T. earlier today and I, ... I helped arrange it!"

"You what? Izu, … no!"

"My uncle will kill you if he hears this! And J.T., I thought Sika was with him."

"He was. You know Toma?"

"Of course. We go way back to our early school days. I did what I had to with my father and uncles and of course, he did the same with his father. He's a sharp and clever man but that doesn't mean I trust him."

"Well, I did. Especially when he risked his neck and life trusting me. I could have easily killed him earlier today but I decided to trust someone who I've only considered my rival and combatant. He proved out Eishi."

"Look; I appreciate what you're trying to say, I think, but like I said, this is all easily fixed with one simple call to my father Ito. The Shigemura's have always respected you and your family and you're like a brother to me. Don't worry about Toma. As far as Dr.

Tai and Kim go; that's a problem but more importantly, is my uncle's son, J.T. We have to work to get him back and you must help me do that before my uncle decides to kill Sika and maybe even you as well for today's mistakes."

Eishi stands up confidently and starts leading the way out of his command quarters. Izu remains seated.

"Izu. What are you doing? Let's go. It's late but let's have dinner."

"Eishi. Please friend. Sit. There is more to talk about."

"More? Whatever it is, my father…"

Before his friend can continue to site his father's support, Izu sternly announces, "He's dead Eishi!"

Raising his fists, Eishi yells, "What is this? Bullshit!"

"I'm so sorry Eishi." Izu's solemn look and destroyed spirit tells Eishi that what he's saying is the truth.

"Izu, tell me. What happened? Tell me now!"

Izu starts to explain, "Boss Saitonaka had Miss Kim. She was dancing for everyone in one of your uncle's dinner performances. The other bosses were all there. Your father, Boss Ito took a few liberties with Miss Kim in front of Boss Saitonaka that he didn't like and then it happened; he killed him."

"How? How could my uncle get the move over on my father? My father is easily twice as fast with his long or short-sword as any man alive, including my uncle Saitonaka!"

"Kim's dance was a little unexpected and went farther than usual. Everyone was drunk and then your father approached Kim on the top of the black onyx table she was laying across. Your uncle didn't like it because he hadn't had Kim yet and didn't think anyone else should mess with her before him. With the saké flowing and this situation escalating right in front of him, he drew his sword behind your father and decisively pierced his skull."

"He struck and killed my father from behind?"

"Yes. It was probably the only way for your uncle to take your father out because like you said, in a fair fight, even drunk, your father would never have lost any form of battle to his younger brother. It's just shocking that your uncle would kill his own brother over a woman."

Eishi starts to cry and adds, "And over a Chinese woman at that!"

Cautiously but directly, Izu says, "That has nothing to do with it and you know that Izu. The prejudice between us Japanese and Chinese must stop! We're the same! We all come from our Mongol ancestors and the Chinese were FIRST! Why do you think so many things in Japanese culture are so similar to Chinese?"

Eishi looks up and Izu continues. "Our histories, art, music, language, numbers, money, ancient leadership and governments and our stubbornness and inhumanity towards others and toward each other!"

Eishi offers, "You went away to school in the United States. I didn't. I was schooled by my father and uncles and they believed differently; more like Emperor Shōwa and Shirō Ishii."

Izu nods and says, "Okay but look how that went! All that horrible energy and focus on plundering and murder. Shirō Ishii was a despicable man who simply took orders, never questioned them, never thought for himself, and had absolutely no compassion for mankind. I have respect for our country's Imperial past but not for Emperor Hirohito. He had a duty to lead his nation to health and prosperity and he had to have known that by following The Reich leader in Berlin, Japan would cry and bleed for decades to come and we did, didn't we? Emperor Shōwa and Shirō Ishii were and are as bad as Hitler in my mind! God damn Adolph Hitler for turning the world upside-down and for turning Japan into a monster against its own people and for what we did against the United States! And our nation still hasn't genuinely apologized to China for our treachery at Nanking! Those events still haunt me! I was just a young boy when it happened but some of my cousins actually took part in it and I have always denounced them as family for their part. It's time for Japan and China to grow the hell up, heal each other and start working together as the brothers and sisters that we are! We all stand to benefit greatly if we do but we also stand to lose greatly if we continue to argue and fight with each other!"

Passionately, Izu continues, "I understand the environment you grew up in and I'm sorry for you because you never got the full or true story of so many things. What you got was the classic Japanese one-sided, propaganda-laced description of things; of people, places, and events. The world is so different now than it was at the turn of the twentieth century. Eishi, Just look at how China is opening her eyes and working with Russia today; they just signed a nearly half a trillion dollar fuel resource Bill with each other! That's major progress that will benefit a billion plus people around the world, as long as Russia doesn't fuck it up!"

Passionately, Izu continues, "I respected your father, greatly and genuinely but I do not respect your uncle, Boss Saitonaka. He has now made a move against the entire Yakuza and you know as well as I do, only you and your uncle Ric can do anything about it! I'll help with whatever I can but we have to act really fast or it'll be too late. That's why I took a stand for myself earlier today by helping Toma, his Triad brothers and helping the Huang's and Tse's. Now we need to help the Zhang's because they are still in great danger. Miss Misa and her daughter Julie are still under Boss Saitonaka's hand."

Eishi stands and bows toward Izu for having shared such horribly difficult and direct news with him. His prejudices aside, Eishi knows the blame is all on his uncle Saitonaka for betraying his family, his older and younger brothers, one of which now must decide to take Saitonaka out himself or suffer the consequences from the rest of his older brother's Yakuza gang. Once they hear of Boss Ito Shigemura's death, they will demand Saitonaka's head and they may even move against Eishi and his uncle Ric Shigemura as well. Time will tell.

"Jesus! Is that where some of the money for my new Misha Katana3 ship came from? From my uncle and his underground perversions?"

"Yes. All of it; over three and a half million Yen!"

Disappointed and angered, Eishi says, "Okay my friend. I'll make the calls and I'll meet with my father's leadership to work out our next steps. Thank you again for your honesty and trust in me to tell me everything."

Izu bows at Eishi and says, "My loyalties are always with you and Yakuza but we have a situation now that must be resolved or we will all suffer. You've been able to run your ships away from much of this so again, I'm happy to help but I need your approvals for many things because I'd never disrespect your father or your younger uncle's wishes."

"Thank you my friend. We'll work together to make this right and I promise, I'll try to open my eyes to my Chinese counterparts but I can't promise anything."

"Just make a genuine effort."

"Yes. I will."

"There is another matter my friend."

"Can it wait? I really have to make these calls and arrange to meet with my father's colleagues. And, I need to talk to my uncle Ric about all of this immediately."

"I understand. It can wait but honestly, not too long."

Eishi looks intrigued but when he sees Izu's genuine frustration and the stress in his eyes, he clinches his fists with angst.

CHAPTER TWENTY-TWO

September 12, 2008

TAI is finally allowed to visit his father's Canton village home and pay his respects. Escorted by two of Hey Sun's men, Dr. Tai boards the same small charter plane that Sika used to navigate. Tai stares blankly at the pilot's cabin with pure adrenaline running through him. Hundreds of thoughts of a coup run through his mind but then he thinks to himself, "Patience, like Poppy would tell me in this moment. There will come a time when I can make this right by everyone so I'll simply wait for that time and then, I'll seize it!"

Tai sits back in his seat, a half step away from pursuing his gut and decides instead to finish the martial-arts article he started reading.

An hour and a half later, Tai lands at Canton International Airport. It is genuinely shocking to him. All the tremendous growth and change is inspiring. He already has a very special tribute planned for his father for after his visit. The three men enter their rental car and head toward Jimmie's Huang's home village.

As they approach, one of the security men says, "Here we are. Hey Sun…"

Dr. Tai interrupts and asks, "What did you just say?"

"I was saying, here we are and that Mr. Sun requests that we call him immediately so he knows we've arrived. He told me to remind you that we can only be here for a maximum of three days Dr. Tai."

Thinking that the security guard possibly knew his village's real name, Tai asks but now he's glad the guard really has no clue. Tai nods at the guard and approaches his father's front door.

The late morning breeze is present and Tai can pick up the faint scent of Dragon's Tears in the light wind. His eyes tear up as he enters his family home. With every step, he can feel his father's presence. In every corner, in each new space he moves into, he sees his father's face and classic smile. It tears him apart. The furniture is as Toma and his men left it; in support of whatever Mr. Huang wanted during his final days. Tai closes the front door and takes a deep breath. He looks around the room and then he sees his father's favorite chair. He immediately notices that the embroidery on the right arm is complete. He carefully sits down in his father's chair and, just as Jimmie had intended for him to see, Tai immediately focuses in on the final embroidery. Making up the dragon's final five-digit claws, Jimmie embroidered his son's Chinese name into the claw with gold silk thread on top of the underlying blue silk thread. Tai leans forward and lays the right side of his face across the right arm of the chair. After a few minutes, Tai gets up from the chair and walks around for a moment checking things over. He opens the front door. Hey Sun's men are waiting right out front.

Tai says, "Are you two hungry or thirsty? There are a few beers in the fridge."

Honestly surprised by his generosity, one of the men says, "Thank you Dr. Tai, I wasn't expecting…"

"You weren't expecting what? For me to be a nice person?"

Embarrassed, the man takes a step back away from the Huang's home.

Tai waves him ahead and surprisingly and calmly says, "Look, just because you work for a monster doesn't mean you are one, right? Misguided, sure, but that's not your fault."

Then Tai's exhaustion and anger starts to build and he adds, "Everyone makes their own way in life. Maybe someday, you'll learn differently or maybe you'll just fucking embrace your current power position and cut my fucking head off!"

The other guard grabs his colleague and escorts him back out of the Huang's home entrance.

"We'll just wait outside for you Dr. Tai. Please, take your time."

Having lost face, the two men walk away from Dr. Tai and head toward the far left side of the docks to look out into the busy water highway.

Tai grabs his travel bag and heads upstairs to his father's bedroom. As he starts upstairs, he smiles at the growth marks on the left wall. When he reaches the top of the stairs, he brushes the right side wall and smiles at the growth marks on it. He remembers how his father used to joke in telling him that he was always a little taller upstairs. Preparing for a very emotional and sacred visit, Tai undresses and enters the shower.

The floor and shower walls are just as he remembered. He stands there as the warm water jet pattern beats down on his back. Facing the back wall, he notices a loose tile at eye-height. He tries to fix it but it won't go back flush with the rest of the wall. He pulls at the edges with his finger tips to reset the tile but it still won't fit correctly. Not wanting to make it any worse, he turns back around and finishes washing off. He quickly redresses and heads outside to meet with his fellow villagers.

They are all so glad to see him. They mob him and the elder women have all brought small baskets of their traditional Chinese donuts and pastries for him. Tai hugs everyone and they cry together in honor of Jimmie Huang. Hey Sun's men see this reunion and can't help but to smile because they see now for themselves how much Mr. Huang and his son have meant to them. One of the elder Chinese residents motions over at the younger Japanese security guards and asks them to join them. Again, this not being their experience, the two security guards are taken back and humbled by the Chinese man's generosity and recognition.

He asks them, "Do you two play Mah-Jongg?"

The elder security guard says, "Of course. We love Mah-Jongg but in Japan, we play it a little different."

The elderly man smiles and escorts the two men over to the rest of the group and announces to everyone, "Tonight, we play Mah-Jongg for Jimmie Huang and our new Japanese friends will teach us a new style of play."

Everyone nods toward the security guards and they all begin walking back toward Jimmie Huang's home. When they enter, the women start rearranging the smaller furniture so space for several games can take place. The men take their cue and start moving the bigger furniture but no one touches Jimmie Huang's chair. Tai places all of the gift baskets around the front room for everyone to enjoy and then he gets to work in the kitchen making his and his father's favorite steamed Chinese Perch with white rice and vegetables. He can't make his father's famous sauce but he gives it a try and adds his own kick of plum wine and ginger sauce.

Within minutes, the Huang home is once again full of sweet and sour smells that delight everyone. The steamed white rice reminds the security guards of their own home-cooked meals and they are genuinely grateful to everyone in the village and especially to Dr. Tai for his hospitality and exceptional and quick culinary skills. Everyone savors the meal and the women each get up from their positions and kiss and hug Tai. One of them brushes Tai's cheek as she cries.

She's whispers to him, "Like father, like son!"

They smile and hug each other and then she returns to her seat. The house is full of love, respect and vibrant activity and this makes Tai happy because he knows his father's spirit helped guide the day's events. A few moments later, just like his father used to, Tai announces the start of the Mah-Jongg tournament.

"Everyone! Thank you so much for today. If you're ready, let's crack the bones!"

A couple women stand up crying and walk over to hug Tai.

One of them whispers to him, "You sound just like your father and that is exactly what he used to say!"

"Thank you! I can't help it! Now, let's see if I have my father's wits and good fortune at Mah-Jongg as well!"

Tai turns on his father's favorite radio station and in the background now, everyone enjoys the infectious sound of Fats Domino and his *Whiskey Heaven.*

Just then, the elder security guard stands up and requests a moment to address the group. He looks over at Dr. Tai and Tai nods back at him.

"We're honored to be here with you all, especially under the solemn circumstances. Please, allow us to contribute to tonight's games."

The elder guard places five-thousand Yen on the table and says, "Please, divide this up as you will and play with this money tonight."

The eldest villager stands and nods toward the guards.

The rest of the evening is spent in great company and camaraderie with old and new friendships; full of stories about Mr. Huang and his famous and growing legacy of consecutive winning games. It had been sixteen but after a couple hours of saké, plum wine, and many Tsingtao and Buddha beers, it's now up to twenty-nine. Tai takes another moment, as he has done all afternoon and evening. He closes his eyes and thanks his father. Then he winks at his mother Mia and younger brother Qin. Tears stream down his face as he returns to his Mah-Jongg table and throws down the winning tiles once again.

One of the villager's at his table exclaims, "That's fourteen! The record falls tonight!"

Tai reaches across the table and shakes his elder friend's hand. The other tables toast Tai's table as well.

The village and Tai's hospitality has opened the guard's eyes to these Chinese people. They are humbled, grateful and their appetites have never been satisfied any better. If only more of these interactions between these people took place.

The next morning, Tai decides to request the special unscheduled trip in honor of his father and the guards immediately agree to take him anywhere he wants.

Tai enters the upstairs shower so he can refresh, collect his thoughts and prepare for the special flight and then for the long flight back to Amami Oshima Island, Japan. Again, he's bothered by the loose marble tile so he picks at it with his fingertips. He quickly grabs it before it falls to the floor. As he looks to replace it, he sees a slightly squashed folded piece of paper in the wall. He retrieves it and holds it up and away from the water. He replaces the tile with his other hand and pushes it tight against the wall. He unfolds the note and reads it away from the falling water; looking up at it.

For the next few moments, you couldn't distinguish between the shower water and the tears coming from Tai's eyes. As he reads Kim's note, his hangover disappears and his strength quickens. He learns about his son and what his name stands for. This information almost buckles his knees.

Then he learns that his son is already an international lawyer at the age of twenty-two. He's so proud that J.T. graduated from Beijing University as well. As he reads about Hey Sun, Tai's eyes narrow as he pounds the shower wall. It infuriates him to learn that the whole Canton docks police investigation was a complete lie but then he realizes that if Hey Sun wanted to, and he would have, he could have easily called for an investigation that would have resulted in a formal arrest and investigation that would have taken months if not years away from them and their freedom.

It sickens Tai to realize that he was there in Hey Sun's apartment complex and Kim was there just a few hundred feet away from him down the hallway. He would have gladly given his life to save her and end this whole charade right then and there. Tai turns the shower off and checks behind the tile again for a disc or tape. He hopes someone they can trust retrieved it. He turns the shower back on and reads on. He learns about Misa and Yuen's daughter Julie again and is so happy for them. He can't wait to get back to Amami Oshima Island, Japan to share all of this with Yuen.

When he reads the section about Kim's apologies, he kneels to the floor. He pushes the door open so the rest of Kim's letter doesn't get soaked. He continues reading as the water trickles down on his back and all over the immediate outside of the shower unit. He's ashamed more for the things he did and he blames himself for not having the self-control to have stopped, especially the evening with Misa. He hopes Kim can forgive him if they ever talk to each other again. He prays for the day when they can speak so he can apologize and tell her he's sorry about everything that happened. Tai is still tormented because it kills him to not know what happened to Kim's parents either.

As he reads about how Kim told his father about all of this, he's overwhelmed with respect and love for her because he knows it could not have been easy for her to tell him such things. The time he shared on the phone with his father was some of his most sacred. He loves that Kim quoted back to him, his father's request and that she added her own devoted claim to make things right again. Her 'My-Tai' conclusion brings Tai to tears again. He just sits there in the shower, half in and half out and holds Kim's letter.

After ten minutes, Tai gets dressed. He's ready to leave but something is holding him back. Tai sits back down on the bed and just closes his eyes. Five minutes later, as if he had always known, he moves to the head of the bed and pushes the small red-lacquer clothes dresser away from the wall. He stares straight ahead at the wall and after a couple seconds he notices a small notch in a piece of marble. He opens his pocket knife and carefully extracts the tile.

He looks into the hole in the wall and carefully extracts a highly decorated red eight-inch long cylinder. Excited beyond words or expression, Tai opens the top of the cylinder and extracts the scroll inside. The scroll appears like new; when Tai's father carefully considered and wrote his declaration over forty-three years earlier.

After a moment, Tai slowly un-rolls the scroll. In his best calligraphy, like back in ancient times, Jimmie's scroll represents his thoughts and feelings with regards to the horrific treatment of hundreds of thousands of fellow-Chinese men, women and children by the Empire of Japan's World War II perpetrators and it features a special wish and declaration addressing the Nanking Massacre of 1937-1938. Tai's eyes tear up as he reads.

"After all this time passed, all the Japanese Government and people of Japan would have to do is to first and foremost put an end to their denialism and aberrations. It has been time and time continues to injure both China and Japan.

What is long overdue is the most solemn and heartfelt apologies from the hearts and minds of the Japanese people to the hearts and minds of the Chinese people, Japan's most closely related peoples, a genuine declaration of life, with the greatest conviction saying to the world,

'We are sorry to our Chinese brothers and sisters for the horrific events that took place during Japan's illegal occupation of mainland China and her territories prior to and including throughout World War II, specifically and here today, acknowledging the 1937-1938 Massacre at Nanking.

We want to replace the image of everyone's perception of the former Empire of Japan. This Land of the Rising Sun needs to be and must be thought of as a thriving, vital and sincere nation full of people who care and wish for forgiveness for our devastating past. We are sickened and dismayed by our nation's denialism and today, it ends.

We can only hope and pray with you that going forward we can act in peace and work together as great nations full of life because we know we caused you so much death. That is not who Japan is and still today, before this declaration, many of us still hold on to those delusions.

We must embrace this change for many reasons; we both share an adamant belief and take great pride in caring for and respecting our elders. We owe your elders this apology! We now offer this most solemn of apologies to them so their souls can rest and so we can all live with ourselves and hopefully, together, as our ancestors would all have hoped for us.

Instead of spitting fire at each other as we have done for centuries, the time has definitely arrived. Our opposing dragons need to come together; embrace one another and agree on peace and support, for all time!

We will never forget December 12, 1937-January 31, 1938"

The first paragraph was written in black characters. The next four paragraphs were written in Jimmie Huang's own blood and have naturally faded over time to the darker and flat maroon color Tai reads. The final sentence is written in Imperial gold flake.

Immediately, Tai falls to the floor but not out of exhaustive grief or depression. He falls to the floor out of sheer appreciation and in honor of seeing and reading his father's long-lost letter that looks to have been hidden away for decades. Also, in learning of his father's true and genuine feelings and sentiment towards Japan and wishing for acknowledgment from them regarding Nanking. Lastly, Tai realizes how genuinely helpful and hopeful his father was trying to be in penning a letter of hope that he obviously believed would help to heals hearts.

After another moment, Tai stands up and cracks a smile as he re-connects again with his father's indomitable spirit.

He looks up, wipes the streaming tears away from his cheeks and whispers, "Poppy! You said exactly what needs to be said and I promise I will take this and try my best to get your message heard, loud and clear! It's time that this is made right and for our people to be made whole. I just hope our Japanese brothers and sisters agree and in my lifetime."

Tai toasts the sky. His very next thought is to share this incredible artifact with Julie, his son J.T. and with his great friend Sik Yuen as soon as he can but not knowing for sure if that will ever happen, he chokes up but this time in total grief.

Settling his spirit down after a few more moments, Tai is finally ready so he makes his way downstairs to head out for his special trip. The security guards greet him at the car and nod, in appreciation of the past evening's events.

As they head to the Canton (Guangzhou) airport, Tai says, "It's none of my business how anyone chooses to live their life but knowing you are working for a man such as Saitonaka, do you have any other options? I'm just honestly curious."

The elder guard says, "Dr. Tai. We respect you, your family and friends but it's not that easy. A Yakuza boss with his power has a lot to say and do, if you get my meaning. It would be a death sentence to everyone I know and he'd save me for last so I could watch it all unfold before he saw to me."

"I do understand that but this war will only rage on and get worse for everyone if you and Saitonaka's other men don't realize that you are in jeopardy as long as he reigns. We have proven we can work together and you've seen those results. What results do you embrace that Saitonaka can provide or that he has created for you? At least with us, you'll never have to look over your shoulder."

The elder guard nods in appreciation of Dr. Tai's explanation and then he says, "My fate was sealed a long time ago when I first joined the Yakuza. It's not a good life overall but for some, it's the only option, even when that option leads to limited and dangerous choices and a short life."

Dr. Tai looks at the elder guard, not with pity but, with a true understanding of his reality and says, "May I know your name?"

Smiling, the elder guard says, "Oso. Oso Wakashi"

Dr. Tai extends his right hand and says, "Mr. Wakashi. You saw me, my family and friends at one of our most solemn moments. '*In the midst of life, we are in death.*' I don't remember who said that, an American Indian Chief I believe but I've remembered that phrase all my life because it rings true. Everyone's path, especially these days, is different. Like my father told me, own your path and with no regrets, live your life as you see it so that when you reflect upon it, you can smile and know you did well."

Oso is speechless. He nods at Dr. Tai and shakes his hand.

"So, where to Dr. Tai?"

"The National Stadium in Beijing Oso, thank you."

"Yes sir. I've never seen it so this will be special for me and Heroshi too."

"The younger guard is Heroshi?"

"Yes sir, just Heroshi. I've never known his last name."

The three take off and head for Beijing International Airport. Four hours later, they arrive at the airport and Oso arranges for a rental car. As they make their way through the busy city streets, Oso and Dr. Tai trade comments regarding the challenging commute.

"You know Oso and Heroshi, I remember visiting Beijing in the early 1970's. My father used to go crazy talking about all of the overcrowding then but just look at it now."

Oso says, "Japan is very similar. Of course, being so much smaller, the overcrowding appears worse. Japan's angst and war ambitions have always centered around land; like everyone else throughout time."

"True. It's always been about one's space and how much you have and want."

Being such a sensitive subject, Dr. Tai quickly changes gears and starts talking about the amazing Chinese National Olympic venues.

"Did either of you watch the Games this past month?"

"Of course. Japan did very well, especially in gymnastics."

Remembering the contentious issues surrounding the men and women's team events and the controversial scoring, Dr. Tai again changes the subject.

"My father and I watched the opening ceremonies alone but we talked about what we saw on the phone."

Having been briefed by Boss Saitonaka before they left, Heroshi asks, "didn't' you lose everything including your modular cell phone in the house fire years back Dr. Tai?"

Sensing a setup with his inquisition, Dr. Tai quickly says, "Yes, that's true but I developed a custom phone using my former radio transmitter and some chemicals I developed to help transmit a signal that he was able to pick up on."

"Oh, and where was that?"

"Where was what?"

"Where did your father pick up your signal?"

Offended by his determination, Oso says, "Heroshi! That's enough from you!"

As interested as Oso might be, Heroshi has quickly forgotten about Dr. Tai's and his friend's hospitality from the day before. With Dr. Tai still well under Boss Saitonaka's command and control, Oso sees no need to dig for such trivial information; what's done is done.

The group arrives at the Beijing National Stadium and it's a thousand times more spectacular in person than it was on television. The complex is huge and so perfectly designed, it takes their breath away. The weaving of the massive brushed steel beams that create the stadium's Bird's Nest is unlike any of man's creations. It's a modern-day Wonder of the World. The men approach the main gate and Dr. Tai carefully and cautiously describes his visit to the security guard.

"Good Morning! My name is Dr. Tai Huang. I'm a friend of the Association, here to tour the Stadium."

The security guard checks his visitor's list and doesn't find Dr. Tai's name. He says, "What level Dr. Huang?"

"Yes. T-gold from Y-red."

The guard looks down at his list again and signals the gate control guard to open the doors. Then the security guard addresses the group.

"Gentleman, I'll escort Dr. Huang and we'll be back shortly. Please remain here and have some bottled water and almond cookies."

Oso and Heroshi remain standing just inside the main entrance gate while the security guard escorts Dr. Tai to a set of elevators.

Once they are clear of the others, Dr. Tai says, "Dan See, thank you for all this!"

"My pleasure Dr. Tai! Yuen has told me a lot about you and your father, Mr. Huang. Please, let me say that I am so sorry to hear of his passing."

"Thank you! I think the worst part was repeating to everyone that I had to contact, the fact that he had passed away."

"Such a great man; he's with us now to do this special thing in his and in your mother's and younger brother's honor."

"Yes! Thank you for this! It means a lot!"

Having reached the highest floor, Dr. Tai takes a two inch diameter coin out of his pocket. The two-tone gold and silver coin has a Chinese dragon on one side and the Chinese character for 'Huang' on the other. On the dragon side, there is a small but powerful magnet attached.

The two walk down a short hallway and Dan See opens a special access door in the ceiling. He then quickly motions to Dr. Tai to climb up into the top structures of the National Stadium.

"When you get clear, just place it wherever you'd like and get back down here. This isn't exactly allowed you know."

Tai gets clear and finds the perfect place for his tribute coin; right in the corner of two beams that meet at an acute angle. He taps the coin three times and leaves it.

As they walk back to the elevator, Dan See says, "It was an honor to know your father and I'm glad I could arrange this for you."

"Thank you and please thank your wife Nan as well. We received the beautiful arrangement she sent. Please hug her for me from us all."

"I will. Take care Dr. Tai!"

Tai nods and shakes Dan See's hand. As Tai approaches the entrance gate, as much as Heroshi inappropriately wants to ask, Oso has already told him to keep his questions and curiosities to himself. It's simply not for either one of them to know how or what exactly Dr. Tai arranged. The threesome heads back to Beijing International Airport and then on to Amami Oshima Island, Japan in the East China Sea.

CHAPTER TWENTY-THREE

SEPTEMBER 14, 2008 – YOKOHAMA, JAPAN

MISA returns from a lengthy trip visiting with her daughter Julie in Tokyo and Beijing. Julie has a few more details to wrap up in Beijing so she stayed behind as her mother travelled back to Yokohama. Hey Sun calls her from his downtown offices.

"Miss Misa?"

Playfully, Misa responds, "Yes sir?"

"Good trip?"

"Okay."

"Just okay? And how's my brilliant Julie?"

"Our Julie is great. She had to stay behind to finish some research projects that she's signing off on for the school and to speak with the Director about something."

Hey Sun knows exactly what the paperwork is for; it's to have Julie sign off on all of hers and J.T.'s former work to ensure any and all patent rights revert immediately to himself and the dummy corporation he setup; just like how he manipulated Tai, Yuen and Misa out of their patents back in 1986. Twenty-two years later, some things never change.

"So why just okay?"

"Oh shit, I don't want to get into all of that right now."

"At dinner then?"

Frustrated, Misa says, "I wouldn't want to ruin our dinner with this!"

Hey Sun thinks to himself, "Wow, she's really pissed off at something."

He's intrigued so he baits her a little more.

"Sounds serious; should I leave early so we can talk?"

Immediately, Misa says, "That would be nice."

"Okay. I'll be there very soon."

Playfully, Misa says, "Okay sir."

After a very long day and a half, Izu finally reaches Boss Saitonaka's downtown offices. Saitonaka told him to meet him there instead of his palatial apartment complex. Izu secures Sika's body in a fireman's carry position over his left shoulder and looks up at the security camera at the front door. Boss Saitonaka sees him, draws on his Cuban cigar and buzzes him in. His eyes narrow as he walks to the front entrance of his office to open the door for Izu. Izu gets off the elevator and walks in the office. He places Sika's body in a chair at the front reception area and stands behind him. Boss Saitonaka paces the reception area, staring at Sika and then at Izu.

After a very uncomfortable and unnerving few minutes of pacing and staring, Boss Saitonaka finally says, "You shot him?"

"No sir. He shot himself. After what happened, he thought it best sir."

"Is that so? He knew I'd have his head, so he shot himself to avoid the issue?"

"Sir."

"Hmm. Fuck-head coward! Couldn't face his mistake or couldn't face me?"

"Sir!"

Boss Saitonaka punches Sika's bloody head from right to left and shouts, "God damn fool!"

He straightens his suit jacket and wipes Sika's blood off his fist and back onto Sika's shoulder.

"And my son J.T.; his body?"

"No sir."

Boss Saitonaka steps back and starts pacing the reception floor again but faster. He strangles his white snake-headed cane sword and then jumbles it around in his right hand. Izu stares straight ahead, knowing that if his eyes follow Boss Saitonaka around the floor for even a moment, it'll cost him his head.

After thirty minutes, Izu's feet are burning. His back is about to give out on him and his headache is getting worse by the moment.

Finally, Saitonaka says, "Sit Izu?"

Carefully, Izu sits across from Sika.

"No. Please, join me in my office."

Izu stands back up and follows Boss Saitonaka to his offices past the open reception area.

Just before he can sit, in a flash, Saitonaka draws his sword and stops an inch away from Izu's neck.

"He shot himself? You didn't shoot him?"

"Sir!" Izu wants to piss his pants but he strains to hold it in, thinking Boss Saitonaka would take it as weakness, and Izu would be right.

Saitonaka withdrawals and says, "Please. Sit."

In that moment, Izu's heart rate jumped from very rapid to practically out of his chest. He glances over at the small bar and Saitonaka sees this and waves him through. Izu gets back up and fixes himself a drink. He fixes Saitonaka a drink, neat and walks back to his seat. He places Saitonaka's drink in front of him and sits back down.

"Tell me Izu, did you see Kim fall overboard or was she already gone?"

"Already gone sir."

Boss Saitonaka smiles and finally takes another puff on his cigar. A long ash falls right into his drink. Izu gets ready to stand up so he can fix him a new drink but Saitonaka waves his left hand down at him so he sits back down.

Then Izu remembers something.

He says, "There was only her blood left in the boat sir. That's when I returned to port. Another boat followed me for a while but then he broke away."

Saitonaka rears back in his executive leather chair and laughs deeply. He puffs several times on his cigar and it even appears to Izu that his feet left the ground for a moment in delight. Boss Saitonaka grabs his drink and downs it. He holds it up and Izu immediately stands and goes to the bar to pour another drink for him.

"You'll standby for me?"

"Yes sir; whatever you need."

"Good Izu! Thank you. Take care of Sika for us, the God damn fool and I'll be in touch shortly."

"Yes sir."

Boss Saitonaka nods and quickly turns his attention back to his desk papers and computer screens. Izu leaves and heads back to Boss Saitonaka's compound on his own. A moment later, Hey Sun anxiously makes his way out of his office and into his car. He lights up another Cuban and smiles deviously as he steers his custom silver Mercedes 300XL down the road.

Meanwhile, Misa paces in Hey Sun's bedroom awaiting his arrival. She fidgets around with various items, returning to them over and over like an expectant mother awaiting pregnancy test strip results. Hey Sun enters his upstairs compound and Misa runs into his arms like a newlywed wife.

She starts crying and Hey Sun holds her briefly and then steps away and asks, "Misa. What is wrong? Are you okay? Is it Julie?"

Misa starts saying, "Its Julie…"

Furious, Hey Sun walks away and into his adjoining office. He calls downstairs to Izu.

"Izu!"

"Yes sir. Right away."

A few moments later, Izu knocks on the door.

"My daughter, get her from the Beijing School and bring her home right now!"

"Yes sir!" As Izu begins stepping away, Misa says, "No. She's fine. That's not it."

Izu steps outside the entrance and closes the door.

Hey Sun says, "But you said it was Julie."

Misa sits down and motions to Hey Sun to join her on the bed.

She wipes her tears away and says, "No. I was telling Julie about some old times and I remembered a terrible time that just hit me. I guess I put it out of my mind but as we talked, I remembered being furious at Kim for something and then it all came back in a flash."

"Go on." Hey Sun offers.

Misa sighs and says, "Oh God! We were all together working late on a project when Yuen pulled out a bottle of plum wine. We had pulled all-night study sessions before but this was the first time in the summer. It had been very warm all day and that evening, it hadn't cooled down. Both Yuen and I were sitting together and Tai and Kim were across from us. Yuen was closest to Kim and I was closest to Tai on the other side of the floor. Research papers were in piles all over the floor as we continued working on our part of the project. We decided to enter the paper as a group and accept the split credit. As soon as Yuen pulled out that fucking plum wine, I knew things were going to get awkward. I should have said something or as I remember now, I should have just got up and left the damn room!"

Growing anxious, Hey Sun blurts out, "What? What happened next?"

"Shit! I don't want to talk about this anymore!"

Misa stands up from the corner of the bed and starts walking away. Hey Sun is practically drooling for more information.

"Misa! Come on! If you talk it out like you did before about Julie, you'll feel better! I always feel better when I talk things out!"

Misa sits back down on the bed and says, "Okay, but I know how much you like Kim. After you hear this, you might not like her so much."

Hey Sun shakes his head and says "Go ahead; get it out."

"Okay. We're in Tai and Yuen's room. It's late and we've been working hard on our papers when Yuen pulls out the plum wine. He takes a big drink and then passes it to Kim. She takes a big drink and passes it to Tai. He just passes it over to me so I take a big drink. After a couple more rounds, it's gone and the three of us are pretty drunk but Tai is completely sober."

Hey Sun repositions himself on the bed; he knows the nasty stuff is coming.

Misa continues, "Suddenly Kim takes off her shirt and Yuen does the same so I do as well. Tai ignores us. Then after another moment, Kim stands up and drops her shorts down and again, Yuen does the same. This makes me really uncomfortable but I go ahead, stand and drop my skirt as well. Tai does nothing. I notice Kim and Yuen staring each other up and down."

Hey Sun says, "And then?" He hangs on Misa's every word like a pubescent little school boy.

"So there we are, the three of us sitting in our underwear and bra's with Tai fully clothed. Kim leans over to her left and says something to Yuen. A moment later he pulls out his dick. Then Kim leans over to her right and starts kissing Tai. With Yuen exposed, I figured I'd better do something so I start to move over to him to grab him but before I can, Kim pushes my hand away from Yuen's erection and she starts stroking him as she continues kissing Tai. Tai's not saying anything and isn't even bothered by the fact that his girlfriend is jerking off his best friend right in front of everyone."

Hey Sun is really starting to get aroused. He repositions himself again and takes off his dress jacket.

"This goes on for several minutes so I start to give Yuen a kiss but he avoids me by sliding forward towards Kim and then leaning back and lying down on his back so Kim can reach him better. He's getting off and Kim is getting him off and at that point they are both ignoring Tai and me. Well, just me because this whole time, Kim is still occasionally sucking on Tai's tongue. So this ménage a trios of sorts that should be a foursome goes on for several more minutes until Yuen comes. Then he just gets up and goes into the bathroom. Kim stops kissing Tai and they return to their research like nothing ever happened."

Hey Sun takes off his shirt and pants and sits back down in the middle of the bed.

"Shit! So there I am sitting on the floor half naked, a little wet and drunk and I got absolutely nothing! What the fuck is that? That fucking bitch just jerked off my boyfriend right in front of me and her boyfriend and no one even touched me! Not even a kiss God damn it! Then Tai gets up and walks into the kitchen so I leaned over and asked Kim, 'what the fuck was that?' She slaps me and says, 'you should have jumped in and did something! Your loss bitch!'

"Speechless, I got up, got dressed and went back to my room. I sat there the rest of the night drunk and alone wondering what the fuck just happened and why. Maybe it was just a moment thing but even then, what a fucked up thing to just suddenly do in front of each other, right? No one ever spoke about it again. Then a couple weeks ago when Kim and I were in Tokyo together, she kept saying we should get some plum wine and that turned my memory back on about that time."

Hey Sun leans back on the bed and Misa starts masturbating him.

He climaxes quickly and she says, "Thanks for hearing me out."

Hey Sun says, "No, thank you dear!"

He walks into the bathroom to clean up and returns to the bedroom after a moment.

"I have to tell you something Misa."

Looking frozen and stunned, stuck back in the past still mentally, Misa casually says, "Yeah, what is it?"

"Kim is gone."

Again, casually, Misa asks, "What?"

"Kim's gone."

"Oh, where did she go, to see J.T.?"

"She's dead."

Now Misa is frozen with fear. She can't believe what Hey Sun just said. She looks over to him and starts crying. Her heart starts pounding like crazy and she starts to breathe heavily.

"Dead? What? How?"

"She left a note."

Hey Sun hands Misa the tri-folded piece of paper and partially coherent, she reads it aloud;

> Dear Misa:
>
> I can't live this lie anymore. My life is not my own and it hasn't been since 1986. My death can be mine though, so it will be.
>
> Tai and Yuen stole our work. Hey Sun told me and showed me proof. This betrayal breaks my heart and from people I used to love so dearly, I don't want to think about them anymore. It hurts too much.
>
> Sika helped me as he has done all these years. My affair with him led to J.T. Please take care of J.T. for me now and forgive me if you can.
>
> K

Misa continues to cry, less and less, and then she crumbles up the letter and throws it at the wall.

She yells, "Coward! Weak woman! She leaves me! She leaves her son and her lover over what, the past?"

Hey Sun sits up and just listens to Misa's ranting.

"I'll bet Sika has more guts than this bitch! J.T. must be so disappointed with his mother! Does he know or should I call him?"

Hey Sun waits and then after a moment, he says "J.T.'s gone too."

"Gone, like away or dead?"

"Dead."

"Jesus! How?"

"Sika shot him."

Hey Sun's blunt honesty is disturbing to most but to Misa, even in this moment, it's accepted and appreciated because it's helping her to flush out her true feelings to get to the root of her past and existing anger at Kim and her whole former college experience.

Misa just stands up from the bed and asks, "Sika shot him. Why?"

"Sika confessed to me that J.T. was his child; the night I brought them here, he slept with Kim in her room and never told me until now. He never wanted to tell me but I noticed Kim and Sika looking seductively at each other a few nights ago during dinner so I confronted Kim and she confessed to me that it was true. Then I approached Sika and he confirmed the story."

"So how does J.T. end up getting shot?" Misa asks.

"I guess Sika told J.T. that he was his father instead of me and J.T. lunged and punched him. Then Sika told him that his mother asked him to end her suffering so he did. Probably not the best time to tell your son that you just killed his mother. Furious, J.T. lunged at Sika again. Sika tried to push him away but he refused to back off. Then J.T. got a hold of Sika's side arm and when the two fought over controlling the gun, it went off, shooting J.T. in the chest and through his back. He died instantly. Distraught, Sika ran outside and into the limousine. After a moment, he shot himself in the head. In fact, Izu is still cleaning the seat."

"I want to see their bodies!"

"I'm sorry dear. After all that, Izu took care of everything and disposed of their bodies."

"So you have no evidence to back this all up?"

"I guess if you really want, you can see Izu as he finishes cleaning out the limousine."

Without shedding a tear for J.T., Sika, or the whole matter, Misa defiantly walks downstairs, out of Hey Sun's bedroom suite and outside to the parking area. Hey Sun follows closely behind her.

She immediately sees Izu washing down the passenger seat and she yells, "Izu! Stop!"

He steps out of the passenger seat and looks at her as she approaches him. She looks Izu up and down and walks past him to look inside the passenger seat of the limousine. In the top left hand corner, nearest the door, she sees a blood stain that extends down eight inches from the high part of the head rest.

Izu steps forward and says, "I'm sorry Miss Misa."

"Sika's?"

"Yes ma'am."

She pauses for a moment and then says "A foolish man to tell his own son of his mother and then of himself; all their lies caught up with them!"

Misa slams the passenger door shut and says, "I want new seats in this thing before I'll ride in it!"

"Yes ma'am."

Izu looks back at Hey Sun and sees his partially-hidden 'thumbs up' signal. Izu walks around to the driver's side, enters, and drives away.

As Misa walks back inside, she grabs Hey Sun's hand and says, "Ready for dinner?"

Surprised with her new resolve, Hey Sun puffs on his illegal stogie and follows her inside.

Like nothing happened, Misa changes the subject and says, "I'd like Julie to visit. She has something to ask you."

"Anything for my Julie, you know that?"

"Anything?"

"Name it!"

"She wants to become a doctor and study in America."

"Of course!"

"Just like that? It'll cost $300,000 to $350,000 US dollars."

"It's done! If that's what she wants, she'll have it!"

Misa hugs Hey Sun and the couple trade quick kisses.

Hey Sun then gets very serious and says, "Misa. I have to tell you something now so listen close."

"My work; I have to go away for some time for my work with the Chinese Government and I'll be away for quite a while."

"How long?"

"Maybe four or five years."

"Four or five years!" Misa's heart begins to race. "What the hell?"

"Let me finish Misa. Julie will be away in America at college, safe. I have to go away where I'll be safe."

"Yeah, and what about me?"

"I've arranged for a new place for you in Sendai; in the North Country."

"Sendai? What am I going to do up there?"

"Whatever you want! Saka will go with you to look out for you so you'll be safe."

"Honestly, I'd rather go look over your interests on Amami Oshima Island."

"Really?"

Boss Saitonaka thinks to himself for a moment and his eyes widen as the idea starts to appeal to him; a spy who is well-familiar with Dr. Tai and especially with Yuen and who can report back to him on their research and experiments in his absence.

"You'd do that for me Misa?"

Hey Sun is really testing Misa's loyalty to him.

She grabs the front of Hey Sun's pants and says, "Of course. After everything, of course! You've been the only upfront and honest person in my life. Besides, it might be good to see Tai and Yuen again after all these years but as far as I'm concerned, we've all moved on with our lives and I still can't get some bad things out of my mind. That's changed everything for me."

Hey Sun nods and says, "Okay, but after the New Year. Saka will go with you. Only report back to me from your home or from a restaurant called the Ding-Ho. Saka will show you. The Chinaman running the place is named, 'Jos', he works for me but only Saka and I know this. Now you know this too."

Misa calls her daughter to tell her the great news.

"Jewel?"

"Mom!"

"Great news. Mr. Sun said yes sweetheart! You're going to Boston College in the States!"

"Oh Mom! That's great! What about you?"

"I'll be fine. You can't know where right now. Remember what we talked about when you were younger?"

"Yes."

"Okay. All of that is about to start up now. It's something I simply have to finish."

"I understand mom."

"And Saka is going with me."

"You'll be okay mom?"

"Sure. I know how to take care of myself and anything else, Saka will destroy! And he's good for a romp once in a while too!"

"Mom! Too much information!"

"Sorry. I had to check if you were really paying attention to me still! You just study hard and become the brilliant doctor I know you'll be and we'll be in touch plenty too. Mr. Sun has already pre-paid for everything so you have absolutely no costs. If anything does come up, just let me know and I'll wire you whatever you need."

"Awesome-sauce Mom!"

"What?"

"Awesome-sauce; I heard it on TV."

"Okay… Just remember what we talked about and everything will be fine. I just have to do this last thing to try to make things right before it's too late. It's just business."

"Fuck mom! You sound like a fucking hit-man or something!"

"Jewel! You know I don't like hearing you swear!"

"Sorry. I meant fucking hit-woman!" Julie covers her mouth laughing.

"Julie!"

"Sorry! I love you! We'll talk soon?"

"Okay then. Yes. We'll talk soon sweetheart. Now, get back to your fucking books and study girl!"

"Mom!"

Mother and daughter stay on the line listening to each other laugh hysterically and then hang up.

Hey Sun calls Misa from his limousine phone.

"Everything okay now?"

"Okay? Yeah, I just spoke with Julie. She's thrilled of course but where are you?"

"I told you; I had to leave. I'm nearing the airport now."

"Where…"

"Like I said Misa; for my work, it is best you don't know. Do your work for me and tell me how things are going once you get settled in. Any real problems, just let Saka know and he'll fix them! And promise me you won't kill Yuen as soon as you see him. What happened between the two of you took place a long time ago so just try to get along and if the time comes, I'll give you my approval to do whatever you want, okay?"

"I promise, for now, but my skin still crawls every time I think back on it. Four to five years? That's a long time. I'll miss you terribly!"

"I know but it's necessary right now. I'll be fine; staying with friends up north that know what this is all about. Okay Miss Misa, we're about to take off. Take care!"

In the background Misa can hear gun fire and then Hey Sun's cell phone cuts out.

A week later, Julie is flown from Beijing University to a top medical college in the Boston area, where she enters their respective advanced medical program three weeks late. Unbeknownst to her, her roommate Jessica is a youthful-looking spy for Boss Saitonaka. It makes no difference what grades Jessica earns or if she even attends classes. Her tuition is also paid in full and at thirty years old, she could care less about her course studies. She spends her time sleeping around with frat guys and sorority girls and drinking; she has an open license to party, so she does.

CHAPTER TWENTY-FOUR

September 14, 2008 – Yokohama, Japan

EISHI contacts his uncle Ric Shigemura and passes his Yakuza reign over to him so he can work to restore order to the Yakuza. Eishi is genuinely grateful to Toma and his Triad brothers for their bold but honest moves and for providing the proof of Boss Saitonaka's betrayals and treachery for him to share with his uncle Ric Shigemura to see for himself.

"Uncle, thank you for coming to see me."

Eishi looks down at the ground as his eldest uncle walks by him. Ric is the youngest of the Shigemura brothers, then Saitonaka, and then Ito.

Ric looks around the captain's deck on Eishi's ship and immediately notices the new control-panel and tracking system.

"Eishi! Nephew! How are you? Are you ready for the upcoming season? I know your uncle Naka usually steps in to help but I'd like to know what I can do for you too. Anything I can't help with, of course, your father will. He's been gone a long while now. Tell him to call me. We have much to discuss."

"Uncle, please sit down."

Ric Shigemura is unusually tall and thin while his older brothers are more filled out. At six-foot two inches tall, everyone in the Shigemura family marvels at Ric's height, quick wit, and genuine intelligence. As the owner of three different legitimate businesses, Ric is extremely busy but he always makes time to visit with his nephew Eishi because Eishi is the only son from the three Shigemura brothers. Ric has two younger daughters and Saitonaka has no children, at least none that the Shigemura's are aware of to date. Ric adores Eishi but not as much as he admires and loves his oldest brother Ito.

Initially, Ito steered away from the trappings of the Yakuza as the Shigemura's grew up. He even took care of the family during World War II. His father was killed at the Battle of Iwo Jima so Ito stepped up to take care of his mother and two younger brothers. On a couple of occasions, Ito would travel over ten miles on foot to secure whatever medicines and food he could to help his mother and brother's fight off sickness. It was a scary time for all of them. Almost everyone they knew was either dead or imprisoned. After the war, like most others, they lived in extreme poverty as Japan slowly began to rebuild Tokyo and all major surrounding cities. Nagasaki and Hiroshima lie in almost total ruin for decades. It wouldn't be until the spring of 1958 until the population would again reach the levels it had before Little Boy was unleashed. With that daily pressure; his family's very existence hanging in the balance, Ito finally joined the Yakuza and did their bidding. Ric only has Eishi to share those stories with because they are much too graphic for his daughters to handle and although Ric acknowledges his older brother Saitonaka, he's never respected how he conducts himself. He knows of stories that would scare even the most dedicated of Yakuza gang members and Bosses.

He knows firsthand that Ito has always been a fair man; a patient man, all things considered and all about business, like America's Charles "Lucky" Luciano, again, all things considered, in their chosen lifestyles. Ito always tries to keep the relative peace so that business can be conducted. Only in the direst of circumstances would Ito approve the killing of any man and even then, he'd call for a vote among all Yakuza leaders to approve such an act.

Whenever Ric sought advice regarding his investments or businesses, he looked forward to speaking with his brother Ito because he knew how proud Ito was of him for staying out of the life of Yakuza and for making his own way; the way Ito knows their father would have liked. It brings great shame to Ito knowing that his father would greatly disapprove of his and his middle son's involvement in the Yakuza. After his death, Ito tried his best but things very quickly spiraled out of control when Emperor Shōwa signed Japan's Terms of Unconditional Surrender to the Allied Forces on the forward deck of the USS Missouri on August 6, 1944.

Many Japanese citizens today are very distraught over their nation's involvement in World War II. Many blame their former Emperor Shōwa and rightfully so but most blame the Reich Fuhrer and his minions. Had it not been for their unquenchable thirst for power and pure greed, the German blitzkrieg would have failed early on and Japan would never have attacked and committed so many atrocities of their own, namely against their own Asian people, the Chinese. The Massacre at Nanking still stands and will always stand as the utmost horrific offense against the Chinese people in their long and rich history. Especially with how strongly his friend Izu feels about this issue, Eishi has made this time to meet with his uncle so he can conclude these delicate and emotional matters with him before Izu returns to discuss some more things with him. Eishi has no idea things are even worse than he currently believes.

"Uncle. A drink first?" Eishi extends his small tray of collector saké cups and a few pieces of sushi.

"A drink? You know I don't drink Eishi-san. Come on, what's wrong?"

Eishi breaks down and says, “It’s my father!”

“What about Ito? What’s wrong?”

“He’s murdered uncle!”

Ric draws his short-sword and drives it through the storage unit next to Eishi’s captain’s chair.

“Murdered! What? How the hell does that happen? No! Not Ito!”

Ric breaks down and falls to his knees. His nephew joins him on the floor and the two grieve together.

Ric repeats, “Not Ito! Not my brother! Not Ito!”

After a few minutes, Ric says, “Who was it Eishi? Who is the walking dead-man who killed my brother Ito; your father. Who was it? Death won't be good enough for him!”

Eishi can hardly catch his breath. He stands back up slowly and sits back in the assistant’s chair, leaving his captain’s chair empty for his uncle.

“Please uncle. Watch this video. It shows who did it and you need to see it for yourself because you wouldn’t believe me if I told you what happened.”

Ric slowly gets back to his feet and staggers into the captain’s chair. He wipes his tears away on his dress shirt and tries to focus in on the video that is beginning.

After ten minutes, Ric says, “Eishi, I know about my brother’s perversions. I don’t need to see this shit!”

Ric’s eyes grow wide as he watches the figure in the tape approach the woman lying on the table. The figure tilts his head up slightly; just enough to identify himself to the camera above him.

Ric stands up and says, “That’s Ito! Are you telling me he had a heart-attack fooling around with this woman?”

“No uncle. Please watch.”

Eishi has watched this footage a dozen times. He turns his head away at the deadly moment.

Ric shouts, “No!” as the blade enters and extends through Ito’s head from back to front. The screen shows the deadly event but you can only see the killer’s right hand in the frame.

Ric falls back down on the floor and Eishi promptly says, “Uncle! Now, watch!”

As Ric gets back to his feet he peers over at the screen again and even through his tears, he can see the man standing behind the deadly implement.

Ric grabs the small video monitor and yells mercilessly at the screen, “Saitonaka! You killed your brother! You killed your father’s first son! You killed your mother’s first son! You’ve killed us all Naka!”

Ric collapses on the floor in total grief. Eishi hands his uncle a glass of water.

Then Ric says, “Where is he? Where is my beloved brother Ito’s body?”

"I don't know uncle. I have to assume uncle Saitonaka still has him."

"He's killed us Eishi. I now have to kill my brother to avenge my oldest brother's murder. I'll never see my parents again because the Shigemura brothers are going to hell! I knew this day could come and now it has. Your uncle Naka has always been jealous of Ito because he knew with Ito in charge; he'd never rise to the top position in Yakuza."

"You don't think the girl made or asked him to do it?"

"No. Naka has had dozens of woman and no one could ever make him kill his own brother. This was all Saitonaka's doing. It's all his drinking and those damn drugs Eishi!"

"Drugs?"

Ashamed, Ric nods. "I'll tell you something you didn't know about your uncles. Ito took Saitonaka to the United States back in 1965. America was a crazy place back then; over-sexed and out-of-control teenagers and young adults ran wild. They experimented with all kinds of drugs and had sex with strangers they came across. Your uncles stayed in America until late 1969 and soaked it all up, becoming addicted to everything but especially to marijuana because it was the easiest and cheapest drug to get and use. It continues to plague the United States today and in many ways, has gotten worse. I fear for their future."

Ric continues, "People in favor of its use think it's harmless and have fought vigorously to make it legal in America and so far, some States are allowing it. But make no mistake Eishi, it is a drug that should be illegal for several main reasons. If you talk to any random twenty people in any prison in America, at least fifteen of them will tell you the primary reason why they are in prison is because of drugs and if you ask them what they think about marijuana, they will tell you it was the gateway drug that elevated their interests in getting 'higher' so it was what caused them to experiment with more powerful drugs that led to their various more serious crimes, including murder and murder for hire in order to secure and maintain their 'high'."

"It is absolutely NOT like alcohol, as so many users would have people believe. We know this because we've drank saké all our lives and that sedative is nothing like the sedative in marijuana (THC). For one, alcohol makes you full and after a while, it makes you throw up. Overuse of marijuana doesn't. It makes most people hungry or they simply pass out because they become so inebriated from the THC. The other big issue with marijuana is simply the product itself and the crimes of opportunity that it presents."

"When is the last time anyone robbed a liquor store Eishi?"

"Actually, it happens quite often uncle."

"Yes, that's true. And what do they steal?"

"Money."

"Exactly! Money; not the liquor. Now, ask yourself why?"

"Because liquor stores bring in a lot of money for the alcohol they sell uncle."

"Yes but there is another reason why they don't steal the liquor itself."

"I don't know uncle."

"When was the last time you saw some asshole rob a liquor store and run away carrying a couple cases of Kirin under one arm and a barrel of plum wine under the other? Right? Alcohol is too fucking heavy to steal but is marijuana?"

"You're right uncle! Marijuana is very light weight and very easy to carry, in just about anything!"

"Exactly Eishi! So, it creates many more crimes of opportunity because it's a one-stop shopping place for thieves. They can grab all the cash and the marijuana from each place and just move on to the next place and if someone gets in their way, they kill them instead of just running away because again, no thief is going to risk his ass trying to drag away a couple cases of America's favorite Wild Turkey or whatever the fuck they like to drink!"

"How do you know all this uncle?"

"Because your uncle Naka and I got caught trying to steal drugs and alcohol just before America's famous or infamous Woodstock Music Festival in Portland Oregon. We spent the next three months in jail instead of going to the concerts and every day when I look back on that, I'm grateful because our getting arrested saved our lives. It definitely saved your uncle Naka's life because he could drink and do more drugs than me and when he was drunk, as you see, he sometimes does nasty and horrible things! And just like so many people in America, our troubles in life all began soon after we started smoking marijuana!"

"Why do you think I've avoided getting involved in your uncle's Yakuza activities?"

"Because of all the crime?"

"Crime is the effect. The cause is drug use. It simply escalates from there because it's like any addiction; after a while, you want something better; something stronger and you want more of it. It's not like alcohol. Alcohol is addictive but there is the 'throw-up' factor. A lot of people lessen their drinking because they simply get tired of throwing up their guts every time they drink too much and for the criminal element, alcohol is too 'inconvenient' to steal. Just remember our image of some fuck-head running down the street trying to get away after robbing a liquor store. He fumbles down the street trying to hold a case of beer and a barrel of plum wine in his arms, as he also tries to hold up his fucking over-sized sweatpants! I have to be honest; I'd really like to see that myself!"

"It's simply not worth the risk like stealing drugs is. You smoke marijuana for a while, pretty soon, you want something stronger and more of it. Then you mix them. Before you know it, you're addicted to several drugs. Then comes heroin, meth, crack, and you're hurting people you can't even remember to get it. And where did the money come from to afford the more expensive drugs? Easy, since marijuana is so much easier to steal and more widely available now, thanks to all the efforts of all the fuck-head people in support of it, more people are stealing it and all the cash is just sitting there along with the product in nicely labelled little baggies and glass jars! So, they have the money and the weapons to buy the more expensive drugs to back-up their insidious behavior. And, the more they steal, the better they think they are getting at their 'craft' so their confidence in stealing grows and their appetite for other crimes grows as well. It's a vicious cycle. What do you suppose happens when it's your 'job' to conduct such business in the first place, like your uncles? You think you can get away with it all, always! In a nutshell, that's your uncle Naka."

Eishi stands up in front of his uncle and bows. "I'm so sorry uncle. What will you do now about uncle Saitonaka?"

"There's only one thing to do but first, I must ask your permission Eishi."

Shocked, Eishi immediately says, "My permission? You don't need anything from me!"

"I do nephew. Ito was your father and your father was the head of all Yakuza in Japan. No matter who killed him, that person must pay the ultimate price. It's just a thousand times sadder for us that the person responsible was your father's brother. Ito's men need to hear your wishes directly because they served him and now they will serve you if you wish. This is how Yakuza operates Eishi."

"I'm sad to say that I do want justice, Yakuza justice, for my father but I don't want to be in Yakuza. I have my fleet to run and my men to lead. We have all the problems we can handle with Australia's Sea Guardians and I have over five million Yen invested this season. People are depending on me uncle."

"Yes. I realize that. You know I have to do something in honor of my oldest brother and I hate that it comes down to having to kill my other brother but Naka has left me no other choice."

"What if I pass my wishes on to you uncle?"

"You can do that but that would make me head of all Yakuza in place of my brother Ito and I know Saitonaka would immediately come after me as well. He's clearly capable of killing anyone; we just saw that so you are in danger as well. We must be very careful."

"Accept my wishes for you to avenge my father's death, uncle?"

"Yes nephew. I accept. We need to meet with Ito's top people and inform them of this as well. Then we must form a careful plan. Your uncle Naka may be crazy but he's crazy-smart too. If he sees anything or any one of us coming at him before we are truly prepared, he'll adapt and change his strategy to take us down."

"Uncle?"

"What Eishi?"

"Remember my friend Izu?"

"Of course; uncle Naka's new right-hand man, right?"

"Not exactly. We met and talked earlier. He's supposed to be here soon to tell me something else he wanted to say earlier. Uncle; Izu gave me the video of uncle Saitonaka killing my father."

Shocked at the risk he took, Ric says "So, how did he get this video?"

"From the Triads, uncle."

"Shit! Not possible Eishi! Why in hell would the Triads get this and give it to us?"

"It was Toma, uncle. Toma called my friend Izu and told him that he had something we had to see for ourselves. He said it was worth other lives so Izu arranged it. They put on a fire-fight at sea with speed boats and Izu fled the area after the rescue. Then he told uncle Saitonaka the woman, Kim Tse drowned. Sika also joined Toma's efforts and told uncle Saitonaka that he had to shoot his son, J.T. and that he fell into the water and was irretrievable."

"So where are these two now?"

"I'm not sure but I know they are siding with Toma. Uncle Saitonaka has kept Miss Kim prisoner for over half her life and for all of J.T.'s life. She has friends that have also been held captive. One of them is Miss Misa uncle."

"Are the other two, Sik Yuen Zhang and Tai Huang?"

"Yes. You know them uncle?"

"Yes! Your uncle Naka told me a little about them. They were all top Chinese chemistry and marine biology students. He kidnapped Miss Kim and lied to her about many things so she'd stay with him. He sent her friends Yuen and Tai away but he kept Miss Misa for his own perversions. I believe she's still with him after all this time. God damn it Naka! He told me and said it so casually, I should have known something was wrong. This is big fucking trouble Eishi, big trouble!"

"And uncle Saitonaka?"

"Shit! He's everywhere and nowhere nephew! He has so many hiding places; I wouldn't even know where to start looking! Being number two man Yakuza, he always made sure he went bigger and bolder than your father because he just had to make that statement. Your father ruled Yakuza as a relatively fair and reasonable man, all things considered. You uncle was the opposite. He ruled with fear and blood! Fuck! This is such big trouble Eishi! I just want your father's body so we can give him peace and then I'll deal with your uncle Naka myself!"

One of Eishi's men calls up to the captain's quarters.

"Eishi sir; it's Izu."

Eishi tells him to allow Izu to board the vessel.

Izu arrives at the entrance of the Captain's quarters and the three men bow. Izu is surprised to see Ric Shigemura there. He had hoped to speak with Eishi privately.

Ric says, "Izu, please sit."

Izu immediately sits down.

Ric continues, "I don't know what game you are playing but I know it's the most dangerous kind and with the most dangerous people. Before you say anything to me, let me just say that I am indebted to you for risking your life in retrieving and giving your recording of my brother's death to my nephew Eishi. Again, thank you for that."

Izu nods and remains silent. He knows Ric Shigemura is not Yakuza but whether Ric knows it or not or whether he likes it or not, he is Yakuza because for decades, his older brother Ito protected him and setup various business deals that directly resulted in everything that Ric has today.

"Eishi has passed his leadership of my brother's now former Yakuza family on to me and I'm glad you are here to personally witness this transition. Obviously, you know who is responsible for my brother's death so all I need to know from you is this one thing; will you update my brother Saitonaka of this event or do right by my oldest brother and your former Yakuza top Boss and help us to settle affairs on our terms? You have already helped the Triads with their cause so I'm asking you now if you'll help us with ours."

Izu stands up and bows to Ric and then to Eishi.

"I made my decision to help you as soon as I accepted Toma's call. I helped him arrange the fire-fight boat scene just north of Okinawa and I knew as I drove back to port, my resulting lies to Boss Saitonaka may cost me my head at any moment. My friend Sika took his own life after he decided to help Kim's son J.T. I foresee other possibilities for my life. I don't ask for your protection but I would ask for your patience in waiting to see what Dr. Tai and Sik Yuen may have planned for Boss Saitonaka. This started with them and I think we owe them that respect and an opportunity."

Ric shakes Izu's hand and motions for him to sit back down.

"You came here to speak with Eishi about something else and it sounded serious. Will you tell him now in front of me as well?"

"Of course Mr. Shigemura."

"Thank you Izu."

Eishi interrupts briefly and says, "Izu. Call my uncle Ric, Boss Ricmasa from now on."

Izu bows and exclaims, "Yes. Boss Ricmasa!"

"I had other sad news but I couldn't bear to share it earlier; adding it on top of your extreme sorrow over your father, Boss Ito's passing. Again, I am so sorry. Your uncle and my boss, Boss Saitonaka has informed me that at the mid-point of this coming Misha Katana season, if you do not meet or exceed your quota for that time period, he has ordered your death."

Izu immediately bows and steps back, taking his seat again.

Eishi immediately looks over at his uncle Ric. Ric lowers his head in shame over his brother's continued treachery.

This 'hit' on Eishi; it's real?" Ric asks.

"Yes sir. I'm sorry. He told me in person a few days ago."

"Crazy bastard! My brother Naka has truly lost all his senses and over what? His obsessions over this Chinese team of chemists? I must learn what they worked on that my brother demands so!"

"Boss Ricmasa. There is more trouble. Saitonaka has also placed a price on the head of the Sea Guardian's captain, Australia's famous Captain Darren Hall."

"I know of Captain Hall. He's a true pioneer in both heart and spirit. He can help us when the time comes. Until then, I'll have some of Ito's men look after him."

Eishi interrupts saying, "But uncle; Captain Hall is all about stopping my efforts directly. How can we work together and still accomplish our separate goals?"

Ric counters with, "Just prepare and set out to sea for your job as usual. We must keep up all appearances because again, if your uncle Naka suspects anything different, I fear he will start chopping heads until he gets the answer he wants or until there is simply no one else opposing him, myself included. He must always think he's running things until we can seize a moment or two away from him to regain power for ourselves. If he knew part of the end-result was that we were getting help from and giving help to Chinese people, he'd just start killing everyone around him to start over from scratch!"

"He's that far gone?"

"Yes Eishi. That far and one true positive note from all of this when it's over; it's time for Japan and China to start working together because we have been at each other's collective throats for centuries. I'm sick of it! I have many tremendous Chinese business partners and friends! It's critical that we don't end up like so many nations in the Middle East who know nothing but war, oppression, and death."

Izu smiles because Boss Ricmasa's words could not have been said any better.

"Eishi?"

"Yes uncle?"

"Get back in touch with Toma so I can speak with and maybe meet Tai and Sik Yuen. I have a lot of catching up to do before your uncle Naka takes his next step. Remember; keep up all appearances no matter what. Now dinner, eh?"

CHAPTER TWENTY-FIVE

SEPTEMBER 15, 2008 5 P.M. – AMAMI OSHIMA ISLAND, JAPAN

AFTER Dr. Tai's return, he shakes Oso Wakashi's hand but Heroshi just nods over at him. The two security guards promptly leave Dr. Tai's company and make their return to Yokohama to report their trip to Boss Saitonaka.

As soon as Dr. Tai enters his rebuilt residence, he collapses.

Yuen runs out from his back bedroom and yells, "Tai! What's wrong?"

Tai catches his breath, sits upright and says, "Long and difficult trip. I guess it all just caught up with me."

"Let me get you some Myst1 and an aspirin."

Yuen leaves for a moment and gets the small bottle of elixir from the kitchen. He's made a new batch of the formula as a part of the current agreement with Boss Saitonaka to resupply Yuen and Tai's fellow villagers back in Canton. He's also created a small clear edible enclosure for each aspirin so it can easily be attached to the top of each bottle cap.

Tai opens the bottle and takes a drink; the elixir is exhilarating and quickly helps to revive all of his senses. Then he picks the aspirin off the bottle cap and swallows it.

"Xie-xie!"

"Unpack later. Come over here and sit down on the sofa for a minute so you can recover. I caught dinner already and there's someone I want you to meet."

"Carmela?"

Yuen smiles. "Yes. How did you know?"

"I saw the look in your eyes before I left. You sneaky devil! She's a nice lady."

"I think so too. We started talking more after you left and I told her about things."

"What? You trust her that much to challenge everything we've worked so hard for?"

"Tai, wait. I'm sorry but yes I trust her that much. She's Triad too. My family has known her since we were kids. She lives on Okinawa, just south of Uruma and she visits Amami to get away from things. And, she loves sharks and cooking! She can out-cook me right out of the kitchen!"

"So, she's coming over for dinner tonight?"

"Yes, but not for a while. Enough time for you to tell me about your trip."

Yuen's eyes tear up and then he asks, "Your father?"

"On the hill right above his home. He rests now forever."

Tai rears back in the sofa and sighs deeply. Then, he sits forward and drops his head into his hands; crying uncontrollably. Yuen stands up and tries to console his friend as he cries harder and harder.

"I'll never recover from my father's passing; all that time away from him is messing me up! We've got to start making things right with Saitonaka!"

Yuen clears his eyes and says, "Whatever you want; tell me!"

"I'll tell you all about Saitonaka's men; Oso Wakashi and his little buddy Heroshi but for tomorrow, okay? Tonight is for Carmela!"

Yuen smiles; he smiles whenever he even thinks about Carmela. She is a very strong-willed Chinese woman. She's highly intelligent, entrepreneurial and focused on whatever task she has at hand. Like Yuen, she is well-acquainted with Japanese Yakuza and the manner in which they operate; their deceptions and devious patience to wait out an outcome in their favor or their blatant attacks to simply take what they want, at any cost. The Triads consider themselves more of a reactionary force. Still illegal and operating under the cover of night as far as legitimate businesses in the world go but still, considered a much more deliberate group that serves it's people and others, for a price; like Italy's original *Black Hand*. When there was a little more honor among thieves and the rules were set in stone and followed.

Sensing his remaining slight distress over Carmela's Triad past, Yuen offers, "What is referred to commonly today as a 'gang' is nothing more than what has existed ever since there were enough people in the world to create politics; two people. As soon as we had two unique opinions about a key subject, we had politics. Their 'gang' was created when each 'politician' had a single supporter and there you have it; one faction versus the other arguing over whatever issue was at hand and in those earliest of days, it was likely over which twosome got more food than the other two.

All conflicts between people are nothing more than these same gangs but on much larger scales; the clans of early man like Neanderthals versus Cro-Magnons, fighting against each other for space and resources and then man simply grew smarter, or dumber, depending on your view. We developed weapons in order to destroy more opposing men without sacrificing the same number of our own men; the Mesopotamians, then the Egyptians, Mongols, Chinese, Japanese, Romans, Greeks, Spanish, English, French, Russians, Palestinians, Jewish, Americans, Hitler's Nazis, Vietnamese, Libyans, Iranians, Iraqis, Al Qaida, Mexicans, Central Americans, the Congo, South Africans, North Koreans, and Syrians. It will never stop as long as there are at least two people with varying opinions and each has at least one supporter."

Tai pauses and then sarcastically smiles and says, "Uh, professor; is this intermission because I really have to pee."

Yuen smiles but then darts his eyes down to the ground and snarls at Tai. The two friends are just glad to be back working and living together and sharing their time because the years that have passed were especially difficult on them; each having lost touch with one another and with their loved ones; their soul mates and as they have each now learned, their children. Tai's son and Yuen's daughter are both now twenty-two, about the same age as Tai, Yuen, Kim, and Misa were when they ventured away from their school days and began their lives together as friends and colleagues. They vowed to stay together but Boss Saitonaka ruined all of those plans.

A moment later, Carmela knocks on the door holding a bottle of wine and a basket of pastries she made for dessert. The trio share a great dinner together and Carmela continues to bend Tai's and Yuen's ears about their former research work and Yuen's shark research while he was in exile on Okinawa. That whole time, Yuen was that close to Carmela in Uruma City and he never knew it until they met on Amami Oshima Island a few months back.

The next morning, Kim and J.T. are up two hours earlier than normal; both can't wait to see Tai and Yuen. Kim has been so distracted; she's constantly forgetting details or leaving things behind. J.T. literally follows behind his mother wherever they go to make sure nothing is left behind; like her cell phone, her small contact/phone book or her silk red dragon coin purse. Toma and his men have prepared the small charter plane that will take Toma and two of his men and Kim and J.T. to Amami Oshima Island, Japan. In a little over an hour, Dr. Tai will lays his eyes on his soul-mate for the first time since 1986 and he'll see his son for the first time. Everyone takes their seat and Toma and the pilot check their weapons just in case they run into any trouble from Saitonaka's faction anywhere along the way. The only real threat is right now, as they prepare to take off and once they land and travel the short distance to Dr. Tai's and Yuen's custom built home.

During his post-fire time away from everyone, Tai rebuilt his home and cove deck using positive energy he stored up for when he would see Yuen again. Since they have been back together, the two friends have spent their time talking about practically every memory from their college days, their earlier days before they knew each other and their favorite times with Kim and Misa. The upgrades they have made to their home include tribute areas, in each corner, to their parents and in the other corners, tributes to Kim and J.T. and to Misa and Julie. This morning, Tai and Yuen decide to walk down to the cove's improved deck to test out the small platform Yuen has been building at the mid-point about twelve feet away from the facing edge. He figures this platform might come in handy for future fishing experiments or something. Tai just thinks it looks cool, better than the original one he fashioned, especially with the light Yuen installed so you can use and see it at night. Carmela usually gets up early but with all the wine and great food from last night, she's sleeping in.

A small charter plane roars overhead. Yuen looks up and smiles at it because that's the image he knows that usually brings Carmela to him every other month. He wishes she could stay longer.

As Tai and Yuen walk down to the cove, Tai says, "I'm glad you met Carmela. She's good for you!"

"Thanks. If it's too much, just let me know but I would like to ask her to stay."

Tai immediately says, "That's great! This way she and I can team up and kick your ass at Mah-Jongg night after night!"

Yuen smiles and pats his dear friend on the back in appreciation for making what he thought would be a difficult question and favor to ask, so simple.

As he's done all his life, Tai takes off his shirt and basks in the sun. He's wearing his father's 3D gold dragon necklace and kicking his feet in the cool waters of the cove. Yuen is staring at the platform he built and trying to figure out what else to add to it to finish it off.

Tai suggests, "A darker stain?"

"Yeah, that would be good but then we'd have to stain the rest of the deck."

"You going somewhere?"

Yuen smiles at Tai's creative sarcasm and then he says, "Actually, yes. I forgot my favorite bait. Without that, you might not eat dinner with Carmela and me!"

Tai angles over on one side and kicks water all over Yuen. "Yeah, well, go and get it or you and your girlfriend will never know the secret to Huang's secret Chinese Perch and Rice sauce!"

Soaked, Yuen makes his way back up the slight hill from the deck and is greeted by Carmela at the back door. She sees him dripping and quickly kisses him on the cheek and closes the door.

"Hey!"

"No! You're all wet and I just cleaned the floors!"

"But I live here!"

"True but maybe I should to, to keep you guys in line."

"Fine. Maybe you should."

Shocked, Carmela opens the door. She stands in the doorway and looks to Yuen trying to figure out if he's serious.

He smiles widely and she runs into him and hugs him.

She says, "Yes! I'd love to live here with you and Tai!"

"One condition though."

"What's that?"

"You two can't team up on me at Mah-Jongg!"

Carmela kisses Yuen, slaps his butt and says, "Ha! No promises there my love!"

Tai's fast asleep in the morning sun. He's still recovering from his trip and his mind continues to spin around his father's passing.

Carmela starts fixing lunch and Yuen is in his and now, Carmela's back bedroom changing his shirt and shorts for dry ones. A knock comes to the door.

Carmela shouts out, 'I've got it."

Carmela quickly finishes setting out small lunch plates and drink glasses for five people around the living room table and for three more in the kitchen area and then she runs to answer the door.

She covers her mouth with her right hand index finger extended up and opens the door quietly. The five visitors enter and quietly sit down at the table.

Yuen calls out, "Who is it Mela?"

She doesn't answer; not because she really doesn't like the nickname but for a better reason.

Yuen calls out again, "Mela? Who's at the door?"

No answer.

Finally, Yuen heads out of his back bedroom a little flustered and starts saying, "What the…"

Just then J.T. says, "Hey uncle Yuen!"

Carmela starts crying. Toma is crying. His two men are crying. When Yuen pans to his right and sees Kim sitting on the corner chair, the two burst into tears. Kim runs into Yuen and they hug like grizzly bears.

After a moment, Kim pulls back and wipes the tears off Yuen's face and says, "And you've already met my son, J.T."

The group stands and walks into each other. They hug and hold each other for a few minutes.

Yuen steps away and says, "Oh my God. Tai. He'll be so happy to see the two of you that you might give him a heart-attack! He just got back from his father's village yesterday!"

Kim and Carmela think and Kim suggests something. The group prepares quickly and then Toma and his men walk around the house to initiate their plan.

Yuen pokes Carmela in her ribs and says, "And I thought I was the sneaky one. How did you know about all this?"

Toma called a while back but you were away fishing with Tai so I answered and told him who I was. We worked on their return together. I called a couple Triad friends of mine to occupy Saitonaka's men at the docks so they wouldn't really put on any rescue efforts for Kim once Izu returned.

Toma sees Tai sleeping in the sun. He and his men walk down to the cove deck. Tai's still asleep. He doesn't even feel the vibrations from the wood planks as the men approach. Toma stands over him and bends down.

"Dr. Tai?"

Tai moves a little; picking up on an object blocking the sun.

"Dr. Tai?"

Tai squints and says, "Yeah? What? … Toma?"

Formally, Toma says, "Yes. We just got here and need to update you and Yuen on a few matters so, … please."

"Yes. Of course."

Tai leaves his shirt lying on the deck and walks alongside Toma and his men back up to the house.

Tai enters and sees all the place settings at the table. He figures they are for Toma and his men so he doesn't say anything about it. Yuen and Carmela are standing somewhat nervously in the kitchen area covering their mouths and it looks like Carmela is crying.

"Carmela? You okay over there?"

She clears her throat and quietly says, "Oh yes. I just … ate a hot pepper is all."

Tai pans the room a little more, sensing tension or something. Then he notices a figure in the far corner. A young man turned away from Tai sitting in his favorite chair.

Tai starts to say, "Excuse me? Who are you there?"

Toma and his two men walk over to the young man as if to check on him for Dr. Tai. A moment later, Kim Tse walks right past Tai from out of the hallway bathroom.

She looks back at him and calmly says, "Nice nap honey? … have some tea?"

She smiles casually. The whole room bursts out laugh-crying as Tai falls to his knees. J.T. gets up and runs over to join his father who is now covered in Kim's tears. The couple grabs each other and then J.T. and time stands still for them. Everyone else in the room comes closer together but allows the three their space.

Kim and Tai are dripping with tears as Kim props up J.T. and says, "Our son! James-Tai! Jimmie's grandson and your son my love!"

Tai whispers to them but loud enough that everyone can hear him, "If I'm dreaming, never wake me. I can finally breathe again!"

He hugs Kim and his son and moves them both to stand up. They hold each other as the group closes in on them. Now, it's a giant scrum. Everyone's wearing a smile that will last for days.

As the reunion scrum begins to break up, J.T. looks at his father and notices all the pressure of the hugs have cut his chest; his 3D dragon necklace has embedded slightly into him, breaking the skin.

"Dad! Look! That is awesome!"

Tai cherishes being called 'dad' for the first time by his son. Then Tai and Kim look down at Tai's chest. His blood has traced part of the outline of the imprinted dragon pendant.

Tai proclaims, "You know what I'm going to do? To honor the day, I'm going to get that blood dragon outline tattooed on my chest as soon as we go into town!"

J.T. immediately says, "Me too!"

Kim adds, "Me too!"

"This is so amazing! You two are so amazing! Look at you!" Tai holds Kim's hands and just stares at her obsessively.

"You amazing woman, look at you! I'm so sorry for all this; all the time we lost but I wouldn't trade it for anything now because you're here with me and nothing and no one will ever take you away from me again!"

The look in Tai's eyes absolutely stuns Kim. Not only is he overwhelmingly grateful to see her again, he's obviously not at all concerned with anything that took place in the past. That soothes Kim's heart, mind, and spirit and she now finally breathes a deep sigh of genuine relief.

J.T. can't take his eyes off his father. The two sound alike, just like Tai sounds like his father. Tai gives Kim a big hug and kiss and then steps in front of J.T.

"James-Tai! My God, look at you! My son!"

J.T. smiles as tears roll down his face. He's speechless and just stares at his father.

"I'm so glad you got to meet your grandfather. Whatever the two of you spoke about, I hope you'll take whatever advice he offered because your grandfather was a great man; far wiser and more patient than me. Keep what he told you in your heart and let it guide you. That's my only wisdom for you son!"

"I love you Pop!"

Tai loves being called, 'pop'.

"I love you so much son, I can't stand it!"

Tai and J.T. hug like a father and son who have been together all their lives. All the time apart from each other just melts away.

Then Tai says, "Now what's this shit about you beating my scores in school Counselor?"

Kim and Yuen burst out laughing. Yuen grabs Carmela's hand and brings her closer to the group.

"J.T. This is my girlfriend Carmela."

"Sweetheart, this is Kim and Tai's son, James-Tai."

Carmela and J.T. shake hands and then hug each other.

She whispers to J.T., "I'm so glad I could help you and your mom get back to your dad honey!"

J.T. hugs her again.

Then Tai announces, "To Toma and his men and to Yuen. I can't thank you enough for bringing us back together. So much time has been taken from us all so let's not waste any more of it!"

Just like that, everyone grabs only what they need and piles into the two cars just in front of Yuen and Tai's home. In their minds, Yuen and Tai immediately start planning the expansions they'll need to accommodate Carmela, Kim and J.T. With that exact thought in each of their minds, they crisscross in front of the cars and pat each other on the back. Toma sees this exchange and smiles as he gets into the driver's seat of Tai's car but running in the back of his mind is the scary fact that if Boss Saitonaka ever learns that Kim and J.T. are alive, heads will literally begin to roll; right off the end of his white snake-head cane's blade.

At forty-eight, Kim looks stunning. She's stayed in great health and is as sharp as ever. Her long black hair still styles as it did before and she still smells of light strawberries.

J.T. takes after his mother with his great intelligence, patience and demeanor but physically, he takes after his father with his sleek and muscular build. He's a little taller than his father and a little heavier at this age than his father was; heavier being one hundred and sixty-five pounds compared to Tai's one hundred and fifty pounds at that time. Today, Tai and his son are like clones with one being a little past middle age and the other being a young man. They sound alike and J.T. is already acting like his father in many ways. This fact hasn't been missed by Kim who marvels at the two men.

Kim sits in the back seat between Tai and J.T. The threesome holds hands as Toma drives them to Tong's restaurant in town; a Triad-owned property so Toma and his men are immediately at ease. Yuen and Carmela sit in the back seat of their car driven by one of Toma's men while his other man sits shotgun. Yuen has something special to ask Carmela but he doesn't want to step on the group's reunion; it can wait.

The small caravan arrives at Tong's and everyone makes their way inside the ocean-front restaurant and bar. Toma and his men make their way to a separate table and Kim immediately grabs Toma by his right arm and leads him over to a mix of tables that Tai and J.T. are re-assembling into one giant horse-shoe shaped table. The waitress Mary greets everyone and kisses Toma on his cheek.

She says "And how's my crazy son?"

Shocked, everyone smiles and moves to pat Toma on his back, including his two men. Toma has moved his mother around from place to place, protecting her from a past gang feud between rival factions of the Triads. Toma's father Kona was killed during one of those uprisings. Mary used to work in Uruma until things started to get out of hand so Toma moved her to Amami Oshima Island for a new and much safer start. Mary is a relentlessly hard working woman. Fiercely independent, the sixty-eight year old embraces each day with a smile.

She likes staying busy and loves hounding her son about when she might finally become a grandmother. In Toma's line of work of constant danger, it's not easy for him to meet a woman he can trust with his life but he continues to try. Mary understands but she still enjoys ribbing her son about his family plans when she sees him.

Mary announces to the group, "Tsingtao all around or Buddha?"

Yuen claims, "Yomama! Bring both every ten minutes until everyone passes out!"

Everyone laughs and Mary says, "I'm not your Yomama! I'm his Yomama!"

As she points at Toma.

"And, you still owe me $200 from Uruma Sik Yuen!"

Yuen bends over laughing and walks over to Mary. He kisses her on her cheek and hands her his debt, plus an extra fifty note for being late.

Mary says, "See! Good boy! And a new girlfriend I see. Soon they'll have a kid. See Toma?"

Toma wishes he could disappear as everyone looks over at him and smiles.

J.T. nudges his mother and asks, "Yomama?"

Kim shrugs her shoulders.

Toma overhears J.T.'s curiosity and says, "It comes from back when I was younger, I'd call out to my mom, 'Yo! Mama!' so soon after, 'Yomama' stuck after that.

J.T. says, "Cool!"

Toma says, "Yomama?"

"Son?"

"Tong in the kitchen?"

"Always."

"I'll go say hi. Everyone, please excuse me. Tai, Yuen… come with me?"

Tai and Yuen excuse themselves and accompany Toma into the kitchen.

In the kitchen, three large woks are crackling and sizzling with all kinds of amazing smelling entrees including Sweet and Sour chicken, pan-fried shrimp and Chinese Perch, and in the third wok, half the deep concave pan has white rice and the other half is full of various vegetables jumping about. Standing in complete command of all woks, managing everything in his classic apron is Tong. Tong turns around as the three men approach and waves at them.

Toma says, "Dr. Tai. Yuen. This is Andy Tong."

The men exchange handshakes as Tai and Yuen embrace the aromas being created and sent into the air above and all around the kitchen.

"Like my father." Tai offers.

Yuen nods.

In broken but decent English, Andy offers, "I was very sorry to hear of your father passing."

He bows at Tai.

"Thank you Andy." Tai bows back.

"Hey, get back to your group. Your food's almost ready."

Andy smiles and Tai and Yuen make their way back to the horse-shoe table. Toma stays behind to talk to Andy.

"They are back together. Dr. Tai, Miss Kim and their son J.T., Sik Yuen and Miss Carmela."

Toma reaches into the back of his shirt and hands over his 9mm handgun to Andy. Andy nods.

The early evening sets in and the amazing food just keeps coming. Andy invites Kim and J.T. back into the kitchen to watch how everything comes together. Carmela joins them and the three watch in wonderment at how quickly and automatically Andy prepares and mixes everything together. He begins fixing his specialty; Ginger Sesame Fish with snow peas and water chestnuts.

J.T. says, "I could eat that every day!"

He watches intently so he can learn how to make it for everyone else back at home. Andy notices J.T. watching his every move so when he gets to the crucial sauce mixing part, he looks over at J.T. to make sure he's picking that up.

The whole restaurant smells incredible. Other patrons begin coming in and immediately smile at the fantastic scents that fill the air. Then Dr. Tai decides it's time for a bit of a show. He nods over at Yuen and the two walk over to the off-center bar. Just then Kim, J.T. and Carmela come out of the kitchen and stand in front of the bar across from Tai and Yuen. The rest of the restaurant patron's crowd in front of the bar as well; they've seen this show before but they are always grateful to see it again.

From one end of the bar, Yuen counts to the crowd aloud, "Seven, eight, and nine."

Tai nods and starts lining up Martini glasses in a long row on the top of the bar at the opposite end of Yuen. Andy peeks out from the kitchen and smiles. He mixes up the last of the entrees from his woks and spoons them out on several plates on a larger serving tray.

A moment later, from inside the kitchen, Andy orders, "Go!"

Tai and Yuen start tossing liquor bottles across at each other. As they catch each flying bottle, they quickly splash the various liquors into the Martini glasses. Tai and Yuen flip them back to each other once they have used them and then they slide the bottles to the far end of their section of the bar. It's a wild display. As the Martini glasses begin to fill, the patron crowd grows anxious. Kim, J.T. and Carmela just stand in awe over the bizarre activity.

Andy calls out to the restaurant floor again, "Now!"

Mary cuts the lights and several people, including Carmela make startled sounds. In the darkness, Yuen and Tai make several passes across the top of the glasses. A moment later, Tai starts to light the top of the glasses closest to him with a small lighter and Yuen does the same on his end. The nine glasses start to catch fire and glow. The outer-most glasses glow green, the next glass glows red, the next glows orange, and the next glows yellow.

Tai calls out, "Kim?"

Mesmerized by the glowing liquors, Kim says nothing. J.T. nudges his mom and says, "Ma?"

Still entranced for a moment finally, she says, "Oh, what?"

Tai asks, "What color do you want for the center glass?"

She quickly thinks and says, "Uh, … blue?"

Tai passes his hand over it and Yuen lights it.

A second later, the glass glows turquoise blue.

Mary turns the lights back on and everyone claps and whistles as loud as they can. Kim walks around to the inside of the bar and gives Tai a hug and kiss and then she hugs Yuen and says, "How did you guys do that?"

Yuen says, "We've been practicing for some time. We've gotten pretty good huh?"

J.T. high-fives his uncle Yuen and his dad and says, "Awesome guys! Awesome!"

Tai announces to the other patrons, "Drink up!"

A moment later the flames all go out by themselves. Andy walks out from the kitchen with family-sized plates full of his famous Ginger Sesame Fish, rice, and vegetables and says, "Here you go gang!"

Toma and his men walk over to Tai and Yuen and collectively say, "Too cool!"

Toma leaves an envelope full of cash on the top of the bar for Andy and calls back to him as he prepares various plates, "Andy! For you my friend! Thanks for everything tonight!"

Andy finishes serving the last plate and walks over to the bar. He puts the envelope in his back pocket and waves over at Toma. Toma bows at him and sits down.

Kim starts crying and says to Tai, "Is this all real My-Tai? You're right. If I'm dreaming, don't ever wake me!"

Tai smiles and says, "It's going to be like this from now on, I promise. We'll be together no matter what!"

Carmela wipes the tears away from her face and says, "To you all! To us all!"

The whole restaurant toasts the inner group. The night is capped off with everyone dancing inside the horseshoe and toasting the night away.

Six weeks pass by like nothing. Yuen, Tai and J.T. have made great progress on the two additional rooms and extra bathroom added to the home. It now serves as a duplex home with one fully functional side for Yuen and Carmela and the other side for Tai, Kim, and J.T. The house is now in the shape of a 'Y' with the additional bedrooms being the high points. The cove inlet and long stained deck still remain the top features on the property.

OCTOBER 31, 2008 AT 12:00 A.M. – AMAMI OSHIMA ISLAND, JAPAN

Yuen gets a call from Toma.

"Yuen. Sorry to call so late but you have to know this now. I confirmed that Saitonaka thinks Kim and J.T. are dead so he and his men must continue to think this if they were to ever visit Amami, got it?"

"Right? What about Mary and Andy Tong? Are they safe?"

"No. I'm taking care of them right now, moving them out of there so don't be alarmed the next time you guys visit. My second cousin Jos, from Uruma is running the place now. He's a great cook too but not as good as Andy. He knows about you and Dr. Tai so you'll be fine. He honestly doesn't know anything about how Kim and J.T. got to the Island so keep it that way."

"Jos? Oh, right, from Jos' Grille…"

"Exactly."

"No problem. So, where is Saitonaka now?"

"That's just it. I don't know and I haven't been able to reach any of my other contacts lately either. It's like everyone just disappeared. And I don't know where Eishi, Izu, or Saka are either. None of my contacts have seen them around. Keep your weapons close by just in case because if something hits, it'll be fast and furious!"

"Trust me! Especially now, Tai and me are ready for anything. We'll gladly die defending everyone!"

"Okay then. Goodnight my friend. I need to lay low for a while so I can see how things shake out. Something's going on. I need to be around Hong Kong and my people are in Tokyo to listen and see what's what over there."

"Okay. Congratulate us now then."

"Congratulate who? You?"

"Yes. Me and Dr. Tai."

"For what?"

"For marrying Carmela and Kim!"

"Really? That's great!"

"Yes! Long, long overdue for them and I've wanted to propose to Carmela for a while now but it wasn't the right time. Now it's the right time for us both. Tomorrow morning, we've got some cool things planned and J.T. is helping us setup Carmela and his mom for it."

"Oh man, that's great. Can you tell me now because I won't be able to get back there for your dual weddings?"

In advance, Yuen tells Toma his and Dr. Tai's pending wedding proposal plans.

October 31, 2008 at 9:00 A.M.

Yuen's wedding plan commences. The small radio alarm in Carmela and Yuen's bedroom has been set to an Oldies station and at 9:09 A.M., The Beatles' *Love Me Do* starts playing. Carmela reaches over to hit the snooze button but Yuen intercepts her.

He says, "Morning! Great song huh?"

Carmela nods and tries to go back to sleep.

Yuen holds her up and says, "No, sleepy head. We've got big plans this morning so up and at 'em Miss Mela!"

Carmela sneers at Yuen and staggers into the bathroom for a shower.

Meanwhile, on the other side of the 'Y'-shaped home, Tai's wedding plan commences. The small radio alarm in Tai and Kim's bedroom has been set to another Oldies station and at 9:09 A.M., Fats Domino's *Blueberry Hill* starts playing. Kim reaches over to hit the snooze button but Tai intercepts her.

He says, "Morning! Great song huh?" Kim nods and tries to go back to sleep.

Tai holds her up and says, "No, sleepy head. We've got big plans this morning so up and at 'em Kimmie!"

Kim sneers at Tai and staggers into the bathroom for a shower.

While all this is going on, J.T. has been running all over the kitchen and living room cooking up breakfast for everyone and setting the living room table with small plates and champagne glasses half full of semi-frozen Mimosa. There's a radio on one side of the table with an alarm set to play at exactly 9:33 A.M. and on the other side of the table, that radio alarm is set to play at exactly 9:55 A.M.

On opposite ends of the house, Carmela and Kim emerge from their respective shower rooms at almost the same time. Yuen walks past Carmela to take his quick shower and Tai does the same, walking past Kim for his. Five minutes later, they re-emerge as well and get dressed.

Carmela says, "Yuen? No kiss good morning?"

Ironically, on the other side of the house, Kim asks the same question of Tai. Both men look at their watches and say to their respective mates, "Tough schedule this morning. Let's get moving and get through breakfast. Lots to do you know!"

The women look up at the ceiling and think to themselves, "… whatever."

It's 9:32 A.M. and both couples make their way to their respective living room side entrance doors. Yuen wipes the remnant shower water and sweat off his forehead and grabs Carmela's hand. She opens the door and the radio alarm goes off. The Beatles' *Love Me Do* starts playing again. A moment later, Tai and Kim enter the shared living room.

Tai says, "Hey, nice song huh?"

Kim agrees and says, "Morning you two." Then she looks over to the kitchen and says, "Morning sweetheart."

J.T. waves back as he finishes fixing the last breakfast plate. Tai gives him a 'thumbs up'.

As the song plays, Carmela says, "Wait, they played that song earlier this morning?"

Yuen says, "Did they?"

Looking suspiciously over at Yuen, Carmela says, "Yes, they did. In fact you wouldn't let me go back to sleep because it was playing and you wanted me to listen to it, remember?"

Cleverly, Yuen changes the subject. "Look honey, J.T. made us breakfast."

Kim thinks to herself for a moment and then says, "J.T.? Did you put all this together for us?"

J.T. looks over at the time on the radio and hurriedly says, "Yep. Everyone sit and eat while it's hot."

Its 9:40 A.M. – Everyone sits down and Yuen says, "So, love, love me do?"

Carmela looks at him and casually smiles and then she looks down and sees the four karat diamond wedding ring Yuen's holding in his right palm. Carmela starts crying and just nods her head up and down. Yuen raises his right palm up and as soon as Kim sees the ring, she starts crying.

Kim says, "Hey! Alright you two! J.T., get a picture of them sweetie!"

J.T. grabs the digital camera off the corner of the kitchen island and takes a few pictures of Yuen and Carmela and then of the two couples. The women continue crying and hugging each other as the guys look anxiously at the other radio alarm.

Its 9:54 A.M. – The group just settles down and then a moment later, Fats Domino's *Blueberry Hill* starts playing again.

Yuen says, "Hey, great song, right?"

Carmela agrees as she and Kim gawk at her new wedding ring.

A moment later, Kim looks up and curiously stares at Tai.

Then Tai starts singing, "I found my thrill... on Blueberry Hill…and I hope she'll say 'yes' because I … can't remember the rest of this song!"

Kim starts walking over to Tai. She looks down and then up at him lovingly and as she looks at his chest, she notices that his 3D dragon pendant has a huge sparkling accessory next to it; a four karat diamond wedding ring in a different style and setting than Carmela's. Kim bursts into tears and drops to her knees. Carmela looks over at Tai and sees the wedding ring around his neck for Kim and she starts crying again.

J.T. hugs his dad and shakes his uncle Yuen's hand and says, "You did it!"

Yuen smiles and says, "We did it!"

Tai breaks away for a moment and joins Kim on the floor. He looks deep into her eyes and whispers just for her, "I waited twenty-two years for you and I would have waited twenty-two thousand more! I figured you could wait another twenty-two minutes after Yuen's proposal this morning, for mine."

Kim cries harder and buries her drenched face into Tai's chest, this time avoiding his sharp 3D gold dragon, just like she did when he proposed to her the first time.

J.T. moves the Beatles radio alarm into the kitchen area so everyone can hear it when they are closer to that area and he moves the Fats Domino radio alarm a little further back in the living room corner so everyone can hear it over there. Then Yuen and Tai celebrate with J.T. by finishing off the Mimosa Champagne as the women stare and marvel at their respective monster weddings rings.

Kim asks, "When? When are we getting married Tai?"

Yuen looks at his watch and Tai says, "In about forty-three minutes, the Justice of the Peace will be here to marry all of us so go get dressed you two."

J.T. adds, "Your wedding dresses are under your beds! I snuck them there last night!"

Carmela points cleverly over at J.T. and shakes her finger. Kim grabs her son and hugs him fiercely and then heads back to her bedroom. J.T. left a gift card on each wedding dress box.

The note on Carmela's box reads,

"Aunt Carmela:

I can't thank you enough for looking out for me and my mother; and for reconnecting us with my father. She needed that more than anything else in her life; God Bless and congratulations today and every day… aunt Mela!

...sorry; Uncle Yuen told me to write that!"

The note on his mother's box reads,

"Mama-Mia!

Wherever you are, I am. Wherever you go, I follow!

The 'Good Son'!"

Her salutation brings her to tears because that was J.T.'s grandmother's name and the first line of J.T.'s note is such a solemn and heartfelt message but then his 'Good Son' line makes her laugh because it's a play on the opposite of the Hollywood movie they once watched together when J.T. was younger.

At 11:11 A.M. The Justice of the Peace proclaims Yuen and Carmela Zhang happily married and Dr. Tai and Kim Huang, finally, happily married.

J.T. takes pictures of both newlywed couples and the Justice of the Peace takes pictures of the whole wedding party and of the Huang's together officially for the first time.

CHAPTER TWENTY-SIX

JANUARY 26, 2009 – YEAR OF THE OX

YUEN and Toma have arranged for J.T. to practice international law remotely through a firm based out of Taipei, Taiwan. He keeps a low profile and works on a wide variety of less urgent projects and parts of projects that have very little exposure. The work affords him the opportunity to practice his craft and to learn about the international community. He's enjoying the work but he's starting to get more and more interested and involved with his uncle Yuen's and aunt Carmela's work because he finds it much more interesting than international law.

Tai and Kim go right back into their routine of developing new and improved ointments, compounds, and elixirs to help the local people with a wide variety of ailments and inconveniences. So far, they have developed a powerful insect repellant spray and ointment to protect people from the many dangerous insect bites that can occur on the island including but not limited to the occasional plague-infected fleas and flies that transmit cholera, compliments of the inhumane and infamous former Lt. General Shirō Ishii, who used these entomological weapons to infect the population in China during World War II. The spray helps to prevent the sting or bite and the ointment is for treatment after being stung or bitten. The whole group participates in the distribution by loading up the supplies in their cars and driving all around the island delivering and sometimes helping to apply the various products. J.T. finds all of his parent's work interesting too but it doesn't compare to uncle Yuen's and aunt Carmela's work on shark teeth, age analysis, migration patterns and breeding habits.

The Zhang's and Huang's continue to make Myst1 and CDT wash for the Canton villager's. To avoid any possible conflicts and to prevent Kim or J.T. from being discovered by any one of Boss Saitonaka's men, Toma plus one or a couple of his men pick up the resupplies and they deliver them to the Canton village monthly. Thanks to Kim's amazing memory of bank account numbers, Toma has arranged sporadic withdrawals from Saitonaka's banking accounts and redirected those funds to Julie's Perth account. With Boss Saitonaka's hasty retreat to North Korea and all the withdrawals that he makes from each of his accounts to pay off his various supporter's each month, it's very difficult for him to track or even notice any of these activities.

FEBRUARY 2, 2009 – BOSTON, MASSACHUSETTS, U.S.A.

Jessica checks in with Boss Saitonaka.

Playfully, she asks, "Saitonaka-san?"

"You know you don't have to call me that Miss Jessica."

"I thought you liked that?"

"Stop jerking me around!"

"I thought you liked it when I did that for you too?"

"True, but not over the phone!"

"It's been three months and Julie hasn't told me shit!"

"Nothing?"

"No sir. The girl eats, sleeps, and drinks school work and that's all!"

"Maybe it's still too early?"

"Uh, no! Maybe she's just the most boring fucking student in the whole school!"

"Just hang tough and maybe she'll open up in a little bit. Give it time. See anything else?"

"Okay. Uh, not really; she's got a cute little body. She's shy. Most of the time she changes in the bathroom and whenever she showers, she usually comes out already dressed."

"Her mother had some pretty juicy memories from her former college days. Give it some time and I think Julie will loosen up and start creating memories of her own."

"Speaking of loosening up sir…"

"So, fuck some college frat kid and enjoy yourself! You're on my dime!"

"But sir."

"What?"

"I was saving myself for you!"

"Nice! Check back with me later this year or next. I'm busy babysitting the local Magistrate; taking him to the States pretty soon to visit some places. I'll try to stop by and see you before we leave."

"But I thought you were supposed to get paid for babysitting sir, not pay someone who you are babysitting!"

"Bitch! And remember, if I do visit…"

"Yeah, yeah, you're my uncle Hey Sun. You don't have to remind me every time!"

"Sorry. It was just that the last time we talked about it, you had your mouth full. I wasn't sure if you heard me."

"Yeah, well you sure didn't have much to say once I got going, did you?"
"You're lucky you still have your looks girl!"
"Yeah? You're lucky you're rich!"
"Bitch!"
"Yes! But your favorite!"
"True enough!"

While this conversation is taking place, a little off campus, Julie is studying hard when she starts looking for her favorite sweater. She sees what she thinks is her sweater sticking a little outside the bottom drawer of Jessica's dresser so she retrieves it. As soon as she takes it out, she notices a diary underneath it. The sweater is very similar to hers but not hers so she puts it back and closes the drawer. After a few moments, she can't resist and takes the diary out of the drawer.

> "Arrived: bitter fucking cold here! How do these people put up with this? Sendai can get cold but nothing like this! My face froze walking from class to class the other morning! My roommate is pretty. As the 'ugly' roommate, I'll do my part and take her calls as tons of guys call for her. Maybe this will be the year but at this point, I just want to get it over with. I can 'fall in love' after I've been fucked at least once!
>
> I'd settle for some of the guys I've seen around but if they see Julie, they'll want her and not me. Shit! Here we go again! No good sushi places here and no saké so I'll have to look around and find a liquor store that sells it. Fuck it! Bossy-san is paying! Warm saké and my vibrator, that's what I need!"

Julie calls her mother Misa and shares some of the details from Jessica's diary with her.

"Hey mom!"
"Julie! Sweetheart! How are you? How are your classes going?"
"Fine. I miss you!"
"Wow! Three months already. How do you like Boston?"
"It's cold! I agree with my roommate!"
"Oh, is she there?"
"No; she thinks the same."
"Do you two have a lot in common?"
"Some things but I'm sneakier."
"Sneakier?"

"Yeah, I found her diary just now and I've been reading it; that's how I knew how she felt about the weather here and a bunch of other things."

"Julie! Put it back! You wouldn't like it if someone read your diary, right?"

"I don't keep a diary mom."

"That's not the point and you know it."

"I know but she thinks…"

"Julie? Put it back right now before she catches you reading it!"

"Okay mom but listen; she thinks I'm pretty and she's just my 'ugly' roommate. She thinks she'll be taking messages from all these guys for me while she meets no one. And, she says she's a virgin who just misses her saké and her vibrator!"

"Julie!"

"What? I'm just paraphrasing what she wrote mom."

"Every young girl thinks like that. We're all full of doubt and misconceptions, especially if you haven't had sex yet. At nineteen, these days, that is a little unusual but who cares. It's 'her' sex just like it's 'your' sex. You own it so do with it what you want. I just hope you're smart and wait to meet a boy that means something to you and not just some guy who's walking after you with a hard-on!"

"Mom!"

"Like we talked about Julie; to guys, it is more of just something to get 'rid of' or 'get over with' with but for us girls, it's very different. There's a connection and deep memory for most of us when it comes to our first time. You'll remember that guy for the rest of your life, just like I did with your father."

Julie just listens as her mother offers her honest sex and relationship advice.

"Your father was just as self-conscious as every other guy during his first time but that's how I knew he was the right one for me to have sex with for my first time. We both liked each other. We were both attracted to each other physically and we were both nervous as hell. So, we took our time; looking at each other, kissing, and hugging each other. We fumbled around a little bit but when it's the right time and you're with the right person, none of that other stuff matters. What matters is that you're sharing each other and then after the first few moments, you just settle into each other and it's what you both had hoped for."

"…then he fucks your brains loose?"

"Julie! My God!"

"What?"

"No! … then I fucked his brains loose!"

"Mom!"

"Hey, you asked! Your father was fun and very loving; how do you think you got here?"

"Okay mom. Now it's getting awkward!"

"Fair enough!"

"… thanks mom!"

"You're welcome. Don't worry about Jessica; she'll find her way too. Now, put her diary back before she walks in on you holding it!"

"Okay. Talk later!"

Just as Julie replaces Jessica's diary, Jessica walks back into the room.

"Hey… I was just…"

"You were just what?"

Quickly, Julie says, "Uh, I thought we had swapped sweaters in the laundry but I saw that yours is a little different so I pushed it back into your drawer."

Jessica slowly looks down at the drawer and says, "Thanks…"

"So, what are you up to?"

"Not much. I know we've been roommates for a little over three months now and we still don't know much about each other so what do you think about checking out the bar around the corner tonight, just us girls."

"Okay."

Julie cleans up a few of her notebooks and papers and the two girls grab their heavy coats.

As they walk, Julie says, "I can't wait for spring. I hear it's really beautiful here."

"Yeah. I saw some pictures online. Still, it's nothing compared to the cherry blossoms back home."

The two continue to exchange pleasantries as they walk around the corner and enter the bar.

Jessica looks at the bartender and says, "Does this place have saké or what?"

The bartender nods and starts pouring a couple warm sakés. The girls take a seat in the far back corner, away from the front door and its relentless drafts.

They talk about this and that, drink and then Jessica says, "Boyfriend back in Japan?"

"No. You?"

"Not anymore. When he heard I was coming here, he broke up with me because he didn't want to try to keep in touch and get that uncomfortable call."

"Uncomfortable call?"

"You know; his girlfriend 'all alone' in her room. We talk and then there's a knock on the door. It's the party girls from down the hall. They're loud and wild. The boyfriend hears all kinds of things like another guy's voice. He asks, 'who's that?' And then something gets knocked over and breaks. He asks, 'what was that?' Then one of the girls starts screaming and acting out her last bad date but the boyfriend only hears, 'Fuck my pussy!' when what she really said was, 'fucking pussy!' Then he hangs up and we spend the next month analyzing everything that actually went on, while he continues to paint all sorts of other pictures in his mind, which results in him hanging up the phone on me and screaming, 'you cheating bitch!'"

"Wow. You know a lot."

"It's happened before and the only thing I learned was that's it's not worth trying to explain things, especially when I found out later, that he was doing the same thing, except that he was actually cheating on me when I called! Little fucker!"

Julie smiles and toasts Jessica's saké cup.

Jessica continues, "Besides, we never went all the way but I jerked him off a lot and I don't miss his stubby little prick anyway!"

Julie laughs, spilling her saké on the table. Jessica fills it back up and says, "Yeah! Stubby and too damn hairy! … made it look even shorter!"

Julie says, "I've only seen two and they were both pretty long I guess."

"How long?"

Julie estimates with her index fingers apart and says, "Like this I guess", as she holds her fingers about six inches apart.

"That's average I hear but I've heard of some guys that are over nine inches!"

"Nine inches? Wouldn't that hurt?"

"Nope. Now, fourteen…"

"Fourteen? That's insane! I wouldn't fuck a guy that big. It would be fun to jerk him off though!"

"So, what's the perfect size?" Jessica asks.

"I only have two to compare against but my last boyfriend was about eight inches and super-hard. It felt really nice in my hands. He was smooth-shaven so he looked and felt really great too. And, I loved his veins so we used to just 'play' a lot."

"Play?"

"Oh yeah; we'd take each other's clothes off and then we'd take turns lying down on our backs for a full-body massage. No sex but everything else goes. He'd trace and kiss my body and every now and again, his erection would brush across me. That was my favorite. I'd return the favor by kissing him all over and trace his cock veins with my fingertips. When he put his fingers inside me, I'd take him in my mouth and we'd just stay like that until we came for each other. We did break the 'rules' once but it was just the one time."

Jessica finishes off the bottle of saké and motions to the bartender for another.

"Nice!"

"It really was. I miss him."

"Does 'him' have a name?"

Julie accidentally says, "J.T."

She squint's her eyes, trying to shake off the overdose of saké.

Jessica inquires, "J.T. What's that stand for?"

Julie recovers and quickly says, "Nothing. It's just JT."

"So, where's mystery meat now?"

"He died Jessica."

Embarrassed by her crass remark, Jessica looks down at the floor and says, "I'm sorry Julie; I didn't know."

Julie starts to cry and nervously says, "I'm going back to the room now. You?"

"No. I'll stay for a bit longer. You go ahead."

Julie quickly grabs her coat off the corner rack and leaves in a hurry as she wipes her eyes.

Jessica watches Julie leave and then closes her eyes tight in recognition that her comment just closed several doors of conversation and camaraderie with her roommate. It's going to be a long year. Time will tell.

When Julie gets back to her room, she calls her mom.

"Hey mom."

"Jewel. How are you?"

"Something's wrong."

"What? Are you okay?"

"I'm fine. It's Jessica."

"What's wrong with her?"

"Maybe a lot. Remember I told you about her diary?"

"Right."

"Well, we just had some saké and talked about guys and she sure seems to know a lot for a girl who's never done it."

"Like what?"

"Size, experience, playing, and a lot of deep relationship stuff. And…"

"And?"

"And, I screwed up but I think I covered it."

"Shit!"

"Yeah, I talked about J.T. but I told her he died mom."

"She bought it?"

“I’m pretty sure because I walked out on her crying and I saw her look down as I left.”

“Julie! No more saké and talk of guys! I told you we have to be careful so I can make my next move before anyone else does… damn it!”

“I know mom. I’m sorry but I think it’s okay.”

CHAPTER TWENTY-SEVEN

February 3, 2009 – Amami Oshima Island, Japan

YUEN announces, "All right! This time, it's the guys versus the girls!"

Kim says, "Fine. Three on two and we'll still win, right Carm?"

Carmela smiles, hugs Kim and says, "Us two girls versus you three boys, fine; we can always use the extra money!"

Kim adds, "It's all ours anyway!" She winks at Tai.

Dr. Tai leans over to J.T. and says, "Pay attention because this is actually how things are in life, not just in Mah-Jongg!"

Kim says, "Hey! I heard that!"

The group smiles as Tai and J.T. mix up the tiles. Mrs. Huang and Mrs. Zhang stare competitively at the mounting cash pool; it's a combination of Yuan and Yen worth well over five U.S. dollars. Yuen retrieves drinks for everyone and sits down on the guy's side of the table. The Oldies station continues cranking out favorites.

Yuen reflects back on classic former games at Jimmie Huang's house and starts to say, "You should have seen your mom play J.T. Her and Mis…"

Tai interrupts just in time and says, "Your grandfather loved this game. He could play all night and never get tired. It was always that 'next' game that he loved the most."

Without saying anything else, everyone toasts Grandpa Huang.

A few moments later, there's a knock at the front door. J.T. gets up and answers it.

Just away from their view, the Mah-Jongg group can't see who it is so Kim calls out, "Honey? Who is it?"

J.T. calls, back, "A Mr. Saka and a lady."

The group looks at each other and Yuen says, "Have them come back tomorrow."

A familiar voice cuts through the early evening air, "But I have waited Sik Yuen; for over twenty-two years… to spit back in your face!"

Misa steps inside the doorway and immediately spots Sik Yuen at the living room table. She locks and glares her eyes at him; staring right through him. Her so-black-its-blue hair shimmers just like it did twenty-two years ago, except now, each strand is like a blade she'd like to swing at Sik Yuen.

Shocked at her comments and bold behavior, J.T. goes to block her full entry when Misa pans the room and spots Kim and Tai. Kim bursts into tears at the same time that Misa does. Misa falls to the floor just inside the doorway and Tai motions to J.T. to help her to her feet.

Carmela stands up and walks over to Yuen's left side. She holds his hand and says, "You're Misa?"

Crying out of control, Misa nods. Saka looks down for a moment and then says, "May we come in?"

Yuen says, "Please!"

Then Yuen walks over to Misa and helps her to her feet.

J.T. holds the door open for Saka as he brings in a couple small luggage pieces.

Tai gets a couple glasses of ice water from the kitchen and places them on the corner of the end table closest to the front door.

Misa can't believe who she's seeing. She grabs Kim's face and kisses her. Then she says, "How are you alive?"

Kim says, "Yes! I'm fine, I'm fine!"

"And J.T…."

"Yes, J.T.'s fine. Why?"

"He said you two were dead!"

Saka looks over to Kim and J.T. and narrows his eyes.

Everyone knows who 'he' is.

Misa clears her eyes and says, "I played his sick game because I had to for my daughter! I tricked him into thinking I was going to do something terrible to Yuen. For even thinking that, I'm sorry. And J.T.; you're fine. You're not killed!"

Misa is overwhelmed with genuine relief but she's mentally and emotionally exhausted like never before. Believing her life-long friend was dead and having cursed her name thinking she had committed suicide only to find her in perfect health as well as her son, whom she had been told was shot to death is more than anyone should ever have to reconcile, especially in a few seconds.

Yuen sighs and says, "The game; we lost sight of his game. It almost destroyed me, twice. He even tried to burn me alive! Hey Sun told you that Kim drowned or committed suicide, right? And he told you Sika shot J.T., right? And I'm guessing that Sika is now dead for real so there's no checking with him what really happened, right?"

Misa looks up and starts crying again. She's hurt to see that Yuen has married someone else but after all this time, she understands.

Tai motions to Saka and says, "This is a lot to take in for everyone. Tomorrow, we can talk things out better and help each other think straight."

Kim and Misa stand up from the loveseat and hold each other as Kim escorts her to J.T.'s room. Saka follows.

J.T. is stunned but happy because this is 'aunt Misa' that his parents have carefully described to him and finally, she's back together with everyone she's loved once again.

With Saka still asleep, the next morning, the group takes turns detailing each of Hey Sun's betrayals. Tai and Kim hand Misa Kim's letter that Tai kept from his father's shower tile wall. Misa looks down at it and just starts crying, missing Mr. Huang so much. Everyone takes a moment because those memories are still pretty fresh and run deep.

Misa gladly explains how she got Hey Sun all fired up over a ton of made-up sex stories from back in their college days. Kim smiles and explains that she used the same tactic with him. When Misa hears that Hey Sun is not at all affiliated with the Chinese Government and that he had nothing at all to do with helping any of them 'escape' but rather that he arranged for each of them to be sent into exile to serve him, she pounds her fists angrily on the kitchen island.

Yuen adds, "His real name is Boss Saitonaka and he's the disputed top boss of the Japanese Yakuza. He has people everywhere so we have to be very careful until we can figure out a way to deal with him. We can never get back all the time he took away from us all but we can start evening the playing field!"

Yuen continues, "When he killed Boss Ito, he took an ultimate risk; if his move against the former Yakuza leader was too early, the rest of his own family will come after him and destroy him! That is, if he's able to avoid Ito's people first! I have a feeling he's fled but to where, I don't know. Toma's looking into it."

Kim says, "And you know about our video sales, right?"

"Yes; sick bastard! How much has he made?" Misa asks.

Yuen counters, "It's a little over eight million Yen right now, spread across all of his accounts, but we've taken away about two million without him noticing because something tells me he's needing to spend a lot of those funds keeping himself alive these days. Wherever he escaped to, it's expensive!"

Misa asks, "And Saka? He's Saitonaka's man. What about him?"

Yuen says, "That depends on you."

"On me?"

"Are you two close or is he just here to look after you?"

"Honestly, when I saw you and Carmela, it destroyed me but I would also have to admit that Saka has been a good man and I know he cares about me. I just don't know if he's willing to risk his life for me."

Tai says, "Now that he knows about Kim and J.T., he's going to have to make a decision and fast because I won't risk losing them again!"

Yuen states emphatically, "It's us or Saitonaka! It's really that simple now. If you trust him, we trust him but if you're wrong, we're all going to pay the price. If he sides with his boss, he can have his people to see to us all in a matter of moments. If he sides with us, we have time to make sure we are all safe and the time to come up with some plan for dealing with him. I'll tell you now, we already have several of his top people working with us; that's how Kim and J.T. made it here in the first place so you know what I'm saying is true."

Tai says, "The stakes are higher than ever now Misa."

A little overwhelmed and scared, Misa asks, "So, what other lies?"

Yuen explains the ordeal at the airport when he spat at her; the fact that he didn't see Misa and Tai together. Naturally, it pissed him off when Misa admitted it but he failed to mention his shortcomings to her as well and just stormed off.

Kim and Tai feel the remaining tension and uneasiness in the air and Kim quickly says, "He did this to each of us and I swear with my last breath, he'll pay for it! Just like you said, you did what you had to in order to protect Julie. I did the same to protect J.T. They were all that mattered to each of us… remember the night of our dance when we both found out?"

Kim and Misa start crying and Misa says, "I'll never forget that night!"

"Me neither because that was the night when we both made a stand and a pact, right?"

"Right!"

"So, it's no different now except for one thing. We're wide open out here and in front of Saitonaka's man Saka."

Misa says, "I trust Saka. He loves me and he loves Julie!"

Yuen and Misa look at each other and without saying a word, and not wanting to make Carmela feel bad or uncomfortable, they simply nod at each other and say they're sorry respectively, with their eyes. Yuen is grateful because he knows Saka is a reasonable man.

He also knows he'd much prefer his life with Misa and Julie over a battle of blades with Saitonaka, who could care less about anything other than himself.

Yuen suggests, "Talk to Saka and let us know where he stands. If he's with us, just keep playing your game and report back to Saitonaka when you call on him so he thinks you're just waiting for the right moment to make your move against us."

Kim grabs Misa's hands and squeezes them. "We did what we had to, to survive. Now, it's even more important because we're back together. We're not going to push him until we have a plan in place so just know that Julie is safe while she's in school. Saitonaka still thinks she's his, right?" Misa nods.

Just then Saka walks into the hallway and heads into the kitchen. Carmela hands him a glass of ice water with lemon. Misa and Saka step outside to the back patio overlooking the impressive cove and beautiful deck in the distance.

Misa explains the new details to Saka and then she sums everything up saying, "I know I can't ask you to risk your life for them."

Saka explains, "I know Sik Yuen. In fact a while back I was sent to confront him and possibly take him out but that's right when his path took a turn and mine did as well. He entered Beijing University and I was told to back off. Soon after, I started working closer with my boss, Boss Ito. I respected that man and when Saitonaka killed him; his own brother, everything changed for me in that moment. He knew my loyalties were with his brother and when he ordered me to assist with Boss Ito's remains; he did that out of spite as well. I survived that horrible night only because as I helped remove Boss Ito's body from the formal dining room. Like a true coward, I looked up and smiled at Saitonaka and said, "Good!" What he didn't see was me crying all the way down the hallway out of respect for my fallen leader. He had Sika carry Boss Ito's head and he required him to carry it by his hair like some kind of dead road animal. I know exactly what Boss Saitonaka is and what he's about! My bottom-line is very simple; I'll gladly risk my own head to protect yours and Julie's!"

Misa and Saka kiss and hug each other as they dance in a small circle. Inside the house, everyone's tension disappears because they can see Saka's decision for themselves. Trusting someone truly outside of their circle is a huge risk but it seems to be the right move now.

FEBRUARY 17, 2009 – AMAMI OSHIMA ISLAND, JAPAN

A few weeks later, Misa makes her follow-up call to Hey Sun.

"Hey Sun?"

"Miss Misa! How are you doing?"

"I'm fine…" She sighs over the phone.

"Come on. What's going on?"

"It's…"

"What?"

"Everyone's changed! I don't know these people anymore!"

Saitonaka smiles to himself and says, "People change dear. It's been a long time since you saw your former friends, right?"

"True but they are so different. Dr. Tai is a drunken fool! All he does is mope around all day, writing in his research books and fumbling around with his so-called experiments. He's a shell of the man I used to know."

Enjoying her descriptions, Saitonaka looks around his palatial room in Pyongyang and sits down in his new favorite chair nearest his bed.

"Is he still making Myst1 and CDT wash?"

"Yeah but that's all he really does."

"And Yuen?"

"Jesus! What a shit-storm he turned into!"

"Really?"

"All he does is fish all day long. He helps Dr. Tai a few times each week with supplies and loading the Myst1 and CDT wash but then he goes right back to his fishing and he fucking stinks like you wouldn't believe! I can't stand being around him! In fact last week, Saka 'accidentally' pushed him into the cove out back just to make sure he got an extra bath that week!"

"Anything else?"

"Oh, Yuen got married to some local woman named Carmela. What a piece of work she is! She knows less than him and does less too! They're perfect for each other!"

Saitonaka laughs out loud and says, "Very good Misa! Just stay as close as you can and watch them for me. And Saka?"

"He's fine; a decent lay but I miss you Mr. Sun and your big…"

Misa hears someone in the background on Hey Sun's phone saying, "Saitona…" and then a second later, their phone connection ends.

BEFORE, ON FEBRUARY 3, 2009 – PYONGYANG, NORTH KOREA

One of the North Korean local Magistrate's guards enters Saitonaka's room and says, "Sir, by order of the local Magistrate, we are moving you to a new location east of the city. Please follow me now! Your belongings will follow shortly."

Having no other choice, Boss Saitonaka gathers a few items including his few boxes of Cuban cigars and follows the guard out of his room. He looks around the hallway outside and narrows his eyes, remaining vigilant as ever. The local Magistrate keeps Boss Saitonaka moving around just enough to interrupt his patterns; keeping him just enough off-balance to maintain his slight edge on the Yakuza boss.

Much like the Yakuza boss himself, the local Magistrate has endless resources to keep this game of his going for as long as he wishes. As long as he continues to be paid for protecting the Yakuza leader, he'll have fun repositioning and controlling his movements. It's a game that Saitonaka is well familiar with but one that he's beginning to grow weary of as well. Until he gets word that things are settling down back in Yokohama, he has no choice but to play the local Magistrate's games.

DECEMBER 8, 2009 – AMAMI OSHIMA ISLAND, JAPAN

Another eventful year has almost passed. The Huang's and Zhang's welcomed back their long-time friend Misa and her guard Saka. Over the summer, everyone pitched in and built a new custom home for Misa and Saka to live in. It's just slightly to the north and west of the unique "Y-shaped" home.

As everyone sits down for dinner, Saka slowly rises and says, "I have to say thank you to everyone for all your support and friendship this year. Misa is obviously very important to you all. You welcomed her back and me as well with open arms. This is awkward for me so please bear with me for a moment."

Saka pulls out a small folded piece of paper and starts reading, "I know my fate dictates that I may never see my own family again but they would approve of my spending my time with you all here. I have changed a lot over the years and I have come to care deeply for Miss Misa. I would gladly protect her with my life just as I would protect her daughter's as well."

Saka pauses, trying to prepare for what he needs to explain next. Tai and Yuen nod toward Saka and he nods back.

Saka is about to start up again when Misa stands up, tears streaming down her face and says, "Yes! I'll marry you!"

Saka breathes a huge sigh of relief and picks Misa up in his arms. As the newly engaged couple kiss and hug each other, the rest of the group stands and applauds them. Tai and Kim then make a call to the Justice of the Peace and requests that he return to the Huang home for yet another special wedding ceremony.

"Another wedding? Maybe we should move all ceremonies to your house Dr. Tai."

Tai and Kim smile and Tai says, "Maybe!"

"What are their names, the engaged couple?"

Tai and Kim don't know so they call out to Saka, "What's your last name Saka?"

Saka smiles and says, "That's part of it! It's actually Yamishinosaka."

They share that with the Justice and he says, "So what time should I be by in the morning?"

Tai and Kim check with Misa and Saka and then they say, "Are you available tomorrow at 10?"

"Oh, so soon?"

"They don't see any need to wait!"

"How about 10:30?"

"Perfect! See you tomorrow morning."

On December 9, 2009 at 11:11 A.M., the Justice of the Peace pronounces Hideko and Misa, husband and wife; the Yamishinosaka's.

December 10, 2009 Midnight – Yokohama, Japan

Boss Saitonaka learns that some of his men are stealing Myst1 and CDT wash to sell on the black markets across Thailand, Laos, Cambodia and Vietnam. It's a huge risk to take but they figure with Boss Saitonaka away in North Korea, they figure he'll never find out. Boss Saitonaka calls on Eishi at midnight for a favor.

"Nephew?"

With his youngest brother Ric Shigemura listening in on their conversation, Eishi says, "Uncle! Where are you?"

"Never mind that. Do me a favor Eishi?"

"Of course." Ric Shigemura starts a trace on the call.

"Go to Misha Katana1 tonight."

"Tonight uncle? It's midnight."

"I know. There's something you must see to before dawn. Izu will meet you there. And keep it quiet."

"Keep what quiet uncle?"

"Eishi! No questions! Just go now!" Saitonaka hangs up.

Ric shakes his heads and stops the tracing equipment. He says, "Damn! Not long enough."

Eishi and Boss Ricmasa head out. An hour later they arrive at the port where the Misha Katana fleet resides. It's cold outside but not as cold as usual for this time of year. As they walk along the port deck, they both get an eerie feeling. The flag ship, Misha Katana1 is at the end of the long port deck. Even though the port deck is solid, it's still very creepy walking around in the earliest of morning hours on the lookout for who knows what. A chill runs through Ric's body because this is exactly the type of setup that usually leads to a hit and he knows it. He checks the position of his Glock 9mm in his back waistband just to be sure it's there.

Eishi says, 'What was that?" as he quickly repositions his flashlight over to his right.

"What?" Ric asks.

"I thought I heard something over there by Katana3."

The two continue walking down the line toward Misha Katana1. As they approach the forward deck, Eishi says, "There it is again."

"I didn't hear anything." Ric says.

"It sounded like a moan or something."

"A moan?"

"Yeah."

"A moan from what?"

"I don't know."

"Well shit nephew! It makes a big fucking difference since we're out here at fucking midnight! Was it an animal's moan or a person's moan?"

A second later, Izu calls out from below the port deck line in a small rescue boat; "Hey you two! Give me a hand." He laughs to himself.

Eishi and Ric jump back a couple steps and Ric says, "Izu! God damn it! What the hell are you doing down there?"

"Boss Ricmasa! Help me and you'll soon find out!"

Eishi and Ric make their way to the short staircase a few feet down the port deck and finally see Izu bobbing around in his rescue boat. As they draw closer, Ric can make out the figure of a body that Izu has propped up.

Eishi asks, "Shit! Who's that with you?"

"Don't be offended Boss Ricmasa. He'd shake your hand, if he could."

Eishi shines his flashlight on the figure. The man is headless and is missing both of his hands.

Izu continues, "It's hard to say but my guess is that no more Myst1 or CDT wash will be stolen for some time!"

Ric and Eishi both grab the man's upper torso while Izu steadies his boat and jumps on the bottom step, holding one of the man's legs.

Ric asks, "No head or hands. Thrown away in the water?"

"That or saved for a later surprise for us."

Ric sighs and says, "Even in Pyongyang, he can touch anyone he wants. Anyone else?"

"I'm not sure. I haven't been on the other boats yet. Saitonaka-san called and told me to come and meet you two here. I got here about thirty minutes ago and started looking around when I heard something knocking up against the front side of Katana1. It was our friend here."

Ric suggests, "Let's check the other boats too."

Eishi says, "Let me grab my navigation logs from the command center first. I'll meet you over at Katana2 in a minute."

Ric and Izu place the man's body on the port deck across from Katana1 and Ric walks back down to Katana2 while Izu quickly boards his rescue boat and searches the opposite side of the smaller 'research' ship.

Eishi enters his captain's command center and everything looks fine. He retrieves his navigation logs and takes a quick look around before leaving. He shines his light around the immediate area and as he turns around to close the door, he yells out in disgust, "Ahhh! Izu! Uncle!"

Ric turns around and runs back to Misha Katana1. Izu hears Eishi and makes his way back to the small port deck staircase. Ric boards the ship and as he approaches the captain's command center, Eishi shines his flashlight, lighting his uncle's path.

Ric notices something very odd about how Eishi is holding his flashlight and as he gets closer he says, "What the hell is that?"

Eishi flips the flashlight right-side up, exposing the severed hand that he is holding that is holding the flashlight.

"I found his hands uncle."

Ric gasps and says, "Stop that!"

"Look uncle. Whoever uncle Saitonaka had perform this task, they even stole the man's gold wedding band."

"That doesn't surprise me. Where did you find the hands?"

"Stapled to the back of my captain's door!"

"…now that does surprise me!"

"I get that you don't steal from uncle Saitonaka but was this really necessary uncle?"

"No. He's sending us a message by sending us down here tonight. And he's just showing off to let us and everyone else know that he can reach across the Sea of Japan to touch anyone he wants!"

Izu finally catches up and stares at the severed hands that Eishi has now placed in a small plastic container.

Ric asks, "See anything else Izu?"

He nods and says, "I need your help again Boss Ricmasa, Eishi; on the backside of Katana2, another body."

Ric looks down, ashamed of his older brother's continued brutality and the three men make their way off Katana1 and over to Katana2.

After ten minutes, Izu returns with the second man's body and waits for Ric's and

Eishi's assistance. They collectively pull the man's headless and handless body onto the port deck and lay him across from the center of the Katana2 ship. Eishi boards the second ship and just like before, the man's hands are found stapled on the inside of the captain's command center door.

Izu asks, "Were these men on your crew Eishi?"

Eishi immediately says, "I guess they could be but as far as I know, all of my men are retired back to their homes awaiting next season to start in late March."

Ric adds, "Call on them to make sure everyone is accounted for and I'll start making some calls… Izu?"

"Yes; I'll make some calls as well."

Izu asks, "What's that?" as he points to the dead man's chest.

Ric reaches down and takes a piece of paper away from the dead man's inside pocket.

"He can't see what he steals anymore and he can't hold it either!"

In disgust, Ric drops the humiliating note. Sternly, Ric says, "Both of you; you hear anything; you call me and only me!"

Eishi and Izu immediately nod. As they walk away with the two men's bodies slumped on top of a small cart, Ric thinks to himself, "So Naka is watching and listening, as always, but who tipped him off to the black market sales?"

CHAPTER TWENTY-EIGHT

February 14, 2010 – Year of the Tiger on Amami Oshima Island, Japan

EARLY in the morning, Tai contacts Boss Saitonaka and tries to arrange for a small research boat. Saitonaka never wanted to commit to a boat because he always feared that with that resource, Yuen and Tai would leave their island home and begin separating themselves from his control.

"Saitonaka."

"Dr. Tai. How are you and Yuen getting along? Island fever getting to you yet?"

"A little; that's why I called."

"Oh."

"We'd like a small research boat so we can begin other shark experiments in the open ocean and to be able to catch larger bait and prey fish."

"To what end?"

"For Yuen's shark aging, teeth and migration pattern work."

"Bullshit! You'll just leave!"

"And go where? My life is here. You know that and Yuen's too. We have no other place to go to."

"What's in it for me?"

"I have several new compounds and pharmaceuticals sir."

"Pharmaceuticals?"

"Yes. I've been working on a hybrid Opium plant from the few plants that grow near here and I think you'll like my findings."

Saitonaka's eyes widen with these prospects. He says, "Interesting doctor! Very interesting! And all you want is a small boat? And Yuen?"

"He wants a supply of syringes, basic medicines including antibiotics and some disinfectant."

"You two aren't becoming fucking junkies or building a meth lab are you? Addicted to your own shit?"

Tai calmly says, "No sir." He turns to Yuen and the two laughs at each other. Kim is starting to laugh so hard, she leaves the room as soon as Tai motions for her to walk away so Saitonaka won't hear her in the background. As Kim walks away, J.T. follows her, hugging his mom and Misa and Carmela hug each other and laugh as they all walk down the right side hall toward Kim and Tai's bedroom.

Saitonaka pauses and then comes back and says, "Agreed but I want you to call me in two months so I can hear for myself if you and Yuen are sloppy fucking drug addicts shooting up all my profits or what."

"Okay, fair enough."

"I'll send my men with your new boat very soon but I want samples of my new Opium in one month. He'll give you a number so call on him in one month and give him the samples. He'll get them to me."

"Fine."

"Remember, no tricks Doctor or I'll reach across the Sea and pull your hearts out; both of you!"

Tai hangs up.

With his black market video sales declining and no new videos being made, Saitonaka looks forward to this new venture because he knows that a powerful new drug's potential is limitless, especially in southeast Asia. Over half the population remains addicted to all sorts of opium products and knowing that Dr. Tai is a brilliant chemist, he can't wait to see what he's come up with.

In the early evening, Tai announces, "Gong-Hay-Fat-Choy!"

Yuen and Carmela respond, "Yes – Happy New Year everyone!"

Tai leans over to Yuen and whispers, "We're getting the boat." Yuen slaps Tai across his back in appreciation.

Misa and Saka stand together and Misa says, "Now… you two" As she points over at Tai and Kim, "It's been a long day so let's go into town for drinks and for some of Jos' special Wor Won Ton soup so you can tell us how you did it!"

The Huang's all smile and J.T. says, "Yeah Mom, how did you do it?"

Kim hugs her son and escorts him out the door. Misa smiles and playfully shakes Kim's left hand as she walks by toward her and Saka's compact car.

As they arrive at Jos' restaurant, Toma and a couple of his men are there as well. The men quickly recreate the horse-shoe table arrangement and everyone sits down. Jos starts preparing drinks for everyone; their usual mix of Tsingtao and Buddha beers.

Everyone sits anxiously as Tai starts explaining, "Okay. Where to start? First, thanks to Misa for telling Kim about Saitonaka's favorite cigars. It just so happens that our host,

Mr. Jos also enjoys the same cigars so I was able to get a sample from him." Tai nods over to Jos, who nods back.

"I created the base drug; just a placebo really, like anything else. It can be whatever we need it to be. Kim added her usual magic and derived a chemical reaction from a tiny amount of actual opium combined with the specific type of tobacco found in these cigars."

Everyone looks over at Kim. J.T. nudges his mom and she smiles.

"Now, when someone like our favorite Boss takes the pill I made exclusively for him, it picks up on any amount of tobacco in his system and mixes, causing an extremely elevated but temporary feeling of euphoria, like the feeling just before you climax during sex but then it's followed by an upset stomach that the taker will never forget because they'll quickly need to find a bathroom or they'll definitely make their mark where they stand!"

Everyone scowls and then laughs out loud. Toma toasts the Huang's from the corner and they toast him back.

"So, as soon as we get our new research boat, I'll get the Bossman his new designer drugs. Kim and I made him a little over a year's supply. If he wants to sell them on the black market, they'll fail once people experience the 'aftershocks' but something tells me, as perverted as he is, he'll keep them for himself because he'll enjoy the first feeling and just deal with the aftermath!"

Yuen announces, "Hey! Another round Jos!"

After a couple hours of celebrating, good food, and drinks, everyone heads out. Toma says his goodbyes and heads out the back way with his men. Jos thanks everyone and starts closing up his restaurant. J.T. and Saka are the only ones sober so they load everyone else up in two cars and drive them back home. A twosome will return tomorrow to retrieve the other car, as they normally do whenever they go out for drinks.

"Saitonaka-san?"

"Huh?" Semi-conscious, Saitonaka leans over and looks at his lighted alarm clock.

"Damn, it's late. Who is it?" The line drops.

Holding the cut phone line in his right hand, Toma says, "Cousin..."

Frozen with fear, Jos can't move. Toma's men enter the hallway from the kitchen, having made sure there is no one else around.

"I could have let you continue talking but you know what that would have meant."

Ashamed, Jos looks down and nods.

"So in exchange for that; you need to disappear. I'll arrange for a new place for you to live and work, back on Uruma if you like. Just know if you do decide to finish your call to Saitonaka, trust me, I'll find out and then we'll revisit option number one!"

Jos nods again.

"There's a boat waiting for you. My men will take you to Okinawa tonight and then like I said, forget everything and everyone you've met this past few years, got it?"

Scared and humiliated, Jos nods again. A small stream of urine begins to flow down the inside of his right leg.

Toma tosses five thousand Yen over to Jos and disgusted, declares, "Goodbye cousin."

February 14, 2010 Midnight – Boston, Massachusetts, U.S.A.

Julie and her boyfriend Keith are working late in the pathology lab. He looks around and then starts grabbing Julie's backside. He reaches under her shirt and she slaps his hand away.

"Seriously? Here?"

"What? … no one here cares."

"I care! I don't want to mess around down here with all the bodies. I told you that before."

Grinning, "I know! It's gross, huh!"

"Jesus! How can you be so cute and so stupid at the same time? No chance!"

She walks away from Keith and out of the pathology lab. Keith just stands there with his erection, alone. At the top of the stairs, Julie shuts the lights off and runs out the front door. As she leaves, she hears Keith say, "Oh shit!" She can hear him running up the stairs.

Later, Julie calls her mother Misa and shares her experience with her. Just as mother and daughter hang up, Jessica enters the room.

"Hey! We've been pretty busy and I haven't really been able to apologize for what I said about J.T. before. I'm sorry Julie."

"I know Jess. You didn't know. It's okay."

"No, it's not. I was a real bitch and I want to get to know you better so please, tell me more if you want because I really want to know you better, if you want to say."

Jessica's redundancy makes Julie nervous; it's exactly what her mother warned her about.

Julie pauses and then offers, "I'll tell you something about me and Keith if you want to know."

Jessica perks up.

"We did it in the pathology lab earlier tonight!"

Jessica's eyes widen and she says, "In the Path Lab?" Julie smiles devilishly and nods.

"See, I knew there was something nasty about you! You couldn't always be just about the books!"

Julie smiles even wider; "Yeah, everyone else had just left so we looked around one more time, taking clothes off along the way and by the time we got back to the center of the room, we were naked and Keith was absolutely throbbing!"

"Sluts!"

"Yeah! So, right there on one of the gurney's we took turns on each other before he finally popped! He's big but stamina-wise, he's not worth a damn!"

"How big?"

"Over seven and decent width."

"Decent?"

Julie estimates about two inches and then adjusts to a little less.

"Nice! You know I saw a guy once that was this wide." Jessica estimates almost three inches wide.

"Julie says, "Jesus! Coke-can cock!"

The girls fall back laughing.

"Hey, I need a shower so maybe we can talk more later."

"Okay. I'm going to check my laundry."

Julie closes the bathroom door behind her as Jessica leaves the room. Jessica enters the laundry room and immediately heads for the phone on the back wall.

"Saitonaka-san?"

"Jess! How's my favorite school girl? Haven't been naughty, have you?"

"Always! Come teach me after school!"

"Oh! So, what's going on?"

"You were right; she's really loosening up. Maybe too much."

"Really? How?"

"Well, for starters, she laid her boyfriend in the Pathology Lab tonight! I certainly haven't done anything like that! Close…"

"That's sick, even by my standards!"

"You don't have any standards!"

"True but I wouldn't fuck someone basically in a morgue!"

"Okay. I'll grant you that one."

"What else?"

"Nothing."

"No talk of her mom or her mom's friends on Amami?"

"Nope."

"Damn! I was hoping by now maybe her and Tai started up again and maybe Yuen was strangling the little doctor fucker as we speak."

"Misa and Tai were together before?"

"Just during one of my famous dinners. I'll send you a copy if you want."

"Want!"

"Okay my little school girl. Get back to your studies and behave!"

"Okay professor! Go suck on another one of your Cuban dicks!"

"... bitch!"

Saitonaka hangs up his phone and lights up another illegal cigar, immediately followed by another one of his favorite and addicting little blue Opium tablets.

CHAPTER TWENTY-NINE

FEBRUARY 3, 2011, YEAR OF THE RABBIT – PYONGYANG, NORTH KOREA

SAITONAKA is growing suspicious of his various off-shore bank account balances. When he tries to access Julie's account to pay Pyongyang's local Magistrate for his continued hospitality, he's getting several errors. He contacts the account manager in Perth, Australia.

"Mr. Stephenson?"

"Yes?"

"Hey Sun here."

"Yes, Mr. Sun. How are you?"

"Concerned; I've not been able to access one of my online accounts; my daughter's."

"Let me take a look for you. Please bear with me a moment as I bring up your account profile."

Saitonaka lights up another cigar and pops an Opium tablet. His euphoria begins.

"I see here that this account has a secondary account where all the funds have been transferred into Mr. Sun."

"What? A secondary account? Who set that up?"

"You did sir. I have a letter from you dated October 31, 2009 requesting the second account and the full transfer at that time."

"Can you send a copy of that and any other requests back to me? I don't remember things back that far."

"Of course Mr. Sun. That will take a little time though."

"That's okay for now Mr. Stephenson because I'm still moving around a bit. I'll get back in touch with you later with a better address for you to send those letters."

"Very good Mr. Sun. Have a great day."

"Yes. Thank you."

Although not as urgent as before, Saitonaka still has to hurry to the bathroom to address his addiction's aftershocks. With his euphoria weakening, his anger begins to build over the altered bank account. He scrambles his mind trying to figure out who all would even possibly know about these accounts because he's only shown them to a very few people including Kim, Misa, Sika, and possibly Izu. With Kim and Sika dead, that leaves just two people in his increasingly frustrated mind. Saitonaka is becoming more and more impatient and for a man that had limited patience to begin with, this is not good for everyone else.

With his monthly payment for January past due, he gets a call from the local Magistrate's captain.

"Mr. Saitonaka?"
"Yes Yoshi."
"Your January funds have not yet been received by his Honor."
"Yes. Yoshi; I know. I'm working on it."
"His Honor recommends that you make your payments timelier."
"Oh, his honor recommends it? Well then I'd better get to it huh?"
"Sir!"

Saitonaka has been moved around three times already and he knows another move is pending so he can't get too comfortable in any one place. If he continues to fall behind with his 'gift' payments to the local Magistrate, his next move could be his last. For the first time in a long time, Saitonaka is getting nervous about this arrangement.

Saitonaka spends the next eight months meticulously reconfiguring all of his accounts in person except for Julie's in order to free up the funds he needs to keep his struggling Yakuza operation going. Tensions with the local Magistrate in Pyongyang are growing and he knows he's wearing out his welcome.

He's also wearing out his asshole because these newfangled Opium tablets have got him practically shitting his pants on a daily basis.

MAY 21, 2011 – BOSTON, MASSACHUSETTS, U.S.A.

Julie runs into her dorm room and immediately slams the bathroom door behind her.

"Julie; what's wrong?"

No response.

"Julie; come on. Tell me."

The shower turns on so Jessica turns away from the door. A moment later, Julie opens the door.

Julie stands in the doorway wearing just her thin burgundy robe. She looks stunning but she's clearly disturbed by something. She starts to cry a little bit.

"What is it Jewel?"

She starts crying a little harder and says, "That's what my mother calls me."

Again Jessica asks, "What's wrong honey?"

Julie parts her robe and slides her left hand down to cover her smoothly shaven pubic area.

"What is it? Did Keith hurt you?"

Julie looks down, ashamed and says, "We were fooling around in the laundry room and I let him touch me. I was getting moist but then after a few minutes he shoved his fingers inside me. It hurt so I yelled, "Stop! But he kept pushing his fingers in deeper. I yelled for him to stop again but he said, "You're already wet! It's okay!"

"Then what happened?"

"I grabbed his other hand and bit him as hard as I could! He got dressed and left, screaming, "Bitch!" as he walked away. I still felt wet so I reached down there but when I looked at my fingers, they were red. I almost passed out. Then I ran up here to clean up."

"So you're okay?"

"I think so but I'm not sure. Look, I don't want to weird you out Jess but would you mind just checking me out real quick? Like a physical. I was bleeding so I just want to make sure I'm not anymore."

"Are you sure?"

"Yes. I don't have any pain. I just want to make sure and sitting and waiting for three hours over in emergency is not an option. Okay?"

"Okay. Get into the shower and I'll have a look."

Jessica undresses and Julie drops her burgundy robe to the floor. Both young women are slightly tanned. Julie is about two inches taller than Jessica and they both weigh about the same at one hundred and ten pounds. Both girls are well proportioned for their smaller frames. The two enter the shower and run their mid-length black hair under the water. Julie grabs her bottle of shampoo but Jessica tells her to wait until she has a look at her vagina; to make sure there are no cuts or scratches that the soap might irritate. Jessica kneels down and gently spreads Julie's outer labia apart.

She checks for any cuts or scratches on the outside and then says, "Okay. Tell me if this hurts."

Julie nods and braces her hands against the wall and shower curtain.

Jessica gently places her right hand index finger and ring finger inside Julie about one inch and rotates them. Then she takes them out.

"Okay?"

Julie nods again. It's a little awkward but she appreciates another grown woman's support and opinion because for one, her mother isn't there to help her directly and two, after being subjected to such a scary event that could have escalated into something far worse, she appreciates the physical examination that will help to ensure there's nothing really wrong. If so, she can always go over to the emergency room for professional assistance.

Jessica stands back up and says, "You're not bleeding and I don't see or feel any cuts or scratches so I think you're okay. Better go see the school doctor in the morning though just to be safe. I wouldn't use any soap. I'm sure the doctor will give you something that won't irritate you, a salve or something."

"Thanks Jess."

"He did scratch your inner thigh though so make sure you clean that out with soap a few times."

Julie grabs the soap bar and offers it to Jessica. Jessica takes it and massages the soap bar between her hands for a moment and then slides her hands across Julie's upper thigh injury.

Julie boldly says, "I'm not gay but this does feel good. Would you mind washing me and I'll wash you? Does that make sense?"

"I know what you're saying. It feels good but 'that's all' right?"

"Right; just in this moment."

"Right."

The girls smile graciously and Jessica continues to wash Julie's legs. She turns her and soaps up her back; massaging the soap across her shoulders and down her spine. Julie turns around and Jessica repeats the soapy process across Julie's chest and down her stomach; no sexual contact. Then Julie returns the favor. The girls exit the shower and put on their evening attire as usual.

May 22, 2011 – For once Saitonaka calls Jessica with an update.

"Miss Jessica?"

"Miss? Why so formal?"

"Listen. Soon, I may need you to do something."

"Dangerous?"

"Very!"

"My favorite! What is it?"

"I'm trying to flush out a rat and I'm going to spring his trap later this year. Will you help?"

"Of course!"

"Someone's messing around with my off-shore accounts and since you have never seen those account numbers, you're the only one I can trust. We're not getting any real information out of Julie and I haven't heard back from Misa in some time. It's time to force their hand to see what they know. I'll have a few of my men in on a plot to kidnap Julie later this winter, during her regular school break. Until then, just keep an eye on her and make sure she's safe until we make our move. If someone tries to make a move on her before we do, that'll narrow things down. Got it?"

"Got it!"

"So, just keep your eyes open and your legs closed! If you see anyone around that looks suspicious, … do what you do!"

"Say it."

"Really?"

"Say it! … after your 'keep your legs closed' crack, you owe me."

"Fine… Queen Mamba!"

Jessica smiles in delight as Saitonaka rolls his eyes on the other line.

"Just remember, whoever our rat calls will be someone really good and dangerous so make sure you've got everything ready and make sure Julie stays put so we can actually get her away safely."

"Yes sir, Saitonaka-san sir!"

"Good girl! One more thing."

"Yes?"

"Look like Julie more, you know what I mean?"

"Really? But I like my hair this length."

"Come on, for me. You've done it before."

"Okay. At least this time, it'll be easy because Julie and I are almost the same height. We are the same weight and all I have to do is cut my hair about three inches and part it like she does."

"Exactly….that's why I asked…"

"Yeah, yeah. I got it."

"Good girl! … Banzai Queen Mamba!"

"Yes! That's more like it! Oh, you just made me wet sir!"

"Oh Jess! And call me after you've struck, Queen Mamba!"

August 30, 2011 – Yokohama, Japan

Eishi's Misha-Katana 'research' fleet returns to port after another lack-luster whaling season, compliments of Captain Darren Hall and his Sea Guardians. As his men clean their respective ships and prepare them for dry dock, Eishi is reminded of what Izu told him before; his uncle Saitonaka's demand for a successful season, or else. With his whereabouts still unknown, Eishi is looking forward to the winter season where he can again keep in touch with his uncle Ric for advice and protection. Just as Eishi is finishing up his work on Misha Katana1, he gets a call.

"Eishi-san?"

"Yes?"

"Listen."

"Who is this?"

"Never mind. Not as important as what I have to tell you. When I finish, call your uncle Ric immediately and tell him, okay?"

"Okay."

"Boss Saitonaka is six miles southwest of Pyongyang, staying in the compound's middle home. He'll be there for the next week, maybe less so you must move quickly. They are already planning on moving him again to the north end of the city. I don't know where yet. I'm close by so I'll let you know if anything changes. I've worked it out with the local Magistrate so you'll have no trouble getting onto the compound but just in case, I've left some guard uniforms by the front gate. Have your men ask for 'Cara' because there is no 'Cara.'"

"Six miles southwest of Pyongyang in the compound's middle home, get uniforms, ask for 'Cara'; go it. Who is this?"

"A friend." The person hangs up.

Eishi lights a cigarette and takes a moment before calling his uncle. A little overwhelmed by the mysterious helper and feeling eerie about his uncle Saitonaka's potential hit opportunity, Eishi starts to shake a little so he grabs the half full bottle of warm saké he stores in his upper Captain's quarters shelf. Then he calls his uncle.

"Uncle?"

"Eishi. Good trip?"

"Not very good uncle. I got a call tonight; I know where uncle Saitonaka is."

"Naka? Where?"

"He's six miles southwest of Pyongyang in the compound's middle home. We have the local Magistrate's support to gain access. Have your men ask for a 'Cara' at the front gate. They have guard uniforms for them and then they can make their move against uncle Saitonaka in his quarters."

"Okay Eishi. Good work."

"Good work?"

"Eishi! He's my older brother. He killed your father! This has to be done. You know this!"

"Yes uncle. For my father; banzai!"

"Banzai! I'll call you when I hear back nephew. I am sorry but remember, Naka put this all in motion, not us and not anyone else. It's time for him to face his fate."

September 3, 2011 – 5 A.M. Pyongyang, North Korea

Saitonaka paces around the outside of his temporary residence. The dark orange pre-dawn light hides a potentially lethal secret.

At 5:05 A.M., the secret is revealed and the pre-dawn silence is shattered with the effects from short bursts emanating from a very high-powered silenced weapon. Saitonaka dives to the ground. He strikes the top of his head against a small stone that splits him open with a half-inch gash. With his heart racing and adrenaline coursing throughout his body, he begins to bleed profusely.

He shouts toward the rear residence, "Izu! Get up!"

In his sleeping quarters, Izu is trying to delay his response by acting asleep. If he gives it another few minutes, maybe then, the hit-men will find their mark and end his boss's deplorable reign.

Saitonaka senses the layout of the hit against him. He quickly recalls a former attempt that almost had him surrounded. His only option is to retreat around the back of his residence and try to commandeer the local Magistrate's private charter jet. He runs around the backside of his residence and yells over to Izu, "Come on Izu!"

Torn between abandoning his boss; allowing the hit to proceed and not being sure if after the deed is done, whether the hit-men will kill him as well, Izu opts to support his boss one last time. He fires back at the hit-men, offering covering fire for his Boss. This allows Saitonaka to reach the charter jet safely. Saitonaka opens the door and quickly grabs the 9mm stored alongside the pilot's chair. Saitonaka then repositions a half-full gas barrel and tips it over. He rolls it down the slope at the rear of the plane, where he initiated from and again, yells out for Izu.

"Izu!" And then something in Japanese to the effect of, "You better fucking hurry up!"

Izu makes his way to the charter jet and quickly enters the pilot's seat. He starts the plane up as Saitonaka retrieves the small staircase. Just before the staircase completely closes, he fires at the gas barrel. The barrel explodes, sending the canister up in the air thirty feet high. A shower of fire and gas mist falls back to earth, forcing the two hit-men to cancel their advance on the charter jet.

Clear and climbing to altitude, Izu calls back in the cabin, "Okay sir?"

"God damn it Izu! You never sleep that sound! What's wrong with you?"

"Sorry sir. I have no excuse."

"Never again, huh?"

"No sir."

Saitonaka starts laughing to himself. "Hey! Look at me Izu! I look like America's Ric Flair after a classic match against Harley Race!"

"Sir! I remember those matches."

"Yes, back in the early nineteen eighties! Our Jumbo Tsuruta and Antonio Onoki sure gave them both some hell!"

"Good times back then sir!"

"I!"

"Where to sir?"

"Friends in Hanoi. I moved all my accounts over to them and gave them a 'gift' so they welcome us now."

"Yes sir."

Saitonaka starts cleaning up his crimson face. He narrows his eyes as he stares at the pilot's cabin. He scrambles his mind trying to think of the short list of people who knew where he was. He barely escaped this time and with only his smaller backpack containing his Cuban's, his few remaining Opium tablets, his bank roll, and his ten thousand dollar Rolex; that's all he owns.

7 A.M. – One of Boss Ricmasa's men report back to him.

"Boss Ricmasa?"

"Tell me my brother Naka is dead!"

"No sir."

"No?"

"He got a hold of a charter jet behind his compound that we didn't know about and got away. Izu flew him out sir."

"A charter jet? Hmm, must have been the Magistrate's. He's done with Pyongyang now so we need to find out where's he's headed to. Find this out for me or don't return to Yokohama, got it?"

"Yes sir."

SEPTEMBER 6, 2011 – BOSTON, MASSACHUSETTS, U.S.A.

Keith calls for Julie but Jessica answers the phone. Julie is off campus putting together the rest of her fall schedule of classes but all Keith can think about is his next chance to score some erotic favors from her. He's completely forgotten about his scary behavior this past May and he has no idea that Jessica even knows about it.

"Julie?"

Flatly, Jessica says, "Keith."

"Hey Jess. Is Julie there?"

"No Keith. Not here. Bye..."

"Wait. When is she back? Tonight?"

"Yeah. Later tonight."

Jessica thinks quickly and adds, "Oh, she'll be here to watch her favorite show at 8 tonight and I'll be with other friends so you can stop by then. I can't stand the show she likes so I leave for an hour or so."

Keith's eyes light up. "Cool. Thanks." He hangs up.

Jessica whispers, "See you later bitch!" as she hangs up.

7:45 P.M. – Jessica gets Julie out of the room for the next hour or so.

"Julie, can you do me a big favor?"

"Sure. What?"

"For my new Psych class tomorrow, I wanted to wear my dark red shirt and black skirt but they need washing."

"Say no more. I need to do a load anyway. Pile it on!"

"Thanks."

"This will take a while. Do me a favor. If he calls, tell Keith I'm doing laundry."

"Will do!" Jessica smirks as Julie leaves the room.

8:01 P.M. – Keith knocks on the door. Jessica cracks the door open, turns the lights off and quickly turns the television on.

"Hey babe! Ready for me?"

"Yeah. The show's a repeat anyway."

"You okay? You sound funny."

"Oh, just a little cold."

"That's okay. We don't need to kiss for what I've got planned anyway!"

Keith makes his way over to Julie's bed and takes off his shirt. He bends down and Jessica grabs his erection bulging from his pants.

She whispers, "First, you do something for me and then I'll do something for you."

"Oh yes! … it's about time!"

Jessica moves to the middle of the bed and starts taking her panties off slowly. Keith helps her; pulling them off rapidly.

"Hey, easy… take it slow."

Over-anxious as always, Keith ignores her and starts groping at her hips and buttocks.

"I like it rough baby, you know that!"

He starts kissing her all over and rubbing her hips and thighs.

"Easy! Slow down."

Keith continues. After a few minutes, Jessica fakes climax and pushes Keith away.

He just stands up and drops his pants to the floor.

She plays along and whispers to him, "Bend over a little babe."

He bends over and she says, "A little more and stand a little wider."

"Oh nice! You never wanted to do this before. Yeah!"

Jessica massages Keith's erection and continues to get him to widen his stance.

He bends over until he's in a football Center player's stance at the scrimmage line.

Jessica takes something out from her silk leg wrapping band and places it against Keith's anus.

He jumps a little and says, "Hey! What's that Jewel?"

Jessica grips Keith' erection harder and emphasizes her other hand a little more against Keith's anus.

"First, I'm not Jewel."

"What?... Jess? Shit! What the hell?"

Jessica grips Keith even harder. She places the cold steel element into his anus about an inch.

Agonizing, he declares, "Fuck! What are you doing?"

"You treat women like shit! Back in May, you hurt Julie and now, I'm here with you to accept your fucking apology!"

"Stop!"

"Oh? Funny; that's exactly what Julie asked you to do but you ignored her so I think I'll ignore you too!"

Jessica sticks her stiletto knife up Keith's ass about two more inches.

"Now, as you stand there clinching your ass cheeks together and bleeding, let me just say this quickly and then you can awkwardly make your way out of this fucking room and out of Julie's life forever. Got it?"

Crying and writhing in pain, Keith quickly nods.

"Grow the fuck up and listen to a woman when she decides to let you touch her. If she says 'stop', that means, 'stop' asshole! Oh and feel lucky that I only went in as far as I did because this will make for a very amusing story for your doctor when he sees and treats your injury. He'll think you forced a hostile gerbil or a big carrot into your asshole!"

Jessica extracts the blade and wipes it on Keith's pants as he collects his clothes and quickly but carefully 'runs' out of the room crying.

OCTOBER 22, 2011 – FOUR MILES NORTHEAST OF HANOI, VIETNAM

Settled in for the time being and hiding, Saitonaka again addresses his concerns over his daughter Julie's off-shore account; remembering that a separate account had been created. Saitonaka contacts his team of Oso Wakashi and Heroshi as well as Izu to discuss an aggressive new plan of action that will yield real results.

With Izu in the room with him, Saitonaka reaches Oso and Heroshi on his conference phone.

"Gentlemen."

Collectively, "Yes Boss Saitonaka!"

"It's time we took the next step. I need help from each of you; not exactly right now but soon enough."

"Yes sir."

"Oso. Heroshi; in December, during her winter break, you'll go to the States, get Julie and bring her here to me in Hanoi. Then maybe I can have a real conversation with Miss Misa about where all of my fucking money has gone!"

The duo responds, "Yes sir."

"Izu; I need you to contact my nephew Eishi. Arrange a call between me and my brother Ito's people. It's time for me to return home but I won't unless we understand each other. They'll either follow my lead or they can deal with my new Hanoi contacts, it's that simple."

"Yes sir. When should I arrange that call?"

"Eh, wait until Oso and Heroshi have finished their task and then set it up."

"Yes sir; very good."

"Yes. That will give me time to meet with my new contacts to gain their support for my return home."

"Until then sir?"

"Until then, I need you in Okinawa to see what you can find out about Miss Kim and J.T. Ask if anyone has seen anything. Maybe part of their clothing has washed up by now or something. The ocean gives up all kinds of things over time."

"Yes sir. I'll leave tonight?"

"No. Give it a week or so. Help me get settled and then leave, right?"

"Yes sir."

Saitonaka throws Izu five thousand Yen and says, "New clothes for us both, my Cubans from my friends and call my drug dealing Chinaman for more O-Tabs and a new supply of Myst1 and CDT wash for my new friends. They will appreciate his work and it'll make me a small fortune as I reside here for the time being."

"Yes sir."

NOVEMBER 22, 2011 – UNDISCLOSED LOCATION IN SOUTHEAST ASIA

Toma gets a call.

"Toma?"

"Yeah? What? What time is it?"

"It's early; 4 A.M. your time. Listen!"

"4 A.M. my time? Who is this?"

"Not important."

"At 4 A.M., it sure as shit is important!"

"It's more important you listen now."

"What?"

After five minutes on the call, Toma hangs up. He dresses quickly and jumps into his car headed to the airport. He buys a round trip ticket to Boston-Logan International Airport. With such a long flight ahead of him, he tries to rest but all he can think about is Julie's safety. He would have liked to have called Misa to let her know what's going on but there simply wasn't time. It's also risky for him to have left without some backup from his men but again, there wasn't time to arrange it.

NOVEMBER 24, 2011 10 P.M. – BOSTON, MASSACHUSETTS, U.S.A.

Toma quickly locates Julie's residence and enters the building from the back entrance. From an earlier tip, he locates her room and in the dark, quickly grabs Julie out of her bed.

She begins to scream but he covers her mouth and says, "You're in danger. I'm here to help. Shush!"

Toma hears voices in the hallway. They are approaching Julie's room. Toma rushes Julie into the closet. Peeking through the key hole, Toma can see Oso Wakashi and Heroshi enter and frantically search the room with their flashlights. A bit later, as Heroshi stands guard at the door, Oso walks through the room checking the bathroom and both beds.

Julie starts kissing Toma and then she sticks her hand down his pants and starts jerking him off. Unable to do anything about it or even make a sound, Toma has to let her finish. A few minutes later, Oso and Heroshi leave.

Toma punches the closet door open and yells, "Julie! What the hell are you doing? Jesus! I'm here to take you back to your mom!"

Toma walks back over to the front door and flips the light on. She is turned away from him, laughing.

She says, "Ha! I thought you'd be bigger…and last a little longer but what should I have expected from a Triad!"

Still shocked, Toma moves toward Julie.

"What? What makes you think I'm a Triad? Did your mom tell you that?"

"My mom? No. No; I killed her long ago!"

She extracts a silver stiletto knife from inside her skirt, turns abruptly toward Toma and yells, "Saitonaka says 'goodbye' fucker!" The blade penetrates Toma's right forearm.

Toma falls back but rights himself before falling completely over. Stunned, he says, "Your hair! You dress like her! You're in her bed! Who the hell are you?"

Jessica advances on him, holding another stiletto knife in her hand. The two are at a stand-still for the moment as Toma tries to recover from his wound. Without the element of surprise and no clear advantage against one of the Triad's better men, Jessica stands firm and just gloats over her initial successful attack.

"Where is Julie you crazy bitch?"

"Ha! Long gone by now Triad! She's heading to Hanoi to be a super sex-slave I'd guess. From what she's told me here in school, she'll make the guys and girls there a fine regular piece of ass!"

Toma staggers momentarily as the loss of blood is beginning to affect his balance and overall stamina.

"We found out about you from a traitor among us. We watched him on a hunch that he'd contact you. When you made your move, we knew he was the one so we made our move first! Oso and Heroshi grabbed that little Chinese bitch about a half an hour ago from the library! They put on a little show especially for me as I jerked you off, just to waste a little more time, and I do mean 'a little'. They left you for me because after all, they don't call me 'Queen Mamba' for nothing!"

Jessica lunges at Toma with her single stiletto fang but he blocks her path with a chair. The two combatants resettle to the middle of the floor.

"Queen Mamba…I know you. Your name is Jessica Snakamoto or Jessie Snake!"

"It's Queen Mamba now and as you can see and feel, I never miss!"

Toma staggers again. He repositions his stance for his own strike at Queen Mamba.

With Jessica focusing in on his bleeding arm wound, Toma slowly rolls his rear right foot up on its toe; unlocking his own secret fang.

"Well, sorry to strike and run but you have to die now Toma! You're making Saitonaka's work too difficult and since you've already blown your little load, I don't have any need for you anymore either!"

In a move that would make any real black mamba proud, Toma pivots and sweeps his right foot across, striking Jessica in the face. When he returns to his position, he sees his strike landed perfectly.

Jessica lets out an agonizing scream.

"Fucker! What have you done to me?" Blood begins dripping down her right cheek all over and down her right shoulder.

Toma stands firm and smirks. He says, "Queen Mamba struck but then, I swept my Dragon's tail!"

Jessica starts to shake a little as she gently feels the lacerated piece of skin dangling on the right side of her face.

"Hey, Queen Mamba. It looks like you're starting to peel! Let me even things up for you!"

Toma spins and repeats his strike on the left side of Jessica's face, landing at almost the same height as before, gashing Jessica's left cheek. Jessica spins around violently and then falls to her knees in complete agony. She makes a last attempt to stab at Toma but with all her blood loss and blood splattered in her eyes, she can barely make out shapes in the room.

Toma pauses and then he says, "Just remember Queen Mamba; I let you live. You owe me a life now! If you have any honor left, you'll side with us next we meet, eh?"

Toma leaves as Jessica Snakamoto makes her way into the bathroom to tend to her wounds.

NOVEMBER 26, 2011 – AMAMI OSHIMA ISLAND, JAPAN

Misa pleads with Saitonaka to return Julie to the States so she can complete her studies.

"I know your name now."

"Yes, I suppose you do."

"I can't believe you're doing this and to your own daughter no less."

"Well, I've been having some bad days lately dear."

"Bad days?"

"For starters, several of my men have betrayed me. Then I had to flee my beloved home to escape assassination. I haven't spoken to my nephew or younger brother in years. Then I teamed up with a rich fool in North Korea who couldn't catch a cold if his life depended on it! My Kim drown! My son was 'accidentally' shot and killed! Then I had to flee North Korea after another attempt on my life. I did blow a couple assholes sky-high with a gas barrel, so that was fun but all this time, I thought blowing me was your job and to top things off, you've been stealing all of my fucking money! So yeah, I've been having some bad days!"

"Oh, and did I mention your mad-doctor-fucker Tai has got me addicted to Opium pills! And all you're concerned about is Julie?"

Misa pauses, allowing Saitonaka to complete his rant and then she says, "Yes. Julie is all I care about! I told you in time, I'd take care of Tai and Yuen myself but it's going to be my way."

"No! I tell you how things go, you don't tell me! One word from me to Saka and this is all over!"

"Instead, how about one gesture for your daughter; send her back to the States so she can graduate and be a doctor!"

Saitonaka's only remaining soft-spot is for his daughter so Saitonaka agrees but he has a few demands of his own.

"Fine but tell the good doctor I want more Opium tablets and I expect something new from him and Yuen in six weeks or else you, my dear, will never see our daughter again! I promise you that!"

"Something new? Like what?"

"Hey, you're the brilliant scientist and chemist assholes! You figure it out! And don't change the mixture of my Opium tablets. I enjoy my sex-like high and my shit-fits afterward! I'm going to market these pills all over Southeast Asia as the new weight-loss miracle of the twenty-first century!

Check out my campaign; "Feel like you're fucking and afterward, no cigarette needed. Just shit your way to a slimmer new you!"

"What do you think?"

Misa hangs up.

Misa immediately tells the Amami Island team about Saitonaka's demands and they get to work producing one thousand Opium tablets as a part of Saitonaka's ransom demands.

As for the "something new", everyone is drawing a blank.

JANUARY 3, 2012 – AMAMI OSHIMA ISLAND, JAPAN

With just a week remaining in Saitonaka's ransom deadline, Dr. Tai and Kim struggle to share their Enhanced-CDT formula with Saitonaka because they know they'd be forced to sign it over to him forever. Saitonaka refuses more research notes from Yuen, Carmela and Misa because they are pointless and have never made him any money. At his Hanoi, Vietnam hideout, he's begun using some of them as toilet paper.

Misa pleads with Tai and Kim to give up their Enhanced-CDT formula because if they refuse, Misa may never see Julie again.

"What else can we do? We're running out of time! We've lost so much time with each other and you know Saitonaka is serious. I don't want to lose that kind of time with my daughter!"

"Please Misa! I know something will come up, I just know it; just a little more time." Tai pleads.

"Haven't you two had enough time already? You've been on this damn island for what, twenty-five fucking years now?"

Crying, Misa runs outside. Kim quickly runs after her. Kim catches her and says, "We can get word to Toma and be a step ahead of Saitonaka this time…"

"He already tried that and it didn't work! Saitonaka will expect that and this time, he might kill her just to show us we were wrong to try."

Kim nods in agreement. The two women hug each other and cry together as they walk around the house and toward the back cove.

JANUARY 7, 2012

The deadline looms when Toma suggests a daring rescue but Misa doesn't want to chance it.

"Miss Misa?"

"Yes Toma?"

"I know Saitonaka beat me to Julie before but I think I have an option that could work."

"I don't want to chance my daughter's life on something that 'could' work!"

"There are never any guarantees."

She thinks for a moment and finally asks, "What is your idea?"

"It's simple. Julie's roommate owes me a life; either hers or another. I figure I can call on her now to help us and by her helping to secure Julie that would repay her debt to me.

She's actually Yakuza; a thirty year-old woman that Saitonaka had planted to spy on Julie at school all this time."

"Jesus! He's relentless!"

"Yes! But I really think this could work."

"And what if she decides whatever you did to her was too much and she decides to support Saitonaka?"

"As I said, there are never any guarantees."

Their options running out, Kim and Tai discuss offering their Enhanced-CDT formula up. Kim talks to Tai again about just handing over their Enhanced-CDT formula to Saitonaka for his greedy purposes; the formula is worth hundreds of millions of Yen because they know all Saitonaka will do is immediately sell it to the highest bidder who can then mass produce it, making even greater profits over time. With the money, Saitonaka can finally buy his protection and safe return back to Yokohama. He'll be able to pay off anyone looking to take him out and he'll be able to settle any and all debts and issues with his younger brother Ric and his nephew Eishi.

"We mock something up and pass it over to him?"

"He'll expect that and he's already shown that he can pretty much reverse anything; look what he did with our first patents."

"If he even knows about Enhanced-CDT, he'll have it stripped down and remade underground and then it could either generate hundreds of millions of dollars for him or it could kill every person they give it to and he'd make sure we hanged for it!"

Completely exhausted and stressed Tai proclaims, "Fuck! I told this man I'd dance with him! Even for just five minutes! Let me just make that case to him! To face him one-on-one, winner take all and be done with it. I'd rather sacrifice my own life for Julie's rather than see this man take what we made together, profit from it, kill us anyway, or blame us when he fails to reproduce it correctly! Fuck him! I'll take him out or I'll die trying! Then I can share all these stories with my father and we'll spend eternity with my mother and brother fishing and playing Mah-Jongg all day!"

Crying, Kim stands behind Tai and just remains quiet as she hugs and holds him. Tai calls in J.T. and Yuen and tells them the plan.

"Brother Yuen. Promise me you'll take care of Kim and J.T. as long as you can. When I call Saitonaka, I'll demand he comes alone but I expect he'll have some of his men here anyway. I'll contact Toma and see if he can be here ready with his team."

Yuen adds, "If it's war he wants, no problem! I can call on my Triad contacts and have as many of them come here as you want!"

"And destroy everyone and everything? No. He'll honor a one-on-one combat because it's about honor. Afterward though, who knows what this psycho might do; that's what Toma and his smaller force are for; to escort Saitonaka's group away after either he or I lie dead. At least then, it'll be over!"

JANUARY 8, 2012

Twenty-four hours to go. Saitonaka calls to remind Misa of his demand and he promises the whole team they will never see Julie again because he'll keep her drugged and offered up to his new Hanoi friends as a sex slave.

Misa says, "You shit-bastard! You could do that to your own daughter?"

Saitonaka says, "Shit-bastard?" Saitonaka laughs to himself.

"That's original Miss Misa. Why not? She's not my daughter! She's Yuen's daughter, but you've known that all along, haven't you, you Chinese bitch?"

Misa falls to the floor crying. She knows now that she may never see her daughter alive again because Saitonaka has found out her biggest secret.

"You see, when we gave her a few new immunizations back in November. I had them run a special blood test that matches against my DNA and it didn't match at all, except for the common Asian markers but not enough to prove that she was my daughter. Plus, she's clearly not even half Japanese, so that rules out you having fucked Saka. That leaves only Yuen or did you fuck countless others my dear? Better yet, let me ask, who didn't you fuck?"

Saitonaka slams the phone down in anger but doesn't hang it up.

Misa pleads on the phone saying, "Please; if I ever meant anything to you, please! Just leave my daughter alone! Let her stay in the United States and become a surgeon so she can help people."

"Oh, she's ready to help people now my dear. With her medical skills, just think of all the people she can help in Hanoi! My new friends will greatly appreciate me all the more for offering her to them all! She's ripe and ready to go! Game over bitch!"

Saitonaka takes a long drag from his Cuban cigar and almost falls back in his chair as his new supply of Opium tablets are taking their affect. He hangs up the phone calmly.

Kim and Carmela try to comfort Misa but she's hysterical. She hasn't slept or eaten for days and finally passes out from exhaustion and dehydration. Saka and J.T. quickly work to stabilize her with medical supplies that Toma provides for the group every time he visits; monthly.

Saitonaka calls for Tai to discuss any last options before he has Julie sent away.

"Doctor?"

"Look, what do you want from us? Haven't you taken enough already?"

"Never!"

"So, what the hell do you want?"

"I think you've been holding back on me for some time now doctor. Maybe you'll stand up and do what's right for your lover Misa, eh?"

"My lover?"

Tai wants desperately to tell Saitonaka that he, Kim and J.T. are all back together now and have been for some time but that would only cause a war they can't win.

"You know what? You're right! I do have something for you but tomorrow is my fifty-second birthday so I'd like to ask for one more day."

"And if you still have nothing?"

Tai asks Kim and J.T. to step outside. Tai returns to the phone.

"Either way; I come up with something or I can't and we finally have our dance but obviously for that, you must be here."

"A birthday challenge from the good doctor, hmm; very interesting!"

"Deal?"

Saitonaka pauses while he lights up another stogie. Finally he says, "Happy birthday you fool! I'll make arrangements to fly out first thing on the eleventh, once you've officially failed."

Tai hangs up.

CHAPTER THIRTY

JANUARY 9, 2012 1 A.M. – AMAMI OSHIMA ISLAND, JAPAN

UNABLE to sleep, J.T., Yuen and Tai walk along the cove deck behind their house. J.T. believes he hears something bellow out near the shore's shallow inlet. It's a fourteen-foot female Orcinus Orca. Being more of a rogue female and not as close to a pod, she swam away so, and thinking she was sickly or dying, her pod left her behind. It appears the killer whale heard humans nearby and sought them out for help. She's suffering from the effects of the increased slime build up now in the East China Sea and needs emergency treatment.

Yuen's eyes light up like never before. Tai's and J.T.'s too. They all know this means something big but they don't know what yet. All they can concentrate on now is trying to save this phenomenal and majestic mammal.

Yuen suggests, "She just shot right up here in our shallow cove inlet and waited for someone to come along."

Yuen's love for sharks extends to whales as well. He immediately but very carefully opens the killer whale's mouth a little wider and notices that her teeth have a green plaque around the roots. He shines the light across the animal's powerful jaws and Tai sees this for himself.

"Quick J.T.! Run and get my Enhanced-CDT case from the closet! I have bottles and syringes ready to go! Bring them all so Yuen can tell us what dose to give her!"

J.T. sprints away as Yuen and Tai try to help calm the Orca, hoping and praying she can survive long enough for the Enhanced-CDT to do its job. Yuen estimates her size at just over fourteen feet and three thousand pounds. On his way back down to the cove inlet, J.T. turns on a lamp light and positions it to shine over toward the Orca. It's the perfect amount of light for the men to work with the Orca and not too bright that it'll scare her. She's very receptive and trusting, allowing Yuen to again open her mouth wider and take a longer look at her tongue and all of her impressive and powerful smooth conical-shaped teeth. They are definitely stained green around the roots, especially her rear teeth and her tongue is badly swollen.

J.T. is in awe of the great mammal, as are Tai and Yuen. They comfort her by splashing water over her massive black head and when the water cascades over her famous white patch and eye just behind it, it looks like she's smiling and winking in appreciation at them for their efforts. She has stopped bellowing and seems a little more relaxed.

J.T. whispers at his dad, "Happy birthday Pop!"

Tai smiles and gives his son a hug. Then Yuen offers his wishes as well. Tai responds to both of them saying, "Xie-xie!"(Chinese for "*thank you*").

The three men look at each other and then at the killer whale and Dr. Tai says "That's your name sweetheart; Xie-xie!"

A moment later, the killer whale starts to slip back into the cove; falling more ill to the sickness that has afflicted her for months now. Yuen jumps past her massive head and braces her body up, grabbing her massive right flipper.

"J.T.! Your dad and I will try to roll her over. Give her the whole bottle I rigged up with the larger needle. Insert it on the underside just below her right flipper and be ready to jump back and away from her mouth when she reacts!"

"How long?"

"Shit! I don't know Tai. With the little fish we tested before, reactions took what, two to five minutes? For her; two and a half tons and if I estimated the dosage right, maybe five minutes. Maybe a little longer."

J.T. completes his task and quickly gets back to shore. Yuen and Tai help right Xie-xie. She is perfectly calm, not reacting violently at all. She rests in the shallows as she did when they first discovered her but now, she's able to maintain her position, not slipping back into the cove involuntarily. She's absolutely breathtaking to see.

After ten minutes, she opens her mouth and starts sticking out her tongue. Yuen figures she's hungry so he quickly runs to the other side of the cove, to the deck side, to get his bucket of fish from yesterday's catch. He has eight good sized Chinese Perch to offer up if she is hungry. With Tai very cautiously remaining in the water holding Xie-xie's right flipper up supporting her, Yuen and J.T. inject the fish using the smaller syringes with Enhanced-CDT as well. Yuen carefully places one of the fish in Xie-xie's mouth. She bounces her whole head up and down so he puts a couple more that J.T. has just injected in her mouth as well. In a flash, she swallows them down.

J.T. yells, "Holy shit! Did you see that? That was awesome!"

Yuen says, "I guess she was hungry! Fix up the rest J.T. and let's get her fed as best we can so she can get her strength back."

Tai adds, "Yeah and hurry up son! I can't feel my balls anymore!"

Yuen laughs and says, "Tai; go ahead and get out of the water now. I think she's getting better!"

Tai gets out, mumbling, "..well shit, I didn't know."

Yuen runs back to the deck side and retrieves another bucket of fish.

Stomping his feet trying to warm up, Tai says, "You know, feeding this killer whale is a full time job. How are we going to manage that?"

Yuen says, "Yeah. I know. They need two to three hundred pounds of fish per day, at a minimum before they start using up their fat reserves."

Yuen continues, "I think once she starts feeling better, she'll be able to survive like she's always done. This cove is plenty deep after you get past the first thirty feet of shore. And look at her, the rocks in front are nice and smooth, the perfect slipway for her to come up for help, just like she did when she heard us talking close by."

"Amazing uncle Yuen!"

Yuen states, "This is amazing! What a gorgeous animal! And she's ours!"

"Ours?" Tai asks.

"Yes! We need to build a protected area for her in our cove. I'd say that makes her ours and if she wants to stay and recover some more, she will."

"And when she wants to leave?"

"Hey, there's nothing we could possibly build out here that would keep her inside if she really didn't want to stay. She makes the rules!"

Yuen again runs to the other side of the cove to retrieve the last of his recent fish catch buckets. He stores them in an ice chest in the small shed at the end of the deck for research experiments he was hoping to conduct over the next few days. He smiles wildly to himself as he thinks about this amazing happening. This wild female killer whale is so trusting and so grateful for the help, she remains in the area when she could easily and more appropriately swim away to seek out her former pod. Yuen returns and remains amazed at how docile she is. She remains close by requesting food. With her jaws agape, Yuen tosses in another large Chinese Perch and she just bounces her jaws up and down slightly, requesting more before she swallows them down. A moment later, she reverses her massive body like nothing and disappears into the glassy black water. With the heavy dose of Enhanced-CDT they administered, Yuen figures they don't need to treat these other fish with any more.

J.T. asks, "Ready Pop?"

"Yeah, watch this?"

Tai slaps the water in front of him and like magic, a moment later, Xie-xie's glossy black head appears from the depths and launches safely up and onto the shore's smooth rocks. The rocks help her scrape off unwanted parasites and just like her extremely ancient land-loving ancestors; she loves the scratchy feeling against her belly. With each hour that passes, the female Orca is feeling and acting better and better but she is still very hungry.

5 A.M. – Kim awakes in her bed and feels across the sheets. She's a little startled to not feel Tai next to her so she gets up. On the other Y-shaped hallway, Carmela senses Yuen's absence as well so she gets up too. Kim checks J.T.'s room on her way to the shared living room and kitchen area but he's not there. The two women meet up in the living room area.

Kim inquires, "Yuen?"

Carmela says, "No. Tai and J.T.?"

"No. They probably went fishing."

"Let's start breakfast?"

Kim nods and heads for the kitchen.

Carmela glances out the back window toward the cove down the gentle slope and says, "Found them."

Holding a carton of milk, Kim walks to the window and looks out. She drops the carton and milk splatters all over the back patio glass and floor.

"Jesus! What the hell is that?"

Casually, Carmela skips over the milk, looking frustrated at Kim's clumsiness, and says, "What the hell is what?"

"Out there!"

"Yeah? So, the guys are getting ready to go fishing, so what?"

"No! Look past the shore line right in front of Yuen!"

Carmela refocuses her early-morning eyes and peers out again.

She thinks she sees something but in the very early dawn, it's hard to make it out.

She asks, "A suit?"

Kim responds, "A suit? Shit! A fin! A big fucking fin too!"

Carmela looks again and a moment later, she drops the small bowl of eggs she's stirring.

"Yuen!"

The two women race out of the patio door and down the walkway screaming non-sense.

Tai, J.T. and Yuen all turn around and say, "Shhh! Shush! … you'll scare her!"

They look at each other as if to say, "…women!"

Kim and Carmela start to tear up.

Quietly, Kim says, "… what the hell did you catch?"

J.T. says, "We didn't catch her mom. She found us. She needed help so we fed her and now, she looks great! Awesome huh?"

Kim stares and then says, "Orcinus Orca… right here in our cove!"

"Watch this mom."

J.T. holds up another Perch and waves it in front of Xie-xie. She opens her mouth and starts bouncing her whole head up and down three times. When she settles down, J.T. tosses the fish in her mouth. Before J.T. can even motion to her that the bucket is empty, Xie-xie slips backward and turns to her left to drop into the deeper waters of the cove; she knew he was out of food.

Tai and Yuen stare at each other and then Tai suggests, "A protected fencing for her?"

"At fourteen foot? No chance. We'd need a tank and besides, I saw "*Blackfish*". I'd never enclose her in a tank and treat her like an exhibit. Trained or not, the instincts of an originally wild animal can never be trained out of her. When she gets frustrated or upset, she has many ways to show it that we can't ever know. We would only find out one time and that would be the end of us, likely in some horrific and gory manner."

"So what now?"

"We just have to hope she'll stick around so we can study her and just learn everything we can. At least now, we have something to really study!"

Tai confirms, "Right! I'll call Saitonaka and tell him about our ultimate bargaining chip for Julie!"

The Huang's all hug each other and they each let out a collective sigh of genuine relief.

As they approach the back door, Misa and Saka are in the doorway. Kim grabs Misa, hugs her and spins around with her. Tai walks past and pats her and Saka on their shoulders. J.T. kisses Misa on her cheek and shakes Saka's hand.

"What's with the 'love-fest'?" Saka asks.

Kim starts crying and explains, "Julie's coming home!"

Misa immediately starts to cry. She falls to her knees and stares back up at Kim and says, "Really? How?"

Kim kneels down to her and says, "Really! When Saitonaka hears about what we just found, he'll agree to let her come here to live with you!"

"Why? What did you guys find?"

Kim stands Misa up and says, "Grab a fresh fish from the fridge and come with me and J.T. down to the inlet."

Saka joins them and the foursome walks down to the cove inlet.

Kim positions the foursome just barely into the water and J.T. says, "Ready?"

He slaps the surface of the water a couple times. Nothing happens.

"What, we have a new pet seal?" Saka offers.

Misa smiles and thinks to herself, 'Would Saitonaka let Julie go for a seal?"

J.T. slaps the surface again. Nothing happens.

Growing impatient, Misa says, "Look guys, I appreciate you trying to make me feel better but…"

Misa and Saka turn around with their backs to the inlet. A moment later, Kim and J.T.

start smiling wildly but Saka looks sick. Misa looks over at him and asks, "Saka honey, are you okay?"

He can't catch his breath. He saw it out of the corner of his left eye. He points his finger frantically indicating something behind her and doubles over with amazement and fear. Misa turns around and like in slow motion, her peripheral vision picks up the shape. Her mind begins to calculate the true size of the animal just three feet in front of her. Her heart is ready to jump out of her chest and run to shore to save itself. Her throat is so dry that her larynx can't contract to make a sound and her bladder just emptied its contents and that is now running down her right leg. All this time, Xie-xie just rests comfortably on the shore's rocks and opens her mouth. She curls her tongue and bounces her head up and down for a moment. She may be laughing.

Saka throws up but a genuine calm comes over Misa. Crying with joy and wonderment, she simply reaches out to touch the female Orca. She touches Xie-xie's nose and then immediately massages the right side of the great animal's glossy black head. Xie-xie blinks and closes and then re-opens her jaws. Yuen is amazed as well but knowing Misa as he does, he knows she's been waiting for a moment like this all her life and she's not about to pass it up.

Kim is shocked as she watches what Misa does next.

"Misa! Stop!"

Misa ignores Kim and continues massaging Xie-xie's head, only now, her right hand is practically in the Orca's mouth. Xie-xie likes it and opens her jaws wider. In total amazement, Kim just keeps quiet, not wanting to alarm the killer whale at this point. One little flinch, and Xie-xie could easily bite off Misa's hand. Misa continues to explore but now she has her right hand completely inside the Orca's mouth. She brushes her fingers and palm across the bottom row of Xie-xie's monstrous conical teeth. Xie-xie allows this and seems to genuinely enjoy the dental inspection. Then Misa begins inspecting Xie-xie's upper jaw. Incredibly, she rubs up and into the roof of Xie-xie's mouth and the Orca props up with delight. Misa's right hand is completely inside the jaws of the killer whale and up to her elbow now. A moment later, she simply starts brushing the outside of Xie-xie's jaws; her upper root line. As Misa passes by the right side, she cuts her palm on a small bone lodged in Xie-xie's jaws. Without hesitation or concern for her own safety, she feels across the area again and simply extracts the small bone fragment from between two of Xie-xie's upper lateral teeth. The killer whale slips back and turns to head back into the cove.

Steadfast and excited, Tai places his call to Saitonaka.

"Saitonaka?"

"Doctor Feel-good? Ha! Hey, it's awful early."

"I know you have an affinity for sharks but do the words *Orcinus Orca* mean anything to you?"

"Bullshit!"

"First things first; you arrange for Julie to be sent here to stay with her mother as soon as possible and YOU now have one week."

"Bold! I hope you can back it up!"

"Bring your Cubans and spread them around because we have something here that will knock you out!"

"And how do you expect to keep a killer whale in your cove?"

"Our issue. Not yours."

"And if it's gone by the time I can get out there?"

"We dance!"

"Interesting; so you're saying you have an Orca to study and I get all research notes, correct?"

"Done."

"And you're saying that this killer whale seems to want to stick around so it may be something that people can be attracted to come and see, for a price of course."

"Done."

"And you don't want anything?"

"Julie! And before you visit to see the Orca!"

"Done doctor! I'll make the arrangements to deliver her to you in a week's time. And no failures or tricks or I'll just have my friends in Hanoi fire off some of their remaining rockets from '72 and blow that whole fucking island up!

Saitonaka hangs up and Tai quickly makes his way back outside to rejoin the group gawking at Xie-xie. Saitonaka knows that with his current black market sales of Myst1, CDT wash and exclusive Opium tablets all over Southeast Asia, combined with this ultimate attraction he will promote once he sees her for himself, all he can visualize are massive dollar signs. With the money he figures he'll raise, he'll be able to buy his return to Yokohama to run his Yakuza regime the way he wants again.

As everyone stands a few feet back from the shore's smooth rocky inlet, Kim whispers to Tai, "You're not going to believe what Misa just did a little while ago."

Intrigued, Tai nudges Kim and looks at her. Kim leans over and tells him.

Tai looks back at Kim in shock and says, "No way!"

Kim closes her eyes in amazement and nods. Yuen, Saka, and J.T. all move over to the deck side of the cove where they can fish from that shallow shoreline for more food for Xie-xie. Each time they catch one, they make their way back over to Xie-xie's preferred landing strip so they can feed her. Each time she appears from the depths, it's an event all unto itself. From nothing but the slightly shimmering water to a rush of momentum that for an instance, camouflage's the great killer whale's glossy black head and a second later, you see her famous white eye patch. For prey, once this appears, you're already in her jaws.

Like a new-born baby, everyone watches anything Xie-xie does with breathless anticipation. When she surfaces and the water explodes from her blow-hole, they are in awe. When her erect four-foot tall dorsal fin breaks the surface, they stare at it frozen in their positions and when Xie-xie runs up the inlet rocks to see her new friends, everyone's heart skips a beat.

Later in the evening, Tai calls everyone together so they can get their stories straight and to properly prepare for Saitonaka's visit. Tai calls Toma as well and asks if he can join them.

"Toma?"

"Tai. How are you?"

"Never mind me, how are you feeling? I heard about the dorm-room fight with Julie's roommate."

"Yeah, she got me real good but I stung her a few times myself. She won't soon forget our meeting."

"If you're nearby, can you join us at your cousin Jos' place?"

"He's no longer there. My mom's running the place fulltime now with a couple of my guys working there as well. Her new sign should be there soon. She's calling the place, "The Grand Café."

"The Grand Café. Nice! What happened with Jos?"

"Let's just say he backed the wrong horse so I strongly suggested that he relocate and he immediately agreed."

"Sorry."

"Don't be. I always wondered what he was up to over the years and the night that you guys had just left after your awesome shot-glass-fire trick, he showed his true colors."

"You didn't…"

"No but I told him if he ever completed the call he was trying to make, I'd find out and then I'd find him. He got the point. He loves scamming and he loves money but not more than he loves breathing."

"And your Uncle Andrew?"

"Yes… my uncle Andy passed away recently."

"I'm so sorry."

"Thanks. He was a great man and he'll be missed. My mom really misses him but taking over his old place will be good for her and it'll help get her off my back about still being single!"

"So, you'll be there tonight with us?"

"Sorry, I can't. I'm in Okinawa checking out a few things but my mom and my guys will look out for you all."

"We have big news to share."

"Yeah?"

"First, Misa's Julie will be joining us soon so please keep your eyes and ears peeled for that. Maybe you can escort her so nothing goes wrong."

"Absolutely! What else?"

"We didn't catch her, she caught us… we have a fourteen-odd foot Orca as an ultimate visitor in our cove!"

"An Orca? … a killer whale, right?"

"Yes sir!"

"Holy shit! I've got to see this!"

"She's amazing! Maybe when you escort Julie back here, you can stay with us for a while and check out, Xie-xie."

"Xie-xie; that's great! Wow! I can't wait for you tell me how that all came together."

"Yes, a great story in itself! So, we'll see you in a week?"

"Yes. I'll check with a few people and make sure Saitonaka is doing what he promised. That'll give me a fix on where the hell he's hiding now too; good for a few other people I know to share that information with because there's a bit of an uproar in the Yakuza since he decided to consolidate. I just hope he doesn't send Oso and Heroshi after her again."

"Why? Oso Wakashi is a good man; he just has a shitty job and boss!"

"Yeah but Heroshi makes me nervous; too ambitious or something. There's just something about the kid I don't like. He's not quiet out of respect. He's quiet because he's plotting. Anyway, say hello to everyone for me and keep my mom occupied with your new stories, … Please!"

Tai laughs and says, "Will do! Thanks Toma. See you soon."

"Yes!"

Tai and Toma hang up and then Tai walks back down the hallway from his bedroom and announces to everyone, "To Jos'?"

They all agree to the familiar namesake so they pile into their respective cars and head into town to now Mary's Restaurant and Bar; The Grand Café. Tai brings Kim and J.T.

up to speed about the change in ownership and about his call with Toma regarding Julie's pending move to join all of them on Amami Island. Kim and J.T. are taking it all in but all they can really think about is Xie-xie and what she's doing at this very moment.

A mile out from their cove and at a depth of a little over five hundred feet, an eight-foot rogue male Great Hammerhead shark glides along effortlessly. He immediately senses some struggling fish ahead of him about four hundred yards away so he narrows his pectoral fins and accelerates toward his prospective prey. Two hundred yards away, the strong scent of blood in the water is like a drug. He quickens his pace and adjusts five degrees to his right side to ensure a proper collision with his unsuspecting prey.

Frenzied smaller blue sharks separate for a moment revealing a wounded five hundred pound female Sun Fish. Swimming horizontally, the Sun Fish has taken on some slight damage to her lower pectoral fin. She struggles to maintain an even swimming motion and this awkward behavior has directly led to her attraction of so many various new attackers seeking an easy meal.

One hundred yards away, the eight-foot Great Hammerhead commands immediate respect in the open ocean by his sheer size and demeanor. The smaller blue sharks take notice and leave the area immediately, scattering away in every direction. The Sun Fish's fate lies solely with the Great Hammerhead and depends now on how hungry he really is.

The Sun Fish begins to recover and she starts to descend to safer deeper waters. Not wanting to miss his chance, the Great Hammerhead adjusts again and starts to pursue the new bearing. Realizing her recovery skills are improving, she pivots vertical and resumes her preferred vertical body position, so she appears larger to prospective predators.

Fifty yards away, the rogue male Great Hammerhead can almost taste the Sun Fish. He doesn't care if she's repositioned herself or not; he's hungry and that's all that matters. A moment later, he is hit with a powerful and stunning blast of sonar that immediately disorients him. A series of clicks follows and they prolong the Great Hammerhead's disorientation. Xie-xie rises from the depths directly beneath the Great Hammerhead and in a mad rush to the surface where he remains stunned, she takes the center of his body into her mouth and practically forces him completely out of the water. Rich shark's blood cascades across Xie-xie's glossy black head and down across her white eye patch. With enough force to bite through a motorcycle, she bites down and extracts a piece of flesh away from the shark that weighs twenty-three pounds.

Without looking back for too long, the female Sun Fish continues on her descent to safer waters as the Great Hammerhead begins to spin in his death circle; the predator has become prey. Xie-xie breaks the surface and announces her kill to the world. After her brief exhibition and shout-out to herself, she quickly dives back down and heads directly toward the now dead Great Hammerhead shark. From the other side this time, she extracts another twenty-odd pound piece of his flesh. She starts to swim away but deciding that he tastes better than she had remembered, she pivots and turns on him again and again. In a matter of moments, the shark is an unrecognizable piece of bloody remnants. As the bloody carcass drifts to the bottom of the East China Sea, dozens and then hundreds of smaller fish converge on the ravaged remains.

Everyone arrives at Mary's Grand Café but the sign on the front door says 'Closed.'" The group drives in a slow caravan in front of the place to confirm the status and begins to drive away when Mary opens the front door and starts waving at the rear car. Misa and Saka see her so Saka honks his horn at the other cars. Everyone parks and goes in. Mary greets everyone at the door and then locks it behind her.

"I'm still fixing up a few things but Toma called me and said you were coming so I've been waiting for you. So good to see you all again!"

Mary grabs J.T. by his face, smiles and shakes him briefly. Kim hugs Mary and then Misa and Carmela do the same. Tai, Yuen and Saka rearrange the tables and J.T. asks, "Mary?"

She nods so J.T. goes into the kitchen and retrieves a half case of Buddha beer from the storage fridge for the group to share.

"Drinking; not too much tonight?"

"Not tonight Mary." Kim confirms.

Tai says, "We've got great news and some quick thinking to do."

Mary joins the seated group and perks up.

Tai announces, "Julie, Misa's daughter, is on her way very soon!"

The group smiles and Misa closes her eyes in quiet prayer.

"And, 'cheers' to our new family member! Xie-xie!"

Thinking he's talking to her, Mary says, "Oh, you're welcome! Doctor Tai, … so nice!"

The group laughs and J.T. says, "No Mary; Xie-xie. That's her name."

"Oh, such a nice young boy! Soon you meet a girl and get married. Not like my Toma, still single. Ahh!" She waves her hand around in playful disgust.

"No Mary. Our new family member is a killer whale. Her name is Xie-xie. She is in our cove back home."

"Oh, Xie-xie, not Xie-xie! A killer whale? Oh, very dangerous! Be careful!"

Mary gets up and simply heads into the kitchen.

She calls back, "Hey! You need something, you know where stuff is! You get it! I have some inventory and food to put away!"

Everyone smiles and Tai says, "Okay. So, Julie will be on her way from wherever they took her but she'll be safe. I asked Toma to look out for her to make sure of it. Next, big issue; Saitonaka can't know about Kim and J.T. at any cost so you two will have to stay out of sight until he leaves! We can't risk what he might do if he knows you're alive and have been here all this time."

Everyone nods and will help contribute to hiding any evidence of their existence. Saka looks Tai over to the side.

"You are good people. I appreciate you all. When Saitonaka gets here, if it's going bad, I'll do what I have to, to protect you."

Tai nods and pats Saka on the shoulder, "Thank you Saka."

"I know Miss Julie is Yuen's daughter but I'll protect her like she's my own!"

"Good man." Tai says.

Yuen stands up and says, "Okay. Like Mary said, 'not too much drink'. We've got exciting work to do, finally!" I'm going to work with Carmela and Misa to monitor and record everything Xie-xie does and to help rewrite a lot of the notes I lost from before. Saka, if you can work with the rest of the guys and fish off the deck side to catch as many fish as you can so we can entice Xie-xie to stay close, that would be great."

Misa says, "I need to look at her teeth again to make sure the Enhanced-CDT is working."

Tai says, "All right, let's head back home and get some rest. Exciting times ahead!" He raises his glass and says, "To Miss Julie; she's coming home!"

Misa and Kim start crying and then Misa says, "Tai, Kim, J.T., to you! For not giving up on me and for working so hard to make things right again, thank you so much! I love you, always! And to Yuen and Carmela, you found each other and I'm so very happy for you. Thank you too!"

Saka raises his arms up and proclaims, "Banzai!"

Then everyone says, "Wànsuì!" — Chinese in origin; an expression meaning to wish the former or sitting Emperor "Ten thousand years" of reign.

Tai calls back to the kitchen, 'Mary? We're leaving. I've got the door."

Mary calls back, "Okay. You guys come back with Julie, okay?"

"Wànsuì!"

For the next three days, Xie-xie makes a few spectacular appearances but not nearly as often as she first made. Misa is completely obsessed with Xie-xie, learning something new every time she sees her; picking up on even the slightest new behaviors, sounds she makes, anything.

In her down time, Misa starts whittling several whistles for calling Xie-xie. She's anxious to test them out to see how Xie-xie will react to the various sounds. She hopes one will bring her to the inlet cove for inspection, affections and play while the other will alert her to behavioral feedings and more aggressive displays that Misa will try to teach her to offer back in the deeper areas of the cove.

CHAPTER THIRTY-ONE

January 12, 2012 – Boston, Massachusetts, U.S.A.

OSO and Heroshi arrive to pick up Julie. In their rental car, they make their way to Julie's university dorm building. Heroshi never speaks out of turn but this whole trade deal has him frustrated.

"Boss Saitonaka wants this trade but who's to say in what condition she arrives, eh?"

Oso glares over at his younger and less experienced partner, Heroshi.

"So, in your vast experience, what would you do with her before she is returned as a part of this deal that you don't approve of?"

Excitedly, Heroshi says, "Just like I said."

"You've merely indicated your intent but you haven't detailed anything. Commit to the details or keep your mouth shut!"

"I'm getting tired…"

"Oh, you're getting tired? Of what?"

"Nothing."

"No, I want to know what my young partner is so tired of because I'll tell you what I'm tired of; your selfishness, your lack of patience, your ignorance, your false bravado, your big talk and your idle threats! Even your intent to threaten Julie is completely out of line, much less what you might actually do if I wasn't here!"

"Well, you asked so I think I should share my details with you."

"Fine Heroshi! Enlighten me with your long-view of what you'd do in this situation. Act as if you're the Boss and teach us your lessons!"

Immediately, Heroshi offers, "First, I'd renegotiate with Dr. Tai and his group and tell him he'll be lucky to get her back in one piece, after I've had my every way with the little bitch! Then, I'd send you and your partner to retrieve her and like in the good ole days, I'd encourage you to have your way with her before and during her transport so she's good and loose when she arrives!"

Growing more and more frustrated, Oso asks, "And then?"

"Then, I'd bolster my ranks by recruiting on Amami Island so I could immediately take over all of their projects and I'd collect all their experiments and drugs to sell on the black market!"

"Yes… and then?"

"Uh, … and then I'd move my operations to Hanoi where I have friends I can trust and I'd buy other friends with the money I'll make from the research and drugs."

"Okay. And then?"

Nervous and frustrated, Heroshi concludes, "And then I'd send for you to join me in Hanoi so you could kiss my ass!"

With a single chop of his right hand shaped like a horizontal knife, Oso chops at Heroshi's throat. The blow sends his head crashing into his passenger window, creating a four-inch diameter spider web shaped splintered crack.

"Now let me tell you something! First, you talk too much! Second, you talk too much! Third, you left out the consequences that will surely come as a result of your actions! Fourth, your rivals will immediately see your weakness and they will move against you because they'll know you can't formulate a real plan; they will quickly replace you and easily take over everything you have and fifth, you talk too fucking much! When I offered you to explain yourself, your answer should have been to quickly say, 'I don't know enough to explain myself Sensei!'"

Oso continues, "I'd never expect you to have every angle covered but your ten-thousand foot overview of this or any other issue is not rational and would never include the insight needed to be successful, understand? Most importantly, your proposed deviant behavior against Julie is not how Yakuza works! That is the behavior of dogs! Such a ridiculous outburst like this in front of your Boss and he'd be laughing at you; staring down at your severed head and then he'd kick you in the ear for bleeding all over his floor!"

In pain and back in his place, Heroshi massages his throat and the back right side of his head as his hard-learned lesson concludes.

JANUARY 15, 2012 AT 8 A.M. – URUMA, OKINAWA

Uneventfully, Oso and Heroshi land with Julie. With Saitonaka's resources running a little thinner, Oso has to rent a local fisherman's boat to make the trip to Amami Oshima Island. He hands the boat owner two thousand Yen for the excursion and the man gladly accepts it. Oso used to have twenty thousand Yen on hand for such needs.

At Noon, their boat approaches the Amami Oshima Island coastline. Yuen and Carmela are fishing off the coast about a mile out to sea. Carmela leans over to bring up another catch.

"Hey! This makes number six for me! I'm winning!"

"I believe our bet also included who could catch the biggest fish for Xie-xie and I still hold that record baby!"

"Baby. Okay. If you called me 'Mela', you'd be dangling with the other fish on the side of the boat!"

Carmela smirks over at Yuen who returns the gesture.

"Since you brought it up, come on babe; bring your fish onboard. Don't let them dangle and bleed in the water. Sharks you know."

"Yeah, yeah. You're just sore because you're losing!"

"Alright. A few more and we can head back in for an early dinner with everyone."

"Sounds good... and this one makes number seven!"

As Carmela begins reeling in her latest catch, something bumps their small research boat. A moment later, something much bigger takes over her line. She immediately flips overboard, falling flat on her back like a reverse belly flop. The impact knocks the breath right out of her.

"Shit! Carmela! Are you okay?"

Yuen throws a life preserver at her but she can't reach it. She's still trying to catch her breath. As she gasps for air, a black fin breaks the water's surface on the opposite side of their boat.

"Okay babe. Just relax and concentrate on trying to breath. Just relax; that's it. Let me get the other vest for you…"

Yuen turns to the other side of the boat and just as he retrieves it from underneath the bench seat, he spots the fin. A second later, the fin disappears. Yuen runs to the other side of the boat and screams at Carmela.

"Get over here Carmela! Now! Swim!"

Sarcastically, Carmela casually says, "You just said for me to just relax."

"Fuck that! Shark! Move your ass now!"

Carmela turns pale. Her arms freeze up. She attempts to swim but the adrenaline coursing through her body is being overtaken by her trepidation.

The fin belongs to a twelve-foot Thresher shark. With a relatively small mouth, this large (Alopias vulpinus) makes up for his smaller jaws with an extensive and extremely powerful and dangerous tail; over seventy inches long, he uses his tail to slap his prey unconscious and then he can simply take his time eating them.

The blood in the water from Carmela's recent catches has stirred up quite a bit of unwanted attention. None of the predators in the East China Sea need incentive but when there is incentive, they respond like rabid Pavlovian dogs.

Another fin breaks the water. It belongs to a ten-foot Short-Fin Mako shark; the fastest shark in the ocean. With her razor sharp teeth and particularly nasty disposition, she doesn't need any easy meals but the way Carmela resembles a sexy seal, she's too easy to pass up. Although smaller, the female Mako (Isurus oxyrinchus) commands the immediate area so the larger male Thresher heads for the safety of the deeper water. He's not about to challenge an angry Mako.

In the water, in their element and one-on-one, man is no match against most marine animals, especially versus a top predator like the Mako shark. Her teeth alone would make most people freeze and mess their pants on sight alone.

"Carmela! Please baby, Swim!"

Yuen starts to break down as he realizes with every moment, Carmela's life could end at any second and in a horrific manner. The very thought of her being bitten scares him senseless so he keeps screaming at her. He throws the second life preserver at her and it rings right around her neck perfectly. It doesn't faze her at all. Her eyes are locked on the black fin that is quickly approaching her. If her presence isn't bad enough, the blood from the dead and dying fish she caught is drifting right over to her and across her path in the water. As far as the female Mako is concerned, she's an injured fish or seal and easy prey.

In a flash, the Mako passes her by, taking in all the information as to her size and shape, the taste of the blood in the water and even the urine that is streaming out of Carmela. One hundred and fifty feet past her now, the Mako has decided that she is worthy of being the Mako's mistaken meal so she pivots and heads back toward Carmela. Carmela's life is passing before her eyes as she watches the small black fin race toward her again. Yuen continues to scream frantically from the deck of the research boat but she can't hear him or anything else.

One hundred feet away from Carmela, the Mako's *Ampullae of Lorenzini* takes over. Pure instinct tells the Mako this prey item is either a large injured fish or a seal, both of which are highly prized. The female shark looks around the immediate area surrounding Carmela to make sure there are no other contenders for her meal; there are none.

Sixty feet away, the Mako prepares for her final angle of attack; millions of years of evolution have taught her to roll to her right or left side slightly in order to properly grasp the best exposed limb of her prey. Her attack will combine a sixty-forty split between power and placement. At the moment of truth, she will roll back her eyes to protect them from any frivolous but still harmful claws of her prey as she makes her exploratory bite. With an impressive and compact bite force, Carmela's body will easily buckle and pull apart at the Mako's will.

Forty feet away; the Mako's small black fin disappears under the surface; on final attack approach. Her jaws widen, exposing an impressive and genuinely terrifying set of jagged razor sharp teeth perfectly adapted to shred and tear flesh from bone.

A fraction of a second later, Carmela passes out from shock. Only the life preserver that Yuen threw perfectly around her neck is preventing her from slipping down into the water and drowning. She's unconscious but alive. It's better that she not be awake for what happens next to her anyway.

Twenty feet away; the Mako is ready to taste her prey for the first time. But something is wrong. The Mako appears dazed. She begins to break off her attack pattern, deciding maybe this prey item is not what she thought it was.

No, that's not it. The preponderance of shock waves hitting her is overwhelming. The great predator simply can't handle the relentless sonar attack. The next moment, seven feet of the Mako shark descends in a tight bloody spiral down to the abyss as the rear three feet of the shark is devoured by Xie-xie.

Xie-xie's perfect vertical attack pattern through the water has forced Carmela's unconscious body much closer to the research boat so Yuen jumps overboard and retrieves her. He's crying and smiling at the same time; in shock and in awe of Xie-xie's completely dominating presence and saving grace. There are no other predators around for almost a quarter of a mile because nothing is foolish enough to challenge the waters around Orcinus Orca, especially this grand dame.

Approaching their research boat now, Oso refocuses his eyes. He can't believe what he thinks he just saw. It happened so fast, he's not really sure so he keeps it to himself. The boat owner knows exactly what that was. He just smiles and navigates his boat. Still sulking from his verbal reprimand, Heroshi remains below deck. Often, he narrows his eyes and remains out of sight. Julie is exhausted from all the travel. She has her head buried in a book. She dozes in and out of sleep depending on the motions of the boat.

The boat owner calls out to Yuen, "You two okay?"

"We are. Thanks! She fell overboard but she's okay now."

"You want me to escort you in?"

"Thanks."

Steadily, the two boats make their way into port; about a thousand yards down the shore from the group's Y-shaped custom home. As they pass it by, the boat owner comments over his CB radio, "You have all done a great job! The house looks great!"

Yuen immediately grabs his receiver and says, "Thanks Cap! Red-one. I repeat red-one."

"Thanks red-one. Out."

The two boats dock and Oso introduces Julie to Yuen. Yuen smiles and starts crying. Not knowing if Oso and Heroshi know that she's his daughter, and not wanting to risk that revelation in front of them, Yuen bows and shakes Julie's hand.

"Excuse me Miss Julie. My wife, Carmela, almost drown earlier so I'm still a little shaken up. Please, we have a car in the parking lot nearby to take you to your mother Misa."

Julie nods and follows Yuen and Carmela. Carmela is truly still recovering from her incident. She has absolutely no idea what happened as the shark approached her from forty feet so in her mind, she remains genuinely scared, cold, and confused.

Heroshi picks up on some chemistry between Julie and Yuen. He sneers and inappropriately walks ahead of everyone. He scopes out the immediate area and farther down shore, he spots a new business sign being installed. He tilts his head and reads it to himself, "The Grand Café."

He mumbles to himself, "Another Chinese fish and piss place!"

Oso overhears his brash partner and offers a look of disgust that Heroshi immediately dismisses; apparently Oso's earlier comments and advice didn't 'take' with his young apprentice.

The five people squeeze into Yuen's compact car and drives the short distance to Yuen's home. The Huang's are all out back near the cove inlet anxiously awaiting another amazing appearance from Xie-xie. Yuen fumbles around at the front door, stalling for time. He realizes if Oso or Heroshi see Kim and J.T., all hell will break loose for everyone as soon as one of them calls Saitonaka.

"Pardon me guys…. I can't get my key to work. I've been meaning to fix this stubborn front door. Please, wait here for a moment and we'll go around back to get in."

Yuen and Carmela walk around to the back side of the house.

Heroshi stares at everything intently; it's making Oso very uncomfortable because it's blatantly rude for him to be staring everything down like some kind of criminal investigator overseeing a crime scene for evidence.

"Heroshi! Stop it!"

"Stop? Aren't we here to see what's really happening? The sneaky Chinamen don't fool or scare me, maybe you."

"Is that right? God damn it! When we get back to Yokohama, we're going to have it out and then we'll see who's scared!"

Again, Heroshi dismisses the words of his Sensei.

Yuen and Carmela enter the back patio entrance and Carmela immediately sits down in the living room to calm her nerves and to collect herself. Yuen quickly gets her a glass of water. Then he sees the Huang's down at the cove inlet. He frantically waves his arms at Tai. After a moment, Tai sees him and is about to call out when Yuen shakes his head frantically from side to side and covers his mouth.

Tai runs up the slope to greet Yuen.

Yuen nervously but quietly says, "They're here! Saitonaka's men are here with my daughter, Julie!"

He breaks down and adds, "I couldn't even hug her for the first time in front of them."

"Shit! I've got to hide Kim and J.T.! Okay, let them inside but close the shared door first so they can't look down the hallway!"

"And J.T.'s stuff sitting right out in the living room?"

"It's mine as far as they know."

"Good. Hey, where is Misa?"

"She and Saka went into town for food and to help Mary with her new sign."

"Okay."

"Okay, go! Hopefully they'll just drop her off and leave. Fishing went okay?"

Yuen stares nervously back at Tai.

"What?"

"We'll talk later tonight."

Concerned and intrigued, Tai says, "Okay. Oh, we haven't seen Xie-xie all day."

"Shit! We did! God bless that Orca, let me tell you!"

Yuen runs back inside and runs down the right side of the house, closing Kim and Tai's bedroom door and the shared living room door. Then he opens the front door for his daughter Julie, Oso and Heroshi. He offers up his hand to Julie and leads her inside. He squeezes her hand proudly.

She starts crying and whispers, "Thank you Mr. Yuen."

Yuen's eyes begin to water. He quickly recovers and asks after Carmela's well-being.

"Honey? Feeling better now?" Carmela offers a careful nod.

Suspiciously, Heroshi looks around the home. His eyes narrow and he smirks as he enters the house. Oso bows and enters, standing behind Julie and Heroshi.

Down the path at the cove inlet, Tai escorts Kim and J.T. to the far end of the deck and into the cold storage shed where all of the past few days catch is kept. Tai reassures Kim and J.T.

He grabs Kim's face, kisses her and says, "It'll be okay!"

J.T. pats his dad on his back as he walks away. Tai heads back up the path toward the rear entrance of the home.

Yuen hurries them along offering, "So, thank you for bringing Miss Julie. I don't know where Misa and Saka are right now but I'm sure she'll be so happy to see her."

Dr. Tai enters and says, "Hello. Mr. Wakashi and Heroshi. Where's Julie?"

Yuen says, "She's just in the bathroom for a moment."

Happy to be away from Saitonaka's men, Julie remains in the bathroom on the left-side wing of the home.

Heroshi interrupts the conversation's natural flow and says, "Saka? Now, I haven't seen him for a long time. Mr. Yuen says he and Misa are away.

"Do you mind if we wait?"

Tai sternly says, "Yes Heroshi-san! They are away getting some things and helping friends. I expect they will be tied up for some time."

Embarrassed, Oso says, "Excuse my young partner; he speaks when he would be better off listening! We won't keep you. I'm sure you all have a lot of catching up to do and I know Miss Julie is probably looking forward to getting some rest after all her travels."

Inappropriately persistent, Heroshi asks, "Eh, can I just use your bathroom? We did just finish a very long and bumpy boat ride."

Yuen says, "Of course Heroshi-san. It's just down this right side hallway about halfway and on your right."

Heroshi stares down everything in his line of sight. He looks like a fire chief inspector looking for the root cause in the dark; looking in every crevice and corner of the home. He enters the bathroom and closes the door. He immediately starts rifling through the medicine cabinet for evidence. He looks in the sink and shower stall. Then he looks behind the door. After a few minutes he flushes the toilet and exits.

Oso offers, "I think we've inconvenienced you all long enough eh?" Impatiently and disgusted, he looks over at Heroshi.

Tai and Yuen escort Oso and Heroshi to the front door when Heroshi asks, "Of course, Mr. Saitonaka looks forward to visiting himself but I'm sure he would like to see evidence of your progress and this big fish you claim to have."

Yuen immediately corrects Heroshi, saying, "Mammal."

"Excuse me?"

"Our Orca is a mammal, not a fish."

With pure resentment, Heroshi stares back at Yuen and says, "Oh, thank you for correcting me. Allow me to correct you Mr. Yuen."

Curious, Yuen asks, "Yes?"

"It's Boss Saitonaka's mammal, not yours Mr. Yuen." Heroshi grins and walks out the door.

Tai immediately corrects Heroshi as well saying, "My deal with your Boss was to give him his O-tabs and resupplies personally. I'm sure you would not want to interfere with his plans Heroshi-san! We don't control the Orca; it visits as it wishes and you can tell him that but rest assured; it's here."

Under his breath, Heroshi says, "I hope so, for your sake!"

Oso is furious. He extends his hand in friendship to Tai and Yuen before they can offer their hands. Oso stomps down the three front entrance steps and stares at the back of Heroshi's head. Oso and Heroshi drive back to port; quickly refuel their rented boat and leave for Okinawa.

With the all clear signal from Carmela, Julie makes her way back into the shared living room and in a flash; Yuen picks her up and spins her around in his arms. The two start crying and hugging each other. Tai yells down to Kim and J.T. Together, they run up to the rear entrance of the house to see Julie. Tai and Carmela hug each other as they watch father and daughter embrace fiercely.

Tai says, "No one will ever get her away from him again!" Carmela's eye well up.

A moment later, Kim and J.T. enter. Kim just stares at Julie; she looks just like her mother Misa did when she was in her early twenties. Slightly taller and with the same so-black-its-blue hair that extends to the middle of her back except Julie has a thin streak of red colored hair down the left side. Also just like her mother, she has a thin frame of a hundred and ten pounds; a total heartbreaker for sure.

"My God! Look at you honey! You look just like your mother did back in the mid-eighties! Stunning!"

"Thanks dad!" Julie explodes into tears and quickly says, "Dad! … I love that I finally got to call you that!"

Kim and J.T. wait impatiently. After a few more moments, Yuen steps back and heads for the kitchen, allowing someone else to tackle Julie. Kim steps in and grabs Julie's face.

She kisses her on the cheek and says, "Welcome home sweetheart, welcome home!"

Julie can see J.T. waiting. His eyes are tearing up. This makes her cry harder. Kim gives Julie another big hug and then she steps away to join Tai and Carmela.

J.T. just smirks and says, "Took you long enough!"

Julie laughs and cries harder as she falls into J.T.'s arms. They hug each other and then Julie pulls away and stares into J.T.'s eyes. She looks down at his lips and closes her eyes. The young couple shares a kiss that would rival the most beloved in television or film. Their passion surprises Tai and Kim a little bit because they had no idea the two were so close. It's been over two years since they've even seen each other.

After a few moments Tai says, "Okay. Misa and Saka should be getting back soon. It's my turn to get someone good!"

Carmela smiles; knowing exactly what to do. She huddles everyone together and after a few minutes, they break apart.

Tai motions over at Yuen; asking after Carmela and he nods that she's fine. Their wild story from earlier today is still pending and it's driving Tai crazy.

The group patiently waits for Misa and Saka to return from helping Mary install her new restaurant and bar sign; The Grand Café. Located on the top right edge of her property nearest the shore, the blood red and white four foot wide by ten foot tall sign was built in the classic design of its 1970's predecessors. Its dual sided face will attract patrons from both land and sea.

8 P.M. local time – Dusk and Misa and Saka's blue compact car approaches the Huang/Zhang/Yamishinosaka shared home.

Misa's holding several bags of groceries and Saka's holding a case of Buddha beer, compliments of Mary for their support and hard work earlier. Carmela opens the front door for them.

Yuen says, "Hey! You're back. Good. We have to go, right now!"

Misa says, "What? Go where?"

"Uh, to Mary's. Yeah, she called and said she had big news to share so let's go!"

The Huang's immediately group up and quickly head out to their car as Yuen and Carmela hurry Misa and Saka along, helping them to quickly put away the groceries.

"But we just got back from Mary's. She got her new sign, that's all."

Carmela says, "Oh, her new sign? That's great! Well… we all haven't seen it yet though so that must be it!"

Yuen calls back and says, "Hurry, before Tai and Kim take your favorite seats!"

Misa mumbles, "Okay, okay. After fooling around with that sign all day, we could use a real drink, right Hun?" Saka nods.

The Huang's are well on their way to Mary's Grand Café.

"Jesus! They could have waited for us." Misa announces.

Julie was hiding behind the front door so as soon as Yuen and Carmela distracted Misa and Saka and got them heading into the kitchen area, the Huang's abducted Julie and they all sped off in their car.

Saka is torn; on one hand, he knows what's going on from a call he got earlier in the afternoon from Saitonaka. The whole issue weighs heavily on him because he is putting on an act for his Boss that could get him killed but he genuinely cares for Misa and for these people now too. He knows an ultimate decision on his part is looming. He'll have to make a definitive choice for one or the other; for his Boss and his Yakuza life or for his new family. He doesn't want to spoil Misa's and Julie's reunion either but that's bittersweet for him as well since he knows Julie is Yuen's daughter. He's just happy for them so he'll sit back and just watch things unfold as they will, with an ever watchful eye.

As Yuen pulls up, they see the new sign at the front top left of the building.

Yuen comments, "Hey! Nice! You two helped install that monster?"

Saka says, "No problem. Mary was great to give us that case of Buddha!"

"Oh yes! Buddha! Our favorite Saka!"

Misa says, "Okay you two. You can talk about your favorite beer all night long. I want to ask Kim why they stormed off! Let's get inside!"

Carmela and Yuen laugh to themselves.

The Huang's rearranged the tables into the group's favorite horseshoe layout and they are seated in their favorite spots, closest to and with their backs facing the bar.

J.T. asks, "Hey you guys! What took you so long?"

Misa smirks and sits across from Kim at the opposite tip of the horseshoe table arrangement. Saka sits down next to her and directly across from Tai, on the inside of the two women respectively. Normally the group's horseshoe table arrangement accommodates the respective seven people; featuring three tables wide with two tables on each end forming the horseshoe but tonight, awkwardly, there is another small table above Kim's table. Misa doesn't notice.

Mary comes out from the kitchen area and announces, "Hey everyone! Good to see you all, … finally!"

Misa has her head buried in her small purse.

"First, let me thank Misa and Saka for their help with my new sign. Did you see it out front? Beautiful! Thank you!"

"And I hired a new employee. She'll be around soon to take your orders so be nice to her. This is her first night. That means you, Yuen! No difficult orders for my new girl or I'll make you wash dishes and clean woks!"

Mary walks over and stands behind the Huang's.

Yuen waves his hands like a white flag and says, "Okay Mary, okay. I promise to be nice."

He laughs but then he starts to choke up a little.

Misa notices this and rolls her eyes. She mumbles to herself, "Ha! He's getting old and so sensitive now."

Misa returns to her dedicated search.

Julie calmly comes out of the kitchen area and says, "Let's see; I got your orders already but those folks are new." She makes her way over to her mom and says, "What can I get you ma'am?"

Misa keeps her head down.

Julie repeats, "Ma'am, what can I get you? Other folks are waiting you know."

Picking up on her cocky attitude, Misa looks up. A fraction of a second later, mother and daughter explode into tears at the same time. Their younger and older smiling and crying faces are as identical as they can be. A second later Carmela, Kim, and Mary burst into tears.

Saka yells, "Banzai!" and Yuen, Tai and J.T. repeat the original ancient Chinese chant of "Wànsuì" two more times.

Mother and daughter just hold each other for the next five minutes, crying all over each other and on the floor.

Finally, they separate a little and Julie wipes her eyes and says, "Shit lady! So what the hell do you want?"

The room erupts with laughter.

Kim whispers to Tai, "Look at her! So beautiful and she's in love with our son!"

Mary walks over and into the back corner, opposite the kitchen corner and turns her new jukebox on. A couple seconds later, Fats Domino's *Blueberry Hill* starts playing. Tai and Kim immediately get up and start slow dancing. Yuen and Carmela quickly join them and then Misa, Saka and Julie join them. J.T. gets up and snatches Julie away from her mom. Misa smiles and starts crying again when she sees the young couple dance and hold each other.

Tai moves Kim closer toward Mary and asks, "The Jukebox?"

Mary smirks and says, "From all that money Toma gave me before, I thought you guys might like a jukebox that played all your favorite music!"

Kim kisses Mary on the cheek and whispers, "Xie-xie!"

The rest of the night, Julie and Misa hold hands as Yuen shares Carmela's and his shocking tale from earlier that afternoon. Everyone's hearts pound as Yuen reaches the climax of the ten-foot Mako's final approach and then he yells, "Xie-xie!"

The elder Mary almost faints from the drama that built up.

"Okay; very long day for me. You all clean up and close my Grand Café when you're ready, okay?"

Everyone cheers and says, "Xie-xie, Wànsuì! Xie-xie, Wànsuì! Xie-xie, Wànsuì!"

Mary makes her way out to her car and mumbles to herself, "Yeah, Xie-xie, and Wànsuì! Crazy! Just don't Wànsuì all over my floor!"

CHAPTER THIRTY-TWO

January 17, 2012 at 10:30 P.M. – Hanoi, Vietnam

AFTER Oso and Heroshi arrive, they to speak with Saitonaka.

"Everything go okay?"

"Yes sir." Oso confirms. Then he adds, "May I have a word sir?"

"Oh?"

"Yes; privately."

"Not with your partner Heroshi-san?"

"No sir; just myself."

Saitonaka motions to Heroshi to leave the room.

"Okay?"

"Julie is with her mother and friends now. I saw no reason to remain to investigate but apparently Heroshi-san did. He made a spectacle of himself and we actually got into it even before we left with Julie. He wanted to have his way with her and I forbade it."

"I see. You were looking out for our best interests?"

"Yes. Exactly sir."

"Did you happen to ask Heroshi-san what he saw in the bathroom during your very short visit Oso?"

"No sir. We didn't talk the rest of the trip. We still haven't sir."

"Well Oso, that would be your fault because young Heroshi-san definitely had a lot to say to me when he called me from the airplane's bathroom!"

"Did you know that Heroshi-san saw quite a bit of ladies garments and accessories around the house?"

"… Yuen's wife's."

"No Oso! Too many! And too many variations for a single woman; different styles and formats. We know women well enough to know that when a girl finds something she likes, she trusts it and doesn't tend to waver. Heroshi-san saw a wide variety, too wide and that tells me there are other women there."

"Sir."

"Heroshi saw three garments and each was a different size Oso."

"Sir."

"So, what else went on between you two?"

"When he spoke of molesting Miss Julie before and while we travelled, I corrected him as I thought you would. That's not how Yakuza works, right sir?"

"Usually Oso but these are unusual times my friend."

"What are you saying sir?"

"What am I saying? I'm saying I like Heroshi-san's attitude and his attention to detail! I'm saying I think I need to split the two of you up before he kills your old ass! And, I'm saying you both should have fucked her brains loose and left her begging for more! That's what I'm fucking saying!"

"Sir."

Saitonaka grips his white snake-headed cane sword tightly and continues, "Heroshi-san may be young and he has a lot to learn but thanks to his investigation skills, he's just uncovered something very interesting going on in the doctor's house and that thrills me! If he fucks up, I'll display his balls on my desk when I get back home and I told him that but I think he's on the right track!"

"Yes sir. I didn't know you two had spoken of these things before we left."

"And who are you that I should consult with before I send you on your next mission?"

"Yes sir."

"Okay then! So, I have actually already split you two up! When I excused Heroshi-san just a minute ago, he was rewarded with ten thousand Yen as a bonus for an excellent job! Now, he's on his way to see his new partner, Izu, back in Yokohama, who is making arrangements for my return home. Is that okay with you Oso?"

Oso says and does nothing.

"Okay then! As for you; a new task, if you don't mind. Very simple: find my younger brother Ric and bring him to me. Actually, no – just bring me his head! And see if you can pry my nephew Eishi away from his tit before you discard my brother's body or poor Eishi may drown! You see, Heroshi-san found out that it was my brother and my nephew who set up the hit on me in Pyongyang. This is information I would have expected you to have discovered Oso, am I correct?"

"Sir!"

"Yes! I am correct but you have been getting soft and I'd just like to know why?"

"I'm not soft sir!"

"You sound sure of yourself but Heroshi-san is convinced that you are. Am I mistaken?"

"In this case sir, yes."

"Very well Oso. But as you know; I don't like being called wrong so bring me my brother Ric's head and my nephew's ears. That should suffice for your insult. If you fail, it will be your head and ears I collect. Fair enough?"

"Yes Sir."

CHAPTER THIRTY-THREE

JANUARY 22, 2012 – AMAMI OSHIMA ISLAND, JAPAN

AFTER a week together, the roommates are having the time of their lives; sharing great stories from their past and reveling in the present. Xie-xie remains a regular visitor but as expected, she ventures out to sea to feed. It's an extra special event when she does appear in the cove. Everyone runs down to the inlet to see her; there's no mistaking her iconic four-foot tall dorsal fin. When that breaks the surface of the water, everyone immediately feels a rush of adrenaline and boost of energy. The group is divided as to what generates their initial excitement more; seeing Xie-xie's dorsal fin break the water's surface or when water sprays everywhere when she expands her powerful lungs at the surface. Julie and J.T. have an exciting expansive announcement of their own.

With Xie-xie nearby and swimming close to the surface, Misa toots her number one whistle. As impressive as her dorsal fin appearance and blow hole explosions are, nothing compares to seeing Xie-xie's glossy black head appear from out of nowhere as she jets up from the depths and onto the smooth rocks of the inlet's shore. At that point, Misa takes over and everyone remains stunned at her total directness to intimately inspect Xie-xie's massive jaws including feeling her tongue, gums, and awe-inspiring smooth conical teeth. Xie-xie's two-inch odd long conical teeth look like bright white shot gun shells. These beautiful and deadly ordinates accent this great mammal's superior marine intelligence but they also mask her fierce and sometimes brutally aggressive demeanor. When a killer whale is in attack mode, absolutely nothing in the ocean is safe… nothing!

In the past three weeks since they came to her aid; administering their Enhanced-CDT shot, Xie-xie has grown another foot and has added about three hundred pounds to her already impressive weight. Yuen and Misa estimates her age to be between ten to twelve years. As a full grown adult they estimate she should top out at about twenty to twenty-two feet long and weigh around three tons, unless she bears young, which could increase her length by another foot and her weight by as much as another five hundred pounds.

The compound offers endless picture post-card moments but it's hard to beat the addition of Xie-xie's four-foot tall dorsal fin in the background as the group looks at her and out into the early morning eastern sky.

With this as the backdrop, J.T. says, "Everyone? Can you come over here with me and Julie for a minute?"

Everyone makes their way over to Julie and J.T. from various spots around the deck and cove. Xie-xie swims calmly in the cove as J.T. continues with his impromptu announcement.

"I've learned so much from each of you and I'm truly saddened to learn how you were all separated for so long from each other. True friends and family should never be apart. These connections we make with each other are for all-time."

Kim nudges Tai and starts crying.

She says, "He talks just like you! So positive and driven!"

Tai smiles and begins to tear up. The couples are all holding hands but after J.T.'s comment, they hold each other a little tighter.

J.T. continues, "When I was away from my father, it was the worst time in my life. When I thought I might be apart from my mother, it was even worse but the thought of never seeing and holding Julie again was the very worst!"

All the women start crying. Kim stares proudly at her son and struggles to focus her eyes. Julie is about to lose all control.

"This is why in front of you all and with our majestic friend in our cove protecting us, I'd like to ask aunt Misa for her blessing as I ask Julie to marry me."

J.T. kneels down and holds Julie's left hand in his right hand. As she looks down at him nodding, tears fall all over his face. A second later, Yuen, Tai and Saka all raise their arms up and say, "Wànsuì!"

J.T. stands back up and grabs Julie in his arms. Tai walks over to his newly engaged son and says, "I have my favorite girl back now forever and you just got yours back! This is yours now son!"

Tai takes off his 3D gold dragon pendant necklace, originally his father's, and fastens it around J.T.'s neck. Father and son share a deep hug and then everyone crowds around the new young couple to share in the moment. A second later, Xie-xie bounds up from the depths and slides up into her favorite smooth rocky spot in the inlet. She opens her mouth and curls her tongue at the group. Everyone bursts out smiling and laughing.

Yuen says, "She wants to be a part of our group hug too!"

For the first time, everyone carefully steps toward Xie-xie and brushes her glossy black head and white side patch. Misa takes full advantage of the opportunity and inspects Xie-xie's tongue and her upper and lower teeth, both inside and outside her gum line. She checks for any loose teeth or any bones lodged that may be troubling Xie-xie. The killer whale genuinely loves all the attention but especially when Misa massages her tongue and gum line.

Misa is fully aware of the fact that with a simple flinch of her jaws, Xie-xie could bite her arms clean off from her mid-radial down but the thought and fear has never entered her mind. Yuen has a couple fish he caught secured in the shallows. He quickly unties them and tosses them in Xie-xie's mouth. Appreciative, Xie-xie backs up her massive body with ease and swims down into the depths of the cove. The compound continues to celebrate. They trade handshakes, hugs and kisses and then Saka pulls a digital camera out of his pocket and says, "Everyone. Please?"

Tai stops him and says, "No, Saka… you have to be in the picture too!"

Tai looks around and finds some used plywood and some rocks. He quickly builds a make-shift table to sit the camera on.

"There! Now, set your self-timer and get over here!"

Facing east, looking out into the cove's inlet with the beautiful early morning sky in the background, Saka sets his timer and races back into position next to Misa; three, two, one, flash and click.

Together, Julie and J.T. says, "One more!"

Saka runs back to the camera and sets the timer again; three, two, one, flash and click. But this time, at the count of one, Xie-xie has breached the surface about sixty feet away from shore and has leapt clear out of the water about fifteen feet high, directly above everyone standing on shore; an absolutely awesome spectacle. Completely overwhelmed and excited, everyone races back to Saka's camera to see if the image was captured. The group cheers wildly when they see the most spectacular picture any of them has ever seen.

Julie says, "Xie-xie! it's like she knew so she gave us this incredible moment!"

Everyone stares back into the cove. Xie-xie has disappeared for now.

The group decides to call the picture, "Xie-xie Wànsuì!"

January 23, 2012 – Year of the Dragon.

Julie's and J.T.'s wedding is all set. Just like their parent's, they prefer a small affair with everyone close attending. Mary offered her Grand Café for the reception and Toma and his men have arrived as well.

In honor of the event, everyone says a prayer together and enjoys the day but at Julie's and J.T.'s suggestion, they prefer to use their wedding day and reception time to collect everyone's thoughts and ideas on how to better manage foreign visitor's, like Saitonaka's men, how to better control information, and how to continue working with Xie-xie so she will be safe in the event they visit while she's in the cove. Rightfully so, no one trusts Saitonaka if and when he actually visits; for all they know and some of them sense it already, Saitonaka may try to kill Xie-xie just to make one of his demented points.

Toma immediately shares the fact that ever since he heard about Xie-xie, he has worked hard to boost Triad support on the island by bringing some of his men to Amami to live permanently. He figures by year's end, there will be a dozen Triad home owner's living on the island that have all sworn to protect the compound's residents as well as Xie-xie, all in honor of Toma's mother Mary. Mary helped raise many of them so they all owe her a great debt and they are happy and honored to serve and support her once again, especially in this amazing environment. Toma also shares an escalation alert code with everyone.

"To begin with, let me just apologize to you all but it has to be this way; you won't know who all of my new men are and that's on purpose. For your safety and for theirs so again, I apologize for all the secrecy but it's required. This way if you're ever asked, you can say and the look on your face will convey the truth, that you honestly don't know. I'd like to thank Dr. Tai for devising these codes for us, based off his Canton village codes for when folks there may have been in need of help with their Diabetes or other medical issues. And speaking of your Canton village friends, they send all the treats in celebration of your special day and they told me to tell you all, 'love and peace!' So, love and peace everyone! Thanks to this group's hard work late last year, the village is now completely self-efficient, from a Myst1, CDT wash and Enhanced-CDT vaccine production standpoint! My men and I made sure they are set with a year in reserves and they have the full production capabilities that all proved out before we left as well."

Everyone in the room stands and bows toward Toma and his men in gratitude for helping this great mainland community, so close to everyone's hearts.

"Red-one; some of you have heard me call that out a few times in the past. Again, that means basically, 'shut-up' when it comes to anything that has to do with Kim or J.T. If we're around Saitonaka or any of his men and this includes Mr. Oso, just assume that Red-one is in effect. Each family will have a new code so disregard anything else we may have used in the past."

Toma looks over at Tai. He nods in agreement.

"Okay. The Huang's, including Miss Julie now are Yellow, in honor of Mr. Jimmie Huang. Yellow-one is Dr. Tai and Kim. Yellow-two is J.T. and Julie. The Zhang's, Yuen and Carmela, are Blue-two and the Yamishinosaka's, Saka and Misa are Green-three. If you hear any of these codes, we either need these couples to see us immediately or there is an issue with one of these couples, obviously depending on the inflection of the call you hear. My mother's code is simply 'YoMama' and the same rules apply with her as well. Xie-xie's new code is 'Oreo'; if you hear this, again, considering the conversation at hand, it means she's either in danger or there is something else going on involving her."

Yuen adds, “And consider combinations.”

Toma says, “Yes! Thank you Yuen! So if you were to hear ‘Oreo-green-three’, there’s an issue with Xie-xie, Saka, and Misa. Now, keep in mind, we’ll never call any of these codes out unless it’s an emergency so don’t worry about hearing stuff like, ‘yellow-one and blue-two went fishing!”

Yuen adds, “And for our foreign guests?”

“Fuck them! They don’t get codes! You’ll just hear their names; especially that little shit Heroshi! Mainly the codes will be alerts to either help hide Kim and or J.T. or to get someone to run interference. And if Saitonaka escalates things, all bets are off and we’ll just fucking kill all of them to protect all of you and your Orca Xie-xie!”

Saka stands up and shouts, “Banzai!”

Once a week, and at Xie-xie’s sole discretion, Misa and Xie-xie put on a special show for everyone in the cove. The price of admission is a bucket of fish that looks to weigh in around at least twenty pounds; otherwise neither of the girls will perform. So far, she’s visiting on average about three to four times a week, as far as they know.

Xie-xie keeps returning to the inlet cove to see her human handlers and especially to visit with her relief savior and trusted dentist, Misa. Misa is hoping that by making herself visible to Xie-xie at the same time each day, it’s possible that Xie-xie may come to rely on her presence at that time so the two can continue to learn from each other and grow their mutual trust.

So far, Xie-xie still appears seemingly at random times throughout the week but maybe to her, that is a regimen. To test that possibility, Misa records every appearance, the duration, and everything that Xie-xie does. Eventually, the two will develop a pattern that they can test out and come to trust.

CHAPTER THIRTY-FOUR

JULY 4, 2012 – HAI PHONG, VIETNAM

FROM their fishing boat a mile offshore from the port city, two local fishermen armed with machine guns fire at the dorsal fin of a fourteen-foot male Great White shark. Drunk, they laugh as they riddle the top predator with bullets along his right side. *Carcharodon Carcharias* darts sharply down into the abyss away from the cowardly pair. As they reminisce about their former Vietnam War camp commanding days, their deadly implements have found their mark, shattering several of the shark's ribs and striking his liver as well. Celebrating their cowardly triumph, the eldest of the two drunks falls overboard but his partner passes out before he notices he's gone.

The injured Great White senses the vigorous splashing and quickly pivots around. From his position now three hundred feet directly below the struggling shape, the shark winces in pain as he tries to adjust and adapt to his new wounds. Inciting his natural instincts to feed all the more and beginning to adjust to his recent pain, White Death races toward the shape, who is splashing helplessly at the surface.

Wearing his life preserver and feeling far better than he should, thanks to the fermented spirits coursing through his bloodstream, the man rests back his head on the back of his life preserver and tries to form the words for help. The shark is closing fast; two hundred feet. Ten seconds later, one hundred feet. The drunk simply bobs up and down like a bobber in a small trout pond. If his foolish friend could wake up, he'd realize he could help his fallen buddy by simply pulling him onboard since he's right next to the boat.

An unnatural chill takes over the man in the water. His dulled senses can still pick up on a presence; a powerful and ominous presence. At the most, ten seconds away. Five, four, three, two, one. Breaching clear out of the water, the apex predator rises in full glory with the drunken man's body spread eagle in the shark's mouth. With an impressive bite force that Great Whites acquired from their ancient ancestors, a human being's body is no match for any shark, much less against a Great White.

The Great mackerel shark closes his extended jaws and engulfs the drunken man's inner thighs of both legs, his genitals and lower intestines extending all the way up to the man's naval and including more than a quarter of his upper intestines. On the other side of the man's body, ninety-nine percent of his buttocks have been removed including the ball-like base of his spine.

As the shark descends back down with his prize, he crashes squarely on top of the unconscious drunk in the boat, obliterating the boat and snapping the man's neck instantly from the shark's sheer girth. With all of the rich blood in the water, the rogue male shark turns around in a fraction of a second and finishes the two inebriate's off. All of this nourishment will help the predator fight off disease and infection for a while but with his liver badly damaged, he doesn't have much time.

JULY 6, 2012, 5:05 P.M. – YOKOHAMA, JAPAN

Having teamed up for the past six months, Izu and Heroshi continue working well together. Arrangements for Boss Saitonaka's return are almost complete. The two are finalizing things in Saitonaka's downtown offices as a welcome home event. It may have been over four years since Saitonaka had to flee from his main operations and location but everything is intact, just as it was when he left. All of his men have made sure no other Yakuza faction or rival group took over or ransacked his property. Izu especially has worked very hard to make sure Boss Saitonaka's prized possessions, like his Megalodon teeth, swords, ancient helmets and rare war items have been secured.

With his return now imminent, Izu and Heroshi are making the last few arrangements for their Bosses momentous return. They accept numerous catered food trays and several liquor deliveries at both the front and rear entrances. Running back and forth constantly throughout the early evening, Izu and Heroshi hardly ever stop long enough to see and talk to each other but as long as the job gets done and on time, that's all that matters.

It's one thing to plan and arrange such an event for Boss Saitonaka but it's something else to fail to deliver on it because as they know, Boss Saitonaka puts on an incredible show when he arranges such events. Everyone in his organization owns copies of those events as proof of their popularity and success. Izu's final task is to order the Geisha girls who will serve as hostesses for the evening's festivities. They will welcome everyone inside and later that evening, they will perform a special ceremonial dance in honor of Boss Saitonaka's return.

6:45 P.M. – Fellow Yakuza Bosses and their family and friends are arriving. The three Geisha's welcome each faction in and personally helps to seat the leader of each Yakuza family. As usual, each Boss and his underboss are leery of the event because in time's past, these events have been used to disguise a coup d'état against one or several of them. It's a classic move that originated several millennia ago when ancient Chinese Warriors attempted to consolidate the best resources in the country at that time. They would invite their rivals to a celebratory feast and at feast's end; they would slaughter everyone from the rival group. The ancient Egyptians did the same thing in their part of the world at this same ancient time and this tradition was passed down to every other ancient powerhouse throughout history. The Romans did it to the Germans and to the Gauls (France) countless times. The Greeks did it to the Romans when they took over Rome. The English did it to the Scots and to the Irish. This pattern repeated itself all over the Old World and across the Atlantic Ocean over to the New World when the young Americans did it to the Native Americans. In more modern times though, this ploy has been thrust into the spotlight by the Italian immigrant's behavior, which formed their La Cosa Nostra in America at the turn of the twentieth century. They used this tactic to eliminate their enemies, thus consolidating and growing their power and criminal enterprises.

7:30 P.M. – With everyone having such a great time, Izu notices the plum wine and top-shelf saké is running low. He asks Heroshi to quickly order some more from a local upscale liquor store just down the block.

"Heroshi-san. We can finally rest for a moment... okay, that's it!"

Izu and Heroshi laugh together.

"Would you mind running down to the liquor store to get some more plum wine and saké?"

"Oh, I would but Boss Saitonaka called me earlier to ask how things were going and he said he'd be calling me back again soon to ask about other guests. He wants me to detail their acceptance of the celebration so far."

"Right. He always likes to hear what people are saying and how they are acting. Better wait for his call. I'll go quickly."

"Thank you Izu. I'll keep the glasses full while you're gone!"

"Very good! Be back soon."

"I."

9 P.M. – In the corner section of the office, Boss Hamata is growing impatient. He only drinks top-shelf plum wine and only in the early evening hours because if he drinks it too late, he can't sleep. At this time, he figures he's got about an hour left to enjoy a drink or two before he has to stop.

In his very deep and demanding voice, "Heroshi-san!"

Boss Hamata motions over to Heroshi with a frantic wave of his fat fist. If he wasn't so overweight, he'd certainly be the top boss over Yakuza but he makes too easy a target for an attack because by the time any attempt against him would begin, he'd be riddled with bullets; unable to move out of his seat in enough time. Instead, everyone knows he's basically 'off limits' because for years, he's been relegated to providing, what else, food and catering services.

He controls most of the food delivery and specialty services like food preparations for weddings and events for the Yakuza.

Heroshi bows and says, "Boss Hamata! Yes sir! How can I help you?"

Frustrated and thirsty, Boss Hamata says, "What? No more plum wine for me Heroshi? Do I have to make more myself?"

"I'm so sorry Boss Hamata! Please, forgive our failures! Izu-san left to get a lot more a while ago. I don't know where he is."

"Izu, ah, good man for Saitonaka! I wish he was with me!"

"Boss Hamata! Again, I'm sorry for your wait. Let me see what I can find for you."

"Good boy Heroshi-san! I'll wait but I have to leave at ten so see what you can do, … quickly!"

"Quickly! Of course! I'll be quick Boss Hamata. Thank you!"

Heroshi bows and steps back and away from Boss Hamata and his three skilled and armed bodyguards.

9:45 P.M. – Heroshi is able to scrounge up a single glass of plum wine for Boss Hamata. He gives it to him and the former third in command top Yakuza boss drinks it and promptly leaves with his entourage. Heroshi breathes a slight sigh of relief, since Boss Hamata didn't yell at him afterward; he must have been satisfied with the minimal offering.

10:00 P.M. – The Geisha's take their place in front of Saitonaka's office and begin their ceremonial dance. Two drummers behind them accent the women's bigger turns, swings and steps. Heroshi watches from the far right corner of the room. He's giving Saitonaka an update as the mystical performance continues.

"Good job Heroshi-san! I hear that everyone is having a very good time."

"Thank you sir!"

"Boss Hamata?"

"He already left sir. As soon as I found him some plum wine."

"Left? Before my girls could dance for him?"

"Yes sir."

Upset, Saitonaka says, "Lazy fat bastard! He eats and drinks his fill like a sow and leaves! If I placed pussy in front of him, he'd look and then leave! But not you Heroshi-san?"

"No sir!"

"You'd stay?"

"I sir! I'd stay and grovel in that sushi!"

Laughing out loud, Saitonaka exclaims, "Banzai Heroshi-san! Banzai!"

"Yes sir!"

"Okay Heroshi-san. Very good!"

"Thank you sir."

Saitonaka pauses.

He takes a long drag on his Cuban and asks, "And Izu? You're okay with that?"

"It is what it is sir."

"Good… good boy Heroshi-san! I'll deal with Hamata later. Just do your next task quickly, huh?"

"Yes sir. Goodnight."

"There's another ten thousand for you in my middle desk drawer Heroshi-san!"

"Thank you but no sir."

"No?" Saitonaka's eyes furrow and his vision gets sharper.

"It was my pleasure sir!"

"Banzai Heroshi-san! … fucking Banzai young man!"

Saitonaka hangs up and gloats. He knows his protégé is coming along beautifully; helping him to tie up a few loose ends and strengthening his return to Yokohama. With such an ambitious and intelligent student at his fingertips, Saitonaka's path to being the recognized top power in the Yakuza is coming together ahead of schedule.

JULY 7, 2012 3 A.M.

Heroshi calls Eishi.

"Eishi-san!"

"Who the hell is this? Shit! It's 3 A.M.!

"Your uncle Naka says for you to go see your Misha Katana3."

Eishi laughs angrily and says, "Ha! Whoever the hell you are, if he heard you call him 'Naka', he'd cut your balls and God damn head off as soon as you finished your insult! Who the hell is this?"

"… I don't think so. Anyway, you should go Eishi-san."

"Right now?"

"As you wish; there's no rush… not anymore."

"What? What is that supposed to mean?"

Heroshi smirks and laughs to himself. "It means you can go now or you can fucking wait because what's waiting for your discovery… can wait."

"Fuck-head! How dare to talk to me that way! Who is this?"

The line hangs up.

JULY 7, 2012 4 A.M. – YOKOHAMA, JAPAN

Eishi tries calling his uncle Ric to ask him to meet up at the Misha Katana3 boat so they can discuss Eishi's mysterious call and caller.

Eishi calls his uncle Ric but there is no answer. He tries several more times with no luck. Finally, he decides to leave a message.

"Uncle. I'm sorry to wake you but I got a strange call earlier this morning telling me to go down to the docks to see my Misha Katana3. When you wake, please come and see me there. It's 4:10 A.M. and I'm leaving now. Okay."

Eishi hangs up and heads out to the docks. At 4:30 A.M., he arrives. In the early morning fog, the docks are especially eerie. Misha Katana3 rests at the far end of the docks. As Eishi walks along the edge of the pier, water slaps all around and against each boat and the pier in a strange rhythmic sequence. Even for the seasoned Captain, the pattern is becoming monotonous and creepy. Half way down the pier, Eishi hears something or someone behind him. He calls out.

"Hello? Who's there? Uncle?"

Silence. Eishi resumes his pursuit of Misha Katana3. Nearing the front of his third ship, he hears a noise behind him again.

His anxieties growing, Eishi calls out into the void again, "God damn it, who is that? Uncle? Is that you?"

An even more eerie silence and colder air takes over the pier.

Fed up with waiting and a little disturbed by the squeaks and mysterious sounds going on at the far end of the pier, Eishi promptly boards his Misha Katana3 ship and warms up in the captain's quarters.

He says to himself; "I'll just wait here for uncle."

He pulls out his cell phone and calls his uncle Ric Shigemura again.

"Uncle. I'm here now at Misha3 in the captain's quarters so as soon as you can, please come down so we can talk. Thanks."

Eishi extracts the small bottle of saké that he knows his captain of the Misha Katana3 keeps in the storage cabinet above the ship's control center. He takes a long drink straight from the bottle and that helps to settle his nerves. Still dark, the strange rasps continue so after every other one; Eishi takes another jolt from the saké bottle.

As nervous as he is about his mysterious caller and the circumstances that have led him down to the docks at the crack of dawn, Eishi is growing more and more concerned as to the whereabouts of his uncle Ric. Whenever he has called for him in the past, he always answers either his home phone or his cell phone and he always returns his nephew's calls. With all that they have gone through over the past few years in particular, Ric has always been back in touch within minutes of Eishi's call.

As he continues to wait, the strong saké begins to take effect on Eishi's early morning condition. Suddenly, he hears another disturbing sound just outside his captain's quarters. He re-awakens, startled and accidently pushes the decorative ceramic saké bottle off the command center table and onto the ground. The bottle breaks in half, spilling out the last third of its contents.

"Shit! That was Kino's favorite saké bottle! Damn it!"

4:50 A.M. – Alert and frustrated now, Eishi decides to walk around outside to get some fresh air and to watch the rising sun of the empire. Maybe the dark mango colored sun will help to calm his nerves. The fog is beginning to lift as well, making the whole pier appear a little less intimidating. Eishi shines his flashlight all around and when the light shines across the ship's mast, he stops and steadies the beam of light.

Twenty feet up on the pole, the item or items are difficult to make out, especially this early in the morning. The next second, Eishi's curiosity turns into horror. As the dawn's early light slowly intensifies, he is able to make out the respective fingers on the pair of severed hands. The severed appendages are affixed to the ship's mast with fishing line. From Eishi's position, it looks like they are just hovering in thin air.

Eishi is too drunk and too scared to climb up there to retrieve them but as he stands there looking up in shock at the dripping hands, his mind immediately begins to race, wondering who the hands used to belong to. He calls his ship's captain, Kino to come down to help him.

"Kino-san?"

"I. Who's this so early?"

"It's Eishi."

"Yes sir!"

"Please, as soon as you can. Come down here to Misha3. I need your help with something."

"Yes! On my way sir!"

"Thank you Kino-san. Please hurry."

5:15 A.M. – KINO ARRIVES.

Concerned he missed one of his duties the last time the ships docked, Kino asks, "Sir? Did I forget to tie something down?"

Curious, Eishi asks, "Or did you just finish tying those up there?"

Eishi points up to the ship's mast.

Kino looks up and then immediately back down, in horror.

"Sir! No sir!"

"Someone on your crew?"

"God, I hope not!"

"They belong to someone Kino!"

"I sir."

"Please, get up there and bring them down so we can see if we know whose they are."

"I sir. One moment."

Kino surveys the immediate area on deck and retrieves a ten-foot long fishing gaff pole.

Kino climbs up a small initial ladder that leads to the area of the ship's mast. How the person affixed the severed hands up so high on the mast is a mystery to Eishi and to Kino. Kino discovers how the severed parts are attached to the mast and uses the gaff to snip the fishing line. As the hands quickly fall to the ground, a small note that had been placed between two digits drifts down to the deck like an early autumn leaf. Eishi grabs at it once and then on his second attempt, he secures it in his right hand. Bloody, he shakes it for a moment and then reads it.

"He tried but he lost! He'll be missed by some but not by others!"

At the bottom of the note, in the man's blood, it reads,

"Some trophies are worth keeping... some are not!"

Kino arrives back on the main deck and offers the hands to Eishi. Eishi waves him off so Kino just continues holding them; a chilling task especially in the early morning hours but the two try to figure out if they know who the hands used to belong to.

"One of your men Kino?"

"I'll have to make some calls but I don't think so sir."

Sick to his stomach and needing any form of mental release from the graphic moment, Eishi says, "Well, if they don't answer their phone right away, just be patient."

Kino cringes and says, "Uh, yes sir."

Kino leaves. Eishi heads back into the captain's quarters, with the hands, to give his uncle a call again.

5:35 A.M. After hearing nothing and receiving no returned messages, Eishi leaves and heads back to his home.

July 7, 2012 Noon – Yokohama, Japan

One of Saitonaka's men enters the formal dining room. He's holding a bag that resembles a nineteen eighties bowling ball bag. In fact, it is a 1984 model bowling ball bag that the man was ordered to buy online for just such an occasion. As he enters, soft white lights turn on, lighting the room at its walls only. He proceeds to his right, passing several very tall and ornate floor vases along the way.

He turns to his left and walks down the far back wall of the room until he reaches the multi-shelf unit that currently features Birds of Paradise on the far edges, an ancient Megalodon shark tooth here and there and several bonsai trees filling most of the other remaining spots. There is an empty space available about chest high to the left center. The man claps his hands once and a naked woman appears from the opposite wall carrying a 12" diameter saucer. She places the saucer on the empty shelf and retreats to her former position.

The man unzips the bowling ball bag and grasps the severed head by its hair. He strategically places it on the saucer and after a couple readjustments; he's content with how it rests. He leans down, closes up the vintage bowling ball bag and walks out of the formal dining room, locking the door behind him. A moment later, one of the naked attendants walks over to the multi-shelf unit and cleans up a single drop of blood on the floor. Then she returns to her quarters.

July 14, 2012 5 A.M. – Amami Oshima Island, Japan

Dr. Tai, Yuen and Carmela discover a fourteen-foot male Great White shark in their cove's inlet. The great apex predator is dead.

"Carmela? Run and get Misa. She knows a lot more about a shark's reproductive abilities than I do."

Carmela runs back up the hill to the rear entrance and retrieves Misa from the kitchen, who happened to be there watching these early morning risers.

Misa strains her eyes to see what Yuen and Tai are hovering over. As soon as she makes the giant shape out, her eyes widen.

Misa quickly makes her way down to the cove.

"What the hell happened?"

She pats the Great White across his *Ampullae of Lorenzini.* She starts crying.

Yuen says, "Look at his back."

Misa tears up more as she sees the horrible damage done to him. The bullet wounds along the shark's right side have become infected and quickened the shark's death.

"Some people are so God damn disgusting! When people act out like this, it makes me sick! I'll be glad when mankind finally dies out in a thousand years or so and just the animals remain! Then they can live out their lives in peace and continue to evolve without our ignorance and selfish interference! Like it was before we evolved and started killing everything in sight!"

Yuen pats Misa on her shoulder, in complete agreement and understanding of her genuine passion for these and all animals.

Yuen asks, 'So, I'm wondering how long he's been dead because look at his claspers."

The shark's long white claspers are swollen; full of crystallized sperm as he lies on his right side, having succumbed to his injuries. Misa inspects the shark's awesome and terrifying looking jaws. Even in death, the shark commands immediate respect. His partially extended jaws accentuate his death mask and this makes Misa furious as she stares down at the top predator.

She continues her inspection and when she investigates the shark's swollen claspers she says, "It looks like he died recently so that's good with respect to his sperm. We need to collect as much of it as we can; freezing most of it and putting some on ice so we can study it before it dissipates."

Misa shows Tai and Yuen how to gently spread apart the various folds of the shark's claspers to extract sperm. Carmela returns from the kitchen with various sized containers to place the samples in. Half-filling one of them, she runs back up into the house and places the specimen container in a separate freezer unit, used solely for everyone's respective marine research projects. Strangely, it also houses Yuen's favorite flavored ice-cycles.

The running joke in the house is actually a bet as to when Yuen will mistakenly grab something else from the freezer and start sucking on it thinking it's one of his flavored ice treats. The Huang's are all betting it happens later this year, during the winter months when Yuen doesn't sleep as well. Julie believes her dad will make his raunchy error before the end of summer and Saka and Misa just love the whole idea and possibility that Yuen may soon make his horribly-flavored mistake. Carmela is just flat out grossed out that Yuen would even keep his treats in that freezer in the first place when there is plenty of room in the regular shared kitchen freezer.

Yuen helps to fill the smaller container for storage in the deck's ice storage unit for immediate study. Then the group just gawks at the awesome shark and starts mumbling to one another. At the same moment, they concoct a plan; they have been meeting secretly away from their other team members, discussing their interests about breeding Xie-xie with another Orca but none have been in the area so this opportunity is too good to pass up; take the sperm from this dead Great White Shark and use it to inseminate Xie-xie. Xie-xie already trusts Misa to approach her intimately so this move would be no different as far as she (Xie-xie) would be concerned. Misa knows from her research how much of the Great White shark's sperm to use to impregnate Xie-xie with so as soon as she can, Misa plans on performing this delicate and intimate task.

With Yuen and Misa leading the way, Dr. Tai and the pair have also secretly been treating Xie-xie with a revised formula based on their former Enhanced-CDT (Crystal Dragon's Tears) vaccine; a hybrid vaccine that will help to protect these much larger apex predators. In preparation for Saitonaka's visit, which could occur any day, they want to ensure that Xie-xie can withstand an attack from both Saitonaka and his team's weapons or if she happens to be in the cove's inlet performing an inspection, so she can withstand a slash from Saitonaka's cowardly white snake-headed cane sword.

During Misa's regular inspections of Xie-xie, she has noticed the slight re-development of the slime build up in and around Xie-xie's gum line. They aren't taking any chances with her health declining so it's perfect timing and logic that they have been busy developing and administering the new Enhanced-CDT vaccines to her, specifically geared for Xie-xie and animals in her size and weight class.

With endless variations of their Enhanced-CDT vaccine now at their disposal, the secret team each has their own visions of developing a Super-Orcinus Orca for some time but now that this Great White shark semen has become available, they have quickly changed their plans and are now energized and determined to help create a new and even more, ultimate predator.

CHAPTER THIRTY-FIVE

July 20, 2012 Midnight – Amami Oshima Island, Japan

RESTLESS, Misa is in the kitchen getting a glass of water when she thinks she sees moonlight glimmer across Xie-xie's four and a half foot tall dorsal fin patrolling the cove about thirty feet out from shore. As everyone else in the compound sleeps, she quickly and quietly alerts Yuen and Carmela and then Tai to join her down at the cove's inlet.

Misa begins by sharply sounding her whistle; one clean toot is all it should take for Xie-xie to respond since she's so close and it's never failed before. Sure enough, a moment later, Misa sees Xie-xie's dorsal fin turn toward the inlet. Misa steps back from the edge of the inlet in anticipation of Xie-xie's amazing and sudden arrival from the depths. How Xie-xie can always perfectly estimate exactly how far outward to go continues to amaze Misa in particular. With her increasing weight and length, you'd think she'd over-estimate even just one time and land a few yards too far; out of the water and onto the sandy shore itself but so far, she's always landed right around the same spot on her favorite smooth rocks in about three foot deep of water.

Misa is thrilled to see Xie-xie as always but tonight, the two will make history; although admittedly, unbeknownst to Orcinus Orca. Misa immediately rubs Xie-xie's tongue that she has immediately offered up to Misa. In this way, the two are like mother and daughter but who's to say who's who. Yuen, Carmela, and Tai look on in amazement of how Misa works with Xie-xie. They are so grateful for her work because there's no way either of them would attempt Misa's behaviors with Xie-xie.

Yuen makes his way over to Xie-xie's right side and caresses her right pectoral fin. This signals Xie-xie to roll toward Yuen, tipping over and exposing her genitalia for Misa to examine. Using an improvised plastic turkey-baster utensil that Yuen developed, Misa successfully inseminates Xie-xie with the Great White shark's semen that the group had on ice. As a further boost of energy and super protein source, they also reward Xie-xie with thick cut strips from the deceased Great White shark, including its few bones, also treated with their newly Enhanced-CDT vaccine; injected directly into the meat and marinating the numerous bone fragments.

The real-life possibility that Xie-xie could one day give birth to a whole new species of Killer whale combining her ultimately superior attributes with those of the top predatory fish in the ocean is captivating to the small inner group. For two species that have forever collided, maybe now, they will fuse together and become one – something the world has never seen.

By the end of July, all of the specially treated Great White shark meat is depleted. Unaware that content was used to feed her, everyone else resumes taking turns feeding Xie-xie whenever she appears in the cove's inlet.

Saitonaka secretly arrives back at his palatial apartment complex. He settles in and then visits the head that has been waiting for him almost all month long in his formal dining room.

He stares deep into the severed head's eyes and mumbles to himself, "See? Now you can watch everything else unfold at your leisure!"

He laughs, demonically as ever and pops another O-tablet.

CHAPTER THIRTY-SIX

February 10, 2013 2 A.M. Year of the Snake – Amami Oshima Island, Japan

MISA is genuinely agitated. Completely in-tune with the likelihood that Xie-xie may give birth any day now, she hasn't really slept all month. She quietly exits the back patio door and walks down to the deck to the right side of the cove. It's an unusually warm morning for this time in the year but that suits Misa just fine. Wearing her favorite light flower print sweater and blue jeans, she's perfectly comfortable at this early hour.

Impatiently, Misa walks up and down the deck, admiring the six by six-foot observation platform that Yuen built. Cleverly, he anchored it to the shore using a simple set of steel beams that are secured to each side of the wooden platform and then run diagonally down to a hefty metal cage that Yuen built and affixed to the shore's rocky bottom. The end result is that the square platform essentially serves two purposes; as an observation deck that appears to just hang in mid-air and as a springboard. Although with Xie-xie in the cove, no one has tested out the platform's springboard abilities yet. To do so and scare Xie-xie could result in complete disaster.

2:22 A.M. – Still wide awake, Misa spots Xie-xie coming into the cove. She's a couple hundred yards out but Misa can clearly see the moonlight cascade across Xie-xie's glossy black dorsal fin. A moment later, Xie-xie lets out an unusual moan; something Misa's never heard before. Misa runs down the deck and over to Xie-xie's favorite spot in the cove inlet. She toots her whistle but Xie-xie remains in the cove; her dorsal fin remains at the surface and she continues to moan.

With her refusing to submerge and make her typical appearance on shore in the shallow water so she can rub her giant pearl white belly against the smooth rocks, Misa becomes very concerned. She toots her whistle again but now Xie-xie begins circling in the cove about thirty yards out. Misa runs back over to the main deck and jumps over and onto the small springboard observation deck. With her flashlight, Misa searches the cove again for Xie-xie's current position. She spots her on her left, as she makes her way in front of the small platform.

Like she's seeking approval or something, Misa leans down and caresses Xie-xie along the top of her head and down along Xie-xie's right side as she swims by. Xie-xie circle's back around and repeats this behavior two more times. Misa starts to panic a little because she's not picking up on what may be wrong with Xie-xie. Then, as Xie-xie passes in front of Misa for the fourth time, Xie-xie angles toward Misa and Misa sees that her Orcinus Orca is bleeding; she's ready to give birth to her pup. Misa starts crying and smiles. She can't do anything for Xie-xie because the killer whale must simply perform this relatively simple procedure herself.

To give birth, the killer whale just needs to swim in circles just like Xie-xie has been doing and just contract her reproductive muscles so her baby will release from out of her womb. Misa stands there on the springboard platform and just cries because she just wants Xie-xie to have a successful birth. Xie-xie continues to circle and moan but now, she sounds more like she might be in some genuine pain. Frantic, Misa dives off the springboard platform and starts swimming over to Xie-xie.

On one hand, it's good she's doing this alone because if her housemates saw her jump in after Xie-xie, they'd all be screaming and going crazy trying to recover her. On the other hand, she's now about to be face-to-face with a near sixteen-foot, two and three-quarter ton apex predator, who's genuinely agitated, pregnant and in pain.

2:43 A.M. – Completely at ease, now that she's right in front of Xie-xie, Misa caresses Xie-xie's nose and brushes her across her left white eye patch. Xie-xie groans but it's not that distressed groan. In an instant, Misa dives below Xie-xie and brushes across the killer whale's privates. She can feel the pup beginning to appear. She brushes across the pup's head again and then resurfaces.

Crying, Misa tells Xie-xie, "Go sweetheart! Give birth to your baby and I'll stay right here for you!"

A moment later, Xie-xie swims away.

After five minutes, nothing; no signs of Xie-xie at the surface as far as Misa can see with her flashlight and she can't see any moonlight catching the side of Xie-xie's dorsal fin either. Ten minutes and nothing still.

Misa starts to cry out of fear that something has gone terribly wrong. After twenty minutes, Misa is shivering. She has no choice but to get out of the water or she might drown from the effects of hyperthermia. She strips off her wet clothes and just stands there naked on the springboard deck in the moonlight.

3:13 A.M. – In bed, Saka rolls over but expecting to run into Misa and not, he wakes up. He staggers down the short hallway and into their side of the compound's separate bathroom. Then he walks down the rest of the hallway and into the shared kitchen and living room. At the kitchen window, he glances out and down toward the beautifully moonlit cove. He immediately spots Misa's naked figure standing in the middle of the small springboard observation deck and immediately runs out the patio door.

Nearing her, he nervously says, "Misa? What are you doing out here all alone and naked?"

She just stands there shivering and crying. Saka makes his way over to the closest point near the platform and Misa shines her LED light on the rocks for him.

Saka says, "No. Just light up the front of the platform for me."

She does so and he jumps across. Misa blocks his body with hers and he picks her up as he runs into her so they both don't fall over and into the cove. He takes off his shorts and T-shirt and immediately hands them to Misa.

She puts them on and tells him, "Xie-xie's trying to give birth but she's having trouble! I think maybe she drown trying! … God! Please! No!"

Saka hugs Misa and rubs her back, shoulder, and arms frantically. Another ten minutes passes and Saka motions for Misa to return to the deck and get inside so she can get a hot shower before she gets sick.

3:33 A.M. – "Honey, please. You need to get inside and warm up. I'm so sorry but there's nothing we can do. You did more than enough from the looks of it."

Crying harder, Misa reminisces, "I jumped in and felt Xie-xie's baby! It was wonderful! I'll never forget it and I'll never forget her!"

Misa buries her face into Saka's bare chest and nearly collapses from her grief. After a few minutes, the two carefully slip into the water, closest to the main deck and wade across. They walk back down the rest of the length of the deck and as Misa reaches Xie-xie's favorite spot in the shallows where the Orca used to love to rub her belly against the smooth rocks, Misa walks into the water and reaches down. She picks up the first smooth rock she touches and kisses it. Saka grabs her hand holding the rock and he kisses it too.

Completely heartbroken, Saka helps Misa back up the path, into the house and into the bathroom. The couple takes an extremely somber shower together. No one else is awake; they have no idea what has just happened.

CHAPTER THIRTY-SEVEN

6:45 A.M.

KIM and Tai awake and stir around for a minute in bed; each thinking about the newlyweds down the hall. They're also obsessed thinking about all the fun they look forward to having later today trying to spot Xie-xie while they fish for more food for the pregnant killer whale. Down the hall, Tai can hear their compound's separate shower running. He sneaks down to the next room and peaks in the door that is ajar; J.T. and Julie's room. Both of them aren't in bed. He sneaks back toward his bedroom and as he walks by the bathroom again, he hears Julie and J.T. moaning so he walks away and heads back into his bedroom laughing.

"What? Why are you laughing?" Kim asks.

Tai pauses and then says, "I think J.T. and Julie are about to become parents! Well, not for about nine months or so but from the sound of it, they are making sure of it right now in the shower!"

Kim smiles and then she stares at Tai with her head tilted slightly down.

Then she says, "Sounds like a good idea."

Immediately, Tai adds, "Really?"

Kim nods and says, "Just lie back and let me know when, okay?"

Tai closes his eyes and falls back on the middle of the bed.

He says, "I can still hold it off a long time you know."

Kim nods as she begins her magical masturbation techniques and says, "We've got all morning!"

J.T. and Julie have been having sex all late night and early morning long. J.T. is exhausted but Julie is still alert and aroused. As J.T. weakens, Julie takes over and makes another erotic pass up and down J.T.'s body. They're enjoying each other, as they should.

8 A.M. – Everyone except for Misa is up now and wandering back and forth between their respective bedrooms and bathrooms. Saka is sitting in the living room reading the

newspaper. Yuen and Carmela start making coffee for everyone and Yuen motions over to Saka.

"Cup?"

He gratefully shakes his head and returns to his paper.

Tai and Kim walk into the shared living room.

"Morning everyone!"

Saka nods and Yuen and Carmela say, "Morning!"

Tai offers, "I thought this morning we'd take turns fishing from the boat in pairs or threes max to catch some more fish for our pregnant little lady."

Yuen and Carmela smile.

J.T. and Julie enter and Tai says, "Hey you two! Gee son, you look really tired. You okay?"

Kim nudges Tai in his ribs and frowns at him and then smiles.

"Morning Pop! … Ma!"

Julie says, "Morning everyone! Do we have a mini-Orca yet?"

Saka gets up from his living room chair abruptly and closes the shared door on his side of the complex. Everyone watches him as he repositions himself in the kitchen and turns around.

"I'll just say it; Misa was trying to help Xie-xie last night. We think she was trying to give birth but she may have drowned. We waited for over a half an hour after Misa jumped into the cove to help her but we never saw her resurface again... I'm so sorry."

The room fills with depression and exhaustive grief. Stunned, Tai and Yuen are speechless. They close their eyes in disbelief. J.T. starts crying as he consoles Julie who is crying uncontrollably. Kim and Carmela temporarily freeze in their positions cooking in the kitchen and then collapse into each other crying. The worst day in the group's life gets even harder when the side shared door opens and Misa stands in front of everyone crying her eyes out. She collapses to the floor and just keeps mumbling, "But I felt it! I felt her baby! It was magic! I want her back!"

Julie immediately runs over to her mother and wraps herself around her. Everyone's crying harder at the very image that Misa just painted for them. After a few minutes, Kim and Carmela help Julie and Misa to their feet and escort them over to the living room sofa. They fall into it and curl up into two balls together.

Saka motions the guys to go out to the back patio so he can explain Misa's details and his actions to them from earlier in the morning. He points down at the small springboard observation platform and talks with his hands as he describes Misa's dive into the cove and her subsequent smooth rock souvenir. The men just walk around in random circles, sick to their stomachs as they imagine Misa's and Xie-xie's final moments together.

With his back to the cove, Yuen clears his throat and then offers, "I think we should all pick stones from Xie-xie's rocky inlet and I'll get them to my Triad friends. They'll do something very special with them I'm sure; setting a special stone inside each or something and for Misa, I'll have them make a full set of jewelry with a black onyx and pearl Orca in the middle of a pendant for her."

Saka, Tai and J.T. begin to nod.

"Uncle Yuen?" J.T. asks

Yuen says, "Yeah J.T."

Saka and Tai's eyes widen and the biggest smiles come across their faces.

Exuberantly, J.T. shouts, "That won't be necessary! Yah!"

J.T. erupts into elation and starts running down the path screaming, "Yah! Woo!"

Tai and Saka run after him also yelling "Woo!" and "Wànsuì!"

Startled, Yuen turns around and sees Xie-xie's gorgeous and nearly five foot tall glossy black dorsal fin out in the cove about a hundred yards away. A moment later, he sees her signature blow-hole explosion, more powerful than before; sea water bursts out and away in an amazing and wider spray than ever before. That sight was always spectacular but what happens right after that is even better.

Just as the guys reach the cove's inlet, another glossy black dorsal fin about one and a half foot tall rises up and soon after, a fantastic smaller blow-hole explosion appears at the water's glassy and shimmery horizon.

Kim wipes her tears away and her and Carmela retreat back into the kitchen so Julie can continue comforting her mother on the sofa. Dehydrated, Kim quickly runs the faucet, filling a glass with cold water. Carmela joins her. Kim hands Carmela the first glass and fills another for herself. Just as Carmela finishes off her drink, Kim's glass crashes to the floor. Kim can't even form any words so she just screams and runs out the patio door. Carmela chases her as the two run down the path screaming. Julie falls off the sofa and runs to the kitchen window. Expecting to see something horrible, she starts laughing and yells for her mom to join her.

"Mom! Quick!"

Julie waits for her mom but she can hardly contain herself.

Julie repeats her command, "Mom! Look! Xie-xie!"

That gets Misa's immediate attention. She falls to the floor so her legs can re-adjust from being balled up and limps over to the patio door. Not able to form any words either, Misa just screams bloody murder and runs down the path with Julie toward the cove's inlet. The guys stand there completely stunned, smiling and relieved like never before because they've seen it all but the girls have just begun to see everything unfold.

Misa screams, "Xie-xie! Way to go sweetheart! Way to go!"

Saka adds, "Banzai!"

Kim joins Tai and J.T. and then Julie joins them. They all hug and Julie points out into the distance at a very proud and protective mother Xie-xie and her fantastic Orca pup.

J.T. whispers, but loud enough for everyone in the group to hear him, "Wait for it..."

Three seconds later, the smaller blow-hole explosion appears.

Yuen and Carmela hug Misa and Saka and again J.T. says, "Uh, wait for it!"

Three seconds later, a third foot and a half tall dorsal fin rises and another small blow-hole explosion appears and announces itself to the world and to the Amami Oshima Island team.

Misa says, "My God! Look at them! Xie-xie and her TWO beautiful pups!"

Yuen suggests, "Now we always say it three times; Xie-xie Wànsuì! Xie-xie Wànsuì! Xie-xie Wànsuì!"

Everyone remains mesmerized. Their eyes are glued to every move Xie-xie and her pups make as they come into the cove; closer and closer to the group. The pups are perfectly healthy but everyone can tell how tired Xie-xie is so the guys run and get all the fish they've caught including everything from the refrigerator in the house. Careful not to scare any of them, the women start tossing the fish into the cove from close to the springboard observation deck and again, Misa leaps over to it. Xie-xie picks up on Misa's move and steers her pups over to the food.

10 A.M. – Yuen joins Misa on the observation platform as everyone continues taking turns carefully tossing fish into Xie-xie's and her pup's future path. The twosome absorbs everything they can from what they can make out in the water; the pup's approximate lengths and weights, their markings and it's great to see they have a very healthy appetite. Yuen has been stockpiling fish on ice in the deck shed so when he brings out several four foot-long strips from Chinese Perch he caught days before, these are really proving popular with Xie-xie and her newborns. That kind of immediate heavy nourishment is critical for their survival.

For the next two hours, the group feeds and monitors the Orcas. In complete wonderment and overwhelmed with joy, Misa can't stop crying but at least now it's out of jubilation and pure adrenaline. At Noon, the entire group takes a break so they can eat lunch and recover from the morning's uber-excitement. Everyone is dehydrated and out of breath so J.T. and Julie start making their now famous mega-citrus mixers and Tai and Yuen break out Myst1 bottles for everyone from the kitchen's secret storage space under the sink.

Yuen and Misa collect their thoughts and Misa offers, "Xie-xie gave birth to two killer whale pups. That's extremely rare because for one, she was only a little over six and a half months pregnant when she gave birth earlier this morning. And second, Killer whales almost always only give birth to a single pup, as far as we know."

Tai and Yuen immediately look at each other and then they look over at Carmela, who then looks over at Misa.

Yuen adds, "We had a ton of work to do before with just Xie-xie but now, we have even more than three times the amount because we have to capture absolutely everything from her behavior as a mother now and every possible second of her incredible youngsters!"

Yuen pulls two high-definition digital cameras out of his pockets.

Everyone raises their arms up and cheers him.

"Okay. So, Misa will keep one with her at all times, I'm sure. The other one is for the rest of us. If you're in the kitchen and casually looking out the window and see them, don't waste time running down to the cove. Just zoom in and start snapping pictures and video right from here! I'm already working on getting six more so everyone will have one they can keep with them at all times!"

Julie asks, "Their names? What should we call Xie-xie's new pups?"

Yuen says, "I was thinking the same thing sweetheart!"

Misa says, "I've got a couple ideas too but how about we wait until I can work with them to see if they are male or female and then our names will fit better."

Everyone toasts that idea from Misa with one of the mega-citrus mixer drinks J.T. and Julie left on the counter for everyone.

February 14, 2013 – Amami Oshima Island, Japan

It's been four days and still Xie-xie won't leave her pups behind to visit with Misa for her usual physical examination. Misa doesn't blame her because with all the top predators lurking everywhere in the East China Sea at a moment's notice, she'd never risk leaving their side. Her bulk is more than imposing enough to back off even the biggest predator that could pose a threat to her pups including any fellow adult Orcinus Orca.

Admittedly, Misa had been reckless before with her behaviors around Xie-xie; boldly diving into the cove to swim with the female Killer Whale. Now that Xie-xie has two pups to care for and guard, Misa knows better to avoid contact with her and her pups in the open ocean. Misa and the rest of the Amami Oshima Island team will have to be content waiting until Xie-xie and her pups are able and willing to appear for a group inspection. There is room on the shoreline for the three of them but Xie-xie must first teach her pups how to control their burst from the depths so they don't beach themselves.

The newlywed couple doesn't know it yet but last night and earlier this morning, they kicked off the magical process of becoming new parents themselves, in about nine months. Their baby was conceived the same morning that Xie-xie gave birth to her pups.

February 15, 2013 – Yokohama, Japan

At Midnight, in a Japanese-style blitzkrieg, Boss Ricmasa calls and orders his top men to assault his older brother Saitonaka's secret apartment compound.

"Destroy everything in your path and bring me that fucking sword that Naka took from my brother Ito! I will avenge my oldest brother's death and respect my father's original wishes! I will move forward with all of my brother Ito's plans, starting with righting this terrible wrong! And don't forget the other. Now go and send this message for me and make sure Naka knows it was from me!"

"Yes Boss Ricmasa! Banzai!"

"Yes! Banzai! Banzai! Banzai! Now, Go!"

As he hangs up, Ric continues shouting, "I will avenge you Ito! … Naka! … I'm coming for you brother! I'm coming for you, with blood!"

As Boss Ricmasa's men arrive, they simply slaughter everyone in their path. Not expecting such immediately aggressive behavior, the first guard outside attempts to stop the lead motorcycle-riding assailant. With a quick slash of his long sword, Boss Ricmasa's man strikes the guard down, leaving him in a pool of his own blood. The second guard meets an even gorier end as his head lies on the ground three feet away and staring back at his own body, twitching. Walking swiftly down the entry hallway, Boss Ricmasa's men throw fire bombs in each room as they pass and simply continue moving forward. Men and women run out of each room seconds later screaming as they try frantically to put out the fires. If they run toward any of Boss Ricmasa's men, they earn a slash from one of their long swords.

The total of ten men don't pillage, they simply destroy, as ordered. There are two unique items one of Boss Ricmasa's men was tasked with retrieving; items that rightfully belong to Boss Ricmasa now. This man makes his way all the way through the compound, seeking these items. The rest of the men continue fire-bombing the compound. They reach Tai's, Misa's, Yuen's, and Kim's former rooms and in a flash, they are in flames. At the end of the hallway, the lone man retrieves his first item from a protective glass case at the entrance of the dining room; an original Samurai sword from the fifteenth century. Then he kicks the formal dining room doors down. He immediately runs over to the multi-level shelf unit.

Standing in front of the severed head, he bows three times and then gently picks it up and places it in a small cloth bag. With a few lashes of his long sword, he demolishes everything else resting on the shelf. He bends over and picks up one of the large shark teeth. He walks across the orange and white koi rug and stops underneath and just to the right of the ornate and intricate strobe light and ball on the ceiling. Like a throwing star, he hurls the one point five million year-old five inch tooth at the ball, shattering it into a million pieces. As the mirrored and colored glass showers down, the man has moved over to the decorative bar and starts decimating everything in sight. A moment later, two naked female attendants come out from the back area and one of them jumps on the man's back, slapping him all over the top of his head. He swings her around and then slashes her across her torso. The other naked woman screams and runs back behind the bar wall.

As the lone man exits the formal dining room, he throws a fire-bomb deep into the room, igniting the far wall. Then he tosses two more fire-bombs in the room; one over into the far right hand corner of the room, shattering the remnants of the multi-level shelf and its contents along with the expensive art pieces hanging on the wall. As he walks away, the second fire-bomb shatters the dining room table and bar area. Glass shards scream out in all directions. The lone man heads upstairs to Saitonaka's private bedroom suite.

As soon as he ascends the stairs, he spits on the short wall to his left. As he enters the office area, he smirks and simply throws a fire-bomb towards the back wall. The grenade lands on top of Saitonaka's desk and explodes, engulfing everything in a ten foot circumference in fire and smoke. The man makes his way into the bedroom and throws a fire-bomb on the bed. As he walks out, the bed bounces up off the ground four feet and crashes back to the ground, blazing. As the suite burns, the man makes one last pass by Saitonaka's office. He takes his long sword and drives it down through the seat of Saitonaka's slightly burned black leather chair. Then he takes a small fresh orange out of his pocket and places it in the bottom of the seat next to the edge of the sword. The sword's end-cap is clearly marked with Boss Ricmasa's name in Japanese and the small orange signifies sweet revenge by a man, once soured.

CHAPTER THIRTY-EIGHT

April 6, 2013 – Amami Oshima Island, Japan

AT almost two months old, Xie-xie's pups are doing very well. One of them is a little over five feet long and weighs about four hundred pounds and the other one is about five feet long and weighs just under four hundred pounds. Xie-xie regularly takes them a few miles out into the open East China Sea to learn how to hunt and the smaller of the two pups is catching on quickly, having already made its own first kill; an eighty pound yellow-fin tuna. The most impressive aspect of the smaller Orca pup's first kill is that not only that it's a first kill at such a young age but the fact that it was able to kill one of the fastest predatory fishes in the ocean.

With the smaller Orca pup's size, the yellow-fin tuna would very easily avoid capture in any sighted attack so that means the Orca employed a sneak attack from below. Xie-xie is surprised at her smaller pup's early ability to fend for itself so she spends a little more time with her larger pup, teaching it these same critical survival skills.

Today's lesson is a special treat; something all Orcinus Orca's enjoy. They pass this skill on from pod to pod and have done so for centuries. Xie-xie leads her young back in closer to shore; about a half a mile off shore. In these relative shallows, in a unique little cove unto itself, Xie-xie has discovered some of her favorite prey but before she approaches, she backs off her young to make sure they watch her first. This trick of sorts is very dangerous but for Killer Whales, it almost comes naturally once they see it performed. It instantly ignites their natural instincts of curiosity and playfulness, not to mention their appetites.

With a simply flick of her tail, Xie-xie inverts herself. Effortlessly, she repositions herself and hovers nose down above the sea floor. Maintaining a height of about six to eight feet above the sea floor, she exhales water from her mouth, basically spitting. Almost instantly, a very dangerous but short barbed tail rises from the sand, pinpointing perfectly where Xie-xie's favorite stingray treat is located. As soon as the defensive weapon begins to lower, Xie-xie simply navigates to one side or the other of the stingray and grabs it by its outer fluttering fin. Having no bone structure at all, Xie-xie bites down easily and draws more and more of the stingray into her mouth until she's eaten roughly half of it. At that point, the fish is no longer a threat to stick her so she quickly consumes the rest of the animal being careful to eat everything except for its tail. A moment later, the stingray's barbed tail floats harmlessly down to the sea bed like an ugly dart.

The smaller Orca pup immediately takes note of this new hunting technique and signals her mother that she'd like to try it. Xie-xie rights herself back to a normal horizontal position and steers her larger pup away. Like a seasoned pro, the smaller Orca performs the technique flawlessly. She gobbles up her stingray treat like she's been doing this for years. The larger Orca pup makes no move toward wanting to try this technique right now so it'll wait for another day. Needing more food, Xie-xie escorts her pups back into the cove inlet so her favorite humans can gawk and marvel at the three of them some more. At this stage of their development, Xie-xie is grateful for the easy food because trying to teach and protect two young is very taxing and stressful.

As the three aquatic marvels close in on the cove's inlet, something is closing in fast on her smaller Orca pup. Its instincts are in over-drive. Three hundred feet away; the predator can easily sense the smaller size of its intended prey. With Xie-xie swimming in front and about thirty feet ahead of her smallest pup, the predator feels comfortable it can strike and be out of the area in a flash before being spotted by the prey's protector.

Two hundred feet away; the predator dives deeper to avoid detection, beginning its attack run. Xie-xie and her larger Orca pup swim close together, preventing any attack on them due to Xie-xie's immense size. Her smaller Orca pup lags behind, savoring the last remnants of its new favorite stingray meal. It especially likes the lack of bones and scales in its meal.

One hundred feet away and the predator rises up from the depths, directly underneath the smaller Orca pup. The pup is completely unaware of the threat directly below it. Forty feet away and the predator makes its final adjustments to its attack trajectory and with a swipe of its tail, increases its speed. As nimble as a Colorado Brown Trout, the eight-foot long predator begins to glisten as he nears his prey. With his jaws agape, he prepares for his first bite. It's not going to be an investigative or exploratory bite either. This will be a full-on kill bite because he hasn't eaten for several days. That's the primary reason why he's seeking out this victim; due to its smaller size compared to himself and the seeming lack of security from its much larger protector.

The predator's plan is to make a kill bite that so severely injures the smaller Orca that its mother must abandon it in order to continue protecting her other young. With the massive blood loss the predator plans, so many other predators will be drawn to the prey that the mother won't be able to save it from the onslaught of attackers its blood will attract. After all, nothing ever goes to waste in the ocean.

The predator adjusts slightly and finalizes its attack plan; to bite off the smaller Orca's tail, making it impossible for it to survive. This will be a devastating blow to the young

Orca family; losing one of her pups, especially this way and being forced to watch it be devoured by all the other predators the attack brings.

Twenty feet away; the predator readies his powerful jaws, preparing to jet them forward to grasp his prey. Ten feet away; the predator prepares to taste his prize. His eyes begin to roll back in his head as the smaller Orca pup's hind quarters, just above its tail come into view; three, two, one.

In a flash, the smaller Orca pup pivots around, sensing the threat from as early as thirty feet away. The predator committed to its deadly course and the smaller Orca pup is taking full advantage of that fact. With no room to bail out and with the smaller Orca pup's mother directly ahead of him, the predator reveals himself a little too early. He's been had by the superiorly intelligent Killer Whales.

Xie-xie stops on a dime and pivots to her right and dives about ten feet deeper to prevent the attacker's escape anywhere near her. Her larger Orca pup takes up position to the left, blocking off an escape in that direction and the smaller Orca pup's awareness and complete three hundred and sixty degree turn completely startles the eight-foot long Bull shark. He doesn't know what to do so he tries to veer away at his top speed just to the right of the smaller Orca pup. Xie-xie moves another couple body lengths to her right and this shuts down the Bull shark's desired emergency escape plan. Realizing that his surprise attack was all for not, the male Bull shark is in full panic mode now. Thinking he can still slip past the smaller Orca pup, he again flicks his tail and attempts to move past his former prey. Prey quickly becomes predator.

The smaller Orca pup anticipates the Bull shark's intended escape route and accelerates to that position in the water. It grasps the Bull shark's left pectoral fin and severs it clean off. The Bull shark begins to spin wildly out of control; spiraling off to his right and down. Xie-xie easily makes her way over to the Bull shark's new uncontrollable path and grabs him in his mid-section. Then she quickly readjusts her bite and extracts twenty pounds from the top predator. Xie-xie's larger Orca pup then closes in and like a surgeon; it lacerates the Bull shark's belly and extracts his rich liver. It devours half of the organ, leaving the other half for its sibling.

On cue, the smaller Orca pup navigates to the bloody organ and devours it. Xie-xie could not be any more proud of her young pups. At this early age, their brash behaviors are a little risky but their advanced instinctive hunting skills more than make up for their novice boldness. They work extremely well together; the larger Orca pup has surgeon-like hunting skills and the smaller Orca pup is a cocky and bold protector of its larger sibling with its particularly aggressive nature. With their impromptu hunting lesson complete and their stomachs full, Xie-xie and her pups make their way into their cove.

APRIL 7, 2013

Misa has continually sounded off with her distinctive whistle but apparently, Xie-xie is still not comfortable leaving her pups behind to take part in her regular physical and personal interactions with Misa. Misa misses seeing and interacting with Xie-xie up close. The bond between them had been so strong but Misa can't help but to be thrilled for the new mother Orca. Watching her with her two pups in the cove as often as they can is just as exhilarating now as it was the first day they saw them all together.

APRIL 8, 2013 10 A.M.

With a single toot of her custom-made whistle, Misa again signals for Xie-xie to join her in her formerly favorite smooth rock shallow area. It's a big risk because she'd be leaving her pups alone in the depths. Julie has accompanied her mother so she can learn from the best.

"Hey ma, when did you start studying sharks and whales?"

"It was actually your father that got me interested in it. Well that and his big fat…"

"Mom! Seriously?" Julie blushes as Misa laughs hysterically.

"Spare me the other details!"

"Fine." Misa smirks and continues, "Actually we were both interested in sharks to begin with. Your father was obsessed and his passion for them attracted me to them as well. Together, we were unstoppable. Tai and Kim were obsessed with their chemistry studies. And as a foursome, we were truly untouchable in school. All of our professor's called us the fearsome foursome!"

"The fearsome foursome, why?"

"There was absolutely nothing the four of us couldn't figure out and then soon master, period! We were two full years ahead of everyone else after our first year together and it went off from there. As juniors, Tai and Kim were actually teaching brand new chemistry classes that the university didn't even offer because they didn't have professors that knew what they knew! Your father and I were so far ahead in our marine biology courses, professors took the classes out on trips so we could all experience the real working environments. They asked us to serve as co-professors leading part of the class on our own so we could all learn more. Basically, we did whatever we wanted, whenever we wanted."

"Shit! You were all fucking bad-asses!"

"Julie! How many times do I have to tell you?"

"… sorry mom."

"…Hell yes we were! … fucking shout it out loud!"

Mother and daughter playfully but lovingly hug each other and then Misa resumes her lessons with Julie.

"Okay, so remember, single sounds from this whistle. It's okay to repeat them but to be safe, not too close together. That's what the other whistle is for."

"The other whistle? I don't think I've ever heard you use that one."

"I have but only a few times. I want to re-introduce it slowly, especially now that Xie-xie has pups. I'm not sure how she'll respond now that she's a mother so it can wait. We still don't even know what the gender of her pups are."

"No way to tell from just watching them in the cove?"

"Not that I know of; maybe your father has some trick he can share with us but as far as I know, a physical exam is the only way."

"Cool. So, can I give the single whistle a try?"

"Sure."

Julie grabs her mom's custom made ornate whistle and blows it sharply once. Misa nods. The two women wait patiently. Misa steps Julie back out of the shallow water to make room for Xie-xie because if she does decide to appear, it is quite shocking if you're not prepared for it; a near three ton Orca bursting out from the depths below and sliding across the shore's smooth rocks closing in on your prone position is quite a spectacle, to say the least. It is breathtaking and she can take more than one's breath away in an instant if she doesn't trust you. It's been a while since Misa interacted with Xie-xie but Julie has never interacted with the great female Killer Whale so who's to say how she'll react to the new human shape standing in front of her.

Misa nods so Julie gives the whistle another sharper toot. The sound carries out across the cove's inlet and seems to remain in the immediate area. A moment later, all three amazing Orcinus Orca fins break the surface together. A second later, their signature blow-hole water explosions appear. Just thirty yards away, the sight is mesmerizing. Misa and Julie embrace as they watch Xie-xie and her young glide effortlessly at the surface. It's like watching a jumbo jet being escorted by two smaller fighter jets. They are as awesome to witness as they are genuinely intimidating. Drawing slightly closer to shore, the three glossy black fins disappear.

A couple moments later, Xie-xie bursts up from the depths and begins her typical slide of about thirty feet into the cove's shallow inlet waters. The smooth rocks brushing across her belly makes her appear to smile. A second later, her larger Orca pup bursts up and begins its slide into position to the right of Xie-xie. Misa and Julie are in awe of the two Orcas; both executing the move perfectly. They anxiously await the smaller Orcas appearance. After a couple minutes, Xie-xie herself calls out; sounding her powerful motherly alert to her smaller pup. A moment later, the smaller Orca bursts up from the depths and slides in on Xie-xie's left side but it's carrying too much speed and Misa can already tell that the pup will over-shoot the shallows and wind up on shore, beaching itself.

Misa braces, moves Julie back and screams, "Oh God! Julie, run and get the guys, now!"

Julie races up the hill toward the rear entrance of the house. Misa actually tries to block the oncoming smaller Orca pup's path but at over four hundred pounds, even she knows she can't do anything to prevent the smaller Orca's beaching. Misa's heart begins to race wildly. She breaks into tears as the inevitable happens.

Julie screams, "Guys! We need you now! It's Xie-xie's pup!"

Responding from all directions throughout the house, Yuen, Tai, J.T. and Saka run out the patio door. They immediately follow Julie outside and down the path leading toward to cove's inlet. To their shock, they see the smaller Orca pup stranded on the beach, a full ten feet out of the water. As it struggles in the hot sand, Xie-xie's jaws are agape, in effect, screaming for help. Saka and Yuen immediately position themselves on either side of the young Killer Whale as Tai and J.T. position themselves directly in front of its powerful jaws.

Filled with pure adrenaline, the four men muscle the five hundred pound plus mammal up and back and push her back into the shallows. Xie-xie begins nodding her head up and down, offering her sincere gratitude. She can tell immediately that her smaller pup is okay. As Misa and Julie cry and settle down from the shock and transition to elation and relief over the quick rescue, Kim and Carmela join the group and Kim points out an incredible feature.

"Great job guys! Thank God! You saved her!" Carmela says.

AT the same time, in amazement, Kim adds, "Look!"

The group turns back toward the smaller female Orca pup and Tai says, "Look at what?"

Kim announces, "Her eye!"

The group focuses in on the small female Orca pup's eye and everyone gasps at nearly the exact same time.

For the team, Kim confirms, "My God! Her eyes are crystal blue!"

Yuen and Tai start splashing water over her head and across her gorgeous blue eye on her left side as Saka and J.T. do the same for her on her right side. The girls move and perform the same service for the other Orca pup, a male. Misa takes care of Xie-xie's cooling. Just then Misa is startled. She points and yells over at Saka.

"Honey? Are you okay?"

Surprised, Saka flatly asks, "What? I'm fine. Why?"

J.T. looks over at Saka's right hand and says, "Because uncle Saka. You're bleeding."

Everyone becomes concerned.

Did the small female Orca bite him while she was being rescued?

Saka looks down and sees that his right hand palm's surface skin is shredded and bleeding slightly from various points.

He just shrugs it off and says, "Ha! I didn't even notice... it doesn't hurt."

Misa says, "Still, you'd better get inside and get some hydrogen peroxide on it so it doesn't get infected."

Saka nods and makes his way out of the shallow water and up the path.

Everyone's heart skips a beat thinking that maybe the female was scared when she beached herself and possibly bit her handler as he helped pick her up and push her back into the water. Misa steps away from Xie-xie, who remains perfectly calm and wades over to see the smaller female Orca.

She approaches carefully and in full view of the young female Killer Whale so as not to startle her. The young female takes note of the human shape walking in front of her and begins nodding her head up and down. Misa cups some water in her hands and gently cascades it across and down the female's head. She repeats the calming move across her left white eye patch. Then inexplicably, Misa reaches in with her right hand and brushes across the top of a few of the young female's conical teeth. A moment later, the young female Orca blinks and Misa smiles and bursts into tears. She whispers something and Kim overhears just the last part of it.

"Misa? What was that?"

Misa clears her throat and says, "Her name. I have a name for Xie-xie's baby girl."

Saka is making his way back down to the group.

Julie asks, "What is it mom?"

"In honor of the New Year, I'd like to call her Snake-Lei."

J.T. immediately says, "That's perfect aunt Misa! Snake-Lei!"

Everyone nods and Yuen says, "Snake-Lei it is young lady!"

He reaches over and pats Snake-Lei on her head.

Kim starts to cry and offers, "For Xie-xie's big baby boy, I'd like to call him Jimmie-Lei!"

Tai hugs Kim and says, "Awesome!"

The other three couples hug one another and they all smile and bow.

J.T. says, "Yeah, that's much better than Grandpa-Lei!"

The group laughs and Yuen confirms, "You are Jimmie-Lei young man!"

He moves over and pats Jimmie-Lei on his head; christening him as well.

All three Orcas remain calm and spirited. Like she's giving her complete approval of her pup's new names, Xie-xie begins nodding her head up and down and then she opens her massive jaws. Jimmie-Lei and Snake-Lei follow suit. The elated Amami team goes into full feeding mode; everyone grabs fish that Saka so graciously returned with from the house. They carefully toss fish into the youngster's mouths and Misa gives the larger fish to Xie-xie. One more time, the Orca's bounce their heads so everyone makes one more pass with the fish and then the Killer whale's pivot, Snake-Lei leading the way to her left, and they wiggle away and back out of the shallows and back down into the cove. A truly stunning display.

For the rest of their lives, the team will never forget yet another precious moment they've all experienced together with these incredible animals. They only hope this wasn't the only time the Orcas will choose to appear to them as a group; the whistle alerts are far from a guarantee.

As everyone makes their way back up to the house for lunch, Misa holds Yuen back. She shows him her concealed right hand. He looks at her with concern and wonderment. The pair talks for about ten minutes and then they too make their way up to the house for lunch. After lunch Misa and Yuen call for a team meeting.

With everyone settled in and listening to the pair intently, Misa starts by saying, "Okay; bear with us here. For Jimmie-Lei, Yuen figures Xie-xie mated with an Orca while she was out to sea and then when we impregnated her with Great White shark semen, that gave rise to what we're calling the hybrid, Snake-Lei, to be born at the same time. We're completely confident saying that the incredible blue-eyed hybrid Orca, Snake-Lei, is the first Orca ever born with crystal blue eyes!"

Concerned, Kim stares intently at Tai and then over at Yuen and confirms, "You impregnated Xie-xie with Great White shark semen? Are you insane?"

Tai offers, "Yes, we did and no, not yet!"

Yuen adds, "We were just about to see if she'd leave finally. I was going to lead her out to sea later the following morning when we discovered a dead Great White in the cove. His claspers were full of crystallized sperm so we froze some… trust me! Don't go into my special freezer looking for ice pops or anything! The rest we put on ice. Later, that sperm on ice was what we used to inject into Xie-xie."

Kim asks, "Inject? Using what?"

J.T. smirks and says, "Trust me! You don't want to use any turkey basters you see lying around!"

Everyone laughs but Kim continues to ask, "What? You were involved in this crazy breeding experiment too J.T.?"

"Yes!

Still upset over the smaller group's secrecy, Kim looks over at Tai and Yuen and asks, "So who exactly took part in this little experiment of yours?"

Tai, Yuen, J.T., Carmela and Misa immediately raise their hands.

"So, Julie and I were excluded. Why?"

Tai immediately offers, "You were asleep and it was so early. I figured I'd tell you later. Time was critical because the Great White was already dead. We had to act fast."

Kim shakes her head, still a little disappointed.

Tai continues, "What was I supposed to say; 'Hey babe, get up so we can all have sex with Xie-xie?'"

Julie starts laughing which makes Kim start to laugh but she fights it off. She shoots Tai her infamous thousand-yard stare that puts him on notice but he smiles it off.

A moment later, he walks over to her and whispers, "Yes. I should have told you earlier. I'm sorry. Do I still get the good lovin' later?"

Kim smirks and playfully pushes Tai away.

APRIL 22, 2013 AT 7:30 P.M.

To the team's surprise, Xie-xie now appears for her check-up and affections in the cove's shallow inlet alone, like she did before. Misa has also been able to call Jimmie-Lei and Snake-Lei and inspect them together without their mother. That's a good thing too because they are all growing so rapidly, it would be very challenging fitting all three of them in the shallows now.

Both of the youngsters have grown a foot and have packed on another hundred pounds or so; Jimmie-Lei remains larger than Snake-Lei. While tending to Xie-xie for her regular checkup after her pregnancy, Misa calls out to Jimmie-Lei and Snake-Lei. Mistakenly, she grabs her other custom whistle; the unique and specific feeding whistle.

Misa quickly learns that a second toot of this whistle makes Snake-Lei very aggressive. When her dorsal fin breaks the water and she blinks her gorgeous blue eyes at you, that look is one you'll never forget. In the shallows, if you're not careful, it'll be the last thing you ever see because Snake-Lei will lunge at anything offered to her as well as anyone who makes the offering. Misa's advanced shark and marine biology studies and recent insatiable research on Orcas has taught her these priceless lessons. As she recounts the episode to her family and friends at Mary's Grand Café, everyone shutters to think what might have happened but Misa eases their tensions by simply saying, "It is what it is"; one of the group's favorite sayings.

Mary exits her kitchen and quickly sits down. She asks, "Go ahead Misa. Tell us about your killer Whale-shark attack today."

The group smiles and Yuen says, "It's not a killer Whale-shark Miss Mary. It's our Killer Whale mother's female pup, who was conceived, in part, with Great White shark sperm."

Mary says, "Oh, that's means a whole lot to a woman who makes Chop Suey all day long!"

The group roars with laughter as Yuen, embarrassed, sits back down.

Carmela says, "Go ahead Misa."

"Okay. I had just finished with Xie-xie. She's doing great; as comfortable with me as ever. She loves it when I massage her tongue and gums!"

Everyone shrills at her bold and blatant behavior.

Yuen confirms, "Yah, that's all you Misa!"

Misa continues, "Then I whistled for Jimmie-Lei and Snake-Lei. They didn't respond so I whistled for them again. That's when I realized I was using the second custom whistle; their feeding whistle and not their first whistle; the inspection whistle. They burst up and slid right toward me. It's amazing to see how they have so quickly learned how to estimate their speed, just like their mother. Jimmie-Lei has always been spot on and Snake-Lei has learned as quickly as she could but she did have that one incident."

Carmela whispers to Yuen, "I love their names!" Saka nods.

Misa continues, "So, there I was in the cove's shallow inlet with two six-foot long and four hundred plus pound Killer Whale juveniles coming at me for what I thought was for their inspections when actually, I had just rang the dinner bell and I was the main course!"

Yuen shakes his head as everyone else's eyes open wider. Misa's heart begins to race as she continues to recount the shocking episode.

"Jimmie-Lei was coming at me on my left and about a half a body length ahead of Snake-Lei, thank God!"

Caught up in the suspense, Julie and J.T. grab at each other. Tai and Kim do the same. Then Carmela and Yuen also grab each other. Poor Saka is alone so Mary walks over to him and grabs him.

"Just as Jimmie-Lei came to a stop, once again perfectly in about two plus feet of water, I saw Snake-Lei head for me with her usual faster pace. It wasn't going to be too fast, like she'd over-shoot onto the beach again but she definitely had some good pace to her and her mouth was open. I've never seen this before because always, Xie-xie and Jimmie-Lei have their mouths closed until after their inspection and then if they want some food, they'll open their jaws so I can give it to them. Not Snake-Lei, she came full blast at me, mouth agape and teeth gleaming at me!"

Just then, an over-flowing pan in the kitchen sink falls to the floor, electrifying the air with its signature ringing orchestral sound.

Everyone jumps and Mary says, "Oh shit! God damn pan almost gave me a heart attack!"

She gets up to collect it and calls back to Saka, "You're on your own now Saka-san!"

"Somehow, Jimmie-Lei and Snake-Lei have learned how to stop their progress just like their mother. They know how to throw out their pectorals to stop their slide at any given time. As soon as they see the area they want to stop in, they simply stop; just like we would!"

"So, that's exactly what Snake-Lei did as she headed toward me. She threw out her pectorals and stopped but then she lunged at me and let me tell you; she may be just a little Orca right now but when those jaws of hers snapped shut, well, let me just say that I had to change my panties as soon as I got back inside!"

Tai confirms, "She snapped at you?"

Misa adds, "And, she shook her head around at me trying to capture me so that told me two things; one, never underestimate our gorgeous blue-eyed young female Orca because even I can't tell what she might do from moment to moment."

Julie immediately asks, "And two?"

"And two, make sure you have an extra clean pair of underwear handy because like me, if you are lucky enough to survive her lunge and jump back out of the shallows to get away from her, you will scrape your knees getting back on shore and you will shit yourself!"

Saka laughs and the group yells, "Wànsuì!"

Just then, Mary walks back in expecting that the group is ready to eat or needs another drink.

Julie processes the genuine horror her mother obviously felt in that moment and walks over to give her mom a big hug.

Then she offers, "Wow! You were right grandma Mary. Snake-Lei could be considered a Killer-Whale-Shark!"

Sarcastically, Mary immediately adds, "See all you doctors and know-it-alls! Mary's not stupid!"

Then Yuen says, "Misa? And?"

"Yes. And there's something else very special about our little Snake-Lei that you'd all better be aware of; Saka and me found out first hand, already."

Kim asks, "What's that?"

Saka stands up and shows off his hand bandage.

More seriously now, Misa explains, "When you guys were lifting and pushing Snake-Lei up and back off the beach and into the shallows, Saka's right hand must have brushed across a few of Snake-Lei's back to middle teeth and cut him."

Carmela asks, "Did she bite down on you Saka?"

Saka shakes his head and says, "No. I'm actually surprised she didn't. She kept her mouth open for all of us so we could pick her up. If she had bit down, I would have lost all of my fingers in a second."

Yuen nods.

Carmela inquires, "So, your cuts are from what, just her weight; the pressure from holding her up and moving her?"

"I thought that too but when I was walking up to the house to treat my hand, I noticed the width of my palm was lightly shredded, not punctured like you'd expect."

Intrigued, everyone walks over to see Saka's wound. He undoes the sterile cloth bandage and shows them his shredded palm.

"It's not too bad but I did need the hydrogen peroxide like Misa said!"

Misa adds, "Then as I was inspecting Snake-Lei shortly after we got her settled down, I brushed my hand across her bottom front teeth and the same thing happened to me with almost no pressure at all."

Misa holds up her right hand and everyone sees how she has shredded striations across the width of her right palm.

Kim interrupts and asks, "So, what are you telling us because I thought all Killer Whales have very powerful but smooth conical shaped teeth."

Yuen says, "That's correct! All Killer Whales, Orcinus Orca's, do have smooth-sided conical shaped teeth but remember, mother Xie-xie and son Jimmie-Lei are Orcinus Orcas. Xie-xie's daughter Snake-Lei,… is not!"

Everyone in the room gasps, including Mary. She covers her mouth and walks back into the kitchen.

Yuen confirms for everyone, "Snake-Lei is a hybrid; the first of her kind! She has conical teeth like Orcinus Orca but serrated or edged, like a Great White's – Carcharodon Carcharias! From her father!"

Frozen in place, Carmela and Julie both ask at the same time, "So what the hell is Snake-Lei?"

Everyone turns toward Misa.

She reaches down and picks up her margarita. She drinks nearly all of it and then slams the glass back down.

She keeps her head down and then after another few moments, she looks up and states emphatically, “Snake Lei is Orcinus… X!”

CHAPTER THIRTY-NINE

YUEN suggests, "Exactly – 'Orcinus Carcharodon', 'Orcinus Carcharias' or 'Orcinus X'. Either way, we just created a brand new species of Killer-Whale-Shark, just like aunt Mary said!"

Collectively, everyone reaches for their drinks as their minds race trying to handle everything they just heard.

Julie leans over Misa, hugging her and says, "Jesus mom! 'Fucking bad-ass' isn't a good enough description for you guys anymore!"

Misa hugs Julie back.

Mary starts bringing out food and everyone's grateful for the timely distraction. As everyone enjoys their dinner, Saka motions over at Tai. The two break away from the dinner table and walk across the floor to the end of the bar.

"Should I tell Saitonaka?"

"Absolutely! This will just give us even more leverage over him because I guarantee you, that sonofabitch will really see the dollars signs flying around his greedy little eyes now! Give it a week or so and then absolutely, call him up!"

May 4, 2013 at 7:00 P.M.

Saka calls Boss Saitonaka.

"Saitonaka-san? Sir."

"Saka! Good to hear from you my friend! Why is it that you are the only one of my people who knows the right time to call on me?"

"Sir!"

"Yes! … respect! How are you doing Saka?"

"Very good sir! I have an update for you."

"Please."

"The mother Killer Whale gave birth sir; two young."

"Two? Hmmm, very rare!"

"Yes sir. And one of them is a hybrid."

"What? A hybrid?"

"Sir!"

"Shit! A hybrid of what? Don't tell me Sik Yuen fucked the mother Orca!"

Saitonaka bellows out a giant laugh and starts choking on his illegal stogie.

Plainly, Saka says, "No sir. Dr. Tai and the Zhang's killed a shark and used its sperm to impregnate the mother Orca."

"Holy shit Saka! It looks like we're finally getting somewhere with these crazy Chinese scientist fuckers!"

"I… yes sir."

Missing the whole point of the hybrid Orca, Saitonaka just asks what else is happening.

"So, anything else? Is the good doctor still making my Opium-tablets?"

"Yes sir! The shipment just went out this past weekend. You'll get them any day now."

"Ah, very good! Very good Saka. Things okay with Misa?"

"Sir!"

"Nice little piece of ass, huh?" Saitonaka bellows out another devious laugh.

Offended, Saka plainly says, "Sir."

"Okay. I still have some things I'm wrapping up here. Most people are accepting my rightful place at the top of Yakuza now but I still have a few more loose ends to address. Keep an eye out Saka; I'm sending Mika in my place for now. I want her to stay with you guys for six months and no longer. She's with me full-time now Saka, understand?"

"Yes sir. Mika's with you now sir!"

"Very good Saka! Very good. And, watch out for the cat-fight between them too because Mika has a big mouth, remember?"

"Sir?"

"Mika's been waiting a long time to tell Misa that she's my girl now so just sit back and watch the hair fly! But don't let Mika get hurt, okay? You can let Misa get hurt, unless you want to step in. I would understand putting a bag over her head while you're fucking her, might not exactly be a plus!"

Sinisterly, Saitonaka laughs.

"Sir."

"Okay Saka. Keep me informed my friend."

"Yes sir."

MAY 22, 2013

After long delays leaving Yokohama and being delayed at Okinawa for three hours, Mika's small charter flight finally reaches the small Amami Oshima Island, Japan airstrip.

To her limousine driver, Koshi, a very drunk and frustrated Mika complains, "It took me forever to get here and all this place is, is a piss-ant little island! I'll bet they don't even have real liquor here yet! Shit! How long am I here for again?"

"Saitonaka-san says six months Miss Mika."

"Oh, don't Miss Mika me you little shit! That's a prison sentence if I've ever heard of one!"

"Uh, … yes ma'am."

"I was a talented and very hot dancer and now I've got to spend the next what, one hundred and eighty days with these science-chemistry geek freaks? I'll tell you this right now; I'm calling my girlfriend Jessica as soon as I can so she can meet me out here. If I'm stuck here in hell at least the two of us can spice things up and teach these people how to party!"

"Yes ma'am."

"Hey, … how old are you driver?"

"Ma'am?"

"How old are you?"

"I'm forty ma'am."

"Well, … I don't fuck fossils like you for free but if you want to have a go, pull the car over."

"Ma'am, Boss Saitonaka would have my head."

"What he doesn't know won't hurt him…"

Sternly, Koshi exclaims, "Here we are ma'am!"

"Fine. God damn it! Let's get this shit over with!"

Koshi exits and retrieves Mika's bags from the trunk. She packed like she's vacationing throughout Southeast Asia. Koshi drags three of her total six bags to the front door of the Amami Island team's house. Wearing his favorite baseball cap, vintage Heavy Metal T-shirt and jean shorts, J.T. is napping on the living room sofa. Only he and Saka are inside the home. Everyone else is fishing for food in and around the cove's inlet in support of Xie-xie, Jimmie-Lei and Snake-Lei. Kim is fishing right in the cove's inlet where Xie-xie normally abounds.

The doorbell rings and Saka casually walks from his position in the kitchen toward the front door to answer it. Normally, he wouldn't look through the small peep-hole to see who it is first but luckily this time, he does – he panics. He tries to wake up J.T. without making too much noise but he can't. The doorbell rings again accompanied by a hard knock on the door from Mika on the other side.

She shouts something in Japanese and Saka immediately recognizes most of it as being along the lines of, "Open the God Damn door you science freaks!"

Saka is almost frozen in place. He knows Mika cannot see J.T. and Kim or she'll immediately contact Saitonaka who in turn would likely send his men here to kill everyone. Frantically, he waves his arms over at J.T. but it does no good. Finally, he grabs his newspaper off the kitchen counter and throws it at J.T.'s head.

"Hey! Uncle Saka! What gives?"

Saka rushes over to the additional banging on the door and quietly says, "Yellow one and two! Someone at the door who can't know you or see you and your mom!"

As soon as Saka opens the door, Mika pushes her way inside and says, "Saka! What the hell? Took you long enough. Grab my stuff and make room for me down there."

She points down the hall toward Tai's and Kim's bedroom.

Looking squarely at J.T. Mika says, "Who's this?"

Quickly, Saka says, "Uh, ...delivery boy from local restaurant... okay then son, thanks! We'll see you next week. Goodbye, now!"

J.T. exits the front door and immediately runs around to the backdoor and down the path toward his mom.

"Ma! Yellow one and two!"

"Who is it?" Kim asks.

"I don't know. Some Japanese woman but Saka told me to leave and thanked me for being the delivery boy."

"Shit! It's probably one of Saitonaka's people coming to check up on us!"

A moment later, a speed boat comes roaring into the cove. Kim and J.T. run toward the far end of the deck, past the springboard platform and into the storage shed that has recent fish catches on ice. They make their way past the small refrigerators and out the back door. Toma stands up and waves over at Kim and J.T. He motions to them to jump into the cove and he'll get over to them quickly to pick them up. Kim and J.T. jump down into the far end of the cove and wade over into the far right corner so they can't be seen by anyone in the house. They continue wading through the shallow water until they finally have to dive into the deeper water. Toma immediately repositions his speed boat and swings by to pick them up.

"Sorry! I just heard that Saitonaka was sending someone in his place to check out the Killer Whales. He sent his favorite assassin and 'wife', Mika!"

Kim is stunned. She confirms, "Assassin?"

As they make their clever speed boat getaway, Toma explains, "Miss Mika is flat-out deadly now! I heard she was somewhat decent when she was younger, a bit of a tramp or a big-time slut according to some but that all changed for the worse when she got arrested for drugs and prostitution in Tokyo about six years ago. I heard Saitonaka left her there but that might not have been his fault because he was on the run. Anyway, that environment turned her cold and heartless. She got an additional year for being involved in a murder but since the officials couldn't prove she was directly involved in the killing they could only add one year to her sentence. I heard later that she absolutely did kill a woman in prison. They were arguing about their former sexual exploits together and Mika's erotic dancing. Apparently, the other woman was a dining room servant to Saitonaka for years and got busted on cocaine charges that Mika setup. Anyway, they got into a fist-fight and Mika broke her neck."

J.T. interrupts, "Where?"

"I'm taking you down the coast to the small port entry about a mile and a half south of my mom's Grand Café. You two can stay with her until we figure out what to do with Mika and Saka."

"And Saka?" Kim asks.

"Yeah, her husband."

Shocked, Kim and J.T. look at each other and just as J.T. is about to explain what he knows, Kim shakes her head at him.

Toma casually continues, "Yah, they were married back in 2006 I think. Their work for their first Boss, Ito Shigemura and then for Saitonaka, kept them apart for a while. When Mika got arrested in early 2007, they just separated but legally, they were still married. I also heard that while she was with Saitonaka in his secret apartment compound, she slept with everyone that ever worked or visited there."

Kim drops her head and starts crying.

"What's wrong mom?"

Kim shakes her head and says, "I'm already missing your father. I feel like we might be apart again for a long time, like before."

"No way! I won't let that happen!" J.T. states.

The reality sinking in, Kim starts crying harder. She says, "Just like before when I was kidnapped, your father had no idea because he was simply waiting for us to be married. Now, he's fishing with Misa and Yuen and again, he has no idea what has happened. This fucker Saitonaka keeps doing this to us!"

J.T. moves over to his mom and hugs her. Then he says, "It's different this time. It's fine; we're with Toma and we'll be safe at Grandma Mary's place. We get to eat the best food and we'll get word to dad, right Toma?"

Toma smiles and consoles Kim. "Already taken care of Mrs. Kim! I know the next six months or so will be hard for you guys but look at it as a vacation. And, have fun with it because for once, we have the advantage over Saitonaka and his assassin Mika! We'll just visit the Grand Café a lot more than normal, that's all. She'll never catch on to that."

Kim wipes away her tears and asks, "Six months?"

"Yah, I heard she's here for six months and then Saitonaka will make his next move. We're keeping a close eye on everyone and with her here now, it'll actually be easier. She doesn't know it but Saka has a bugged cell phone that I gave him to give to her. When she calls Saitonaka, we'll hear and know about everything they talk about. That is, if Saka gives her that phone. I expect him to play both sides but sooner or later, he'll have to make a final choice."

J.T. asks, "Anything else we should know?"

"Yes. Mika knows of me so I can't be around directly but rest assured; I'll be around! And don't worry, I'll get word to everyone about you two so just sit back, relax and enjoy all of my mom's cooking!"

The three collect their things and Toma escorts them to the back entrance of his mom's Grand Café restaurant.

"My single son!"

"Yomama! Don't start!" Mary sighs as Kim and J.T. laugh quietly to themselves.

"There's trouble at their house with the 'guests' I told you about."

Before Toma can even finish his explanation, Mary nods and shows them to their rooms upstairs. There are three bedrooms and one bathroom on the second floor of the building helping to secure the property by having the owner around twenty-four seven.

Having anticipated the need, Toma and his men added the two extra rooms just after the New Year.

Mary confirms their new living space and says, "Now each day, we can drink and eat well. I'll show J.T. how to catch the fish of the day for specials and we can all talk about and wonder how my son still remains single!"

Toma promptly leaves saying, "Thanks Yomama!" as he walks out the back door.

Back at the house, Saka advises his 'wife' Mika to wait until Tai and Yuen return from their fishing trip before she gets settled into an area for her to stay in.

About thirty minutes later, Tai and Yuen return and immediately notice the absence of Kim and J.T. They play along as if nothing's wrong.

Tai asks, "And Saitonaka?"

Mika shakes her so-black-its-blue hair and says, "No! I'm here for him so I am him."

Yuen adds, "You've changed Mika."

She immediately counters, "A lot and in every way Sik Yuen"

She adds, "So this is the crazy Chinese scientist's and chemist's lair huh? Quaint. So, who's all living here?"

Reluctantly, Tai says, "Me and Yuen, Yuen's wife Carmela, Saka and Misa and their daughter Julie; just the six of us."

Yuen adds, "And our three Orcas."

Mika smirks and says, "You mean Boss Saitonaka's Orcas!"

Tai motions to Yuen not to add anything else. He immediately offers, "Let's see; we'll have to make room for you in here. It's a large storage room but it'll make a great bedroom for you and of course, the bathroom is just down the short hall on this side. There's another bathroom and the rest of the bedrooms on the other part of our 'Y-shaped' home."

"Y-shaped? Was that Yuen's idea?"

Agitated now, Tai explains, "Actually no. It just came together that way. You know after the fire that burned my original home almost completely down to the ground, myself included, I started to rebuild and when Yuen joined me, it just came together this way. When Saka and Misa joined us, we expanded and when we got Julie back, we expanded yet again. Is that enough history for you?"

"Oh yes; the fire…tragic!" Mika closes her eyes and looks down to the ground irreverently and then directly over at Saka. Then she pushes past Saka and makes room for some of her luggage in her new space. Saka looks down, embarrassed and proceeds inside with the rest of Mika's bags.

As Yuen steps away in total disgust of his one-time lover's comments and behavior, Tai adds, "You're going to be here with us for some time Mika. You might want to pace yourself!"

Tai shuts the door for her.

Mika skips her first evening's meal with her new roommates and calls Saitonaka instead.

"Naka!"

"Don't call me that! My younger brother calls me that!"

"Oh okay. How about fucker? How could you send me over here to live with these people? It's like the worst reality television show ever imagined!"

"Oh relax God damn it! Your drama after less than one fucking day gives me a headache!"

"Well shit! Dr. Tai is already ordering me around and telling me to fucking pace myself!"

"Well shit Mika! The doctor is right! Fucking pace yourself! Its day number fucking one, isn't it?"

Mika settles down. She calmly asks, "What am I supposed to do here day in and day out?"

"Observe and learn what you can whenever you can. There are three incredible Killer Whales there for Christ sake! How hard can it be? You've got absolute experts in their fields there at your disposal! Don't fuck this up Mika! I wish I could be there but even back at home now, I have so much shit to clean up, I can't get away just yet."

"Okay, okay. Settle down Mr. Fat-stick!"

"Yah, that's more like it! You want it baby? You want me to stick you with my fat-stick?"

Mika starts masturbating and Saitonaka does the same on his end of the line.

Almost slipping out of his chair, Saitonaka says, "Yah! You want me to stick you baby?"

With her left hand index and middle fingers inside herself, Mika says, "Oh yah! Puncture me! Puncture me!"

Climaxing, Saitonaka drops his phone and the line disconnects. He straightens up and texts her back saying, "Thx! Now, get back 2 group & play nice until time 2 not play nice!"

Mika texts him back and attaches a pornographic image of herself to her message.

Saitonaka receives her message a few seconds later and opens the attachment. This time he does fall out of his chair as he stares at the image she sent him; her slightly tanned and shaved vagina with her index and middle finger from her right hand inside of herself and her index finger on her left hand is waving and inviting him closer.

A few seconds later, Saitonaka yells, "Banzai! Banzai! Banzai!"

Later, Mika makes her way out to the shared living room and immediately apologizes to everyone for her arrival behavior; sharing the details of her many delays and wasted travel time and expenses.

Tai, Yuen, and Misa almost immediately accept her apologies but Julie is hesitant. After dinner, Julie talks to her mother about their new guest.

"You told me about Miss Mika but she sure doesn't sound like the same person you described."

"A lot of time has passed sweetheart. I'm sure she's changed a little but at her core, I think she's still the same. You heard about her day and you'd have to admit; that kind of day would get to any of us too!"

"Sure but I'm not talking about her words. I'm talking about her moves; just walking past uncle Tai and dad like that, completely ignoring them and disrespecting them in their house! She has to know she's not exactly fully welcome since she's dispatched here by her lover-Boss whatever his name is!"

Misa tears up a little, proud of how sharp and quick-witted her daughter is and says, 'You know; you're pretty fucking sharp sweetheart!"

Julie smiles widely and says, "Fucking-A right mom!"

"Julie!"

"Hey, you brought it up mom! I'm just agreeing with you"

"Yeah, you're right...fucking-A! I think Tai and Yuen would agree; let's take it easy and make an effort to get along. I'm sure Mika's quite nervous being around the three of us after all this time. We all had short little affairs or episodes with her in our past so it's probably hard for her to look at any of us square in the eye. As long as she doesn't bring those memories back up, I think we'll all get along."

"And Kim and J.T.?"

"I know. I miss them too but it's actually better that Kim isn't here because then Mika would definitely dive into those past tales just to freak everyone out! I do know one thing young lady"

"Yah?"

"Being a little over three months pregnant, you need your rest!"

Misa kisses her daughter on her forehead and rubs her beginning burgeoning belly.

CHAPTER FORTY

JUNE 1, 2013 4 A.M. – YOKOHAMA, JAPAN

AN ancient ritual is taking place. The former top Yakuza Boss, Ito Shigemura, is dead. Ito assumed power after his father; Shinto Shigemura was killed in a clash between rival factions in their same Yakuza family. Shinto was the kind of man to think long and hard before coming to a decision and then he'd think some more. Back in the late nineteen seventies, the world's level of patience was not exactly at their highest. Cocaine and heroin were the preferred drugs both for distributors and users and in the dark alleyways out West, some people were developing a new and even more powerful drug called Crack. Crack cocaine would very quickly destroy families, homes and lives from the first day it officially hit the street to the present day.

Shinto refused to have his people get involved in the drug trafficking business in Japan. Many regions in the country were still recovering from World War II and film makers continued using Godzilla as their sounding board for many issues including protecting the environment and for the respective Japanese guilt the nation still felt over the War. Other Japanese film companies, out of Sendai, joined the cause but focused more of their efforts on conservation and ecology with the continued release of the now cult-status Gamera movies.

Rival Yakuza factions were growing more and more impatient with Boss Shinto's delays and end-result refusals to get involved with drug trafficking. The rival Bosses would meet twice a month to discuss the issue but after a while, Shinto stopped attending. Finally, the rival faction leaders had made their decision and asked that Boss Shinto attend one last meeting so they could make peace with him and so they could ask for his blessing to proceed without him.

They spent tens of thousands of Yen preparing an elaborate dinner and dance performance complete with Geisha's and a very special dragon dance. The night would be capped off with a special ceremony where the other Bosses would literally pay their respects to Boss Shinto by offering him his 'cut' even before any production and distribution began. He received word of this special celebration in his honor where he stood to receive close to one hundred thousand Yen as a peace offering and all he had to do was attend and enjoy the palatial setting; the extravagant food and drinks and lavish festivities. The rival

Bosses also planned the celebration just after the annual Spring Festival so everyone was still very much caught up in the seasonal celebrations as well.

Anticipating a possible kidnapping move or even a flat-out coup de' tat against him, Boss Shinto decreed that his sons; Ito, Saitonaka and Ricmasa be sent away so that if anything did happen, Boss Shinto was guaranteed to be avenged by his surviving sons. Under very heavy guard, Boss Shinto left to attend the celebration. Dressed in his elegant dark green and white kimono, Shinto sat in the driver's side rear seat of his short limousine.

As his entourage of four cars arrived at the gates of the host home, the driveway was lined with the other guest's cars, paving the way for Boss Shinto's arrival and paying their earliest respects to him and his Yakuza family. As the last of his four short limousines entered the driveway leading up to the house, the gates behind them closed. The night promised amazing food and drink, Geisha performances, special drumming displays, and a dragon dance all capped off with a ceremonial and large monetary gift being given to Boss Shinto signifying his blessing of the other Yakuza family's involvement in national and international drug trafficking. Boss Shinto sat up in his seat, anticipating the evening's exciting events.

A second later, a thunderous rumble and explosion took place. The ground under all of Boss Shinto's entourage gave way and crumbled into a chasm. The limousine second from the front caught fire and a few seconds later, it exploded. This caused the third limousine in the caravan, Shinto's limousine, to catch fire and explode as well. In a matter of moments, the evening was shattered by this horrible and tragic accident.

Everyone at the celebration was shocked. After the fires were put out people started passing by the giant pit and tossed flowers at the now entombed victims; their graves were complete and only lacked this final solemn ceremony in their honor. None of the rival faction leaders were ever held responsible for the tragic 'accident' and a month later, Shinto's oldest son Ito was appointed successor to the family. He stepped through the ritual that his youngest brother Ricmasa now steps through.

Dressed out in a pure silk multi-colored hibiscus flower kimono robe and brandishing an original Samurai sword that dates back to the fifteenth century, Ric Shigemura stands in the doorway of his oldest brother's, Ito's Yakuza compound. The ceremonial sword was originally given to Ric's oldest brother, Ito by their father Shinto when Ito pledged his life to his Yakuza family, over his own family. A week later Boss Shinto died under mysterious circumstances.

The very first thing that Saitonaka took from his older brother Ito, after taking his life, was this ceremonial sword. From the very moment that his father Shinto gave the sword to Ito, Saitonaka's jealously began to grow. The sword was his sick symbol of later justification in his mind for something that somehow 'belonged' to him; the superior warrior. When Saitonaka Shigemura killed his oldest brother Ito, Ric was appointed leader of his former Yakuza family by Ito's son, Eishi Shigemura. This ceremony is the long-awaited official assignment of all of Ito's former resources, property and people that are now pledging their lives in support of whatever Boss Ricmasa now decrees. With a ceremonial strike at an ice sculpture depicting a vanquished ancient foe, the festivities officially begin.

For the first time, Boss Ricmasa sits in his former oldest brother Ito's chair in the center of the room as Ito's former body guards and Yakuza family soldiers take turns bowing toward him three times. Several women pass by as well, tossing imported Iris and hibiscus flowers at his feet. Other small gifts are also tossed at his feet as symbols of their respect and loyalty toward his reign.

In the far corner of the room, a man whispers to his Boss, "This marks both the start and the end of the Shigemura Yakuza reign sir."

"I! We'll follow along for now but if Boss Ricmasa is anything like his brother Saitonaka-san, I'll happily take his head myself!"

Eishi waits impatiently as the last of the supporters offer their gifts of respect and loyalty to Boss Ricmasa. Finally he is able to motion to his uncle. Boss Ricmasa stands up and moves over to the far wall with Eishi.

"Uncle! You told your men to tear apart uncle Saitonaka's compound?"

"I! And they did a great job! They brought me my brother Ito's Samurai sword! The one our father rightfully offered and gave to your father in the first place!"

Eishi stares at it, realizing its significance to his uncle. He bows at his uncle in appreciation.

"And uncle Saitonaka will know the damage and plunder was from you?"

"I! My man left a hallmark from me in a very conspicuous place so as Naka looks through his rubble, he won't miss the message from me!"

"Can I ask what it was uncle?"

"Of course Eishi; I'm serving in honor of your father so there is nothing I won't share with you and there is nothing you can't ask of me! Right through the center of his now charred black leather chair and stuck to the ground is one of my long swords, accompanied by a tangerine by the blade's edge!"

"They brought back something else too Eishi-san."

Saddened, Ricmasa escorts his nephew Eishi into the side office. Sitting on the desk is the small cloth bag the lone man retrieved from Saitonaka's multi-level shelf unit.

Eishi approaches the desk slowly. His heart begins to race. As he steps closer and closer, he knows who this must be but he's hoping he's wrong. He draws close enough to grasp the edges of the cloth bag and takes a deep breath. As he touches the cloth, ready as he can be to unveil the severed head's identity, a knock on the door makes him jump back in fright.

Startled as well, Boss Ricmasa says, "God damn it! One minute!"

The merchant couple on the other side of the door scampers away, fearing they have really upset their new Boss. They leave their gift of engraved personalized writing implements on the floor next to the chair that Boss Ricmasa had been sitting in and run away.

Eishi re-approaches and just steps to the cloth bag. He pulls on one saggy side of it, revealing the person's final face; their death face a fraction of a second after the connection to their brain was severed leaving the brain to realize the horror of being separated from the rest of its body. The muscles in the person's face contracted and contorted for the final time, freezing in this position.

Eishi quickly moves to the waste basket and throws up his evening's contents.

"Please uncle, get rid of it! I'll call his wife tomorrow and tell her there was a horrible accident on one of my ships. We were cleaning it and one of the high wires snapped loose and swung across the deck…"

"I'm sorry nephew. He was a good man. He helped our cause but uncle Naka got to him before I could help hide him."

"He may have played both sides but damn it, uncle Saitonaka will damn sure miss him now too! If you get the chance, avenge him for us as well!

"I will nephew! Now, let's go. People are still waiting for us. Do me a favor?"

"Of course."

"Take the many gifts of value and sell them back to some of Saitonaka's contacts. I want to use some of his own money to finance his ruination!"

"Banzai uncle Ric! Excuse me, Boss Ricmasa!" Eishi immediately and respectfully bows.

"To you; uncle or uncle Ric but to you only! Banzai Eishi-san!"

Ric smiles and winks at Eishi!

CHAPTER FORTY-ONE

August 15, 2013 8 P.M. – Amami Oshima Island, Japan

At dusk, Carmela anxiously waits for a surprise appearance by Xie-xie and her six month year-old pups, Jimmie-Lei and Snake-Lei. Everyone else is playing a Mah-Jongg tournament inside the house. As always, their Oldies radio station blares in all directions as the sun sets in front of the house. It's that much darker and cooler down the hill toward the cove's east-facing inlet.

Walking around herself, Mika sees Carmela sitting on the springboard deck and starts walking over to her. Carmela sees Mika approaching and turns away from her facing more toward the entrance of the cove. She hopes a sudden appearance by Xie-xie and her pups will distract Mika from the pending awkward conversation.

"Hey Carmela."

"Hello."

"What are you doing out here all alone?"

"Just hoping to catch Xie-xie and her babies. Why?"

"Oh, nothing. I just thought you and Yuen would have better things to do together that's all."

"Meaning what?"

"Oh no. I just meant I figured you'd be playing Mah-Jongg together or something."

"Uh huh… whatever."

"I probably shouldn't say anything but I figure by now, you two have hashed this all out."

Annoyed, Carmela says, "… And, what's that?"

"You know. The times Yuen and I had when we were younger. All that stuff."

"Since you're obviously dying to tell me, why don't you just save your breath, okay? I'm not interested in your lies anyway. No one here likes you!"

"Oh, is that right? Well then, I will tell you about the fantasy free-for-all fucks the two of us shared in the limousine as I escorted young Yuen to Uruma City back in eighty-six!"

"Is that right?"

"Oh yah! In fact even after that, I visited him a couple times, at his request, for follow-up fantasy fucks! We basically annihilated each other for days!"

"You know, it's not my place and I didn't want to say but you're a real fucking slut and everyone here knows it! That's fine with me because that's how you've chosen to live your life. Obviously, that's not the norm or we'd all be covered in some of the same crusty crabs that you likely have!"

"Oh! Big talk from Miss International Tropical Islander!

"Get the fuck away from me or I'll call for Yuen and he'll gladly kick your ass!"

"No, no sweetheart. One call from me and Saka will burn this whole fucking place down and this time, the little doctor and your Yuen won't escape!"

"What? Saka burned this place down before?"

"That's right! Why do you think he's here? God, you guys are so fucking stupid! He's been our plant here from day one! He only married Misa for a regular piece of ass! And a hot piece she is! I remember fucking her myself. Her and the former Miss Kim! Anyway, he's my fucking husband and it's high time I took him back!"

Carmela stands up and says, "Liar! You are the biggest piece of shit I've ever met! We're going to clear all this up right now!"

Carmela makes her way to the edge of the platform and prepares to jump across.

As she does, Mika catches her with a single sharp chop to her throat; instantly breaking Carmela's neck. The back of Carmela's head strikes the back edge of the platform, breaking her neck in several other places. Her body then slips down and falls into the water. She's face down and floating around the bottom of the springboard's base. Her right foot hangs up on the right rear diagonal steel support that anchors to the bottom of the rocky shoreline.

10 P.M. For two hours, everyone has been searching for Carmela. Yuen calls over to the Grand Café, hoping she went over there for a drink and to update Kim and J.T. on the goings on in the house. It's getting cooler in the evening now. Misa and Tai think that if she's out swimming, she could have been overtaken by hypothermia. They search along the cove's inlet and around the deck area but they don't see her. They go back into the house hoping to hear that Yuen has discovered that she did walk all the way to the Grand Café, although that's unlikely because Mary's Grand Café restaurant is a short drive away but still about seven miles away on foot.

At 10:15 P.M. Xie-xie appears in the cove. There's no sign of Jimmie-Lei or Snake-Lei. Misa sounds her first whistle. She runs over into the cove's inlet and waits for Xie-xie to appear. A few moments later, Xie-xie bursts up from the depths and slides into her favorite position in the shallows. She's restless. Misa knows this behavior from Xie-xie is unusual. Misa massages Xie-xie's tongue like usual but then Xie-xie starts shaking her massive head to her left, repeatedly. Misa thinks to herself, "I hope she's not taking after Snake-Lei."

Xie-xie is clearly distracted and very animated. Misa asks her if she's okay as she massages her nose and brushes across her lower gum line. Xie-xie continues to shake her head to her left; not back and forth but just to her left side. Misa raises her hands and signals Xie-xie to show her what's bothering her. In a flash, Xie-xie backs up and dives back down into the cove. She reappears ten yards away and directly across from the springboard deck. Misa makes her way over to the springboard and jumps across onto the small platform. She motions at Xie-xie, requesting the next clue.

Xie-xie dips her mouth in the water and then spits it across the right hand corner of the platform. If she wanted to play and douse Misa, she would have done so. She aimed her spray specifically at the right corner and Misa knows this. She looks down and around the area of the right corner but she sees nothing unusual so she stands back up and motions over at Xie-xie again. The Killer Whale nods her head frantically and again sprays the right hand corner. Then Xie-xie lets out a somber sounding bellow and generates a huge wave of water, directed into the right hand corner of the platform. This behavior concerns Misa. She drops to her knees crying and starts to feel underneath the right hand corner of the platform. A second later, she feels human hair in her left hand.

She screams, "Yuen! Everyone! Come quick!"

Misa cries harder as she struggles to free the rest of Carmela's body from whatever is holding it back. Xie-xie's wave blast helped to free Carmela's body a little. Frantically, Misa tugs at Carmela's lifeless body, trying to be respectful but also cognizant of her true status and the need to extract her out of the water in case there is a slim chance of saving her. Finally freeing her right foot from the obstruction, Misa pulls Carmela's body to the front of the platform so she can grab her and pull her up on deck. Full of adrenaline, Misa is able to pull Carmela's body up and onto the deck. She immediately takes note of Carmela's fatal injuries to her neck and gently repositions her head straight so her natural state doesn't overwhelm and shock Yuen and the rest of the group when they see her.

Misa screams again, "Yuen! Everyone!"

Unfortunately, there is no need for them to hurry.

Still thirty feet out and starting to swim away slowly, Xie-xie bellows solemnly again and then disappears into the depths. She knows her handlers have suffered a tragic accident or maybe she knows it was murder.

Julie opens the door and calls out into the dark, "Mom?"

10:35 P.M. – Misa repeats her blood-curdling scream and everyone in the house storms out and runs down the path. As soon as Yuen and Julie get within twenty feet of the platform, they crash to the ground in agony. Everyone explodes into tears as they see Misa standing over a body they all know is Carmela's. Saka makes the call into town for an ambulance from his cell phone as Tai tries to help his life-long friend and confidant to his feet. The whole group is completely devastated but especially Yuen because he never thought he'd meet someone so special that he considered an equal soul mate to Misa. In his mind, he split his life into two stages; his younger days with Misa and his closest friends Tai and Kim and his second life that began as soon as he met Carmela in Uruma City.

Tai says, "Saka. Help me bring her across to the main deck so we can carry her inside."

Saka nods.

10:45 P.M. – Yuen again falls to his knees and wails in grief. Julie consoles her father and escorts him back up the hill and into the house. Saka and Misa switch places on the platform. Saka supports Carmela's upper body and head as Tai and Misa hold her on each side.

Misa whispers to Tai, "Her neck is broken all around."

Julie holds the patio door open as the three carry Carmela into the house. They lay her down on the sofa. Five minutes later, the ambulance arrives out front. The driver knows Toma so he alerted him to the call before he left his station. Toma tells him to bring the victim to 'the other' hospital room as soon as he arrives with her.

"Toma?"

"Toss! What happened?"

"Female. Maybe drowned. I don't know yet."

"You're sure the call is for Dr. Tai's house?"

"Yes sir."

"Shit! It's starting. Okay listen. Bring her into 'the other hospital room' first. I want my people to look at her before the hospital's coroner does, got it?"

"Yes sir!"

"Thanks Toss!"

10:50 P.M. – Zen Tossagami (Toss) and his assistant Cori enters the home and respectfully but quickly load Carmela's body on a stretcher.

Tai asks Yuen, "You should go with her or do you want me to go?"

Yuen appreciates the gesture but he says, "I'll go. Lock things up here and meet us later, okay?"

"Of course. We'll see you very soon. I'm so sorry brother!"

Yuen and Tai embrace.

Julie asks, "Can I come with you dad?"

Yuen nods and says, "I'm sorry. Of course sweetheart, please."

As the ambulance drives away, Tai, Saka and Misa gather a few things and prepare to follow.

Tai says, "Jesus! Where the hell is Mika? Have you seen her at all tonight?"

Saka offers, "You two go and I'll wait here for Mika."

Tai and Misa get into the car and head out for the local hospital.

11:15 P.M. – The ambulance arrives at the emergency entrance of the hospital. Toss and Cori immediately unload Carmela and roll her down to that other room Toma described. Waiting for them, an elderly man wearing grey slacks, a white dress shirt with thin black vertical stripes and a black sports jacket takes possession of the stretcher. He immediately begins examining Carmela's body. The man motions to have Toss and Cori help roll her to each side as he checks for other trauma to her back and legs.

As Yuen and Julie tearfully look on, Toss asks, "Her clothes sir? Cut them off?"

"No need. Her neck is broken in several places, especially right in the larynx and the back of her neck. Broken severely in front and even worse in back but I think the traumas occurred nearly at the same time. She doesn't have any punctures or any other lacerations. I'm sure of it and judging from the outside of her clothes, she definitely didn't drown first. Someone or something broke her neck, violently, in the front and then her fall, violently backwards broke it again! If the hospital coroner doesn't come back with these same findings, let me know."

Toma walks out of the adjacent empty room and tells Toss and Cori to take Carmela down to the coroner's offices.

Toma holds Julie and Yuen back to talk to them.

"Yuen. Julie. I'm so sorry. Do you know what happened?"

Julie says, "No. We were all playing Mah-Jongg. Aunt Carmela went out to see if she could catch Xie-xie and her pups entering the cove to take pictures at dusk and that's the last we saw or heard from her until my mom screamed at us two and a half hours later."

"And, where was Mika?" Toma asks.

Yuen says, "I have no idea. In fact, through all of this, I still don't know where she is or has been."

"Your Killer Whales? Do you think they got to them?"

Julie covers her mouth. "Oh my God!"

Toma reassures Julie saying, "No Julie. I'm thinking Mika had something more sinister to do with Carmela's death. She has a broken neck both in front and in back. That's not natural."

Yuen says, "If the Orcas were involved, they would've done worse things to her. She had no bites and no punctures of any kind. And you heard him; she didn't drown first so how does she get her neck broken in front and in back and then end up in the water?"

"Exactly! If she slipped and fell backwards from the shore trying to jump from the platform to the main deck and fell back against the edge of the platform, that's a single neck break that would kill her so why is the front of her neck broken as well? In any case, a true accident would involve only one side to the broken neck, not multiple. Not without help and human help at that!"

11:15 P.M. – At this same time back at the Team's house, Mika approaches the front door, soaking wet and knocks.

Saka answers and says, "What the hell did you do?"

"Oh relax Saka! As far as they know, we went for a swim and she fell behind. She drowned and then their little pets played Ping-Pong with her body in the cove until she got stuck underneath the platform. Done!"

"Jesus Mika! Is this what you're here for; to kill everyone off or what? Tell me now you crazy bitch so I can answer to Saitonaka myself!"

"Hey! Remember who you work for big-man! And what you're doing here God damn it! You work for Saitonaka and I'm his so you work for me while I'm here! Got it?"

Saka pauses and then reluctantly nods.

"Good! She was a freebie and besides, the bitch pissed me off! Everyone else will be much more 'elegant.'"

"Elegant?"

"Sure. Why not? You only die once so it should be either shockingly graphic like a warrior or elegant, out of respect. Of course, since we're dealing with all cowards and geeks, their deaths will be cowardly elegant!"

Saddened, Saka nods again.

Mika concludes, "Just let me put on my little show and carry on for them. Don't watch if it upsets you so much and then things will get back to normal. Then maybe someone will actually show me something of value here so I can leave this shit-hole! This damn constant tropical air is bad for my hair!"

August 16, 2013 12:05 A.M.

Emotionally crushed, Yuen signs the release form so the hospital can make the final arrangements for Carmela's body. Everyone sits silent in the waiting room as the coroner makes his final determinations. He simply rules Carmela's death accidental and marks her file closed. Toma takes Tai aside and tells him that he'll let Kim and J.T. know what happened.

12:10 A.M. – As the group heads back to the house, Toma calls and wakes up his mom.

"Mom?"

"Toma? It's late."

"Sorry. Can you wake up Kim for me?"

"What happened?"

"Mrs. Carmela is gone. It happened this past evening."

"Oh God! I'm so sorry. I'll wake her and start making some tea for her and J.T."

"Thanks mom."

A few moments later, Kim answers the phone, "Toma?"

"Mrs. Kim. I'm so sorry but late this past evening, Misa found Carmela underneath the springboard platform. At first, it looked like she drowned. We're still checking into it but then Misa discovered that her neck was broken in front and back. Again, I'm so sorry. Everyone's heading back to the house now."

Kim wakes up J.T. and tells him. Mary goes downstairs and starts fixing three plates of scrambled eggs and some white tea. The three share an early morning meal and just cry together. Kim knows how special Carmela was to Yuen. She's sick to her stomach over how he must feel and worse, she can't be there for him to help him get through this awful time.

12:30 A.M. – The rest of the group gets back to the house. Saka has stayed up to answer the door.

Mika is asleep.

Julie and Misa start making some tea for everyone. Tai and Yuen start clearing off the living room table that still features the Mah-Jongg tiles scattered across it. Yuen starts to stagger.

He clutches his chest and Tai immediately says, "Saka! Help me get Yuen into the car!"

Julie screams, "Dad!"

Misa bursts into tears and runs to hold the door open for Saka and Tai. Saka and Tai get Yuen into the passenger seat and Julie throws her uncle Tai a bottle of Myst1. Tai floors the accelerator heading back to the hospital with his friend Sik Yuen still clutching his chest. Standing in the doorway, Julie almost slips on her tears pooling on the floor. She collapses into Misa's arms and the two escort each other over to the living room sofa. In her make-shift bedroom, Mika can tell something else tragic just happened so she remains silent in her bed. A moment later, Misa surges into Mika's room and flicks the light on.

"Where the fuck have you been all night?"

Crying and acting injured, Mika whimpers, "Saka told me. I'm so sorry! Carmela and I were swimming near the platform. She wanted to race to the other side; you know behind the storage ice shed and back around to the other shoreline so I took off. I guess she got cornered by one of your killer whales and drowned. One of them was following me too so I swam as fast as I could, staying as close to the shallows as I could but it kept getting deeper and they kept getting closer so I kept swimming, out of fear, you know?"

Incensed, Misa inquires, "And then?"

"And then, what? Isn't that enough?"

Immediately Julie screams, "Fucking liar!"

Mika hatefully glares at Julie.

"Don't stare at my daughter like that you dirty bitch. Glare at me!"

Mika slowly looks away from Julie.

"If you two were together, why did it take you so long to get back around to the house? Why didn't you immediately get back to us and tell us Carmela might be or was in trouble?"

"Like I said Misa, I didn't know what happened to Carmela because we were racing but I do know that I was being chased and stalked by your fucking Killer whales so excuse me but I was looking out for myself in that moment, motherfucker!"

"Wow! Motherfucker? Really? …"

Misa steps back and pauses, taking the ultimate insult in surprising initial stride.

Misa then continues, "Our friend is dead and Yuen is being rushed back to the hospital as we speak, where he just signed out Carmela's body. And then there's you; you're in here cowering in your fucking bed like a scared little girl who just lost her puppy AND you 'mother-fuck' me? … my daughter is right; you are a betraying fucking liar! And it's Mrs. Yamishinosaka, not Misa!"

"Oh, okay. Look, I am sorry but it's not my fault your wild-ass pets did what wild-ass animals do! I know everyone's depressed and exhausted. It's been a long day for everyone.

I'm still pretty shaken up too so I'm going back to bed! You two should try to get some rest. Dr. Tai will probably try to call you soon about Yuen anyway, right?"

Mika walks back into her room and starts closing the door.

In the background, she hears Julie say, "Yeah ma, the bitch is right. We'll wait here for uncle Tai's call."

Then, laughing sarcastically, Misa abruptly reopens Mika's door and says, "And I can't wait for you to try to tell your bullshit story to Yuen when he gets back because we'll all enjoy watching him rip your fucking head off and then, we'll simply sit down for a nice breakfast! So, yeah, get some fucking rest you poisonous bitch!"

Twenty agonizing minutes later, Tai calls Misa.

12:50 A.M.

"Yuen's fine. Dehydrated and sick to his stomach, naturally. He didn't have a heart attack. The Myst1 definitely helped! Tell Julie she helped save her dad's life tonight! We'll be back in a couple hours after a few more tests I asked them to run just to be sure."

"Thank you Tai! You've always been there for us, especially for Yuen."

"We're all one; nothing has ever changed that! He's really going to need us now. We've really got to watch him because I know he'll jump right back into work and not want to really deal with any of this. It'll get worse over time until he gets through it. All we can do is support him and be there for him, even though we can't really do anything physically for him, emotionally, just support him and look out for him. That's what real support is!"

Misa whispers, "Mika's here."

"What? Where the hell has she been all night?"

"She's got a story you'll have to hear for yourself!"

"Bottom-line?"

"She blames the Orcas for chasing them while they swam in the shallows by the platform and then she claims that one of them chased her around the other side and kept stalking her as Carmela drowned out of fear."

"Fucking liar!"

Misa laughs and says, "That's exactly what Julie called her, to her face!"

Tai smiles and says, "Sharp girl... just like her mother! Keep your eyes open and your nine millimeter loaded and ready! I don't trust that bitch for nothing and never have! If she's involved in this at all, I promise you all, I'll send her fucking head back with Saitonaka's next O-tab shipment!"

"And while she made her case to me, I got 'mother-fucked' for my efforts!"

"What? Why the hell would she say that to you? Was she drunk when you talked to her?"

"Not at all; just to spice up her bullshit story, I guess. The conversation had no reason to go there but she took it there anyway!"

"Well, there are some things people do and say in life that they can't come back from and I think that's a perfect example! I'll fix that for us all when we get back and that's nothing compared to what Yuen may do when he hears her bullshit story!"

Julie grabs the other line and asks, "Uncle Tai? My dad?"

"He's fine sweetheart; we'll be back home soon. Upset, naturally and dehydrated, that's all."

"Thanks uncle Tai!"

"Night sweetheart; try to get some rest but keep an eye on that fucking liar in the other room too!"

Crying, Julie closes her eyes and laughs lovingly at her uncle Tai's supportive and honest comment.

During this same time, Mika has been texting Saitonaka. He advises her to leave immediately, citing, if she has to, that her mother has fallen gravely ill back in Tokyo.

Saitonaka immediately contacts his man in Okinawa and has him leave for the small airstrip on Amami Oshima Island.

"Koshi."

"Saitonaka-san!"

"Right now! Go and get Miss Mika and bring her back to me. I'll send her back in a few months when things calm down over there but right now, she's already stirred up too much shit! Go!"

"Sir!"

"Koshi. An extra five thousand if you can get her out of there without anyone knowing! I'll call them later and smooth things over with the good doctor and of course, we still have Saka-san there as well! Now, go!"

Koshi leaves.

2:33 A.M. – Koshi arrives at the airstrip and drives to the team's home.

2:43 A.M. – Already packed and ready to go, Mika grabs half her bags as Koshi grabs the rest and the two slip away undetected as Misa and Julie are passed out in Misa's and Saka's room down the other hallway.

On her way out, Mika smirks and mumbles to herself, "One down, just a few more losers to go!"

2:45 A.M. – As they crest the top of the hill heading east, back to their house, Tai notices another car sitting off to the far side of the road with its lights off. As they pass, he thinks he sees the silhouettes of two people in the front seats. As they continue on toward their house, about a mile back, the solitary car turns their headlights back on and continues heading west, toward the airport.

August 18, 2013 10:00 A.M.

With Mika definitely gone, Kim and J.T. immediately rejoin their loved ones.

Carmela's funeral and burial is appropriately accented by a tropical rain storm that pours off and on throughout the day. There are sixty people in attendance from all over the island and from as far away as Okinawa and Taiwan as well. Carmela was beloved by everyone she met with the exception of Mika. Yuen stands at the front podium preparing to give his wife's eulogy but he freezes up. A moment later, Julie stands up and joins her father at the podium. Briefly, she smiles at the crowd and then she reaches over and wipes Yuen's tears away.

She stares deep into his eyes and says out loud, "No more tears. God is crying for us all!"

On that perfect note, the solemn ceremony concludes. Nothing better could ever be said so everyone walks out of the small church. The tribute luncheon is held at Mary's Grand Café. The front entrance is adorned with flowers and offerings from so many family and friends, they wrap around the sides of the restaurant. Toma appropriately waits but after several hours, he finally approaches Yuen and Tai and asks them to step outside.

"Carmela was a great lady. I'm so sorry Sik Yuen!"

The two shake hands and Toma hugs his grieving friend and confidant.

"My contact at the hospital snuck back into the morgue after the coroner completed his report. He called me with his findings."

Yuen interrupts saying, "And?"

He told me that a well-defined horizontal marking appeared across Carmela's throat. When I asked him what it was; a handle or bat or something like that, he immediately said 'no'.

He said the marking was consistent with the back edge of one's hand, as in a martial arts chop to a person's throat with a partially closed fist. He's seen it several times before and can recognize it quickly."

Again Yuen interrupts, "So, Saitonaka's bitch Mika killed my Carmela, right?"

Toma lowers his head and suggests, "Sik Yuen? I have to ask you right now brother, please, don't call for retaliation just yet. Misa has an idea that I think will work and will certainly exact the kind of revenge you're feeling in your heart and mind right now."

Toma asks Misa over to the table. She quickly details her plan to Yuen and he reluctantly agrees. They break apart so that Saka doesn't notice the obvious planning.

Addressing that obvious loose end, Toma nudges Tai and asks, "And Saka?"

Tai looks at Yuen and shrugs.

Yuen shrugs backs and says, "It's his choice. Time will tell."

Toma nods in agreement and says, "I'd hate to do it but, it is what it is."

CHAPTER FORTY-TWO

November 2, 2013 – Amami Oshima Island, Japan

As Mika returns, the group reluctantly accepts her. Tai and Saka make sure Yuen and Mika are never alone together. Mika welcomes the pending train-wreck and makes no effort to support the separation. With so much work and exciting research to do with the Orcas, it's pretty easy to avoid each other for days on end; weeks on end in fact. People wake, eat or skip breakfast and or lunch, depending on whether or not the Orcas are in the cove and they simply spend as much time with them as the Orcas offer, observing everything they do. Misa conducts somewhat regular physical checkups on each of them. They are all perfectly healthy and vibrantly active mammals.

Xie-xie and Jimmie-Lei remain very patient and model cove inlet shore 'citizens' but Snake-Lei is, after all, a different breed; she plays, eats, and even swims aggressively.

Misa is careful not to showcase any of their behaviors in front of Mika. If Mika even approaches as Misa is performing her tasks, Misa will motion to the Orcas and they will promptly back out of the shallows and dive into the depths of the cove. This behavior took several months to master but it's critical for the Killer Whale's survival in case Mika or Saitonaka ever wanted to harm them. At nine months old now, Jimmie-Lei and Snake-Lei are experts in their own right at hunting and social interactions with other Killer Whales.

Xie-xie has reconnected with her former pod, led by the father of Jimmie-Lei. The pod readily accepts Xie-xie and Jimmie-Lei but they were all a little wary of Snake-Lei initially. Xie-xie used to have to leave her position close to Jimmie-Lei and swim alongside Snake-Lei to help settle the pod's nerves. It's taken a few weeks, especially since Xie-xie breaks away from her former pod to swim back to visit with her rescuer's and handler's but when they reconnect again, the pod recognizes their clicks and welcomes them back for as long as they wish to stay.

The larger pod hunts together and Jimmie-Lei and Snake-Lei show off their skills for stingray hunting to the rest of the pod, helping to teach the younger members of the pod this priceless skill. It took quite a few attempts but finally the pod's leader, Jimmie-Lei's father, fully accepts Snake-Lei so the rest of the pod knows they can trust her. Early on, whenever he would approach Snake-Lei's eyes, he'd back off and go into attack mode;

her beautiful crystal blue eyes startled him. Xie-xie would monitor the interaction and she used to have to alert the pod leader and remind him that Snake-Lei is her pup. He finally got used to her and is ready to accept her as a full member.

2 P.M. – A forty-two foot female Finback whale glides below them with her young. The Orca pod leader decides to teach the young in his pod the art of pursuing, intimidating and corralling one of the bigger prey animals in the ocean. Xie-xie and her pups haven't seen this for a while so they are immediately intrigued. They quicken their pace and take up strategic positions on the far outside of the pod, awaiting their leader's signal.

Just five hundred yards away, the female Finback quickens her pace but she is restricted to whatever speed her young can muster. Alone, her immense size is more than enough to deter every predator in the ocean, including Killer Whales but her much smaller twelve-foot long calf is the perfect non-threatening prey for every predator around. Things get even worse for the gentle giants when they have to surface for air. This highlights their weaknesses and calls it out for the whole ocean to see and hear. As soon as the Orca pod leader sees this, he signals for everyone to take up their pursuit positions; designed to frustrate and disorient the mother Finback so other pod members can scare and confuse her young pup.

The text-book end-result is the corralling that takes place because in order to protect her pup, the mother Finback tries to close the distance between herself and her young. They stick together until they have to surface for air again and then the mother just hopes that her young is able to withstand the torment. This is the moment when the larger pod members snap at the young, trying to inflict devastating injuries. After enough damage is sustained, the young will descend into the depths and drown or succumb to its injuries and the mother Finback has no choice then to abandon her young and swim away so she can survive to bear another pup next season.

In this instance, the Killer Whale pod is executing their pursuit and intimidation tasks perfectly. Xie-xie and Jimmie-Lei eagerly advance and begin distracting the mother Finback. With her extraordinary aggressive demeanor, Snake-Lei and three other pod members are assigned to attack the young Finback.

At three hundred yards away, the mother Finback's senses are overloaded with her recognition of the sixteen-member Killer Whale pod pursuing her and her young. Her man-hole cover sized eyes widen as she begins to strategize her and her young's escape plan; Killer Whales don't typically like to dive as deep as she and her young can so she figures if she can surface one time for a big breath and her young can survive that one vulnerable moment, they can make their way to depths that the pod will not pursue.

The mother Finback signals her young to get as close to her as possible and slightly ahead of her so the pursuing predators can't attack her from below and behind. The mother Finback lost her very first pup fifteen years ago to this same kind of attack and she's never forgotten. As she's matured, so has her survival instincts, evasive maneuvers and strategies.

One hundred yards away and the pod closes in on their prey. Their instincts are in over-drive as well. All eighteen total mammals are at their respective peaks and are driving toward perfectly opposite goals; two are trying to survive by evading predators and sixteen are trying to survive by feeding.

At fifty yards away, the mother Finback begins showcasing the immense power of her massive tail and pectoral fins. One strike from them can easily crack a Killer Whale's head or jaws, causing agonizing or instant death and they all know this. One of the pod members sees an opportunity to snap at and possibly injure the young Finback so he jets forward. Just as he closes in on the young's belly, the baby Finback takes a page out of his mother's defensive book and lashes the young adult Killer Whale with his right pectoral fin. The right upper-cut causes the attacker to fall away further to his right; stinging him for his effort. Snake-Lei notice's this and responds by racing forward to cut off the baby Finback's path; trying to rejoin her mother for protection.

The young Finback defended himself well but in doing so, he's made the juvenile mistake of falling behind. His fate now rests with exactly how hungry the Killer Whale pod is. The pod leader signals Snake-Lei and three other members to go in for the kill.

He's hungry and that's all that is needed to change an exercise into a predation. The four attackers, led by Snake-Lei, launch into their attack positions and ready themselves. Two of them will time the mother Finback's last ditch efforts to save her young by telegraphing her massive tail and pectoral fin strikes and that will clear a path for the other two Orcas to attack the young Finback whale's tail, destroying his ability to propel himself clear of danger and making it impossible for him to resurface for air.

Xie-xie looks on as Jimmie-Lei swims beside her. A moment later, Xie-xie senses a struggle and hears a distress sound coming from directly below her. It's one of the pod members; a pregnant female who is in labor. Three hundred feet away from her, she can easily smell and taste the blood from the pending event. A second later, Xie-xie picks up on another disturbing signal; the heat and body signature from a massive fourteen foot rogue Tiger Shark (*Galeocerdo cuvier*).

He's been patiently patrolling the depths, watching the whole Finback situation unfold and now he realizes his opportunity to feed on a very rare Killer Whale pup. With more than half of the pod pursuing and concentrating solely on the Finbacks, he remains below the pregnant Killer Whale and simply awaits his chance to seize. With his size and the element of surprise, he knows he can strike, extract a deadly amount of flesh, killing the baby Orca, and escape to circle around later to finish it off.

Mother Finback surfaces but her twelve-foot long baby has not. A couple minutes pass and she begins to panic but then a moment later, her young surfaces. The mother immediately signals to him to take in a larger amount of air than normal so the two can flee. Water explodes high up into the late afternoon sky as the two plankton and krill eaters begin their deep dive attempt, trying to elude ten of the sixteen predators pursuing them. They pull in as much air into their massive lungs and descend.

Now three hundred yards away from the Finbacks, the struggling pregnant Orca continues to give birth to her pup. The blood surrounding her is beginning to attract a lot of unwanted attention including that from that fourteen foot Tiger Shark swimming directly below her. He can taste the rich blood in the water. He peers up and begins his ascent toward the preoccupied mother Orca. He selects his initial path of attack on the newborn and locks in his course. With a single flick of his powerful tail, he sets his pectoral fins back and launches himself up at his prey.

He's closing fast; two hundred yards. Xie-xie senses his presence and shoots a sonar wave at him but the Tiger shark is moving too fast. The powerful disruptive signal flutters in the water and falls behind the Tiger Shark's pace. Xie-xie clicks at Jimmie-Lei and the two of them shoot a sonar signal at the large predatory fish but again, his increased speed helps him to elude the potentially damaging signal. This time, the Tiger Shark is winning the match up of the apex predators and it looks like finally, his predation attempt against them will prove out.

Inside one hundred feet and increasing his speed, Xie-xie and Jimmie-Lei break off, realizing they have done all they can to defend their pregnant pod member's newborn but this Tiger Shark is hell bent on feeding and with his attack speed at capacity, even they can't stop him from making this kill. Less than sixty feet away, the giant Tiger Shark begins to open his jagged toothed jaws. As he does, more of the newborn's blood rushes into his mouth making his *Ampullae of Lorenzini* senses go wild.

The pod leader senses his pregnant Orca's struggle and alerts the rest of the pod to break off their pursuit. They collectively turn and race back down to assist her before it's too late. Snake-Lei maintains her attack course and then abruptly adjusts and increases her attack speed. She rushes right past the pod leader and the rest of the group. This is speed none of them have ever witnessed before. She completely ignores the pod leader's rightful position at the head of the pod and continues well past him at increasing speed. With all pursuer's breaking off, the mother Finback and her male pup are safe. They continue to dive to great depths just to make sure.

The Tiger Shark is less than thirty feet away and the pregnant Orca has successfully given birth. She escorts her newborn female Orca to the surface for her very first breath of Earth's oxygen. The pair is elated and the mother can't wait to teach her daughter everything she can so she'll be a productive member of their pod. This is the pod leader's child as well so he is particularly interested in protecting his daughter because she will give rise to a whole new pod's development. Unfortunately, the newborn is about to learn the cruelest lesson in life and death in the ocean; there is always something looking to eat you.

As mother and daughter Orca approach the surface, little does the mother Orca know her newborn female pup is about to have a foot long gash in her side, compliments of a massive and very skilled hunter in the Tiger Shark closing in on her position. He has locked in on her final expected position and his mouth is agape, ready to extract his bloody initial meal.

The Tiger Shark is ten seconds away. Nine, eight, seven; Xie-xie and Jimmie-Lei shoot out a sonar signal, directly at the mother Orca. She signals her young and they pivot. The closing Tiger Shark simply adjusts. Six, five, four; Xie-xie clicks frantically at her fellow pod mother. Three, two… Snake-Lei!

From below and perpendicular to the newborn's position, Snake-Lei clicks a new distress signal that scares the newborn and her mother. In that final second they break left and away and at that moment, Snake-Lei accelerates at an incredible pace, taking up their former space and rams the Tiger Shark of nearly twice her size right in the side of his massive agape jaws. A collision; unheard of and something man will never see, she obliterates the Tiger Shark's entire jaw and skull.

He buckles and wails in agony. He dies three agonizing seconds later from the massive trauma. A few seconds later, the rest of the pod, with their leader at the front, catches up just in time to see the Tiger Shark spin lifelessly down into the depths. He brushes past Snake-Lei in appreciation and dives down to grab the dead fish. Offering her the first bite, Snake-Lei passes and allows the new mother and her newborn to feed. The new female Orca needs the nourishment more than she does. Xie-xie signals to the pod leader that it's once again, time for the three of them to leave. She swims in front of the pod leader and the two brush against each other. With Jimmie-Lei leading the way, Xie-xie and Snake-Lei catch up and head back to visit with their human handler's in the Amami Island cove.

5 P.M. – After a quick and early dinner, Misa aggressively but appropriately invites Mika for a walk around the compound; she wants to better understand the circumstances surrounding Carmela's death back in August.

"Look Mika. I just need to understand. We all do, especially since you were gone a few hours later after you 'mother-fucked' me and never explained anything to Tai or Yuen!"

Crying, Mika says, "I know. I'm so sorry; that day has haunted me for the past three months too and rightfully so. I deserve all the guilt and pain I've felt! I just hope you guys can forgive me and don't hate me now."

"We don't hate you but honestly, we are apprehensive. You understand that, right?"

"Of course. You are all such a tight-knit group. I miss that because with Saitonaka, all he does is order me around; suck it, then we eat lunch or dinner. I'm nothing but a pricy whore to him and I always have been! It's awful but I've survived and tried to make the best of it."

"I'm sorry Mika."

Crying harder, Mika asks, "I wish I had a child to care for. Maybe then, things would be different. Maybe then, he wouldn't treat me like shit! I needed to get away. That's why I volunteered to come here. So I could get a break from all of his bullshit!"

Misa consoles her former friend, feeling like they are finally starting to mend old wounds. The pair walks around in the failing daylight and then Misa offers Mika an opportunity.

"Hey! Tomorrow, how would you like to meet Xie-xie and her pups?"

Wiping the tears away, Mika says, "Really?"

"Sure! I'll introduce you and hopefully, since we look the same still, they'll be as nice to you as they are with me."

Misa gives Mika a hug and pats her back. Then, Mika makes a romantic pass at Misa, kissing her passionately on and in her mouth. Caught off-guard and embarrassed, Misa accepts her kiss initially but then pulls away and looks down.

"Whoa! That was a long time ago Mika. We were kids and just fooling around. Maybe too much but under those circumstances, it was okay. Now, it's not. I'm with Saka and I know he wouldn't approve of that from me. Plus, my daughter Julie would completely freak out. She has no issue with lesbians or the bi-sexual lifestyle either but that's simply not a choice she would respect from me. I have no issue with others who make that choice for themselves but for me personally, it would just make my life much more complicated than I want or need, and more importantly; it's simply not the choice I want for my life, sex life or lifestyle, that's all."

6:30 P.M. – Respectfully, Misa steps away from Mika and walks up the hill and back into the house. Mika walks down the rest of the hill and heads for the far end of the wooden deck. Freshly re-stained, the scent surrounds the immediate area and soothes Mika's stress.

Again, Mika skips her first return dinner with the group and calls Saitonaka.

"Fat-stick mushroom head!"

"Oh! Not yet! First tell me how things are going."

"I've cleared things up with Misa and tomorrow, she's showing me the Orcas. That's when I'll strike!"

"First?"

"I'll make sure the others are away fishing so I can better concentrate on my new training. I'm a nervous new student so I don't want everyone around watching me in case I do something embarrassing. This group will identify with that and oblige my meager request."

"Very good! … next?"

"Next, a devastatingly accurate chop across her little throat and Mrs. Fucking Yamishinosaka is done!"

"Very Good! And then?"

Saitonaka starts masturbating.

"I throw her into the shallows and quickly re-signal the Orcas to surface. They'll grab her and make quick work of that skanky meal! Of course twenty minutes later, they'll be hungry again!"

Mika laughs demonically at her own racist joke.

"Oh! You're making me come Mika!"

"Jesus! Wait a minute fat-stick!"

"Then, I signal for them again and one by one in the shallows, I shoot them up with the overdose I brought with me in my fake strawberry-scented shampoo bottles. As they swim away, they'll quickly get sick and tragically and mysteriously die; like gigantic crack whores! And, when this pathetic group of losers retrieves them and performs autopsies on their precious whales, they will soon discover that it was Dr. Tai's Enhanced-CDT formula that your men cleverly concocted that caused their deaths! He thought all this time he could keep that from you, wrong! Thanks to Heroshi and his bold last visit! You have something now that will make us hundreds of millions of dollars, all over the world!"

"Oh, shit! What a mess! … uh, let me call you back in a few minutes!"

Saitonaka laughs and hangs up.

Mika laughs and says to herself, 'God! He's like a fucking college freshman still; kind of dumb and full of cum!"

7:00 P.M. – She continues voicing her deadly plan to herself saying, "Then, as they split up and frantically search for poor little Misa, I'll join them in their search; slicing and dicing them up one by one! Then, one, two, four and throw them into the cove like chum! As for my new house; a little fix up here and there, get rid of all the science geek bullshit, add some new hibiscus drapes and new plants. Then Saka and me fuck each other's brains loose and I'll finally have my own family to care for and support! Finally, we all just sit back and watch the Enhanced-CDT monies pour in! It's perfect! Thank you Mika! Oh no, thank you Mika! … Oh, yes! You're welcome Mika!"

NOVEMBER 3, 2013 AT 12:30 P.M.

Having shared lunch, Misa offers to teach Mika how to feed the trio of Orcas; how to bring them all up to the surface with a series of little splashes on the surface and a single toot of the custom whistle she crafted. In honor of the occasion, Misa hand crafted a whistle just for Mika. She presents it to her in front of everyone just as their lunch concludes.

"Mika. I made this for you last night. I want you to be my co-trainer and medical assistant to the Orcas."

Mika tears up and accepts the generous hand-made gift. Everyone else claps.

Tai says, "Hey! Congrats Mika! The rest of us are heading into town for the afternoon, to help distribute Myst1 and CDT wash and I've got Saitonaka's next O-tab shipment to send out too. You two have fun. Saka will be here if you need anything from the house, right Saka?"

"Actually, you know. I'd like to join you guys in town if you don't mind."

"Hey! Not at all."

Tai looks sharply over at Yuen.

Julie says, "Have fun mom! See you later this afternoon."

Mika smiles and interrupts saying, "So how long do you guys figure you'll be?"

Yuen immediately says, "Oh, we've got this down pat by now. It takes at least three hours to distribute everything, check up on a few of the elders in the village and then just a quick stop at the post office. We should be making our way back home by around four or four thirty."

J.T. quickly adds, "Hey pop! You still owe me a drink from before!"

"Oh! Well there you have it! We'll probably be at Mary's Grand Café right after the post office so why don't you two just clean up whenever you're done and drive over to join us for drinks and dinner."

Mika nods and says, "Perfect! We'll do that…once we've cleaned everything up here." She winks at the rest of the group and heads out the patio door, waiting for Misa.

12:45 P.M. – Saka and Yuen grab four cases of Myst1 and Tai and Julie grab a couple cases of CDT wash. They load up their two matching silver sedans and take off. Misa grabs a large plastic beverage container full of pre-mixed margaritas, a couple plastic cups and a large box of imported sweet and sour crackers from China.

"Oh! Those are my favorite Misa!"

"Me too! I thought since it's just us girls, we'd party it up like old times; drinking and eating shit that's not good for us!"

Mika laughs and smiles passionately at Misa.

It's unusually warm so, decked out in their bikini tops and shorts, the pair reaches the bottom of the path. Misa puts the container, cups and cracker box on the ground and drags a small table to the front of the cove's inlet. Then she moves the table and one patio chair into the cove, in about two feet deep of water. Mika grabs another chair and joins her. The pair collects the drink container, cups and food and sits down. At the same time, they start kicking the water, smiling and staring up at the sun with their eyes closed for a moment.

"You know it could take some time before Xie-xie and her young appear so that's what the drinks and crackers are for!"

"Good plan!"

For the next two hours, the two trade stories about the past; their time at Saitonaka's apartment compound, the formal dining room performances, and raucous stories about the guards they each slept with back in the day. In Mika's case, which few guards she didn't sleep with.

2:45 P.M. – Most of the afternoon, Misa has been slowly spilling her drinks into the cove.

Acting drunk, Misa says, "There is one other thing…"

Drunk, Mika slurs, "Wha?"

Misa pauses and then says, "I thought we could try that kiss again?"

"Really?" Mika perks up.

Misa stares down then seductively, she looks back up at Mika and nods.

"You sure? I'd hate to shock 'the daughter' by turning her mother lesbian!"

"Hey, what she and Saka don't know won't bother them!"

Mika smiles and gets up from her chair. She kicks the water once more and leans over to Misa.

Just as their lips touch, Misa pulls back and over to her left and shouts, "There they are!"

She jumps out of her chair and walks a few more feet into the cove.

Startled but thrilled with the new developments on both fronts, Mika quickly joins her and hugs Misa around her waist. Amazed, the two watch the three Orcas enter the cove. Misa can't stop smiling and laughing and neither can Mika. They wade into about three feet of water and hug each other as they watch the Killer Whales glide like submarines in the cove, occasionally diving down and then reappearing. As the water explodes from their blow-holes, Misa smiles and drops her bikini top. It falls to the surface and floats over to Mika.

Mika smiles and Misa says, "Hey, it's just us girls, right?"

Mika undoes her top and starts massaging Misa's bare back. Misa continues watching the Orcas as Mika concentrates more on Misa's breasts. She kisses Misa's shoulders.

Misa says, "Wait. Let me teach you something about the Orcas before we get into that!"

She smirks and steps away from Mika.

Misa starts slapping the surface of the water and says, "Now, watch this!"

Still staring at Misa's breasts, Mika finally relents for a moment and says, "Oh, right."

A moment later, Xie-xie appears in dramatic fashion, bursting up from the cove and into her classic position. Mika is completely terrified and starts to run out of the now thigh-high water.

Misa grabs her right arm and says, "No! It's fine! Just wait."

Mika squirms away and frantically makes her way onto the sandy beach. She almost loses her new whistle that Misa fastened around her neck. Mika's eyes bulge out as the now eighteen foot plus long and three ton Xie-xie completes her elegant positioning. Backing out a little bit, in three feet of water now, Misa is dwarfed by her patient. The two step through their ritual health screening and Mika watches at first, in horror and then in delight as she sees how amazingly receptive, calm, and trusting Xie-xie is. With her physical complete and not even asking for a reward, Xie-xie backs up like nothing and disappears.

Misa says, "Now, watch this!"

She slaps the surface of the water twice.

A moment later, Jimmie-Lei bursts up and slides into the same spot that Xie-xie had just occupied. The young male Orca is filling out and continues to grow at a rapid pace. At nearly nine feet long and weighing a little over a thousand pounds, he is well on his way to leading his own pod someday.

Mika starts to approach slowly and Misa says, "There you go! Come on! You can help me give Mr. Jimmie-Lei here his physical."

"He won't bite me?"

"No! We look so much alike, he'll think you're just another one of me!"

Mika approaches and the second she touches Jimmie-Lei's nose, she's captivated. She brushes across the top of his head and down by his right eye patch. Speechless, Mika just repeats her first contact with the young male Killer Whale.

Misa completes her physical of Jimmie-Lei. He dips his head down into the water and sprays Misa's naked torso. Misa bursts out laughing and turns away. She motions with her right hand and Jimmie-Lei backs up and swims off. Mika just stands there staring at her right hand; the one that touched Orcinus Orca.

3:45 P.M. – Three slaps on the surface and eight seconds later, the crystal blue-eyed Snake-Lei bounds up and slides into the shallows. Always carrying a little more pace, Misa braces and waits for her to stop herself. Misa immediately reaches into the female Orca hybrid's mouth and vigorously massages her pink and black tongue.

"Fuck me! Are you crazy? You just throw your hand right in its mouth like that?"

"Sure. You try it?"

"Fuck that! No fucking way!"

As Mika steps back closer and closer to shore, she sees Snake-Lei's blue right eye. She's frozen with fear and shock but mainly fear; eighty-twenty and the disparity increases with each passing second. Still drunk, Mika's stomach starts to get upset as her blood pressure rises and her heart begins to race.

Impatiently, Mika says, "So, finish up with the blue-eyed freak so we can get started! I've waited a long time to be with you again Misa!"

Narrowing her eyes, Misa says, "Patience. Miss Snake-Lei here is very special."

"Special, my ass! Not as special as the new fingering technique that I've got for you!"

Snake-Lei swims away and Misa says, "Jesus! What the hell is wrong with you Mika? We're having a nice time together and you have to go and ruin it with your crude over-sexed big mouth!"

Drunk and embarrassed, Mika yells, "My over-sexed mouth? I remember a time when your over-sexed mouth couldn't get enough of my pussy and Saitonaka's fat little cock!"

"Jesus! Grow the fuck up already! That was over twenty-odd years ago! That's not me anymore!"

"Bullshit! It's you! You just haven't had anyone hot enough around to fuck for so long, you've forgotten what it was about! And trust me, Saka is not the answer!"

"How would you know that? I asked him and he said he never slept with you while you two were in Yokohama!"

"True. We never slept with each other in Yokohama but we fucked regularly everywhere else! You don't think this ring on my finger is just for decoration, do you?"

"What?"

Happy to brag, Mika says, "He was MY husband way before you married him and he's still my husband, on loan to you all this time!"

"Lying bitch!" Go to hell!"

"Ask him yourself when they get back. You know, I had a little plan today but I think I'll discard it. The pending wild drama will be much more entertaining and if it ends with the two of us wrestling on the floor and scratching each other's eyes out; all the better! I might even kick off dinner tonight by recounting some of our nastiest dinner dance performances, especially the time when you ate me out using half a bottle of that delicious orange liquor!"

"You wouldn't! My daughter can't hear about all that shit now!"

"Oh, that's right. Your poor little daughter can't hear about that or how her mother sucked off her uncle Tai's stubborn monster cock back in the mid-eighties!"

Two matching silver sedans pull up to the front of the house.

4:15 P.M.

"Fine! Then I'll tell everyone about the time you couldn't get Saitonaka off the first night you spent together because you didn't know how to blow out a candle much less his dick! And then right after I ask Yuen to pass the rice, I'll caution everyone to stop eating as I tell them about the time you and Yuen were in the limousine together. Remember? You were trying to get into a better position to blow him and when you knelt down in front of his seat, you shit your panties! A real trooper though, he pressed on and pressed your head down on him and you finished him off anyway! But what you might not have seen was him exiting the car, laughing his ass off and desperately pinching his nose closed!"

Mika's eyes glare and turn red, partly from the alcohol and partly from her growing rage.

As she grabs her bikini top and re-fastens it, Misa adds, "Here's my tip for when you get back with little fat-stick! Don't be stupid enough to offer him a hundred percent of yourself until he pays you for it! He thought Julie was his early on so he threw tons of money at me for her. Trust me, we've all here, very much enjoyed it and we continue to do so! And, if you have already given him a hundred percent, that's too bad because I was never stupid enough to do so!"

Mika shrugs her comments off and says, "And here's my tip for you sweetheart! You don't know who I am anymore and that fact will surprise you soon enough, I promise!"

She grabs her bikini top and throws it up the path.

Misa says, "And what's that idle threat supposed to mean?"

"Oh, remember, like you told me; patience dear!"

"You're just pissed off that I played Hey Sun's, excuse me, I mean Saitonaka's little game better than you?"

"You knew about that whole deal? For how long?"

"That doesn't matter now. What matters is that I knew for long enough to get my daughter the hell away from him and you!"

Mika starts yelling something really nasty in Japanese.

A second later, Tai runs down the path and says, "Hey you two! Long day or what? Oh, too many margaritas I see."

Misa walks out of the shallows and marches up the path and back inside the house.

Tai reaches down and picks up Mika's bikini top. He hands it to her and says, "We haven't had the chance to talk yet. Do you mind?"

Mika smirks at Tai and says, "Still nice huh?"

Tai looks down and casually nods. Then he says, "Look; we really need to talk about a few things if you're going to stay here with us again. I actually overheard a little more of your conversation and that's got to stop. It helps no one and solves nothing."

Mika shrugs Tai off and fastens her bikini top back on. She takes another long pull on the margarita bag.

"So, let me guess. You want to grill me over what happened to Carmela, right?"

"Not grill you. I need to understand what happened, from the sole survivor. If these Orcas are in fact dangerous, then we need to know it before something else happens. Just tell me what you remember."

"We went swimming. She kissed me so we started to fool around. We laid-out on the platform thing over there for a while and then she wanted to race around to the other side. I took off and before I knew it, she was way behind me. I started to turn around to go back to her when I saw a fin."

"One fin or two?"

"Just one. That was enough! I'm not like you science geeks. I've never seen a shark's fin before! It scared me so I started swimming away from it as fast as I could, heading back around the cove."

"Away from Carmela?"

"Right, because the fin was closest to her."

"And where was she?"

"What?"

"Where was Carmela when you headed around the corner?"

"When I looked back, I didn't see her. My mind was racing and I figured since the shark was already heading for me, it had already bitten her so I took off and kept swimming around the corner."

"And then?"

"Jesus! … uh and then, I kept swimming but the fin followed me."

"The … shark's fin followed you?"

"Yeah! It kept following me!"

Mika points to the top of the cove in the right hand corner, showing the area where she had been pursued.

"And you couldn't just get out of the water at that point?"

"No! The shallows over there get deeper so the shark was able to get closer to me so I kept swimming, trying to get into more shallow water."

"Okay but after a while, you were able to finally get out of the water, away from… the shark, right?"

"Right! Exactly! It was all very scary!"

"Okay. Well thanks. That all checks out then."

Mika squeamishly nods and drinks the last of the margarita mix.

"You know, tragically, Carmela suffered a horrible 'chop-like' mark right across the middle of her throat. You figure, a big wave from the shark's attack must have thrown her into the steel support beam that holds up the platform?"

"Yep! That had to be it."

"Of course, there's absolutely no room in this cove for that kind of momentum to build up and if it was even remotely possible, that would mean the shark would had to have been between forty to fifty foot long! A true Megalodon!"

"Exactly! … that was probably it then!"

Exasperated with her ignorance and obvious lying, Tai asks, "So, how did it go with the Orcas today? Did you get to touch them?"

"Oh, yes! It was incredible! I patted and held Jimmie-Gee as Misa checked him out!"

"Great! Amazing stuff, huh?"

"Really! It actually made me a little wet… and Misa and I were about to…"

Dusk. Seeing Misa start to walk back down the path, Tai interrupts, waves and says, "Hey!"

He promptly walks away from Mika and runs up the hill to meet Misa half way.

"Okay. Be careful, please! Are you sure you want to do this?"

Misa nods firmly.

She tears up and says, "I owe you. I owe Kim. I owe Sik Yuen!" I knew what kind of person Mika had become but I didn't do anything about it. Now Carmela is gone, my soul-mate Yuen is forever crushed and this bitch is going to pay the price!

Tai whispers, "You're sure?"

Misa smiles and kisses Tai on his cheek. Hugging her, Tai notices that Misa isn't carrying her 9mm pistol behind her back.

As Misa walks down the path toward Mika, Tai calls out, "Hey, we're going to head over to Mary's Grand Café now. You two finish up and join us soon, okay? And no more margaritas! Save that for the bar! We have a couple special guests joining us tonight that will put on a show you won't believe!"

Misa immediately offers her apologies as she approaches Mika.

"Sorry. Tai was right; too many margaritas and the sun got to me and burned my tits and temper!"

Mika nods.

"Hey, want to learn another cool trick?"

"Okay but quick. I want to see that show Tai's talking about and I'm getting hungry too."

"Speaking of getting hungry; it's feeding time for our favorite Orca gang!"

Misa quickly retrieves the bucket of fish that Tai left out for her. She carries it over to the cove's inlet and rests it on top of a large smooth rock; her little feeding table when she's attending to Xie-xie and her growing pups. In the failing light, Misa covers the hole on her whistle and tries to give it a toot. It sputters. She tries it again.

"Shit! My whistle must be broke! Try yours?"

Mika grabs her whistle and toots it proudly.

From a couple hundred yards out in the cove, Xie-xie's huge black dorsal fin turns toward the sound and underneath the surface, Jimmie-Lei and Snake-Lei follow their mother. It's been a while since they heard this unique sound.

"Don't they do any tricks?" Mika asks.

"As a matter of fact, they do. They jump out of the water and grab fish out of your hand but only if they trust you."

"And if not?"

"If not, you'll get one hell of a free shower, especially from Xie-xie! To be safe since it's almost dark. I'll feed Xie-xie in the cove but we can feed the kids from the springboard platform."

Misa quickly and sharply splashes the surface of the water in the cove inlet. A minute later, Xie-xie makes her awesome appearance. With her mouth agape, she readies for food. Misa piles it in her mouth and Xie-xie closes her massive jaws and swallows it down. Without delay, Xie-xie backs off and disappears back into the cove; her beautiful white eye patch offering the only evidence of her massive glossy black presence. Misa and Mika make their way over to the springboard platform. First Misa jumps across and then she helps Mika wade across as the last of the sunlight fades away. Misa turns on the overhead lamp light. It illuminates a radius of about thirty feet and as it sits back on the rear post of the deck, it doesn't bother the Orcas when they perform their trick-jump feeding exercises. Misa has only performed a night feeding from the springboard observation deck twice herself so she's excited to see Jimmie-Lei and Snake-Lei tonight.

"You go first." Mika offers.

"Of course. Whistle for me?"

Mika toots her whistle as Misa holds out a fish. Calmly and with perfect precision, Jimmie-Lei suddenly appears from directly below her and gently takes the fish out of her hand.

"See! It's that simple!"

"Wow! That's amazing!"

"Now, let's try it with Xie-xie!"

"Oh shit!"

"Yah, oh shit is right! I actually haven't tried this with Xie-xie yet!"

Misa kneels down and slaps the water once and then says, "Give me a toot?"

Toot and a moment later, Xie-xie rises from below. The gorgeous hybrid female takes the morsel even more gently from Misa's hands and gently disappears back down into the abyss.

"Hey! I thought you said they would jump out of the water for it."

Misa kneels back down and slaps the water three times.

"My turn! I want to feed one of them!" Mika demands.

With their horse-shoe shaped tables already in position, Mary turns on the jukebox in the far corner and Yuen and Saka start lining up shot glasses on the bar.

Looking back over her shoulder, Kim smiles and then plants a long awaited kiss on Dr. Tai. J.T. walks by and pats his father on his back. Julie waddles in from the kitchen and motions over to J.T. for her second helping of egg-foo-young and heavy gravy.

J.T. holds up a mid-sized plate in his left hand and a larger plate in his right hand. She nods toward his right hand and he smiles.

Saka raises the first of many toasts to come to everyone in the room as Toma's men set the table and place the first round of drinks around it. Kim interrupts Julie's meal and gets her up to dance. Tai and J.T. dance as Kim and Julie dance slowly and safely.

Tai taps Julie's belly and says, "To my… grand-son!"

Saka says, "Wànsuì!"

Julie smiles and shakes her head. She declares, "To your… grand-daughter!"

Already drunk, Saka and a couple of Toma's men say, "Wànsuì!"

Toma offers, "To a healthy baby… boy!"

Saka and his team counter again.

Mary and Kim declare, "Girl!"

Saka and his team counter again.

Tai abducts Kim from his son's arms and spins her around saying, "To you sweetheart!"

Crying, Kim whispers, "To us!"

J.T. joins Julie and says, "For Grandpa Jimmie!"

Julie cries and nods. Then J.T. takes off his 3D gold dragon and fixes it around Julie's neck. Passionately, they kiss. Tai and Kim see the gesture. They smile and cry together as they continue to dance.

Yuen solemnly says, "To Carmela!"

The room thunderously shouts, "Wànsuì!"

Toma immediately corners his mother Mary and sits her down so the two of them can discuss, in excruciating detail, his ominous bachelor status. Everyone turns to see this and bursts out laughing.

Under the mysterious surface, both Xie-xie and Jimmie-Lei suddenly swim away from the platform area; Snake-Lei approaches. With a flick of her tail, she rises up and snatches the dangling fish from Mika's hands. So gently and perfectly, Mika is completely mesmerized.

"Again?" Misa asks.

"Really?"

"Go ahead." Misa confirms.

Misa adds, "This time, extend your hands out full of fish for her."

Struggling a little bit to hold two larger fish out horizontally, Mika asks, "Like this?"

Misa confirms, "Exactly!"

With the full moon above, Mika stares with wonderment out into the abyss.

Misa says a prayer and flatly asks, "You killed Carmela, didn't you? Right here on this platform."

Not hearing her, Mika asks, "What?"

"You killed Carmela! You chopped at her throat, right? Tell me the truth and maybe I'll change my mind."

"Change your mind about what?"

"Change my mind about whether or not to feed you to MY Orcas!"

"Bitch! Come on! They wouldn't hurt me. I'm 'you' to them, remember? Snake-Lei took my food even more gently than the others did from you!"

"And that means exactly what?"

"That means sweetheart; they trust me more than they trust you!"

Misa declares, "Wrong!" and then toots her whistle twice.

Acting scared, Mika says, "Oh, and that double toot means what, double the pleasure?"

Thinking for a second then Misa says, "Uh, actually, yes; double the pleasure!"

"Ha! Just like when you took on both guards that one night! I'll bet you couldn't walk straight for a week!"

Misa flips Mika her middle finger. She whispers to herself, "Game over!"

A moment later, Xie-xie strikes the springboard platform, sending Misa and Mika into the chilly water. Snake-Lei immediately circles around and opens her jaws. She blinks her gorgeous crystal-blue eyes once and closes her serrated conical teeth down on the flailing arms in front of her. Mika frantically splashes around when a look of horror and shock comes across her face. She looks across the surface of the water at her arms and immediately notices the absence of both her hands.

Frenetically, her heart races and then she immediately passes out from the shock and blood loss. Delicately she begins to sink down into the depths of the cove. Misa swims over toward the center of the cove; to its deepest point.

She sees Xie-xie's dorsal fin break the surface and then she hears her trademark blow-hole and the respective explosion of sea water. Misa throws her head back and floats on her back, perfectly at ease.

Jimmie-Lei's dorsal fin breaks the surface alongside his mother and his blow-hole sounds off as well. Mother and son head directly toward a completely prone Misa Yamishinosaka.

Having accelerated from beneath her at an incredible speed, Snake-Lei surges clear out of the water with Mika's body; showing off her bloody prize to her mother, brother and to her real favorite trainer and handler, Misa. The intimately acquainted pair crashes back down into the cove and disappears back down into the crashing and frothy crimson water.

With everyone dancing, eating, drinking, and occasionally playing the Mah-Jongg tiles in front of their spots around the horse-shoe shaped table, the full blown celebration has begun. Tai and Yuen make their way over to Saka.

They bow and Saka immediately bows and says in Chinese words to the effect of, "Please forgive me for not acting sooner. I'll give my life to protect any one or all of you now, my dear friends!"

Yuen bows again and gives Saka a large black and red ancient Chinese coin. Yuen motions Saka to look over to Toma. Toma bows once and waves his hand; open fisted, up and down and then again with a closed fist, slamming his fist downward in the air. Saka has informally joined the Triads and now works for Toma.

"Wànsuì!"

On the top of the bar, nine shot glasses start to catch fire and glow. The outer-most glasses glow green, the next set glows red, the next set glows orange, and the last set glows yellow.

J.T. calls out the center glass, "Crystal Blue!"

Again, thanks to Kim's expert final touches, the flames all crackle like tiny firecrackers.

Together, everyone shouts, "Xie-xie Wànsuì! Jimmie-Lei Wànsuì! ... Snake-Lei Wànsuì!"

After a moment, the Amami Oshima Island Team; Dr. Tai Huang, Dr. Kim Huang, Sik Yuen Zhang, J.T. Huang, Julie Zhang Huang, and now, Hideko (Saka) Yamishinosaka all quietly reflect and think to themselves,

"... Orcinus X!"

APPENDIX A – A BRIEF HISTORY ON SHARKS AND WHALES

EVER since the first *Homo sapiens* narrowly escaped a set of jaws and frantically scrambled out of the water's shallows, we have been fascinated by sharks. As soon as he or she settled down and changed his or her undergarments of the time, we've wanted to know everything about these incredible animals. Let's face, they shit themselves and were likely happy to just let it run down their leg because after all, they were alive!

Without question, the earliest progenitor of these ferocious ancient sharks was *Cretolamna.* Ninety to fifty million years ago, the wildest of new creatures was born. They would be between seven to ten feet in length and would weigh a terrifying five hundred pounds. With large un-serrated teeth, at this time, there was no need for serrations because these fish simply grabbed whatever was in their way. Then, the wonderful engine of evolution took over for these fantastic fishes and with each new version, came a frightening new level of terror and predation for everything else.

Sixty-five MYA - Was it fate or just blind luck when the great extinction event that took out all of the dinosaurs took place? Luckily for us, almost all life had to, once again, start over. What remained of the monstrous and ferocious dinosaurs evolved into our much more limited and manageable birds of prey and animals of today. As we continue to learn, the word 'dinosaur' no longer fits since we now know that the mighty Tyrannosaur lineage were actually 'terrible birds', not 'terrible lizards'. Ferocious as we have always believed, these ultimate birds were extremely colorful and feathered. So, it follows that T-rex was not the top ancient lizard of his day but the top … ancient rooster or the like!

Here's a summary of each animal's incredible reign, keeping in mind, these are millions of years ago.

Otodus obliquus; 60 – 45 MYA. On average, between thirty and forty feet long weighing between five and twelve tons. *Otodus obliquus* was the first genuinely huge super-predator. Built on the evolutionary positives of her parent's *Cretolamna*, this new super-shark took size, shape and appetite to a whole new terrifying level. This ancient relative of *C. megalodon* had un-serrated three inch plus long teeth.

Otodus aksuaticus; 45 – 35 MYA. On average, between thirty and forty feet long and weighing between eight to twelve tons. This ancient relative of *C. megalodon* also had huge un-serrated teeth.

Carcharocles auriculatus; 35 – 25 MYA. What an upgrade! *Carcharocles auriculatus* had teeth that topped out at around four inches long. *Auriculatus* is the earliest ancestor to *C. megalodon* to have serrated teeth. She was on average twenty-eight feet in length and a staggering six thousand pounds. Larger than any Great White recorded by mankind, this beast glided through the ancient oceans almost completely unopposed but on the horizon, there were new species developing. New species that sharks had never seen before. As a species in general, they had been ruling the oceans for hundreds of millions of years but now it was time for some healthy competition.

Carcharocles angustidens; 35 – 22 MYA. A voracious predator in its time. All *Angustidens'* roamed free and devoured everything in their path. The world had never seen anything like her before. With serrated teeth between one and a half to two inches long, this shark declared war on basically everything. A muscular fourteen to sixteen-odd feet long and close to a two ton predator at this time would easily scare any other animal to death on sight. Like glancing into Medusa's eyes, a stone-cold freeze would over-take them. After millions of years, it was time for an upgrade because the chemistry of the ocean was changing and so were animals. Those latter three million years of evolution proved critical as the remaining *Angustidens'* would serve as grandfather to the greatest shark to have ever lived. *Carcharocles angustidens* gave way to *Carcharocles chubutensis.*

Carcharocles chubutensis; 28 – 5 MYA. *Chubutensis* was a particularly nasty version of ancient shark. Like the child left at home while others ventured out to play, she had the nastiest of ancient dispositions and an unrivaled appetite. Roughly the same size as her parent's but bulkier; *Chubutensis* had that demeanor that stood apart from other ancient sharks developing at the time. Her size and bulk suited her well because basically, if she wanted you, she had you. Your only hope and small advantage as a smaller fish at this time was your sleeker size and speed. Forty to forty-five feet in length and weighing an awesome twenty to twenty-five tons. It was *Chubutensis'* stubbornness to adapt that began her down-fall but she gave birth to the world's largest and most awesome shark of the ancient oceans.

28 – 1.5 MYA. Finally, the inevitable; *C. megalodon* was born. The time was right; the climate and chemistry of the oceans, the abundant and growing sea life, new top predators to feed upon and an unrivaled evolutionary path had all taken shape to produce the new kings and queens of the world's oceans.

C. megalodon was born into the most dangerous oceans in the world and for millions of overlapping years, she waged war against everything. *C. megalodon* preyed upon and likely aided in the extinction of her great-grandparents, *Carcharocles auriculatus,* her grandparents, *Carcharocles angustidens* and her parents, *Carcharocles chubutensis.* With teeth topping out, as we currently believe today, at just over seven inches long, this translates into a shark easily in the upper sixty-foot range and maxing out at around seventy-two feet. Of course, as with any animal, there were surely anomalies; those individuals that defied all logic and grew to immense and ungodly proportions; over eighty feet and weighing over one hundred and twenty tons.

The 'average' *C. megalodon* weighed in between a staggering and truly horrifying forty to as much as over eighty tons. An absolutely awesome and freakish sight to behold for any other fish in the ocean or for any mammal on land or sea, *C. megalodon* was everything's nightmare. With a six to seven-foot tall dorsal fin cutting the surface of the water, any land animal had to wonder what in hell that could be and be thankful they were on land. Simply imagine a fleet of city buses gliding effortlessly through the water in most corners of the planet armed with the biting power to actually bite a city bus in half without missing a beat. Thankfully we have perfect evolutionary evidence of these awesome creatures because they left behind millions of their teeth and thousands of bone fragments (many with bite marks in them) for us to wonder, marvel, and learn about.

It wasn't until the latter half of *C. megalodon's* reign that several other species had caught up to the undisputed ruler of the seas. The ancient whales were absolutely ferocious and had been top predators themselves but their evolutionary path had also taught them to adapt to climate changes far better than all sharks of the time. They had a better and more varied diet and as a consequence, they grew smarter, they developed families, or pods, and they were slowly learning how to communicate with each other by a series of clicks, squawks, and chirps.

The evolution of these ferocious whales spurred on the diversity in the sharks. So it follows, with diversity in predators, there was a like-response in the diversity of all other animals as well. The variety of smaller sharks including the early Great White shark would constantly battle over territorial boundaries against an expansive variety of smaller killer whales and other smaller predators like the early dolphins; smaller being the tremendous variety and insane volume of fifteen to twenty-foot predators throughout all oceans and seas of the ancient world.

Most battles were fierce and fast. Like the voracious piranha feeding frenzies that mankind can witness today in any region of the Amazon, just imagine those kinds of frenzies but in place of the typical terrifying 200-odd six to ten inch long piranha, consider 300-odd fifteen to twenty foot long sharks, of all kinds, preying upon an injured eighteen foot Killer Whale. Or the more intelligent early Killer whale pods of around a dozen families corralling, stalking, and devouring a group of twenty older or injured sixteen-odd foot rogue sharks. It was a bloody good time. When the ocean floors again settled and the carcasses and silt stop moving about the sea floors, these were always the only two goliaths "standing". All other smaller predators were either destroyed or devoured; meaning they were devoured because nothing ever went to waste, especially in those ancient days. The defeated sharks or whales nourished its rival and then the body of the defeated went on to feed thousands more. As each dead or dying animal drifted to the bottom of the ocean, countless other fishes and mammals took their portion. Once the dead lay on the ocean floor, anything remaining quickly fed the existing plant life on the sea floor and enriched the water as well.

Yet another explosion of marine life took place at this time thanks in part to the increasingly more oxygenated water throughout the planet. Countless species of new fishes were developing and as they feasted upon the brilliant abundance of both plant and fish life, they grew bigger, becoming more attractive to all predators. This in turn made them grow larger in size and become more attractive to all super predators. This cycle, vicious for some, continues until finally a trigger in each species turns on or off, telling the species to stop because they have reached their "optimum" version for the time, place, and circumstance; this is how we believe evolution works.

Raptorial Sperm Whales; 13 – 10 MYA. *Livyatan melvillei* was between forty-five and sixty feet long and featured the longest teeth of any animal to have ever lived; in excess of twelve inches long. The world had something it had never seen before and they all swam away from it as fast as they could. With foot-long teeth glistening at you and closing in on your position, no wonder there was plenty of excreta (urine and feces) in the oceans as well.

Raptorial delphinids; 11 MYA. These early Killer Whales were getting smarter than any other creature in the ocean. At twenty to as much as thirty-two feet long and weighing as much as ten tons, these early Orcas quickly helped to kill off all remaining *C. megalodon's* by either devouring them or scaring them off into regions where they could not survive for very long. With an attack speed of around thirty knots, there were certainly faster fish in the water at this time but if you were a large fish or mammal in the water at this time, you likely did not escape this ultimate-level predator.

Orcinus citoniensis; 5 – 2 MYA. As far as we know, this was the mother and father of today's *Orcinus orca*. Growing between twelve and fifteen feet long and weighing about two tons, there was clearly room for the next generation to grow bigger so, they did.

Orcinus orca; 2 MYA – current. Making their ancient parents proud, this extant (existing) species of whale is the undisputed king and queen in every ocean, sea and bay in the world today. For how long this will remain true, time will tell. As long as mankind doesn't permanently ruin the world's oceans, they should easily surpass the existence of Homo sapiens. The Orca's gestation period is between fifteen to eighteen months with one single calf born on average each five years. Females can live as long as eighty to ninety years but males range between fifty to sixty years.

For a solid five hundred thousand years, two ultimate combatants lived at the same time. *C. megalodon* and *Livyatan melvillei* would rarely seek each other out but as food resources became less and less at this time, both species began to realize it was time to prey upon each other in order to survive. The distant future human being, Charles Darwin, would have it right; survival of the fittest. These great battles took place in every ancient ocean on the planet and thank God human beings hadn't yet fully developed or we would all have had our hearts attack us and we'd be done.

Luckily for us, our earliest ancestors were barely foraging for nutritious roots and insects at this time. We were staying as far away from large bodies of water as much as possible. Still getting around the savannas on four legs, we stuck to our trees; having a lot of learning and evolution still to get through. Loud and obnoxious grunts, fighting, and holding each other were our only forms of communication. On a positive note though, we were beginning to develop stronger and tougher teeth, some great flexibility, curiosity, a more varied diet and we were beginning to find and eat more protein. Some human beings today fancy themselves as vegetarians but it would be good and smart to remember and pay your respects to your ancestors who ate meat; they grew their brains back then so you could shrink yours today.

Over time, the super-rich protein from meat grew our primitive brains, helping us to become smarter. This led to strengthening our natural instincts of curiosity and exploration and one day, a few of us stood up tall on our hind legs for the very first time. We immediately discovered that we could see a great distance and conveniently, we could see other animal predators taking up positions against us. Seeing the pending attacks gave us the advantage we needed. We were able to quickly strategize and seek better hiding places; taller trees and one day, small areas in rock formations called cave dwellings. We'd learn to paint on the rock walls trying to tell stories to share with each other using these visuals because we hadn't formed a language yet. One day, we officially inherited the earth but at this ancient time, we were small, practically helpless, not very smart, starving and genuinely struggling little pre-humans just trying to survive.

Every creature within ear-shot would react when they would hear some of the classic coastal battles that took place between *C. megalodon* and *Livyatan melvillei.* In some parts of the world today, some people believe if you listen very carefully in certain places and at certain times, you can hear the vicious and relentless roars some of these great predators made in their battle of battles. In the Florida Keys, *C. megalodon* was prevalent in this area as this region and the adjacent Gulf area were its favorite breeding grounds. Many times throughout the ancient season, *Livyatan melvillei* and its immediate successor, the early Killer Whale, would migrate through this area on their way to the western coast of Africa, its favorite breeding grounds. They preferred these tropical ancient coastlines.

Up and down the entire coast of South America, especially in the area of Chile, *C. megalodon* and *Livyatan melvillei* engaged in some of their bloodiest and most spectacular battles for survival. One reason why *C. megalodon* fossils discovered today in this area are tinged slightly red could be because of the gargantuan amount of rich blood content in the water back in those ancient times. In the center of the country along the coastlines today, locals of several villages swear they can hear bellows from ancient dying predators from both factions as they gasp their final breaths. In times past, off the western coast of Africa, formerly called the Ivory Coast, many residents gathered twice a year to listen to the sun "scream" as they all marvel at the sounds they claim to hear during their Spring and Winter Festivals. They pray to these great fish and mammal gods because in their minds, these great creatures symbolize life itself.

C. megalodon met their end due to several main circumstances and limitations that this ultimate predator had engrained in its DNA. First of all, their nurseries died off due to the closure of the Central American Seaway. This led to the nurseries having insufficient protection from the rest of the predators in the area. A bigger factor was that this closed seaway created much cooler water temperatures in the world's oceans and that killed off huge numbers of *C. megalodon* young as well. With no escape and waters too cold to survive in anyway, this species was fast on its way to extinction. In their pod lifestyles, all whales learned to migrate so it was easy for them to avoid any surviving *C. megalodon's* in the immediate area. With newer, smarter, and smaller competition evolving around them, *C. megalodon* actually became prey for the new generation of apex predators like the newly forming *Orcinus orca.* This time frame officially marked the end of the long reign of the sharks and opened the bloody door to the reign of the new king and queen of the oceans, the Killer Whales.

Whatever camp you prescribe to, one fact remains; these creatures are forever in our hearts, minds and imaginations. Mankind will likely never know for sure exactly what lineage *C. megalodon* came from but it is endlessly fascinating to contemplate her origins. She may be extinct, for quite a long time actually, but the future of *Orcinus orca* and *Orcinus X*, is bright, mysterious, ravenous and now!

A little advice; as you enjoy the world's oceans, if you happen to own a whistle, please, … be careful!